IT ONLY TAKES ONCE

VILLAGE OF BALLYDARA
BOOK ONE

SUSAN COLLEEN BROWNE

ISBN: 978-1-952470-17-2

ebook ISBN: 978-0-9816077-2-6

This is a work of fiction. Names, characters, places, and incidents are either the product of the author's imagination, or are used fictitiously, and any resemblance to actual persons, living or dead, business establishments, events, or locales is entirely coincidental.

Published by Whitethorn Press

Cover design by Courtney Lopes

www.SusanColleenBrowne.com

www.susancolleenbrowne.substack.com

ALSO BY SUSAN COLLEEN BROWNE

Irish Village of Ballydara Series

Mother Love

The Hopeful Romantic

The Galway Girls

The Secret Well (Short Story)

A Christmas Visitor (Short Story)

The Little Irish Gift Shop

Becoming Emma

Becoming Emma Special Edition: With Two Fairy Cottage of Ballydara Novelettes

The Fairy Cottage of Ballydara

Memoirs of Country Life

Little Farm in the Foothills: A Boomer Couple's Search for the Slow Life

Little Farm Homegrown: A Memoir of Food-Growing, Midlife and Self-Reliance on a Small Homestead

Little Farm in the Garden: A Practical Mini-Guide to Raising Selected Fruits and Vegetables Homestead-Style

Middle Grade Fiction

Morgan Carey and The Curse of the Corpse Bride

Morgan Carey and The Mystery of the Christmas Fairies

The Secret Astoria Scavenger Hunt

A LITTLE HELP WITH THE IRISH...

Aislin—pronounced "Ash-lin"
   Ghillies—soft shoes used in Irish step dancing
   Feiseanna—pronounced   "fesh-ah-na,"   Irish   dance
festivals/competitions

THE SIGN

*T*he urge to contact an old boyfriend should be approached with extreme caution, I always say. Even if you've excellent reasons, any impulse with such potential for disaster on a grand scale should be either squashed immediately, or given due consideration: i.e., discussed exhaustively with your friends, whom you have bribed with cheap wine and equally cheap Cadbury's to listen to you, and for your trouble, will give you their expert counsel.

In case the confab with friends regarding the ex sets off an uncharacteristic impulse to take action—Saturday night's strategy session with Deirdre and Maggie ended with a rash, midnight phone call to America—you'll want to be on the lookout for signs and portents that you're on the right track.

I was saying exactly that to Deirdre six days later, in the back room of her mam's shop, O'Donnell's Books & Collectibles. "Though I was sure I'd get a sign before now. Especially here."

After all, you'd think a shop stuffed with fairy-themed merchandise—that's *Irish* fairies, mind—in tourist-jammed Temple Bar, smack in the middle of Dublin, Ireland, which is home to spiritual icons galore, would be a magnet for messages from the Other Side, the far corners of the world, or the Infinite.

"Signs," scoffed Deirdre. As my fellow shop assistant, she *could've* been helping me sort through the tatty leftovers from her mam's parish jumble sale, but she was busy Web surfing. "Maybe you're meant to watch for the one saying the call was a waste of time."

"No way," I said, though I was starting to wonder. While I hardly expected a metaphysical memo to waft in, such as, *Attn.: Aislin Moore, Congrats on the genius phone call,* surely a teensy insight into my next move wasn't too much to ask? I gazed balefully at yet another overflowing box, perched on a high shelf. "One more box to go. And the dustiest of the lot."

"Sling it 'til Monday," Deirdre said, clicking madly. "Mammy'll never know."

I sneezed. "I'm for that." I swiped my hands on my jumper, then made the mistake of glancing at the box again. It seemed to droop toward me reproachfully. "Shag it all," I muttered. On tiptoe, I grabbed one corner of the box and jerked it forward. "As if this crusty junk is worth anyth—" I yelped as something thunked me on the head and fell to the floor.

"What?" said Deirdre, eyes glued to the screen.

Rubbing the sore spot, I knelt to pick up the offending item, and almost fell over. "Oh, my God, this is it! The sign I've been waiting for."

Deirdre swiveled round. "A book." She wrinkled her pretty nose. "You can't wear it or eat it—what's the use?"

"Don't you see?" Trembling, I ran my fingers over the title, and lurched to my feet. "My fate is shagging sealed." Deirdre still looked blank. "It's a sign! Telling me to ring his mam again."

"An old book told you that?" Deirdre said, incredulous. "The dust in here has addled your brains."

"*Little Women* is not just an 'old book,'" and I hugged it to my chest, "it's my favorite book of all time." I'd read my dog-eared paperback a gazillion times, and watched all the film versions over and over. "So, I've *got* to keep trying to contact...you know. Him." Spurred into action, I set the book down and pulled my rucksack from under the desk. "It's the least I can do for—"

"Aislin, like I said Saturday, you are *so* going to regret this," Deirdre said darkly.

"Bollocks." Enjoying the novelty of being decisive, I dug out my mobile. "What's the harm, to make sure she got my message? Maybe my phone numbers got a bit garbled."

Deirdre shook her head, her dark, glossy hair swinging round her shoulders. "So what if you meet up with him again, and he turns out to be a loser...or even a gobshite?"

"He's not the sort," I said without thinking.

"Well, people change. But have you considered your worst case scenario?"

"Like what?" Staring at my phone, I could feel my grand resolve weaken. I'd tons of reasons for contacting him—I'd even made a list. What was I waiting for?

"Like...our man could still be carrying the torch," Deirdre said with a melodramatic air. "And in his undying passion for you, he jumps on the next flight to Dublin."

"As if." My stomach tightened at the very thought. "I can guarantee that the last time I saw him, he'd dumped whatever torch he ever had for me." *If he'd had one at all.*

"Or what if he's married, and his wife got all prickly about him hearing from an old girlfriend who looks like Nicole Kidman—"

"I so do not look like Nicole Kidman," I interrupted, secretly pleased.

"Do too—well, okay, a younger Nicole, if she was a foot shorter, and had more than one percent body fat. And if she never used some decent product on her hair. Anyway, what if his wife cut him off in the bedroom! He'd be all cross, and there you'd be, starting off on the totally wrong foot."

"Even if he's married, it's not like I'm trying to mess him about or anything. I'll get his e-mail from his mam like I planned, chat him up online a bit, then throw out a few feelers." I stared at the phone in my hand. "Easy-peasy," I added bravely.

For all my show of confidence, dread pooled in my middle. I was ready to postpone the call when *Little Women* caught my eye. Despite her rocky start, Meg March, my favorite character, had turned out to be the perfect mother. What would *she* do? I flipped up the lid of my mobile.

"You're mad," said Deirdre. "But if you're *so* dead keen on doing this, you might as well ring the woman at breakfast, before she goes anywhere." Deirdre had an amazing facility for time zone calculation. But no head for accounts. Go figure. "But you know, Ash, I don't think I can watch this." She gathered up her handbag and coat. "I've an errand to do."

Which likely involved a visit to Brown Thomas. Phone in hand, I waved Deirdre off from the backroom doorway, amused despite myself at her circuitous route to the front door. Once outside, and safe from her mam's detection, she dimpled at a man in a posh coat standing by the shop window. That's Deirdre for you—she'd flirt with the corpse at a wake. Of course the man smiled back. Wishing that sometimes, my life could be as simple as Deirdre's, I keyed in the number, glad she wasn't here to see I knew it by heart. When I glanced back up, my thumb hovering over the keypad, she and the man were gone.

Well, for all I knew, *he* was the errand. But this was no time to dwell on Deirdre's romantic adventures. I'd a job to do, though I lacked the Chardonnay-primed courage I'd had last weekend. And any minute now, Polly—indulgent boss and mother she might be—would notice both her shop assistants were AWOL. So, ignoring that sinking feeling, rather like a large stone sitting right behind your navel, I pressed the "on" key...

THE STRANGER

From the first page of *Little Women*, I'd taken a mad fancy for the poor but happy March clan. What's not to like? With the absent but adoring dad, close-knit sisters, and the mother who was actually there for her kids, they were like, my fantasy family.

A shame my own bore no resemblance to it. To take my mind off my ex, I'd kept the book close by, to sneak read while Polly wasn't looking. But now, back at the counter after Deirdre had decamped, I set it aside to gaze wistfully through the shop's front window. Though it was not quite seven, Temple Bar's narrow stone streets were already pulsing with activity, people heading for parties and pubs. I hadn't much taste for nightlife, but wouldn't any girl of twenty-six want a break from a seriously Stuck in Neutral life?

A man materialized out of the crowd, and stopped at our front door. Mr. Posh Coat again, mobile at his ear. Tall and broad, he was a bit of a standout; Temple Bar was rampant with not only track-suited tourists, but scruffy artists and eccentrically-dressed oddballs. Since he was hardly our typical customer, maybe he'd returned to get Deirdre's number.

I took a slurp from my third Coke since lunch and took a closer look at him. How...strange. He rather had the look of— My mobile vibrated, setting off a jolt of adrenaline. I cautiously pulled the phone out of my pocket. "Hallo?"

"It's me." Deirdre. Not Annie Carpenter. "Have you heard anything from the mother, back in Minnesota?"

"Not since you rang twenty minutes ago," I said glumly. When I'd gotten Annie's machine a second time, I started to wonder if her silence was...significant. She'd forgotten who I was? That seemed highly unlikely, given our longtime connection. Then, upon leaving her every possible means of contacting me, a far more demoralizing thought struck: what if she'd told her son I'd rung and he asked her not to speak to me?

"Oh, shaggit," Deirdre said. "Maybe it's time you took the direct route—check him out online, get his e-mail that way. Else you'll be a wreck all weekend."

"Google stalk him? I don't think so." For now, I wanted to keep him more... theoretical. Looking him up would make him well, *real*. "I'll read *Little Women*, in the bath," I decided. "A nice long one. That'll calm me down." That and about a half dozen chocolate bars.

"Oh, puh-lease. God knows reading it would put me into a coma."

That's Deirdre—a walking advert for a bookstore. "Sure, I'd drop dead from the shock myself, to see *you* with a book," I teased, "but I wish you'd give this one a try." I got a bit misty-eyed. "When I was twelve, I must've read the part where John Brooke proposes to Meg about a million times."

"Why, is it hot?"

"Get off," I told her. "It was sweet and romantic." To my girlish soul, Meg sitting on John's knee had been incredibly sexy.

"With that boyfriend of yours hardly a great one for

6

romance—or should I say sort of boyfriend—you need all you can get," said Deirdre. "Especially with his eejit hiatus thing—"

"Let's keep Sam out of this," I broke in. In case you're thinking a proper girlfriend would have defended her guy, I'd bigger worries than Sam. Like how late I'd be stuck here. I sneaked another glance at the door. Our man was still outside, still on the phone. "Why'd you ring anyway?"

"To see if Mam ever noticed I left," Deirdre said promptly.

"I doubt it." I finished my Coke in one gulp. "She's been chatting up two ancient ladies from Clare, then she found this old feather duster amongst the jumble. She's been having the time of her life ever since." About twice the size of Deirdre, Polly was whacking the duster round like a Valkyrie going into battle. "Say, before you ring off, there's this guy hanging about outside —I think he's waiting for you."

"Who?"

"Well, you smiled at him when you left earlier. Tall, well-dressed, nice haircut."

"Who?" she asked again. I rolled my eyes. Evidently he *wasn't* her latest conquest. "Look," and I glanced at another of Polly's jumble finds, a cuckoo clock. "It's nearly seven—got to start closing out the register. See you later."

I stowed my mobile, giving it a silent pep talk to ring with Annie, not Deirdre on the line. Then I jerked my head up as the bell jangled, and Mr. Posh all but vaulted inside. Giving him a quick sidelong look, I blinked. *He really does resemble—*

Polly breezed over to the counter, winking at me as she whisked her duster over a display of miniature step-dancing shoes. "Wouldn't you know, just at closing we'd get Himself over there." She jerked her head in the direction of the stranger, now in the book section.

Trying not to mind I'd be stuck here past seven, I grabbed a pile of receipts. "D'you think we should lower the lights to get him out the door?"

"Let's give him another minute or two," Polly said. "The fairies often bring your biggest sales on Fridays." Polly believed the fairies had an active hand at the shop—but then, she was away with the fairies a good part of the time. "If he takes much longer, I'll give him a bit of a sales pitch." She sashayed off to dust more stock.

Sorting receipts, I sensed a tense aura round him—perhaps the result of my recent mystical contemplation. Then I jumped as my mobile vibrated again. Annie Carpenter, at last?

"It's me again," said Deirdre. "I just had a fantastic insight. What if *not* hearing back from his mother was the real sign? That you should drop the idea altogether."

Don't say that! "I won't believe that," I said stoutly. *Little Women* fell on your bloody head, I reminded myself. If that's not a sign I don't know what is. Eager to get home, I glanced at the man to see if we were making any progress, and it struck me forcibly. Holy Jaysus, he was a dead ringer for...*I should really give up Coke—the caffeine's clearly making me hallucinate.*

"Aislin...?" Deirdre prompted.

"Yeah?" I said vaguely. The man didn't appear to be actually *shopping.* He'd pick up a book without looking at it, then put it down.

"Ash! Are you there?" Deirdre asked.

"Oh—sorry. We've a bit of a problem customer here."

"Someone hassling you?"

"Not exactly," I said. "It's that guy I mentioned. He came inside, but he's just wandering round. Seems to be hiding one hand too."

"Maybe he's a nutter," Deirdre proposed. "Loaded, but loves the thrill of shoplifting."

"Shopl—?" I squeaked. Lowering my voice, I said, "He doesn't look the type."

"They never do," Deirdre pointed out. "Maybe you should call the Guards."

All I needed was a big brouhaha keeping me here even later. "Really, if he tries anything, your mam'll be sure to chase him out with her feather duster."

"If you're sure nothing's wrong." Deirdre actually sounded worried.

"Positive," I said grandly, then jumped as the man grabbed another book and strode to the counter. I looked up and met his eyes. "Oh, Jaysus!" I gasped, and promptly dropped my mobile.

"Ash..." hissed from the speaker. "ASHH-LINNN!"

Hands shaking, chest heaving, I retrieved my phone. "I-I-I'll ring you later."

THE REUNION

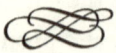

*N*umerology folk hold that the number seven has mystical, magical qualities. You know, the Seven Wonders of the World, seventh heaven, Snow White's seven dwarfs. But seven's never worked out for me. My parents forgot my seventh birthday. I seem to overdraw my bank account the seventh of every month. And whenever my face breaks out, I invariably get seven spots.

Now, as I was caught in Dante's Seventh Circle of Hell, Polly's cuckoo clock chirped seven times.

"Hey, Aislin." The man's voice was guarded. "It's been uh, a long time."

My chest so tight I could barely breathe, I gaped at him. Why, why did I never, *ever* sort out anything beyond ringing Annie...

"Hey—you okay? I thought you knew I was going to drop in," Ben Carpenter said.

I tried to speak but no sound came out. A good thing, since the only thing I could think of was, *What in the bloody hell are you doing here?* Another excruciatingly awkward minute passed, then I managed a faint, "Your mother was meant to send your e-mail address." *Not you.*

I couldn't think of anything else to say. It was a little too soon for, *by the way, I've Something Important to tell you—*

"I would've come sooner, but I was in Galway," Ben said, and lifted his hand. "Uh...these are for you."

He'd been hiding something, all right. Cream tulips, with fuchsia throats. And if I wasn't mistaken, there were seven of them! But guys didn't give girls flowers anymore. Were the tulips *and* Ben simply a product of my over-caffeinated, oxygen-starved imagination?

I blinked, hoping to break up his image, but no. He was still in front of me, solid and all too real. "They're...lovely." Heart-burn flamed in my chest. "Very k-kind of you."

"Mom thought you'd like them." Ben's Midwestern accent sounded flatter than I remembered. "Actually, I was just on the phone with her. She was...really glad to hear from you." Setting the flowers and book he'd chosen on the counter, he looked around, as if searching for an escape route.

I couldn't blame him...but how he could show up in Dublin so fast had to be one of the Great Mysteries of the Universe.

Polly suddenly appeared. "Sir, I'll ring you up, then?" She looked at me. "You're pale as milk pudding, love. You're all right?"

"I'm great," I said feebly, and turned back to Ben. "It...it's g-grand to see you too." My smile wobbled. The nuns at school always said that liars would burn in Everlasting Hellfire, but Holy St. Joseph, I was being punished even before I got there. "Seven years, is it?"

"That sounds about right," said Ben.

Well, *I* knew exactly how long it was. Practically down to the minute. And what did I tell you? Seven, for me, clearly means doom. "So then," I said casually, "here you are in Dublin! On business?"

Ben pushed his hands into his coat pockets. "I always said I'd visit Ireland someday."

Jaysus, never tell me you came all this way on account of a phone message? The shock of it robbed me of speech yet again.

"Well, God love ya!" Polly broke in. Wreathed in smiles, she gazed at Ben, feather duster pressed to her broad bosom. "Are the pair of you long-lost friends?"

"Yep." Ben looked relieved. "From my home town in Minnesota."

Polly peered at him more closely. "You've not been here before? You look famil—"

"It was when I went to America for university," I said quickly.

Luckily, Polly was easily distracted. "A number, were you?" Her voice was arch.

"You mean like, uh…dating?" Ben swallowed. "Well, not officially."

Polly's smile widened, and she gave the flowers a significant look. "Unofficially, then?"

"We didn't get that…uh, far." Now he pulled at his shirt collar. I'd have laughed, if this wasn't so awful. "I was home on leave from the Navy, and Aislin and I, uh…hung out a few times."

That's a great way to put it.

Polly said admiringly, "A military man—fancy that."

"Just a four-year hitch," Ben said. "I helped her with… freshman calc."

We'd sit side-by-side in my parents' showplace kitchen, while his mother Annie, our housekeeper, did the washing up. I'd sneak dreamy looks at him, struggling to keep my attention on dreary equations. Much more interesting was his expression when I'd tickle his knee under the table…

"Grand at the maths, so," Polly was saying. "The good Lord's blessed you with looks *and* brains."

Lovely. Polly's flirting routine, honed at St. Brendan's jumble sales, was shifting into high gear. With Ben of all people!

Ben looked flushed. "Actually, Aislin and I go way back—we were pals when we were kids, before she left to live in Ireland. Mom doted on you, Aislin. Remember?"

"Sure, your Mam was sweet to me." I fumbled with the receipts. He was as...nice as I remembered. Nicer, even. Which made my plan sort of...unethical? I sent a furtive glance at the tulips. *How about completely rotten...*

A substantial elbow nudged my ribs. "Aislin." As I looked up blankly, Polly said, "Why don't the pair of you go out for a bite, and catch up a bit?"

"Well, I..." I began. "Actually," Ben said at the same time, "I've got to—"

"There's a grand little pub across the way," Polly told Ben. "They do lovely sandwiches."

Hello! I thought resentfully. *I'd like to see* you *eat with this heartburn.* Before I could stand my ground, Ben said, "I don't much care for pubs. Anyplace else?"

Polly looked at him as if he wasn't quite right in the head. "Well, the pubs are full of racket anyway, but there's a coffee place round the corner."

"Great," said Ben. Give the man credit, he was a lot more gracious than I could ever be. Especially since he obviously hadn't wanted to be here—he'd needed two tries to come inside. "How about it, Aislin?"

I ventured a look at Ben's face. *No way. Not ready.* "I can't, really." I plucked at my seen-better-days jumper. "Look at the state of me."

One advantage to working at O'Donnell's was no spending money on power suits—but couldn't I have been more put together than today's ensemble? Which was a tatty cardigan with baggy pockets, jeans frayed at the hemline. As if my hair knew it was being depended on to carry the day, it began to slip from its knot. I reached up to check how badly it was drooping, and felt a wad of frizz. *Brilliant.* Dressed like a tinker with hair to match.

Polly elbowed me again. "You've no need to dress up for a quick coffee."

I snatched my hand down, in case she thought I was primping. "Really, that's not the point. I just have to get home."

Ben drummed his fingers on his book. "Your...husband's waiting for you?"

"Ha, that's good one," Polly snorted.

"I'm not married," I said stiffly, "but I have a...a—" I couldn't quite get the word out.

"A date, huh?" Ben's fingers stilled. "Maybe another time—"

"You've plans?" Polly looked affronted. "Since when? I thought you and Sam—"

"I do not have...whatever!" Jaysus, I sounded like a right fool. I took a deep breath, reaching for my rucksack beneath the counter. "But maybe we could meet next week." *Or next month. After I've sorted out what to do with you...*

"I'll count on it." Ben handed Polly his credit card.

Scanning the card, Polly annoyingly asked, "And what brings you to Ireland, Ben?"

I resisted the temptation to sprint out of the shop. What wouldn't I give for the placid, boring life I'd enjoyed before my eejit phone call. But regrets were shag-all use to me now. I'd made this sorry mess—and I'd have to see it through.

IT'S TOO LATE (TO TURN BACK NOW)

$\mathcal{B}$y all accounts—that is, people unaware of my situation—I should have been mad for Ben Carpenter. You see, seven years ago he'd rescued me from the kind of Embarrassing Moment that's like having "Failure" stamped in block letters on your forehead and haunts you forever.

I was performing in the freshman "Retro Night" talent programme at college, and figured my Irish step dance was about as retro as you could get. Save for the previous act, a trio of girls gyrating to "Like a Virgin." I mean, there were no virgins on campus, as far as I could tell. Except me.

The Madonna wannabe's had gotten a rousing response—no doubt in direct proportion to the rate of BBPM—Bouncing Boobs Per Minute. But as the last notes of my fiddle and bodhran CD faded and I took my bow, not a soul applauded. I could only stand there, my face flaming. Then suddenly, a young man—who, despite the military haircut, was clearly a crazed non-conformist, bless him—stood up in the middle of the audience and started to clap. The crowd got the idea, and as they joined in, my hero threw in an ear-splitting whistle.

I could have kissed him. In a few short moments, I'd gone from Total Reject to Off the Applause-o-Meter. Beaming, I scanned the audience and found my savior. To my utter amazement, I recognized him—it was Ben! Our housekeeper's son—the "older" boy I'd fancied at age six. And as it turned out, not long after, I *did* kiss him...

Ben's voice pulled me out of my time tunnel. "...University after the Navy...Seattle IT job...Stock options...brainy Irish guy...Ireland's software industry...new design firm..." Yada, yada, yada... "Our office near Intel..."

Shite! He lived here!

Suppressing a gasp of horror, I clutched my rucksack for something to hang on to. Deirdre's imagined problem of Ben hopping on a plane to Ireland had nothing, I mean, absolutely *Nothing*, on The Real Worst Case Scenario: Ben actually *residing* in Dublin!

"The Celtic Tiger gave Ireland some good times," Polly said. "Not so easy now, but I've no doubt you'll be a grand success. And did you hear that, Aislin? Ben has a *business*."

"Lovely," I managed. God help us, Polly was at it again—the woman could smell a matchmaking opportunity at thirty paces. When she actually wiggled her eyebrows at me suggestively, I sent her a pleading glance. *Please. Not the eyebrows.*

But to no avail. "Ash, love," she wheedled, moving in for the kill, "Ben's brought you *flowers*. Has Sam ever troubled himself?"

"Well, no," I admitted. "But I've a million things to—"

"You're not to worry, I'll finish up here. My Maggie won't mind keeping the b—"

"But it's getting late," I interrupted, feeling frantic.

"If this isn't a good time," Ben said, "we can—"

"It's a great time," said Polly. "Aislin, run to the back and get those flowers in some water."

I glanced from Polly's determined face to Ben's impassive

one. "Right," I mumbled, resigned. I'd go out with the devil himself if it would shut Polly up. And while I was in the loo, maybe I could sort out a quick escape—which Ben would likely welcome as much as I would.

Polly handed Ben his credit card slip. "You'll like *Wicked Game*," she said slyly. Ben looked blank. "But I'd never've pegged you as the potboiler sort."

"Potboiler?" Ben said in a strangled voice. As he glanced down at his book, I did too. A red-haired cover girl wore a sultry smile and strategically placed handgun—and nothing else.

I forgot my turmoil and stared at him, fascinated, as a fresh swath of color—actually more like a Sherman's March through Georgia—marched up his neck to the tips of his ears. "I thought I picked up the new Grisham book."

I'd heard that one before. So had Polly. "No need to be embarrassed." She chuckled. "Why, three guys from the parish bought this title last week—and all three said it was for his wife!" Then coyly, "Why not get *your* wife to buy your books?"

Ben smile looked glued on. "This one's fine. And I'm not married."

I took pity on him. Besides, practicing my retail skills in the middle of a nervous breakdown might come in handy someday. "Don't be silly—you'll want a store credit." I snatched the awful book, shoved it under the counter, and pulled out a credit form and a pen.

"Actually, I'll take...these." Ben plucked a pair of the mini-dancing shoes off the display, then met my eyes.

I was the first to look away. As I stuck the pen into my hair at the temple, I caught Polly waggling her eyebrows at me again. *The loo*, I thought desperately, then my mobile rang.

It had to be Deirdre. "What is it?"

"So, what's happened with that nutcase—"

"Sorry for not getting back to you," I broke in cheerily, "but everything's great."

"You're not being held hostage, forced to make phony 'Nothing's wrong' phone calls?"

"Honestly, Deirdre, you watch too much telly," I said with false gaiety. "See you tomorrow night!" Ringing off, I realized the desperate need for a new plan, before I could possibly be alone with Ben. "Look," I said to him. *That's it. Don't let Polly run your bloody life.* "It's just not on, after all. Going for coffee, I mean."

Ben pushed his hands in his trouser pockets. "Then how about a ride home?"

"Would you hear that?" Polly beamed. "A nice change from the bus, so it is." Then to Ben, "Good job Sam's not the jealous type."

Another spurt of acid hit my middle. "My flat's awfully far—the bus is more convenient."

"Then I'll walk you to your bus stop."

Polly nodded approvingly. "Temple Bar's a mad crush, this time of night."

"But...I...I..." A short walk, in a public street—what could go wrong? Anyway, I'd need to be on Ben's good side soon enough, even if the Universe had it out for me tonight. "Okay, then. Be right back."

I stashed my mobile in my jumper pocket, and grabbing the tulips, dashed to the loo. Filling the sink, I dunked the flowers in it, ready to hurry out. Unfortunately the plugging device was as paltry as my excuses, and the sink promptly emptied. Ah, hell. Re-jigger the drain and run more water? I asked myself. Or get this bloody ordeal over with? I pulled out the dripping flowers, and reaching over the toilet, tossed them into the bin next to it. *He'll never know.*

Still, I stared down at the tulips. *What an utter cow I am, when bringing flowers is such a Little Women-ish, John Brooke-ian thing to do...* I leaned over, poised to fish them out, when I remembered that last, awful moment with Ben seven years ago...My knees wobbled, and I closed my eyes, reaching for the wall for support.

There was a thunk, then a splash. I popped my eyes open.

My mobile was in the toilet. "Shite, shite, shite!" My lovely phone, only three months old! Then I remembered Ben. He'd probably heard me—what if he thought I was swearing about him? Too late now. I dug out the rubber gloves we kept under the sink, strapped on the right-handed one, and gingerly fished my phone out of the water. Pressing the power key, I prayed for a signal.

Nothing. So I'd just ruined my one-hundred euro new mobile, when I hadn't any money to buy another, and it was all Ben Carpenter's fault. I perched the phone on the sink and peeled off the glove. Maybe after the phone dried out a bit, there was hope for it.

I left the flowers in the bin.

After snatching my raincoat, I marched back to Polly's side as she was wrapping up Ben's tiny shoes. "Thanks for..." *complicating my life...* "closing up." I grabbed *Little Women*, to stow next to *Wicked Game*.

"Take it home, if you like—but better not read that old thing in the bath," Polly said merrily. "It'll fall to pieces."

Feeling my cheeks scorch, I jerked my coat belt so hard I got a stitch in my side. "Thanks, but I've my own copy." *Lovely of you to share my bathing habits.* "I'll sort out the receipts Monday."

Polly handed Ben his parcel. "I haven't a doubt of it." Clasping her hands across her ample middle, she smiled beatifically, the one she normally saved for Father Flaherty at St. Brendan's. "Off you go."

With Polly looking like the cat who'd swallowed a lorry of

cream, Ben and I stepped into the misty April twilight hovering over Crown Alley, and my heartburn turned into a forest fire.

BEN HAD NEVER BEEN drop-dead handsome, the kind where you do a double take on the street. Which appealed to me, because film-star looks meant every other girl was staring at him too, and soon the guy got a big head from the attention. I was all for the sort of guy you didn't realize was good looking until you'd got to know them a bit.

Like Ben. Brawny and easy to look at, if you like the rugged type. And I had. Apparently I still did, because as I walked beside him, my hormones were on high alert.

Sort of like my hormonal rush the night of my step-dancing triumph, when Ben had found me backstage. "You were great," I said, so happy to see him I'd got a lump in my throat. "I thought I'd made a mess of it, 'til you started the whole lot applauding." I gave him a sidelong glance, completely forgetting about Kelly, the boy meeting me here. "And haven't you changed in the past thirteen years."

"I hope that's good," he said, his dark eyes intense. Then he smiled, his eyes going sort of sparkly, and I saw he hadn't changed at all.

"Oh, definitely," I said. "*Verrry* good—I think thirteen's my new lucky number." I'd never really flirted before, but with him it came naturally. Along with a lot of other things that...came naturally...

I came to, there on the cobblestones of Temple Bar, just as Ben was reaching toward my head. I jerked backward. "Sorry?"

He dropped his hand. "Your pen—it's still in your hair."

The old me, the Natural Woman, would've leaned toward him with an inviting look, and said, "Take it then. And whatever else you'd like." The New Me grabbed the pen, nearly poking myself in the eye. What was wrong with me? Here was an opportunity to start chatting Ben up. I could ask him about his mam, or how he liked Ireland. Even have the laugh about Polly's matchmaking. But I couldn't manage even a minimum of repartee. And the longer I let this farce go on, the more likely he'd wonder why the bloody hell I'd asked his mother for his e-mail —then give him the silent treatment to his face. "I just remembered…an errand I've got to do. I'll take the bus from there."

Ben frowned. "Let's get you a pedicab, then. The fare's on me."

Why did he have to be so noble? But then, except for once, he always had been…Suddenly, the old memory of our non-goodbye flashed into my brain again, with the regrets, the could-have-beens, and I felt tears at the back of my eyes. Shivering against the April chill, I yanked out my gloves, the crowds and the noise and the garish lights of Temple Bar closing in on me. I had to escape…

Like an answer to my prayer, a young man with a plastic cup in his hand blundered toward us. Used to the Bar's rowdy party-goers, I quickly stepped back, but Ben didn't. The man splashed his drink all over Ben's overcoat. Beer.

"Damn," Ben muttered, as the young man said, "Sorry, mate," then staggered on.

Poised to bolt, I realized my flight from Ben would be temporary, since I'd given his mother enough personal information to steal my identity. But flee I would. "I'm sure you'll want to clean up your coat." I took another backward step as he bent to the cobblestones.

"Aislin, you dropped your glo—"

"Sorry, got to go—nice of you to call in at the shop."

I sensed Ben's bafflement, and my former life as a natural woman rose up to haunt me again. But I *had* to sort out what I was getting into. I darted away from him, stifling a fist-shaking-at-the-Almighty-moment. *Why? Why does my life always turn to crap?*

Had I really thought contacting an ex-boyfriend only took a bit of caution? Seeing Ben had exposed the truth of it: To keep from remembering what it was like to be completely mad, head-over-heels for a man, you'd want to stuff your heart and your memories into a mental Haz-Mat suit.

Especially if you'd borne your ex a child.

MAMMY KNOWS BEST

I'd never really believed the old wives' tale that you can't get pregnant having sex just once. But there's small comfort in disproving a time-honored superstition, when you'd no intention of putting it to the test in the first place. Having an unplanned baby, whose welcome is shaky at best, means you start motherhood off on the wrong foot. And often are left hopping around on said foot for the rest of your days.

Still there's something about motherly love that eventually gets the better of you. As I approached our flat, Kevin, eyes sparkling, raced up to me outside the door. I glued on my Happy Mammy face, wishing I could wrap him in my arms and hold him forever. Make up for all the times I'd let him down without meaning to… for all the times I'd been a less than perfect mother. Which started about the minute I'd given birth to him. No, wait—from the minute I'd discovered I was pregnant.

But not wanting to be one of those awful clingy mammies, the sort that squeezes the life out of her son so the poor little fella is forced to squirm away from her tentacle-like grip, I only kissed the top of his head. "Hallo, love." I unlocked the door, easing his schoolbag off his shoulder. "Watching for me, were you?"

"G-guess what happened today!"

My life turned into a *really* bad joke… "Let me think…" I stalled. "Something good?"

Even Kevin's freckles looked sort of sparky. "There's a new boy at school, he's called Sean, and he's short! The smallest b-boy in the c-class now! Even Chris said so."

"Grand!" I slung off my coat and switched on the electric fire, ignoring the usual detritus strewn across the threadbare carpet. "Chris knows what he's about."

Kevin's face suddenly clouded. "But the boy c-called me 'st-st-stupid st-stutter nutter.'"

Ire swelled in my chest. "That little gob—" I broke off. That's the other thing about being a second-rate mother. You want to whack any kid who hurts your child. "That wasn't very nice," I said instead. Small for his age, Kevin having a stammer—speech disfluency, the experts called it—created even more of a handicap. "Perhaps that Sean's a bit of a thick," I added kindly, smoothing my son's carroty hair, several shades oranger than mine. "He doesn't know stuttering is caused by…by…having tons of smart thoughts in your head."

Kevin scowled. "If I had a d-d-dad, he could c-call round to Sean's and th-thrash—"

"No one's going to thrash anyone!" I interrupted, and a fresh wave of maternal guilt struck me. Look what else Ben Carpenter had made me do: break the No Interrupting rule for a stammering child. But at the same time, I got the pleasurable image of big shouldered, square-jawed Ben giving out at the misbegotten Sean *and* his parents…

I couldn't help glancing at the fridge. Sellotaped front and center was the haunting little drawing of Kevin's, that had led to last weekend's confab with the girls. I swallowed against the tightness in my throat. "You'll soon tower over that pipsqueak

Sean," I forced out, to squash my own Daddy Fantasies. Kevin still looked glum. "Well, you will," I insisted, and tickled him under the chin. "Hey now—when we need cheering up, what do we do?"

Kevin pulled a face, but said dutifully, "Slip jig."

"Then give us a beat!"

"Aw, Mam," he said, but commenced clapping. I curtsied, then tried on a few steps, but his half-hearted clapping sort of dwindled. Just like my jig. As I fumbled a final bow, a slip of paper fell out of my jumper pocket. I grabbed it before Kevin could see it. "Well...time to call round next door with Maggie's pay."

"I've a new p-picture at Maggie's," Kevin said, brightening. "Me 'n Chris 'n Janey drawed after school."

Oh, no. "Another fairy picture for Polly?" I asked hopefully, stuffing the paper into my jeans pocket. "She's sure more fairies visited the shop this week."

Kevin peered at me uneasily. "Well, n-not exact—"

There was a single rap at the door. Maggie, Deirdre's sister and Polly's eldest, poked her head in, waving a crayoned drawing. "It's me—here's your picture, love," she said to Kevin, handing it to him before I could see it. As he trotted to the kitchen, she came inside, and fixed a stern look on me. "Still got that list around?"

I patted my pocket, more trepidation filling me. "I've kept it on me all week."

"You'll need it," Maggie said. "That drawing—it's another one. Of his *dad*."

THE LIST

Reasons to contact *him*:

 # *1* : K's stuttering improving. Better able to handle life changes. Plus daddy fantasies getting out of hand.

#2: Sam thing not going well. Totally man-free life not best for all concerned.

#3: Chance of more $ coming in. Awful of me but true. But it'll be spent on speech therapy. Not awful of me since true.

#3a: Sam's all for me having more $ as well. But no great new job has fallen into lap. And both too depressing to include as regular item on list.

#4: Recently added item, after getting *Little Women* sign: My family will never be like the Marches. Family-free life not best for all concerned either.

KEVIN HAD ALREADY AFFIXED his new picture next to last week's and was off to his room by the time I'd sat Maggie down at my kitchen table. Smelling faintly of onions, cooked lamb, and dishwashing liquid, Maggie Tobin was not just my neighbor and

Kevin's carer, but my second best friend, next to Deirdre. "Well," she said, gazing at the drawings. "You've a matched pair."

I winced. Both drawings featured Kevin's imaginary dad. You could hardly miss the self-portrait—red hair and freckles—only bigger. "The fantasy problem was first on my list, you'll remember."

Maggie, brunette like Deirdre, but a rounder, jeans-clad, flour-dusted version of her sister, gave me a penetrating look. "Deirdre rang a few minutes ago—said you haven't heard a peep from the mother."

"Not...yet," I said, avoiding her gaze. Well, *technically* I hadn't.

"Still, no way round it—the boy needs a father."

Maggie was the most together person I knew, so I was more inclined to take her advice over anyone else's. Still, I wasn't ready to spill the whole Ben story. "Sam hasn't made much of an impression on Kevin, I'm afraid."

"Sam isn't quite daddy material—which can't be news to you."

"Of course it isn't," I said. "I put it second on the list."

"It wasn't a proper list, as I recall," Maggie said.

Maybe that's where I'd gone wrong: a list of all "Pros" and not a "Con" in sight. But I'd guess the bigger problem was that I wasn't particularly good mammy material myself. "I suppose you've made a lovely supper for Bill and the kids," I said, to change the subject.

It worked. "I'll bet you can smell it on me." Maggie grinned, brushing at her jumper. "Eau de stew. Kevin seemed to like it—he had two servings."

What did I tell you? Maggie was the sort of homemaking diva who'd already fed her family—and it being Friday, my late night at the shop—my son as well. And she'd already finished the washing up before eight pm.

I jumped up and went to the fridge, trying not to look at the drawings. "You're a regular Martha Stewart and that Nigella What's-her-name rolled into one. And thanks for giving Kevin his tea." Pulling some potatoes out, I grabbed a paring knife. "I haven't even thought about mine." Normally, I'd be ravenous by now, but the Ben business had really put me off my food.

"I'd love to look like Nigella," said Maggie, not meaning a word of it. She might not be as pretty as Deirdre, but then, she didn't care. Besides, her sister still lived at home, and with Polly picking up all her expenses, Deirdre had plenty of money to spend on cosmetics and facials.

As I began peeling, I felt her eyes on my back. "You seem a bit knackered tonight, love." Maggie hadn't inherited her mother's obtuseness—which was inconvenient at times. Like now. "Did Mammy put you through the ringer at the shop?"

"Nothing like that." I thought fast—maybe I could give a bit of a hint now, and tell the rest tomorrow. "Actually... someone I used to know called round before closing."

"Girlfriend?"

I shook my head, and glanced over my shoulder to make sure Kevin was still in his room.

"Boyfriend, then?" Maggie dropped her voice and giggled. "Or lover?"

I almost dropped the knife. Maggie's horniness didn't quite jive with being a homemaking wunderkind. "Aren't you the loopy one." For something to do, I started on another potato. "This one was never a...real boyfriend, but he looked great. While I acted a real eejit." Not surprising, given my dreary track record with men, but still.

"Why should that bother you? Unless you're keen to impress him," Maggie said slyly.

"Him? God, no," I hooted. Then realized I was doth protesting too much. "It's just that—well, after so long, I didn't want to look like such an ould hag."

"You? Ha." Maggie propped her feet on the opposite chair.

"Even if you don't fancy this one, you know my motto: men can do wonders for tension."

"To create it or release it?" I asked mockingly, peeling madly. Now that I thought of it, Sam was much better with the former than the latter.

"You've too many responsibilities, love. You need to relax a bit."

"My granny says that too." I hacked the potato in two, nearly whacking off my index finger. "But I know how to have fun."

"Do you now," Maggie observed. "I'd like to see it."

According to Maggie and Deirdre, every girl should have a time when you just live for the moment, with no worries whatsoever. They'd enjoyed a carefree youth, at least during the six months they'd shared a flat before Maggie met Bill. For the O'Donnell girls, having fun meant keeping all your clothes in a heap on the floor, so all you had to do to get dressed was pick through it each morning, with a fridge that held only beer and moldy cheese, because you couldn't be bothered to go to the shops. Not to mention, as the sisters would giggle, occasionally waking up with a guy you'd met the night before in bed with you.

Whereas I'd lived with my parents before *and* after Kevin came along, with no chance for that sort of craic, or any other highjinks. "Okay, no need to remind me again," I said, concentrating madly on my peeling, "that I'm way out of the mainstream."

"I know—a single mam with the father gone missing." Maggie sobered. "Sure, Kevin's progress with his speech makes up for the difficult times."

And with Ben Carpenter in town, those times were just about to get harder...

The phone rang. Before I could set down the knife, Maggie jumped up and grabbed it. "Of course she's here. Would I call round if she wasn't?" She held out the handset. "It's Mammy."

"Shop business, I'm sure." I wiped my hands, then reluctantly took the phone. "Polly?"

"You'd a nice time with Ben then?"

"Lovely," I said brightly. *All five minutes of gut-churning nerves.* Then it occurred to me how fast Ben's presence could get blown out of proportion. "But if you could sort of not mention..." I noticed Maggie was listening without shame, "You know, at the shop—"

"Not mention himself to the girls? I'm silent as the grave. You'll want to tell them your exciting news yourself."

"That's it," I said, relieved, though it was debatable, how long Polly could keep from broadcasting Ben's visit. Discretion was, most assuredly, not her strong suit. "Anything else?"

"You'll want to know Ben came back to the shop—"

"C-came b-back?" I stammered.

"Did you forget? The beer on his lovely coat? I sent him to the loo so he could clean up."

Bollocks. He couldn't have missed the flowers in the bin. Or my abandoned phone. "Did you...chat a bit?"

"He had to rush. But I wanted to let you know, of course I didn't mention Kevin."

"Oh." Relieved, I sagged against the counter, then glanced at Maggie again, wondering what she was making of the conversation. "Any...special reason?" I held my breath.

"Ash, love," Polly sighed patiently, "I didn't want to scare him off. A lot of men aren't too keen on...you know. Single moms."

No kidding. "Really, Polly, there's no question of..." I couldn't say, *me fancying him,* not with Maggie there, "...any involvement. Anyway, I don't have anything..." I turned away. "to hide," I whispered.

"Of course you don't," said Polly. "You'll see him soon, then?"

"I'm sure I will," I lied. It got a bit sticky sometimes, having your boss play your surrogate mammy. Though surely, I wouldn't *always* be working for Polly... "I'll see you Monday," I said, and rang off.

Now I'd one more thing to fret about. Not only how to spin Ben turning up to Maggie and Deirdre, but do it before Polly did...

"Aislin?"

I blinked, meeting Maggie's curious gaze. Before she could ask what her mother wanted, I said, "Are you still up for coming here tomorrow night? We'll get a video, and order Chinese."

"Instead of O'Fagan's? Deirdre will complain that there won't be any guys around," Maggie said. "So to entertain ourselves, we'll want to hear what Sam's about with this hiatus idea. And we can sort out your next move with the Minnesota fellow."

My move? On Ben? My stomach started churning again. Then I remembered she didn't know about him. "You mean," I said weakly, "since his mam never rang."

"What else?" She gave me another assessing look. "Is there something..." she began, then checked her watch. "Will you look at the time? The kids'll be waiting for tucking up."

"Kevin too," I said, and opened the door. Good job motherhood always came first for her. While I was glad for Maggie's sisterly concern, she often saw more than I'd like.

"No rest for the wicked, my granny says." Maggie laughed, and disappeared next door.

Definitely a cliché I'd never believed applied to me. Now, given all the ways Ben Carpenter could complicate my life, it just goes to show how wrong you can be.

THE STEP DANCE

I took the last bite of my General Tso's chicken, clicked "Stop" on the remote, and curled my toes around the edge of the coffee table with contentment. "Time for dessert," I said.

"Already?" Maggie picked up her knitting needles. You had to admire people like Mags, who did the washing up straightaway after dinner, then solved half the world's problems before they thought about pudding. Sadly, I wasn't one of them.

Pressing "Rewind," I waved a small paper sack. "Fortune cookies." I disregarded my tight waistband—had to be water weight from the salty Chinese food. Quantities of which had still not helped me forget about Ben.

"What'd you think of the film?" asked Deirdre as my old video player whirred. "Do I know how to pick them or what?"

"Kate Hudson's Irish accent wasn't half-bad," said Maggie, knitting away in the corner of the couch.

"Well, call me retro," and I surreptitiously unfastened my jeans button, and pulled my t-shirt over it to conceal the deed, "but I'm not that keen on sex farces." Why watch one when you can live one?

"Now that surprises me, since you put up with Sam," said Deirdre.

"He has many good qualities," I said loftily. "So stop slagging him, will you?"

Deirdre snorted. "You're not still thinking of taking a weekend with ol' Mr. Romantic—what, to have one for the road?"

"You've a dirty mind," I chided. With Sam, I'd never been big on having *one*, much less for the road. "After he mentioned this hiatus thing, it could be a grand opportunity to sort out—"

"What's to sort? If you ask me, he thinks he's too good for you—"

"Back to the film," Maggie broke in, her fingers slowing. "What's with that fellow sleeping around with this one and that one, taking advantage of the girls' weaknesses?"

"*About Adam* is a chick-flick," Deirdre explained. "The characters are meant to be...well, really confused. You know, like Ash is about Sam."

"Like real life," I contradicted, refusing to rise to Deirdre's bait. "Only in films, it's funny." Actually, this could be an excellent lead-in to Ben, but I couldn't quite make myself do it.

"Or not." Maggie's hands stilled, and she closed her eyes. "What's the time?"

"Wake up." Deirdre nudged Maggie with her foot. "We've got to analyze our fortunes."

Maggie opened her eyes reluctantly as I opened the sack. "Look at this! They've given us an extra cookie."

"Kevin would tell us to save it for the fairies," Deirdre said, "but I say we split it."

"I always seem to get a fortune that completely relates to my life," I confided as I passed the cookies round.

"Sheer coincidence," Maggie said, and broke hers in two to pry out the slip of paper.

"No, Ash is right," Deirdre said. "It's a metaphysical thing. The cookie is giving you the exact message you need."

"You're bats," Maggie said. "Here's mine: 'You are the master of every situation.'" She crumpled up the paper and tossed it into an empty carton. "Sure, I've got it all covered, whether I'm scrubbing the loo, or picking up Bill's underpants."

"Haven't you always got the carpets hoovered, the meals on time?" I pointed out quickly. "And not just fish fingers or beans and toast. You've always clean knickers for everyone, and help your kids with their lessons." If I had it together half as well as Maggie, I would have found a better job *and* a stepdaddy for Kevin ages ago. And wouldn't have dropped my mobile into the toilet.

"And you never run out of toilet tissue," Deirdre added.

Well, yes," Maggie admitted, and bit into her cookie. "But Aislin, you go out to work."

"Doesn't matter," Deirdre put in. "What about Aunt Bridie? She's home all day, but she couldn't do a decent tea if the prime minister came to call. Too busy yakking."

"Auntie does mind Granny O'Donnell," Maggie said, but she chuckled. "Deedee, your turn."

"Don't call me that," Deirdre said, and opened her cookie. "'Your attention will be deeply returned.'"

"I sense a mystery," I said, as Maggie commanded, "Tell all."

"Well..." Deirdre's eyes shone. "Remember that goal-setting seminar I went to last week? I met a fellow called Adrian, and we had coffee yesterday."

The girl had no shame. "And here I thought you were out on shop errands," I said, and set my cookie on the table.

"He actually gave me some grand promotional ideas," Deirdre said virtuously. "The thing is, Adrian was *deeply* attentive. Hardly took his eyes off me the whole time."

"Maybe it was something to do with that cleavage-baring top you had on?" I grinned.

"A girl's got to leverage her assets," Deirdre said. "I'll never meet anyone at the shop, that's sure. All we see are the fairy fetish types, and old ladies hip enough for Temple Bar."

"But Aislin," Maggie said, "what about that guy who came in yesterday, who—"

"That nutter?" Deirdre said. "I can't believe I almost forgot about—"

"I'm interested in...setting some goals too," I said quickly. Well, I was. For starters, to be a better mother.

"Oh. Cool." Happily, Deirdre was easily distracted. "I've a new goal myself."

"Great!" I said. Maybe I could finagle some way to...leverage Ben's appearance without even mentioning his name. "Let's all share a goal, then a talent to...you know, reinforce the goal." I'd read that in a self-help book somewhere. "Deirdre, you first."

"Well—and don't give out at me—it's more a group goal..." Deirdre fiddled with a perfectly curved fingernail. "We should add someone new to our Girls' Nights."

"Why?" Maggie narrowed her eyes at Deirdre. "We're not entertaining enough for you? Just because I close my eyes for a minute late at night—"

"It's only half eight!" her sister retorted. "If you're going to snore off halfway through our one night together, wouldn't we have more fun with a fourth?"

"Maggie, I see what she's about." I patted her arm. "If she ditches us for Adrian, she wants the pair of us to do something other than sit at home, comparing potty training stories."

"That's it," Deirdre said. "I have only your best interests at heart."

As for me, if I was going to improve my mothering skills, my Girls' Nights might be numbered. "Maggie, haven't you a goal to share?"

Luckily, Maggie was too good-natured to stay insulted for long. "You mustn't tell Mam—she'll be all over me with advice."

"Ooh, sounds good," said Deirdre. She and I leaned forward in anticipation. Maggie having goals was a good sign—that being a good mammy didn't mean your life was over.

Maggie lowered her voice. "Bill and I are trying for another baby."

Deirdre and I jerked back simultaneously. "Jaysus," said Deirdre. "She's like that mam on *Leave it to Beavis*."

"That's *Beaver*," I said slowly, reeling a bit with Maggie's announcement.

"Whatever. She's June Cleaver, come back to life."

At least June had the sense to stop with the Beav. "So…a baby—that's grand," I lied. With a newborn to care for, Maggie would probably give up minding Kevin—*and* Girls' Night.

"But a *baby*, for God's sake," Deirdre said. "There's barely room in your flat as it is."

"Now, Deirdre," I began.

"I should have known you wouldn't be happy for me," Maggie snapped. "What's it to you if I have two kids or ten? Unless it's Mam spending her extra money on them instead of you."

"Maggie, you cow—"

"Deirdre, stop it!" For a minute, I was afraid she'd regress and pull Maggie's hair. "We're meant to support each other, not get into a barney."

Deirdre curled her lip. "Sure, I can support my sister. Feck's sake, Maggie, why a *baby*?"

"You've two great kids, and you said you're on easy street since Bill's promotion," I pointed out. If Maggie was going to all but disappear from my life once she had another baby, she'd better have some bloody good reasons.

"True," Maggie said, sounding appeased, "but I've missed having a little one in my arms. And I—well, it probably sounds a bit mad to you, Deedee, but I love that connection you get from breastfeeding." She ignored her sister, who pulled an even more grotesque face. "Ash, don't you miss it too, sometimes?"

"I… didn't breastfeed," I said.

Maggie looked shocked. "Whyever not?"

I wanted to make some excuse about bottles being more convenient, but couldn't lie. Not to Maggie, at least. "Actually, I…couldn't."

Maggie frowned, and picked up her cookie again. "I thought that was a myth."

"It's not," I said flatly. "But we're on *your* goal, not mine. What does Bill think?"

"He's all for it." Maggie's smile was a dead-on Mona Lisa's. "Since we're having it off almost every night. With no condoms to fuss with, Bill thinks he's died and gone to heaven."

"You've been using condoms since Janie came along?" I asked, then clamped my mouth shut. *Sure, you can always count on a condom.*

"Eeuuww." Deirdre stuck her fingers in her ears. "Bill and condoms? Let's not go there."

"Right, none of our business," I managed. This was no time to think about condoms, snogging, or the rest…

"I must say," Maggie went on, dreamily biting into her cookie, "going condom-free is *fantastic.*"

"No more!" Deirdre begged. "I can't take it."

"If I get preggie as fast as I did with the other two, the fun won't last long," Maggie said, laughing.

Deirdre still had her fingers in her ears. "Yuck! Please, Ash, make her stop."

So, it looked like I'd be out my child minder and friend sooner rather than later. Is this what I get for wanting to change my life? I looked at Maggie, missing her already. Still, there could be an upside to this pregnancy business. *Now that we've accounted for the extra thumping against my bedroom wall, once you conceive, I can get a bit more sleep.*

Maggie pulled her sister's hands down. "I'm done—what about your sex life, Deedee?"

"Wait, Maggie," I said. "What about your talent? Besides the clean loo and underpants."

Maggie picked up the needles and yarn in her lap. "Baby blanket."

Deirdre rolled her eyes. "Deirdre," I said hastily, "you've shared your goal, but not your talent." Her frown vanished. She extended her hands, fingers splayed.

"Nail varnish?" Her well-manicured nails were painted red, with teensy white swirls painstakingly applied on top. "Fabulous," I managed. "Must have taken hours."

Maggie took a quick look and snorted. Deirdre ignored her. "It did," she said with pride, then reclined back in her chair. "Adrian was quite keen. But Ash, it's your turn now. Don't say your goal is to get Sam back."

"No," I said, not pointing out, *But we haven't really broken up.* "My goal is to someday…" I took a deep breath. "You know, ages from now…have my own business."

The two girls exchanged glances, then looked back at me. "Aislin, that's great," they said in unison. "Really, Ash," Deirdre added.

"You're not just saying that so I'll leave the shop and Polly will promote you to manager?" I teased. We all knew Polly planned for her youngest to take over when she retired.

Deirdre looked alarmed. "God, no—we couldn't do without you."

"Good job Aislin isn't going anywhere for now," Maggie said. "So, what would you do?"

"You'll think it silly, but…maybe something fun, or touristy. Like a chocolate shop?"

"That's a grand idea," said Deirdre. "We'll be your first customers," Maggie added.

So far, so good—they hadn't teased me about not making a

profit because I'd eaten all my stock. "Or I could teach step dancing."

"You've certainly the talent to get paid for a bit of dancing," Maggie said. "Michael Flatley's got nothing on you."

"I wish," I said. "But all those *feiseanna* I competed in when I was a kid might be good for something."

"Your poufy hair's perfect for step-dancing too," Deirdre said. "And doesn't Sam want you to make more money?"

I pretended not to hear that. Bad enough it was on The List. "With my trick ankle, I'd still need to be careful, even with teaching."

"Why not give us a demo?" Maggie glanced at her watch. "Bill won't mind a bit of racket coming through the walls."

Sporting of him. I stifled a grin. Since he sure doesn't mind making it himself. Before I could change my mind, I dashed to my bedroom. Shucking off my jeans, I pulled on some Lycra shorts, laced up my ghillies, then ran back to the front room.

"Don't forget," Deirdre said, "we've still got to look at your fortune, Ash."

"I won't." The possibility of getting the key to my entire life was my favorite part of the ritual. Quickly replaying the steps through my mind, I slid a bothy band CD into the player, rustled in the top desk drawer for Sellotape and a bit of loose change, and struck a pose against the far wall. "Right, Deirdre— take it away."

SATURDAY NIGHT FEVER

I was in The Zone.

Or the...whatchacallit...Flow. Where your creative energies are at their peak, and the San Andreas Fault could split the earth under your feet, and you'd hardly notice.

So when Deirdre went to the door, opened it, then glanced back at me, her eyes the size of footballs, I pranced on. Absorbed in one of my fave moves, a twirl, ankle sway, then leap in place, I only sensed Maggie joining Deirdre at the door, and the person framed in the doorway.

But as the music abruptly stopped, I simultaneously zeroed in on Maggie's bugged out eyes, and my tall, dark-haired visitor. "It's *him*," Deirdre hissed. "*Him!*"

Oh, no. I froze. Ohno, ohno, ohno...Maggie and Deirdre *knew* who Ben was. *Instantly*.

I met Ben's eyes, feeling my face—no, my entire body—overcome with heat. Like the time I'd mistakenly ordered five-alarm curry takeaway. And let me tell you, I haven't had curry since. Swallowing hard, I whispered, "I can see that."

Was this the Universe's idea, to bring Ben to my *home*? As

Nature abhors a vacuum, had *She* come up with another plan in place of the one I hadn't?

The problem was, I *still* wasn't ready to see him, chat him up, or so much as think about him. Especially in my sweaty and vastly underdressed state. But what else could I do but gasp, "Hallo…Ben."

While my ghillies seemed glued to the carpet, Maggie had the gall to smile at him. *Traitor.* "So—you're called Ben, are you?" Before I could intervene, she said, "Come in, won't you."

Oh, great. Just bloody great. The jig was up, in more ways than one. Ben stepped awkwardly over the threshold. "I've, uh… come at a bad time." He looked at me, then Maggie. "I got the address from my mom, but…I should have phoned first."

Dead right you should, I longed to say, only here was Maggie, interfering again. "No need for that." She ushered him inside.

"You couldn't have picked a better time," Deirdre had the effrontery to add.

"I'm an old…uh, friend of Aislin's," Ben said. He didn't seem to remember smiling at Deidre outside the shop yesterday—not much of a girl-ogler? "You two must be related."

"Sisters," said Deirdre, showing her dimples again. "I'm called Deirdre, and that's Mags."

"Maggie," she corrected, and smiled at Ben. "Did you say you're an *old friend?*"

As I blushed deeper, he said, "Uh…yeah."

She threw a sharp look at me over her shoulder. "And did you," Maggie continued, "by any chance, happen to call round at O'Donnell's Shop yesterday and see Aislin, and our mam? She owns the place."

"That's right," Ben said.

Deirdre looked mystified. "And Mammy didn't tell me? Too weird for words."

Maggie sent me a glare, with a tiny jerk of her head toward Ben. So I'd no choice but to proceed with the Walk of Doom

41

and hold out my hand. "What a...lovely surprise," I lied. Oops. I stared at the coin taped to my palm. "Sorry." I snatched my hand back before it touched his. "Forgot about that."

"You like to wear your money?" Ben asked politely.

"It's a step-dance thing," Deirdre piped up. "Trains you to hold your hands just so. Isn't that what you told us, Ash?"

"That's right," I said faintly. Could people expire from embarrassment?

"That's the bit I don't understand about step-dancing." Deirdre, drat the girl, gave him a roguish grin. "How you've got to keep your arms stiff, down at your sides."

"How's that?" Ben asked, and stuffed his hands in his pockets.

"What if you got so good at it, you'd get inhibited when it was time to put your arms round your boyfriend?"

"Really, Deedee," Maggie said, but she laughed.

I didn't. "I think I'll just..." I slowly backed away, "change or something."

Shite. One stray word could let everything out. But this situation was clearly out of my hands. As I left Ben and the girls to skulk down the hallway, I had to hope the Universe would for once be on my side, and save me from a catastrophe.

THE GENTLEMAN CALLER

*L*ooking back, the weeks I'd spent with Ben seven years ago seemed to pass in time-lapse photography…where a flower blooms in three seconds instead of a day, or the sun rises and sets in the time it takes for a good sneeze. We'd no sooner met backstage at the college talent show, then it seemed like a minute later, Ben and I crossed paths in town.

Regrettably, Kelly Keenan, a wannabe boyfriend and my father's intern, who'd escorted me home from the show two nights before, had tracked me down that afternoon. Even more unluckily, Kelly, his gingery hair sticking straight up like he'd put his finger in a plug socket, was slightly pissed from a few mid-afternoon pints. As Ben providentially appeared outside Ace's Hardware, Kelly was trying on an unwanted snog.

I confess, at nineteen, fresh from Irish convent school, I must have had all the emotional maturity of a twelve-year-old. Because when Ben showed every sign of wanting to take on my horny escort—manly clenched jaw and fists, that sort of thing—I found it wildly thrilling.

Instead of egging the fellows on, however, I took the high road and sent Kelly packing. I'd like to say I was being noble, but he was about a foot shorter than Ben and half his weight. Which wouldn't have been very sporting, now, would it? I hardly saw him slink away, though, when Ben offered to walk me home. Two days after that, he kissed me...

I'd instantly decided I was *made* for snogging. We were at it constantly, and one night, almost three weeks into it, Ben pulled away, with what sounded like a painful laugh.

This is killing me, he said against my hair. *I'm not in high school anymore.*

Neither am I, I said, and kissed him again...

But what a time to remember *that*. Entering my bedroom, I stared at my duvet, bought at a second-hand shop, and wondered if Ben had noticed how the mighty—me—had fallen. From my former home with my parents, the grandest house in Eagle Prairie, with a vast, well-manicured garden, to a dingy flat filled with cast-off furniture in North Dublin.

"What brings you here, Ben?" Maggie asked, her voice carrying into the room. I kept the door open, determined not to miss a word. And to prevent any loose-lips commentary from the girls, if I had sprint back to the front room in my knickers, I would.

"I was...doing some errands and I thought, well, why not drop in." Ben sounded sheepish. "Actually, I was on my own all day, and figured I'd start talking to myself any minute."

The girls giggled. "I talk to myself all the time," said Deirdre. "I don't even need to be alone."

Okay so far. I yanked my shorts off.

"You're not married, then, sounds like," said Maggie. *Oh, not so good—shut up, Maggie, will you?* But it got worse when she asked, "So why aren't you out with a girl tonight?"

"Uh, well..." Ben's voice trailed away.

"Sure, you're rather new to Ireland, aren't you?" Deirdre said. "If you don't know any girls, you can post a personal ad."

"I don't think they're for me," Ben said.

That's one thing we can agree on. I stepped into my jeans, tried to button them, and failed.

"Actually, that's grand," Deirdre said, "because we were just saying, weren't we Maggie? That we needed a fourth for our Saturday nights. And here I thought that being at Ash's flat instead of O'Fagan's pub meant no guys. Little did we know, eh?"

"Little did we know," Maggie confirmed.

"Even better, tonight we got two for one, a fourth *and* an actual *man*." Deirdre giggled again. "It's lovely to get the male point of view now and then."

"Since husbands don't count," Maggie added. "At least mine doesn't."

"Gee, I didn't know you stopped being a male when you got married." Ben sounded like he was smiling. I slipped on a shirt. Maybe tonight wouldn't be a complete disaster after all.

Deirdre put in, "Tell us, Ben, if you're not married now, have you ever been?"

My fingers fumbled with my buttons. Ben, divorced?

"Nope," he said. "Never took the plunge."

I exhaled slowly. So, he'd never loved a girl enough to marry her. Which for some reason made me...happy.

"Contemplating it, then?" Deirdre asked immediately.

"Well, I..."

I held my breath as the silence stretched on. Ben engaged, or worse, having a new wife, would really bollux up the works for Kevin. "Yes, I am," Ben said finally, sounding determined. "I've got a girlfriend back in Seattle, and we've talked about it."

I sat abruptly on my bed. Oh, great. Not just a girlfriend, but a potential stepmammy for Kevin. Well, someone as nice as Ben would get married eventually, wouldn't he? I looked down at my shirt, with the buttons straining a bit over my boobs and tummy. *You just better remember he's taken.* I crawled off the bed and chose the baggiest sweater it was possible to wear without it falling right off me, and pulled it over my head.

"Thinking about marriage...that's lovely." Maggie sounded as if it was anything but.

"Lovely," echoed Deirdre, who didn't seem too pleased either. "She's a longtime girl?"

"A couple of years," Ben said.

That sounded serious. Perhaps I should fabricate a tummy-ache? Spend the rest of his visit in here, and pretend my eejit idea to get a father for Kevin had never occurred to me?

"Actually," said Deirdre, and I heard a decisive slap on the coffee table, "that's great. You being a man of the world and all that, we've a question for you."

I suddenly got a bad feeling, and headed back to my guests. Deirdre's questions had mucked up my life more than once.

"We have?" Maggie asked as I sidled into the front room. I couldn't miss the polite, inquiring look on Ben's face.

"It's about time you got back," Deirdre said as I sat across from Ben. "I was just saying to Ben, we need a man's opinion on something."

"Do we really?" Still smelling trouble, I'd all the enthusiasm of a depressed Basset hound. And Ben could tell. He tightened his jaw and reached for his jacket. *Good. You're leaving. With you gone, maybe I can sort out what the hell to do next...*

Convinced I was almost home free, I froze as Deirdre said, "What does a guy really mean when he says 'relationship hiatus?'"

THE FORTUNE COOKIE

*D*eirdre. *You wouldn't.*

But she had. And Ben was apparently playing dumb. Though how he could miss Maggie shaking her head at Deirdre like a bobble-head doll was a shagging mystery. "In what context?" he asked.

"I'm sure Ben has better things to do than discuss silly theories," I threw in, to stem the tide of humiliation eroding the shores of my life.

"I like theories," Ben countered. "Ask away."

"What do you think," Deirdre began as I sensed impending calamity, "when a guy's been going out with a girl for a while, and one day he ups and says they should go on 'hiatus.'"

Too late. I could only sit there, the red-hot curry sensation flooding through me again, and silently curse Deirdre's indiscretion.

I felt Ben's curious look—he had to have guessed I was the Hiatus Girl. *Well, here's your Moment of Triumph: you can get back at me for running out on you in Temple Bar.*

"I say, it means he wants to have it off with someone else," Deirdre added helpfully.

"Not necessarily," Ben said carefully. "Maybe the guy just wants out, but doesn't have the guts to just come out and say so."

A bit floored by Ben's decency, I felt awful. Because I hadn't been too decent to him.

"Maybe he's the sensitive sort," Maggie put in. "Needs time for personal growth and all that. Not to go for another girl."

"Uh uh," Ben said. "If he was so *sensitive*, he'd be up front and say what he means. Not make you guess."

"See, Ash, what did I tell you—"

"Deirdre!" Maggie looked ready to take a swing at her. "You've a gob on you like—"

"Fortune cookie time!" I said brightly, to hide my mortification, and pawed through the cartons to find the two remaining cookies.

"Just so happens that we've an extra," Maggie said, looking relieved. "Deirdre and I finished ours."

Fortunes would be a brilliant way to bring this unfortunate evening to a close. I passed Ben a cookie without touching him. "You first."

Ben broke open the cookie. "Read it out, Ben" said Deirdre. "I agree with Ash that every fortune you get is connected to your current situation."

"'Perseverance will bring desired results,'" he read, and downed the cookie in one bite.

"Well?" asked Maggie. When he didn't answer, Deirdre said playfully, "You've been persevering with the girlfriend?"

"I've...uh, been putting in a lot of hours at work," Ben mumbled around his cookie, "and it's paying off."

"I think fortunes mostly refer to personal stuff," Deirdre said, with a sly look.

"Uh, not this one." Ben looked a bit squirmy all of a sudden.

"I mean your girlfriend," Deirdre prompted. "If you persevere, you'll be engaged before you know it."

48

I sensed Maggie watching me with sympathy. Apparently I wasn't the only one who could see how horrible this was. I finally managed, "And won't that be lovely." Ben seemed to be looking everywhere but at me, so I popped a piece of cookie in my mouth and unrolled my fortune. "You should..." crunch, crunch, "...not return to a—argh!" A cookie crumb caught in my throat. "Ahhhh...ahem!"

Overcome by coughing, I covered my mouth, praying I hadn't spewed bits of half-chewed cookie on Ben. Apparently not, as he jumped up at the exact moment Maggie did. Mags was quicker, and got in a few good whacks on my back as Ben sat back down.

Deirdre had leaped up too. How sweet, I couldn't help but notice through my coughing fit. But instead of ministering to me, she knelt and was fumbling with something on the floor.

Finally, though, I got control of myself. I held up my hand, and Maggie stopped her thumping. "I'm okay," I said in a gravelly voice. "Sorry. Really, I'm great." I sifted through the cartons. "Did you see where I dropped my fortune?"

"I've got it," Deirdre said, waving the paper.

"Give it back," I said, reaching for it. "It's nonsense."

"Is not," Deirdre contradicted. "It's actually quite intriguing." She read, "'You should not return to the past—'"

"Deirdre, give it back!"

" '—to renew an old relationship.'"

Ben appeared to freeze. Maggie said, "Deirdre!"

I wanted to die. I felt a new hot flash—though surely I wasn't meant to have one of *those* for another quarter century?—so extreme I could be the heating source for a small village.

Ben was looking plenty red by now himself. He had to be wondering, *How much do your girlfriends know about us?* But he'd get nothing from me. He was out of the loop, and until I sorted out what to do about him, he'd have to stay there.

And thankfully, he'd jumped off the couch and was shrugging into his jacket. "Sounds like you have your answer, about that hiatus thing," he said in a fake-hearty voice. "I'd better be going."

Deirdre looked contrite. Which did not make me feel better. "I guess Ash's fortune means she should tell Sam to piss off."

"I vote we drop it," Maggie said, clearly uneasy, as Ben reached for the knob.

Ben was leaving, salvation was nigh... So close, I could almost taste it...

When disaster—true disaster—struck.

MISTAKEN IDENTITY

"$\mathcal{M}$ ammy!" Kevin burst into the flat. "I forgot my Spidey t-torch."

Oh, God. Ohgod, ohgod, ohgod...If my powers of speech had been out to lunch when Ben arrived, they deserted me entirely as my Spiderman-pajama'ed son skidded to a stop. Kevin looked at Ben solemnly. "Are you m-my mam's friend? I'm c-c-called Kevin."

Ben flashed a strained smile at Maggie. *Maggie?* "I'd like to be."

"You m-m-mean, you're her new b-boyfriend?"

Ben looked at Maggie again. "Didn't you say you were..." As the word "married" just hung there, I was powerless to correct his mistake.

"Close the door, love," Maggie said to Kevin.

Ben frowned at her. "Yours?"

I knew it was too much to ask Maggie to cover for me—though I hoped she'd say *yes, I regularly engage in a ménages à trois with Bill and other men, then have their love children.* Of course Maggie shook her head. "Only on weekdays, 'til suppertime."

"He's my son," I choked out.

51

Ben blinked, while all four of us were absolutely silent. I waited for the axe to fall: Ben would recognize Kevin, all hell would break loose, and my baby would be in stuck in the middle. It had to be The Worst Moment Of My Life.

All I could do was focus on Kevin's tense little face. God knows I'd be nervous too, if I was small, and there was a strange and very large man in my house, whilst he and my mammy and her friends were looking at me like I'd turned into a werewolf.

I tried on some telepathy for Kevin: *It's all right, love, no matter what happens, it'll be all right.*

Ben, amazingly, was the first to break out of our collective trance. With a kindly look at Kevin, he said, "I like your jammies." His face suddenly changed. "Did you...say your name was...uh, *Kelly?*"

The emphasis jolted me. "He's called Kevin."

"Kevin," Ben repeated, still looking intently at my son. "What are you, Kevin—uh, four, five years old?"

Kevin's lip trembled. He shook his head.

"He's six," I said defiantly.

Ben's Adam's apple bobbed. But he didn't have quite the gobstruck look of a man who'd just discovered he's a father. So I knew *exactly* what he was thinking. That I'd shagged Kelly Keenan the Intern right after Ben had left town. Which was right after I'd shagged *him.* But Kevin was the priority here. "Run and get your torch, love," I said, with extraordinary calm. "It's in your top drawer."

Kevin raced down the hall. "He's sensitive about his height," I told Ben coolly, and decided, to hell with subtlety. "Didn't you say you had to go?"

Maggie and Deirdre were still letting me handle this, thank Jesus. If I'd had to monitor what the pair of them might say, I'd lose my cool altogether. As Kevin trotted back into the front room, clutching his torch, I knew we were almost home safe.

But Ben apparently couldn't just let things lie. "Where's your dad, Kevin?"

I made a small sound as Kevin ran to me. "I d-d-don't have a d-d-d-d—"

"It's okay, love," I interrupted, and curved my arm round him. Looking out for Kevin in the long term, as opposed to the short—being very inadvisable to cut off a speech-disfluent child mid-stammer—I stared back at Ben, still defiant. Then looked significantly at the door.

But Ben was *not* taking the hint. "Damn it, Aislin, why didn't your dad make that little intern jerk pay child sup—" He broke off, looking mortified.

It was about time someone else beside myself was upset. But right now, I needed to give myself a good shake and make sure Kevin was all right. "Bill and the kids will be wondering what you've got up to," I told my son. I kissed him, then walked him to the door and gave him a tiny push. "Off you go, love."

Kevin dashed out, and I didn't look at Ben until I heard the bang of the Tobin's door.

"Goodnight, Ben," chimed Maggie and Deirdre simultaneously, who would've probably agreed with me that the discomfort level in the flat, on a one to ten scale, had to be nineteen. "Lovely meeting you."

"See you later, Ben," I said in an expressionless voice, and opened the door wider.

Ben carefully stepped past me, as if I'd a contagious disease. Not that I blamed him. On the stoop, though, he surprised me by turning around. "You still want my e-mail address?"

For all the finality implied by practically kicking Ben out of my house, I knew—of *course* I knew—I would be seeing him again. I swallowed, hard. "If you want to give it to me."

Ben slid a business card from his wallet and gave it to me. Clutching the card, I couldn't watch him leave, so I carefully closed the door, to keep from slamming it. And since Maggie and Deirdre had their eyeballs glued to me, I managed to restrain myself from giving it a good boot.

Jaysus! Didn't they say trouble comes in threes?

Trouble #1: Ben had met Kevin before I could...prepare the way.

Trouble #2: BUT, he'd been too blind to see that Kevin was his own son.

Trouble #3: THEN! He'd hurt MY little boy's feelings, the bollocks!

Sensing Maggie and Deirdre's sympathy, I could think of only one thing to say. "What in the feck do I do now?" I wailed, and burst into tears.

THE SEVEN YEAR ITCH

*a*fter five minutes of cleansing, noisy sobs, I sort of got a hold of myself. Still shaking, I rounded on the traitors, Maggie and Deirdre. "How in the holy hell could you invite him in?"

"How in the holy hell could you not tell us *he* was the 'nutter' who came into the shop yesterday?" Deirdre began indignantly. "Leave us out of it like that? We think—"

"Hush," Maggie told her. "If you can't be supportive, just shut up." She disappeared down the hall, and returned with a wad of toilet tissue. "Here." She handed me the lot. "No question of not letting him in, love. He is Kevin's daddy, after all."

I tried to swallow the lump in my throat. "But I wasn't ready to actually *see* him...I mean, I was going to take it gradually— Jaysus, I don't know what I'm saying, only that it was too soon. Instead of making Kevin's life easier, I've just screwed it up even more."

"At least Ben didn't suspect," Deirdre said, evidently chastened. As if that was a comfort. "Even if he seemed a bit freaked out."

"Well, yeah..." I sniffed. It was obvious what Ben hadn't

finished asking, about the purported father Kelly paying me child support. Really, anyone with two eyes could take one look at my flat and think, uh-uh. This place hasn't seen a shred of fatherly cash flow. "But if anyone should be losing it, it should be me!"

"It *is* you losing it," Deirdre pointed out. "At least, he fancies you enough to call—"

"Don't be fecking ridiculous," I said shortly.

"The way Ben was checking out your bum," said Maggie, "he fancies you all right."

"Who cares? He's got a *girlfriend.* Anyway, I could see him doing the math—and I know exactly who he thinks fathered Kevin."

"Who?" Deirdre asked interestedly.

"It doesn't matter," I said, dispirited. "Ben's going to get married. And he thinks I'm a slut." The lump in my throat swelled. So much for the best-laid plans.

"He won't if you tell him the truth," Maggie said. "ASAP," Deirdre added.

Dread closed in on me. "And how am I going to do that?"

"Easy," Deirdre said. "Just go back to your original scheme."

"No way," I said.

"'Way," Maggie said. She picked up her knitting needles. "E-mail Ben straightaway."

"Start from scratch, and chat him up online, like you'd planned," Deirdre put in.

I looked from Maggie to Deirdre. "That plan was crap! I need a whole new one."

"What could be better than the God's truth?" Maggie asked. "As soon as you and Ben get reacquainted?"

Trust Maggie to show me how fecked-up my strategy was. "What about the way he'd upset Kevin? And if he thinks I'm a slut—"

"Will you stop obsessing about the slut thing?" Maggie's

fingers picked up speed. "It'll clear up when you tell him the lot. And Ben, God love him, never meant to hurt the boy."

"How do you know?"

"Men." Maggie waved one hand. "They don't mean to, but they can be such clods—"

"Ben's not a clod!" I burst out.

Deirdre hooted. "You haven't lost that lovin' feeling after all?"

"Of course I have," I snapped. "You know bloody well it's been seven years—"

"Right, there's that famous *Itch* and all," Deirdre said, still laughing.

"Stop it!"

Maggie was trying to stifle her grin. "If you let nature take its course—"

"As in hormones," Deirdre interjected.

"There are no hormones involved," I said heatedly. "Absolutely none. Nada. Zero—" I snapped my mouth shut.

"Maybe not on your side," Maggie said, "but I keep telling you, from the look on Ben when he saw you in those shorts—"

"What look?" I couldn't help asking. "Remember, there's the girlfriend—"

Maggie laughed. "You know what I mean. The *Look*. And his girlfriend hasn't a thing to do with it. So take it from me—one e-mail, and he'll be eating out of your hand."

THE NEW GIRL

*M*onday afternoon, in the back room of the shop, I flexed my fingers like a piano maestro preparing for a concerto, and positioned them over the keyboard. Deirdre hung over my shoulder. "Do it, Ash."

"Don't rush me," I grumbled. "I can't believe I let you and Maggie talk me into this." I was already out of sorts, after checking my phone in the loo, to find it deader than Marley's ghost.

"You've got to get something down, before you lose your inspiration. And before anyone else comes into the shop."

Except for regular Mary Lynch, who could spend hours in here without buying a bloody thing, the shop was empty. And with Polly out and therefore unable to scold us for neglecting our customers, we could safely leave Mary to her own devices. So I typed, *Hello Ben.*

Then stared at the screen, stumped.

"That's it, you're doing grand," Deirdre urged, as the bell over the door tinkled. I almost leaped up, but Deirdre put a restraining hand on me. "I'll go."

Since closing wasn't far off, and Deirdre wasn't going to let me leave until I'd e-mailed Ben, I narrowed my eyes at the screen, and tapped out, *Lovely of you to call round Saturday night...*

I frowned. That was a total lie—hardly a grand start to this enterprise. I backspaced to *Hello Ben*, and began again. *I'm not a great one for surprises...* (Especially you showing up out of nowhere, and catching me dancing with my bum hanging out to dry, but I've got to focus here...) I typed, *So I shouldn't have—*

Deirdre bounced in again. "I *so* hate to interrupt this, now that we're making progress—"

"'We?' Please, don't hesitate to take credit for this," I said. "And you've interrupted my flow."

"Sorry," Deirdre said, clearly unrepentant, "but you're needed out front."

"A customer asked for me, then?"

"She's keen on fairy figurines, and I said I'd fetch our in-house expert on mystical stuff."

That's what I got for all my signs and portents foolishness. I was almost through the doorway when I looked over my shoulder. "Feel free to read what I've got so far," I said sarcastically, as Deirdre slid in front of the computer.

"Thanks, I will," Deirdre said without looking up.

I sighed. With a "you're okay, then?" to Mary Lynch, I rounded a high shelf to find a thirtyish girl with dark-hair, in a generic-looking business suit that didn't quite fit. "So, you'd like to see our fairy stuff?"

Giving me what seemed to be a searching look, she said, "Um...since I've come to Ireland, my mom back in Seattle has turned into quite the collector."

"Seattle, is it?" I said absently, my mind still on my e-mail. "I know someone from—" I cut myself off, feeling superstitious about mentioning Ben. "Anyway, they're over here."

As we made our way to Fairy Central—what Deirdre and I

called Polly's prized fairy section—we exchanged names, and she mentioned being from Seattle too, how her kids were adjusting to Dublin, and her Irish husband was starting a new business. Liz McCarthy, she was called, stopped in front of a little nun figurine, sprinkled with green-shamrocks.

"It's not a fairy, but Mom'll love this." Liz stroked the smooth porcelain. "I must say, this is a great place to unwind after work —you know, before facing everything at home."

For some reason, I felt rather drawn to this stranger. "Whoever invented the term, 'working mother' had to be completely bonkers," I said. "Don't we work all the time anyway?"

"The worst part is, you feel guilty at work for not being home," Liz agreed, "and guilty at home for not working."

A lose-lose situation, we concluded, making our way to the counter. As Liz set her handbag down, I smiled at her, sensing a kindred spirit. "I hope you'll come back. We've more fairy junk —I mean, merchandise than anywhere else in Temple Bar."

"Oh, I will. Mom's got plenty of room on her mantel."

She sounded a bit homesick. It couldn't be easy, making friends in a new country. "We should do coffee sometime," I said impulsively.

"I'd really like that," Liz said, "but—" An odd look came over her face.

"You're too busy? I totally understand, really." Obviously, I'd been too forward. "Well, it was nice seeing—"

"No, it's not that," Liz interrupted. "I won't beat around the bush. I'm a friend of Ben's."

Jaysus! "Ben Carpenter?" Acid spurted into my stomach. And here I'd thought I'd like to know Liz better.

"He's my husband's business partner." Liz fidgeted with her handbag. "We—my husband and I—have known him since he and Dan started working together three years ago, but he's like family. I'd do anything for the guy."

"Does that mean Ben sent you over here to…"

Liz looked genuinely shocked. "He'd kill me if he knew I was here. To be honest, I suppose I was just… curious."

"Right," I managed.

"You see, we had him over for dinner last night, and he was sort of quiet," Liz said. "Afterward, Emily was fussing big time, and Ben pulled these little dancing shoes out of his pocket, put his fingers into them, and started tapping out this little dance, and got Emily giggling. When he saw me watching, he turned bright red, and stuffed the shoes back into his pocket." Liz's eyes suddenly danced. "So naturally, I had to worm out the rest."

"The rest?" I said faintly.

"You know, that he'd bought them for his mom at O'Donnell's in Temple Bar, and run into someone he knew from Minnesota—who obviously was a girl. Of course I had to come."

"And check me out, naturally." I tried on a light laugh. "And your… verdict?"

"You're so much…um, you don't mind if I'm candid here?"

"Not at all," I said. Oh, God, these straight-talking Americans made me nervous. "In fact, I love candor," I added, lying through my incisors.

"Well, you're much nicer than his girlfriend. She couldn't be more wrong for him if she was Buffy the Vampire Slayer."

I had to laugh. "That wrong." I hesitated. "Did Ben tell you we used to…know each other?" I managed not to say "biblically." As Liz nodded, I swallowed hard. "Any…details?" I tensed, ready for the worst.

"Not one, darn him," said Liz.

I practically collapsed onto the shelf in relief. "So whatever you find out about the pair of us can come from me first."

Liz laughed. "Sounds good to me. If you want to get started, can I buy you a latte?"

All of a sudden, the thought of getting out of the Burmuda/O'Donnell Triangle was quite appealing. "Hold on." I ran to the back room. "That girl out front knows Ben," I told Deirdre. "We're going out for a bit. Just round the corner—"

"You are *not*." Deirdre slapped her hands on the desk. "You've promised to do this e-mail."

"Hang the bloody e-mail. I can do it later—"

"If you don't do it, like you promised," Deirdre threatened, "I'll send him one myself. And sign it, *Passionately yours, Aisl—*"

"You little beast," I said, laughing. I *had* promised, after all. "I'll fix another time with Liz."

Just then, the shop's bell rang, and a flurry of footsteps came inside. "Ah, crap," I said. "Maybe we're too busy for me to leave anyway. Come on, give us some help."

I reached the front, only to hear a familiar voice. "And kids, don't get into anything or Mammy will have my head on a platter." Maggie. With the kids. Including Kevin.

Maggie found me as the children's chatter filled the shop. "Hiding out, were we?"

Oh, God…Panic swept over me. Ben's friend Liz was here. Kevin was here. Avert possible disaster by sending child to loo. "Not anymore," I said, trying to sound calm as I sidled around the counter. "I've got to—"

"Hang on," Maggie said. "Mam set aside a book for me, a new one on women's health. I'll want to grab it before Deirdre sells it by mistake."

"That would be a stretch, but Deirdre, could you find it?" I said, intent on—no, actually, on a mission to save My Life As I Knew It—getting Kevin out of sight.

"Don't you know everything about having a bloody baby already?" Deirdre said as I crept down the main aisle, guided by Kevin's little voice.

"Mammy says fairies are like half angels, but very naughty…" Please, *please* have him chatting with Mary, and have Liz on the other side of the store…

No such luck. There they were, Liz and Kevin side-by-side, discussing the fairy display. "Mam!" Kevin said. "The lady likes fairies too."

I hardly heard him. I saw Liz's gaze linger Kevin's rapt face, then she looked up at me, a bit googly-eyed. "Oh," she said.

THE NEW GIRL...KNOWS

J grasped Kevin's small shoulders and turned him toward the front counter. "Go see Deirdre, there's a love. She's got...got some chocolate for you."

"Nice talking to you, honey," Liz said. Kevin waved back, and as soon as he was out of earshot, Liz gave me a level look. "He's...um...Ben's."

I nodded miserably. What else could I do?

"And...oh, God. I get it. Ben... doesn't know?"

I shook my head. "Please...don't—please don't say anything."

Liz touched my arm. "Of course I wouldn't. But you're going to tell him, aren't you?"

"Of course I am. Really." I casually extended my elbow to rest it on the shelf and missed. Catching myself, I said, "I mean, really soon. Actually, when you came in, I was sending him an e-mail."

Liz's jaw dropped. "You're telling him *that* in an e-mail?"

"No! I mean, I wouldn't *dream* of it—I'm just figuring out how to work up to it, that's all."

"It looks like the latte thing isn't going to work out after all." Liz looked disappointed.

"Sorry—with my son here, I'll be trooping home on the bus with him. Another time?"

"Sure," Liz said, with a blank expression. She picked up the figurine. "I haven't paid for this yet—"

"Wait," I said. I liked Liz already. And not because the woman could put in a good word for me with Ben. Meeting his friend had to be a sign—a good one—that I was doing the right thing. Telling Ben that he was Kevin's daddy, that is. "Are you free Saturday nights?"

"I can be," Liz said, her face brightening.

"Well, then, sometimes we—that is, I and the other shop assistant and her sister, who's that other dark-haired girl at the counter—get together on Saturdays," I said. "Deirdre and Maggie and I go to the pub, or stay in and watch telly, split a bottle of wine, get pissed on chocolate. You know—have wild craic. We'd love for you to join us. In fact, I'll introduce you now."

"I'd like that." Liz opened her handbag, extracted a piece of paper, and scribbled a number on it, handing it to me with a searching look. "You're not inviting me because...."

I knew what she was trying to say. Time to give my new honesty-is-the-best-policy a run for its money. "Buy your silence? Frankly, it occurred to me for about a second, but in this case, I think we've got to trust each other." I held out my hand. As we solemnly shook on it, I said, "I'll be in Galway this weekend, but Saturday next, we'll expect you."

I LEFT MY HEART...IN BALLYDARA

*L*aying low at my granny Moore's house in the country seemed like the best idea I'd had since Ben showed up. While Polly O'Donnell was often like my substitute mam, Granny was as good as the real thing.

You see, I was the age of six when my mother (of the Chicago Hennessys, pals of all the Moore relations in the city who'd emigrated too) had some sort of health crisis. I was never told what it was—so much for the reputation of the legendarily loquacious Irish. But I was promptly packed off to Ballydara, a village in County Galway, to live with my granny Edith.

Which wasn't the hardship you'd think. Granny's people were the Currys, and she was as fun and spicy as her name. She had flaming hair—of *course* dyed—the color of Kevin's, and accessorized her flowered housedresses with purple trainers and a Minnesota Twins ballcap my father sent her. Instead of a rocking chair, Granny kept an exercise bike. Used it too. And she'd been the one to give me my first copy of *Little Women*. She was like a sister—that my real sister Grace had never been—if you didn't count her gray roots.

After the near-debacle with Liz, I needed a sympathetic ear.

Or another one, since I think I'd nearly worn out Maggie and Deirdre's. So, as soon as I arrived home from work, I sent Kevin back to Maggie's to lend her a cup of sugar—our agreed code when we needed a bit of privacy from our kids—and rang Granny straightaway.

"Is that you, child?"

Hearing her voice, a wave of homesickness swept over me. "You're home from your travels, then."

"You're a good girl, to ring your old granny."

A good girl. I didn't *try* to pull the wool over Granny's eyes, but she *would* persist in thinking the best of me. "You, old?" I scoffed. "The village hottie?"

Although Granny was on the far side of seventy, she didn't look it. She had legs so shapely that Pat Hurley, down at the village pub, gave her a wolf whistle every time she passed by. She'd stop, give a Maureen O'Hara-ish toss of her hair, lift her dress a bit, then cock her knee. Inspired, she told me, by Claudette Colbert in *It Happened One Night*.

"Silly girl," but Granny giggled. "I suppose you're wanting all the news from Chicago."

"That's it. How is…" I gulped, "the family?"

I used the term loosely. For most of my early childhood, Mother was often in a martini-fogged state or had a terrible head on her, my father was absorbed in his Irish Immigrant Success Story, and Grace pretty much lived at boarding school. At the time, though I was so little, the hardest part about leaving home was that I wouldn't see Ben and his mam anymore.

"They're grand," said Granny. "I saw most of the cousins, and…" I tensed, but she only said, "…everyone."

"I'm glad you're home," I said fervently. Had it been only a fortnight, since I'd seen her off to America? Goes to show how fast time passes when your life has become a train wreck.

Granny must have picked up the undercurrents. "Aislin, love, is everything all right?"

"Ah...had a...a frantic week, that's all. But I was wondering... could Kevin and I spend the weekend with you?"

"Isn't the door always open for you? But darling, you sound a bit low."

Tucking the phone under my ear, I swept some stray grains of sugar off the scarred countertop and shook them into the sink. *Change the subject.* "I've been wanting some peace and quiet. Dublin's getting so...crowded."

"Maybe you've lived in the O'Donnells' pockets long enough," my granny guessed.

I'd occasionally thought the same, with Maggie and her family next door, and Polly and Deirdre three doors down. "I love them all to pieces," I said, feeling a bit disloyal. "But it gets a bit...overpowering."

Granny chuckled. "Don't I know it, with Nora and Bridie O'Donnell a stone's throw away? Though Bridie was good enough to pick me up from the airport yesterday. But how about a different flat, a bigger—"

"This one's fine, really," I said, instead of *it's all I can afford.* I shouldn't like Granny to worry about my finances, since that would make two of us miserable, instead of just me.

But there was no fooling Granny, who could often read between the lines. Or hear between them, anyway. "I'm told Dublin's full of young people. It wouldn't be too hard to find a flatmate, would it?"

Sam would have been a good candidate—tidy, regular paycheck and all that. That is, if I'd wanted him to move in— which I wasn't so sure I did—and, of course, if he hadn't announced the "let's go on hiatus" thing. Anyway, with Ben's appearance complicating my life like nobody's business, I couldn't think about planning a weekend with Sam anytime soon.

"I don't know—most of the people I see around Temple Bar are wild keen on stag and hen parties." *Except for a certain nice and noble guy who doesn't even* like *pubs*. I felt teary, though you'd think I'd have run out of tears after Saturday night's cloudburst.

"I shouldn't want you to be a recluse," said Granny.

"I'm not," I said. "I like going out with my friends as well as the next girl, but as for the rest, I don't see the point, really."

"An old soul, that's what you are."

Translation: no fun. All right for your own granny to think so, but not your boyfriend. Needing something to do other than discuss my shortcomings, I opened the fridge. Slim pickings, as usual. I reached for a half-full jar of spaghetti sauce that, if I recalled correctly, wasn't too ancient. "Anyway, I'm not sure I could find the right sort of flatmate," I said.

"Perhaps you're waiting to share your place with a husband?" Granny teased. I pretended not to hear that too. "And Sam doesn't quite fit the bill?"

I didn't know what to say. I hadn't told Granny about our hiatus, or planning a weekend with Sam either. Not that she'd reproach me—she'd always been sadly indulgent—but no proper granny would approve of an illicit getaway with a man who wasn't completely and totally mad for you. Unscrewing the lid of the jar, I peeked inside. I was in luck. No blue fuzz.

"Meanwhile, there must be some young fellow you'd like to go round with."

I dropped the jar. It smashed, spewing sauce and glass all over the worn linoleum.

"What's that? You're all right, love?"

Eyes burning, I stared at the new red polka-dots on my socks and the hem of my jeans, then the clots of sauce on the floor. "I just, em... b-bumped something." I swallowed hard. "But we've got sidetracked—tell us all the family gossip."

"The cousins tell me your mother hasn't come to see you in ages." Granny's disapproval zinged through the phone line.

"It's all right," I said carelessly. I'd learned long ago not to expect anything from my mother. And once I had Granny, it didn't hurt. Or hurt so much.

"We tried to welcome Rosemary into the family, but she always was a flighty little madam." Granny sniffed. "Good job you don't take after *her*."

"Meaning I take after my fath—" I clamped my mouth shut. I don't *think* so.

"Your dad drove down from Minneapolis," said Granny. "With a gift for everyone."

"Lovely," I said though my teeth. More unsettled than ever, I grabbed a piece of newspaper, then knelt to pick the broken glass off the sauce-splattered floor.

"Aislin," Granny said patiently, "I've something for you, from him—"

"Thanks, but I don't want it." I painstakingly set each shard of glass on the paper.

"Now, love—"

"He knows I don't want anything from him." *And if he's after worming his way back into my life, he can forget it.*

"There's more at stake than what's good for you, love." That was as close Granny had ever come to a scold.

"I know. I...I'm sorry, Granny." I wasn't up for discussing my father. Especially not after the turmoil of the past days.

"Sure, he has faults."

"Yes, and plenty of them." I tried to make it a joke, but there was no hiding from Granny.

"But he's my son. Someday you'll know—"

"Granny, I've got to fetch Kevin," I forced through the lump in my throat. "At Maggie's."

"I'll say it again, then," Granny said almost sternly. "You'll *know*."

Know your child will disappoint you, because you disappointed them first? And often? "I'm sure I will," I agreed, so I could ring off with a minimum of guilt. "See you soon, okay?"

I replaced the phone in its cradle, swiped my sleeve across my nose, then surveyed the floor, still strewn with what would have been our tea. And speaking of muddles...how had I mucked up this business with Ben so badly?

The reason for contacting him in the first place had been like a Message from Above. When I'd driven Granny to Shannon airport a fortnight ago, then said my goodbyes, I turned round and there it was. The Message: Three little boys running to their daddy, clinging to him like monkeys, the joy in their faces like a slap in mine.

I tried to see the positive in Ben's mother Annie sending him round right away: maybe she still liked me. But as far as my experience with fathers—that is, my son's and my own—well, let's just say it was a bit Jerry Springer-esque. How I would manage first, telling Ben about our son, *and* second, having him be a part of Kevin's life—in an emotionally healthy, non-dysfunctional way? Now *that* was a real long shot...

My stomach squeezed as I pulled my underused mop out of the closet. Anyway, how could I worry about the Future, I asked myself, when my Present was in such a state?

YOU'VE GOT MAIL

"*J*esus, you look like death," Deirdre said the next morning.

"Thanks, I needed that." I cast a longing glance at the back room, but I was determined to stay away from the computer for…well, at least ten minutes. "If you must know, I've not been sleeping too well."

"We're lucky then, that with Mam out, we can slack a bit. But at least we'd got the e-mail off to Ben yesterday," Deirdre added smugly.

I like to think I'd set the right tone:

TO: Ben @ MacCarSoft.ie
FROM: Polly O'Donnell
SUBJECT: Saturday night at Aislin's
Hello Ben,

It's me. Not Polly. I'm sending this from the shop computer since I don't have one at home. That is, yet. Kevin will probably need a computer soon, since I understand even the youngest kids at school type their homework now, and teachers are forgetting how to read handwriting.

Speaking of Kevin, I could see you were surprised. To find out I have a child, that is. I'm not a great one for surprises myself, so consequently, we rather got off on the wrong foot when you called round Saturday. But I shouldn't have got my back up about your remarking on Kevin's size. Which I did, a bit. Mothers tend to take on their children's hurts and disappointments, but then I don't need to blather on about that.

Anyway, good luck with everything.

Aislin.

I YAWNED, as Deirdre urged, "Now, go and see if he's sent you one back."

"It's too early," I protested. "He runs a business, hasn't time for social e-mail—"

"Go," Deirdre ordered, and pushed me toward the computer.

I resisted. "He has a girlfriend, so why would he be keen to—"

"Jesus, you're dense," Deirdre said, and pushed me harder. "Now go!"

I sat in front of the computer, Deirdre hanging on my shoulder. "Must you lean over me, like a bloody vulture?"

"Yes, I must," Deirdre said, grinning. "Get on with it."

Booting up too forever. But what do you know, there was an e-mail in the Inbox!

FROM: Ben Carpenter
SUBJECT: Saturday night
Aislin,
Dropping by last night was really out of line—and I really

put my foot in it with your son, implying he was short and all. If there's any way I can make it up to him, let me know.

Ben

"That's terse," I said. "How am I to take—"

"Ash—look, his e-mail's from Sunday, it must've got hung up on the server or whatever you call them."

"Well, so..."

"Jaysus, you *are* short of sleep. He made the first move! It's like mind-meld or something. Or. syn...synchron...synchroniss...what do you call it?"

"Mad," I said. "Look at this, he wants to make it up to Kevin, but not to me—" I shut my mouth. It was what I wanted, right? And if I was going to bother with any fellow, it should be Sam.

"Synchronicity!" Deirdre said triumphantly. "So. Fix a date with Ben, right now, let him make it up to Kevin, like he said."

"No," I said.

"Ash, when fruit is ripe you pick it, for God's sake. Not wait until it rots and falls off the tree—"

"No," I repeated, and slid out of the chair before Deirdre could wrestle me down. "I've got to think about this."

Ten minutes later, Deirdre screeched from the back room. "Ash, an e-mail!"

I confess, I came running.

FROM: Ben Carpenter
SUBJECT: Saturday night at Aislin's
Hi Aislin,
Can't say I blame you. For getting bent out of shape, that is. As you said, comes with the territory of being a mother.

I had originally dropped by to give you the glove you dropped in Temple Bar last Friday, but it slipped my mind. Let me know if there's a good time to get it to you.

BEN

"See, he wants to see you," Deirdre crowed. "I was right."

"Jaysus, can't I have any privacy?" I asked. "I appreciate your support and all that, but—"

"Ash, you've got to get off your bum and tell Ben about Kevin fast, before he realizes it himself. The pair of them—they're the spit image of each other."

I cupped my chin in my palm. I didn't think so, but if Ben eventually saw the resemblance, I wouldn't have so much to explain. Maybe the thing to do was throw the pair of them together, so the truth would dawn on Ben sort of... naturally. *Organically.* So by the time I made my big confession, he'd hardly be surprised.

Yesss! Good plan. So I fired off another missive. And ended up spending practically the whole day with e-mails...

TO: Ben Carpenter

SUBJECT: Missing glove

Hello Ben,

Kevin and I are off to Galway this weekend to see our Granny. Since April in the West isn't much warmer than

January, and the fact that wearing one glove makes you look a bit daft, I'd be glad to have both. Maybe we could meet you before we catch the bus. My mobile's not working, but you can reach me here at the store.

Aislin

PS... Saturday night was rather a one-off—I don't normally put on dances for my friends.

FROM: Ben Carpenter
SUBJECT: Saturday
Hey Aislin,

I can meet you Saturday a.m., but I'd like to do something special for your boy. Any ideas?

Ben

PS... ANY REASON FOR POLISHING YOUR DANCING SKILLS?

TO: Ben Carpenter
SUBJECT: Saturday morning
Hello Ben,
How about Stephen's Green, around eleven? It's not far to the bus station, and Kevin likes to feed the ducks.
Regarding your PS, I'd been telling Maggie and Deirdre I was after making some extra money, and they talked me into demonstrating one of my few semi-marketable skills. Feel rather silly about that too.
Aislin
PS... Feel free to drop the glove in the post, if you think your girlfriend will mind your seeing us.

FROM: Ben Carpenter
SUBJECT: Stephen's Green
Aislin,
I'll be there.

BEN

PS... Courtney isn't the jealous type.

THE WISH

I hate to admit it, but Saturday morning, when I saw Ben coming toward us at Stephen's Green, my heart went a-flutter. *I'm just tired*, I told myself, *this little carryall weighs a ton*, but even I didn't quite believe it. I felt all motherly pride as Kevin shook hands with Ben, very man-to-man. But when Ben handed me my glove, a girlish, *Little Women* reverb tingled through me—definitely reminiscent of the Meg and John Brooke mystery glove bit.

As I thanked Ben, Kevin looked confused. "How come you had Mam's g-glove?"

"I dropped it," I said quickly.

"She forgot it," Ben jumped in at the same time.

Kevin's face cleared. "Mam's always f-forgettin' stuff. Once she bought heaps of fish fingers for our tea, then left the whole p-parcel at the shop." He smiled shyly at Ben, and I felt another tweak in my chest. "Do you forget t-too?"

Ben didn't look at me. "Sometimes—like the other night, when I forgot my manners." He hunkered down to Kevin's level. "Can I tell you a story?"

I tensed as Kevin nodded, eyes wide.

"When I was a boy, I was shorter than all the kids in school," Ben began. "Everyone called me 'Shrimp,' and I hated it. But my mom would say, 'it's okay, you'll be tall someday,' because my da —because it runs in the family. Know what?"

Kevin looked positively fascinated. "What?"

"When I was about fourteen, what do you know, I started to grow like a magic beanstalk."

Kevin's eyes went all sparky. "Like in the fairy t-tale?"

Suddenly, I saw it. *Deirdre's right—The Spit Image!* But the man was having quite a time with his tale. "You betcha. Pretty soon, I was taller than most of the guys in my class."

"Wow!" Kevin was practically wriggling in delight. I couldn't have come up with a better story myself. And Ben's was probably true.

"So," Ben finished, "the moral of the story is—"

"Boys should listen to their mammies," I finished. I couldn't help smiling gratefully at Ben.

"That's right." Ben smiled back. "And that sometimes your dreams do come true."

How impossibly maudlin, Pollyannish…and I loved it almost as much as Kevin. "Then every night, I'm g-gonna dream I'm t-tall," Kevin concluded, and squinted up at Ben. "You're a Yank?"

"I am," Ben said. "Is that okay with you?"

"You bet-betcha." Oh, my. He'd got the American accent just right too. "I usta b-be a Yank too," Kevin went on. "When I was a baby. We lived in America."

With things off to such a good start, I didn't need them to get mucked up with a trip down memory lane. "We haven't much longer," I broke in. "You've your bread ready, Kevin?"

Kevin split his supply with Ben, an excellent sign for the future—as he didn't share his duck food with just anyone. Then the pair of them began flinging crumbs at the ducks. "Do you like visiting your grandma?" Ben asked him.

"She's grand," said Kevin. "She always has chocolate b-biscuits. Didja know a g-great lot of fairies live in Galway, near my granny?"

Now I was the one listening with fascination, as Kevin took to Ben like an old mate. And with hardly a stammer out of him!

"I didn't," Ben said. "Any fairies in particular?"

"Well, there's Finvarra, the K-king of the Western Fairies."

"And what does this Finvarra get up to?" Ben looked quite... well, charmed. "Cast magic spells or something?"

"Lots and lots of 'em—he made a d-deal with the fellows at Castle Hacket, so they never run out of wine!" Kevin wrinkled his nose. "If I got p-presents from the fairies, I'd ask them to bring me puddings, not yukky drink."

"Me too," Ben agreed. "But I thought leprechauns were the big thing in Ireland."

"*Leprechauns.*" Kevin pulled a face. I could see Ben stifling a grin, and we actually exchanged amused looks. "It's fairies that are the important ones," Kevin added, eyes on the grass.

"He's quite taken with the Other Crowd," I said to Ben in an undertone. "Polly's fairy addiction is a bit contagious." I checked my watch, glad I'd an excuse for it, then saw Deirdre scurrying toward us, her own carryall slung over her shoulder.

"Whew," Deirdre said as she joined us. "Sorry I'm late. I got caught up trolling round Grafton Street."

"You remember Ben, don't you?" I said, feeling tense again. God knows what Ben would be thinking: *Girl meeting fellow asks friend to come along, in case she's having a really bad time.*

Deirdre gave Ben an artless smile. "Hallo—in case you're wondering if Ash asked me to meet her here, you're right."

Ben didn't look at me. "You and Aislin think I'm a potential kidnapper or something?"

"Oh, n-no," I stammered, but Deirdre rather saved the day. "Ah, sure, there's that." She grinned, and I relaxed. "We're actually traveling together—I'm to visit my granny too. Lives next to Aislin's, in the toolies west of Galway City." She pulled a face.

"Not exactly the most exciting way for a girl to spend her weekend, but you know. Family obligations and all that."

"Yeah, there's always family," Ben said. Was that a shadow in his face?

I felt quite forlorn all of a sudden, at having to leave, then Kevin popped up between us, his palm outstretched. "Mam! Auntie Deirdre! Look what I found!"

In Kevin's small hand were two four-leaf clovers. "Very clever, love," I told him.

"*Totally* cool," said Deirdre.

Kevin gave Ben another shy smile that squeezed my heart again. "Lookit, Ben. Shamrocks!"

"How about that," Ben said, smoothing the shamrocks on Kevin's palm. "Two of 'em." I didn't know a man could be so gentle, and my nostalgic, weepy feeling intensified.

"Mammy calls me Super-ShamrockMan, 'c-cause I always find four-leafed ones."

"That is *amazing*," Ben said, and he and Kevin smiled at each other. "You must be especially lucky."

"Make your wish, Kev," Deirdre directed.

"I wish—"

"Wait." I suddenly remembered Kevin's previous wishes. "You're not meant to tell anyone about your wish, if you want the luck."

Kevin ignored me. "I'm g-gonna be lucky anyway," he crowed and looked up at Ben. "I wish for—"

"Kevin," Deirdre began—maybe she sensed trouble too. "We're meant to—"

"I wish for a da—"

"Kevin!" I snapped. "Your wish won't come true!" As Kevin's face fell, I felt like crying again. But in a bad way.

I reached for him. But before I could give him a reassuring pat, Ben leaned down to Kevin, touching the bits of green one more time. He gently closed my little boy's hand round them.

"They're great, Kevin," he said, not looking at me. Can you blame him? Giving out at my son for apparently nothing? "I'm sure *all* your wishes will come true."

"Can we c-come back here tomorrow and I'll find a shamrock for you?"

"I think you'll be at your grandma's tomorrow," Ben said, "But I hope to see you soon."

The yearning in Kevin's eyes was painful to see. "Will you… be my mam's b-boyfr—"

"Kevin!" Deirdre said gaily, and took his hand. Say what you will about the girl, but she'll rescue you in a pinch. "Let's get a head start to the station, shall we? Your mammy'll catch up in a minute. Bye, Ben."

"But Auntie Deirdre," and Kevin pulled on her hand, "I want to—"

"Say good-bye, Kevin," she said firmly.

Good job my boy liked her so well. "Bye, Ben," Kevin said obediently, and Deirdre herded him away. I slung my carryall back on my shoulder, unable to look at Ben.

"Uh…" Ben finally said, "kids say the darnedest things, huh?"

I hadn't expected it, him being easy on me. Particularly since we'd somehow ended up alongside a bed of tulips. "Thanks for… meeting us," I mumbled. Between snapping at Kevin and being reminded of mistreating Ben's flowers, I was pretty well guilt-wracked.

"No problem," Ben said like he meant it. Maybe he'd forgiven me for the tulips after all. "About Kevin—I wasn't just saying that—I really would like to see him again."

This whole Kevin-Ben thing was swiftly taking on a life of its own. "We'll fix a time next week," I whispered, and before I could stop myself, I kissed Ben's cheek and hurried away.

Well, there you go. My plan was working. But Ben's compassion with my son made me wonder: were any more surprises coming my way?

TIME WAITS FOR NO GIRL

*K*evin was asleep, a crayon still clutched in his hand. "You've been a darling to entertain Kevin for me," I said to Deirdre, and sniffed hard. "With his 'Ben this,' and 'Ben that,' it must've got on your nerves."

Deirdre looked up from her *Cosmo*. "It's okay. You were getting a bit...emotional."

I'd fought tears all the way out of Dublin. As the bus lumbered westward, past grazing sheep and rock-strewn hillsides, I thought I'd pulled myself back together, but then I'd think of my son and his daddy back at Stephen's Green, and my eyes would fill again.

I had just about succeeded in blinking away another bumper crop of tears when Deirdre giggled. "Great article here, Ash." She showed me the magazine. "How to find your G-Spot."

"I'll think I'll pass." I tried to smile. "I found mine last week, ha, ha."

Deirdre laughed again. "You want to talk about it?"

"No, I do not!" I said with mock-affront.

"Very funny. I meant Ben."

"Well…" I couldn't help myself. "Oh, God, did you see the pair of them?"

"Turned out pretty well," Deirdre said, "all things considered."

"It was straight out of that film," I said. "You know, the one with Tom Cruise and Rene Zellweger and her little boy."

"Jerry something."

"That's it—*Jerry Maguire*," I said. "When Rene's son totally bonds with Tom, and it's so sweet you could cry." Call me susceptible, but Ben and Kevin would've been great stand-ins.

"Even if Kevin blurted out the bit about Ben being your boyfriend," Deirdre agreed.

I had to confess. "Deirdre, you won't believe it—I can't believe it myself—but I got sort of overcome. I…em, planted one on Ben."

Deirdre's eyes rounded. "You bloody kissed him?"

"Don't get all hot and bothered—it was just on the cheek. But who knows what he's thinking…that I go round kissing fellows, just for being nice?"

"In case you're still worried about the slut thing, the easy-virtue types don't kiss men on the cheek," Deirdre said wickedly. "They go for frenching, balls-out."

"Jaysus, Deirdre! I would never—I mean, there's still Sam."

"Sam can—" Deirdre pretended to stick her finger down her throat.

"Go on," I said, as the idea of frenching Sam was replaced with…*oh, no.* I stared at a deserted hut along the road, one of the zillions dotting the Irish countryside. People said it was bad luck to tear them down. As the bus rumbled along, it occurred to me that even if Ben seemed to get into the Irish-fairy-luck and shamrocks stuff, he might not be around as a long-term daddy. What if he stayed in Ireland only long enough to get his business off the ground, then returned to the States? And the girlfriend? Where in hell would that leave my son?

I'll admit, I'd suddenly got rather attached to the idea of Kevin having a real daddy. Ben couldn't have faked being so patient, so interested, could he? As the bus hit a pothole, I rescued Kevin's drawing, lying face-down on his lap. "Deirdre, did you notice the really big thing about Kevin?"

"He hardly stuttered?" Deirdre closed her magazine.

"So that only means..."

"You've got to come out with it," Deirdre finished.

The bus jounced again, rousing Kevin. I felt another clutch of tenderness at his otherworldly look, before he came to full consciousness. "Didja see my picture, Mam?"

I helped him straighten out the paper, then met Deirdre's eyes. A stick figure with red corkscrew hair like a Slinky toy, was off in the corner. I tried to be philosophical—after all, mammies you see every day are a dime a dozen. While a very tall stick man—hair represented by very creative spikes of black sticking out of head—had joined hands with a small boy with red spikes. The boy's free hand, a circle with five lines coming out of it, had two green dots in the center.

"It's grand," I managed.

"Like I said, Ash." Deirdre's look was sympathetic. "Clock's ticking."

BLAST FROM THE PAST

I flung myself onto Granny's flower-patterned sofa. "There you have it, Granny. The whole story." Well, the essentials, anyway. With Kevin tucked up for the night, I'd told Granny about seeing his daddy again. Though of course she knew a bit about my...past, I'd never divulged the when, where, and how of Kevin's conception. And the unfortunate incident after...

I shuddered. There's only so much you can tell your granny, no matter how hip she is. All she said was, "I always knew Kevin's father would turn up sooner or later, child."

"You're a mystic, is it?" I had to laugh. Rosehill Cottage made a strange dwelling for one. No beaded doorways or Tarot cards round the place, just a country home with your usual cutting-edge Irish interior design—JFK photo, crucifixes galore, and Sacred Heart of Jesus. Tonight, my eyes lingered on Granny's piquant touch of a rosary draped across the handlebars of her exercise bike, and vase of lucky bamboo on the kitchen table. I ignored the family photograph collection on the wall whenever possible.

Granny chuckled. "I knew he'd be the decent sort. You'd never have taken up with some dreadful boy."

"Ben isn't a...saint, Granny. And don't be thinking that once I tell Ben, it's going to turn into wedding bells and the perfect family. He has a girlfriend. And marriage isn't for me." If I wasn't mistaken, Granny rolled her eyes." But back to Kevin—I'm sure it's the right thing to have him see Ben, if his stutter improves."

"He's such a quiet little soul, that one," Granny murmured. "But he had a real sparkle in him today."

When I'd gone upstairs earlier, to tuck Kevin up, I found him surrounded by the childhood toys I'd brought from Minnesota. "Lookit, Mam." He opened his palm to show me an old, tarnished American silver dollar. "Can I k-keep it?"

A gift from one of the Chicago uncles. I'd forgotten about it. "Of course."

He rummaged in my old jewelry box—covered in fake pink satin, it was the latest in '80s chic. Or so I'd thought. "This b-box is awful girly, but there's lots more c-cool stuff in here."

I knelt down, gathering up toys. "It's time for bed, love. We'll poke through it tomorrow."

"Wait, Mam—lookit this gold c-cross. If we sell it, we'd get lots of money."

I'd won the trinket at a parish bazaar. I felt a bit rotten, that Kevin already knew our family finances were crap, but he was already on to the next item.

"And here's a pit'cher of a boy. Who is it?"

I glanced at him and froze. He held a school photograph of Ben, that had made my six-year-old heart skip a beat. I knew it would hurt to look any closer, remembering what a serious, watchful boy he'd been—so much like Kevin. "Great," I said, stuffing toys into the cupboard.

"Who is it, Mammy?" he repeated.

I couldn't lie. "Ben—you know, the man we saw—"

"Wow," he breathed. While I couldn't—breathe, that is—waiting for the question: *why do you have his picture?* But thankfully, he didn't ask. "Can I keep it?"

"Sure, but under the covers now." I hardly knew what I was saying. Because Deirdre was right. I really *was* running out of time...

Granny's voice pulled me back to the present. "...Kevin'll get a boost," she was saying.

"Sorry?"

"I was saying, Kevin'll get a real boost, having a daddy around."

I twisted my fingers together. "Please don't get your hopes up. I've no idea when to tell Ben, or how he's going to take it."

"It'll come out right, I'm sure. But love—"

I jumped up from the couch. If I wasn't careful, Granny would have me blubbering out all my worries. Such as, what if Ben's good at being a nice guy, but awful at being a father? Then a *bigger* worry than Ben heading back to America hit me. What if he got so attached to Kevin he'd want to take my child with him?

No—no, and no. I can't go there. I dropped a kiss on Granny's flaming hair. "I'll put the kettle on." Desperate measures called for the universal Irish restorative.

Granny rose from her chair. "I can—"

"No, you don't," I said. "Let me."

Granny ignored me. "I'm no Nora O'Donnell—God love her, but she's all for having Bridie and everyone else running off their feet for her."

I threw a grin at her on my way to the kitchen. "I'll bet Deirdre's already worn to a frazzle and the weekend not half over."

While Granny rustled in the small pantry, I made tea and found some ready-made biscuits. By the time I brought the tray back to the front room, I was on my second biscuit—and feeling much revived, thank you—when Granny said, "I've something to show you."

She didn't look quite...right. Suddenly, the biscuit was like chalk in my mouth. "Everything okay?" I set the tray down with a thump, then noticed an overstuffed scrapbook on the tea table. "What's this?"

"Open it, love." Granny's face suddenly looked pinched.

Mystified, I lifted the cover—and seeing the first photo, couldn't stop a painful sigh. "Oh, Granny." It was the man I'd worshipped from afar. My father. And Granny had assembled an entire "This Is Your Life" scrapbook of him.

The veritable tome of photos and newspaper clippings showcased John Moore's political career. I flipped through the first couple of pages, seeing his brash charm and confident smile, then looked back at Granny, feeling six years old again. When I'd first dimly realized loving my father carried its own brand of hurt. "I really can't—"

"Please, Aislin."

Shaking, I forced myself to start at the beginning. For Granny's sake.

Eagle Prairie attorney elected to state legislature...Before I was born.

John Moore wins seat in Congress...I noted with irony that no newspaper had picked up the exclusive, *Wife takes to the drink*.

The memories of my early childhood sort of blurred, save for a few blips of clarity when my sister Grace came home from school. My life really came into focus when Annie Carpenter had come to work for us, when I'd felt that inexplicable sense of safety with Ben. Then my sixth year lapsed back into the mist, summed up by *Congressman's wife convalescing after undisclosed illness*, before I came to Ireland.

While I lived with Granny—visits to my parents getting more infrequent as the years went by—she'd apparently continued to accumulate stories of my father's accomplishments, including an Oval Office visit with the President. Which, if I recall correctly, made the rounds down at Hurley's pub.

I turned another page. Amazingly, my father had also won a number of amateur tennis tournaments. I tasted bitterness in my mouth, as if I'd sucked on a penny. I suppose when you farm out your children and eliminate the distractions of fatherhood, there's no limit to the heights you can reach, right?

Still another page. *Moore seeks Senate seat.* That was my life at nineteen, when Ben and I found each other again. And after Ben left town: *Rep. Moore quits Senate race, indicted for misusing campaign funds...*My eyes blurred. I forced myself to keep turning the pages until I reached the end of the scrapbook. The end of my dad's public life. One that began with such promise, sliding into disgrace and obscurity.

I slapped the scrapbook closed, my throat thick with tears. "Why did you want me to look at this, Granny?"

"You know why," Granny said, grief in her eyes. "Because I love you both."

I clenched my hands. You can always count on love to get you into trouble. "Granny—"

"A festering wound will never heal, darling."

"I'm not festering—" I intercepted Granny's most patient look. "All right—I've a few scars, but I'm handling life all right."

"We've none of us escaped the hurt." Regret was etched in her wrinkles. "I can't forget how I let you and Kevin down."

"Don't say that." I went to Granny and put my arms round her. "You took us in—you've always been there— "

"Don't be thick, love." Her smile was bittersweet. "I never should have allowed your father to take advantage of the situation the way he did. Or almost did."

Suddenly, illogically, I wanted Ben here with me. "It's not like he was one to take advice."

"I should've stood my ground. But old habits die hard, child. I spoiled my boy dreadfully."

I hugged her, hard. "Like you spoiled me."

"Ah, well…" Granny patted me, and I let go of her. "Your dad was so determined, so successful, I thought indulging him hadn't done any harm. But he was done in by his fatal flaw, never happy with what he had."

"It doesn't matter now," I said. "I'm fine—I never even think about him." Well, hardly ever.

"And that's such a good thing, to shut your dad out of your life?"

The way I've shut Ben out of Kevin's… I wanted to weep, have a real, proper cry, but I couldn't fall apart in front of Granny. The only person, save for Kevin, who truly loved me.

"It is for me," I said with difficulty. Really, it wasn't my fault that Ben hadn't been told about Kevin at the time. Anyone in my situation would have done the same. Having had my fill of the past, I gave Granny's thin shoulders a squeeze. "I'll concentrate on Kevin. On the future."

"You're a good girl. But you'll want to know that your dad's been…em, a bit under the weather lately. Might you ring him?"

Because he has a cold? Not bloody likely.

"And there's…something else you'll want to know," Granny said. "He'd like to—"

"Granny." I pushed a cup of lukewarm tea at her. "Maybe you need to talk about him, but I can't—put your hopes somewhere else."

Not on me. I won't mean to, but eventually I'll let you down. Like I do with everyone else.

ON HIATUS

I arrived at the shop early Monday—amazingly, I wasn't the first one in. "What are you doing here?" I asked Deirdre. "I'd thought you'd be positively knackered from running circles round your granny and Bridie."

Deirdre yawned. "I am, but that's easy, compared to walking my aunt's beastly mutts." She gave me a look-over. "Jaysus, you look like shite. What'd you do, stay out all night?"

"That's me, the big party girl," I returned. "Hard to believe, but I was simply up late."

As in, unable to sleep. Again.

Granny had asked me to take her infamous scrapbook home, with the parting advice: "You might need to talk to Kevin about his grandfather someday." Hence, the insomnia.

Which was also brought on because I'd deceived my own grandmother and stuffed the scrapbook in the depths of my old closet at Granny's. If I hadn't, the scrapbook would be sitting in my bottom drawer in my flat, emanating deadly vibes rather like Superman's kryptonite. And how could a girl sleep anyway, when she simply *had* to figure out a definitive, can't-fail plan for telling a man Something Big?

"I've something to cheer you up," Deirdre said, grinning. "I came in early to get on top of the e-mail situation—and we've got mail, Ash."

Shoving my worries aside, I hurried into the back room. "Never tell me you're reading my e-mails before I do? What a nerve—"

"I didn't," Deirdre protested. "What do you take me for? Anyway, I had an e-mail myself." Her voice was smug. "From Adrian. And in case we try anything kinky online—"

"Deirdre, you're *so* disgusting!" I laughed. "Like what?"

"That's for me to know. I've already rung our Internet provider, to get us separate e-mail."

"It's about bloody time," I said, planting myself at the computer, and clicked on Ben's e-mail. Sent Saturday afternoon, which was rather nice.

FROM: Ben Carpenter
SUBJECT: Galway
Hi Aislin,
How was Galway?
Ben

DEIRDRE SEEMED AS DISAPPOINTED as I was. "I was hoping for something more... personal, Ash."

So was I. If Ben keeps his distance, how can I create opportunities for him to *organically* realize he's a daddy? Ready to hit, "Reply," I paused as another e-mail came in. From Ben again!

PS FORGOT TO ASK—ANY reason Kevin sees me as a potential boyfriend when you already have one?

. . .

97

"WHOA," Deirdre said. "Now *that's* personal. We need to come up with—"

"No, *I* need to," I said, wondering how in bloody hell I'd answer this. Before I could so much as set a fingernail to the keyboard, Polly burst in the front door. "Away from all that Internet business, girls," she called. "Deirdre, love, you've those errands today. And the dust's an inch thick in here."

" AREN'T YOU THE LUCKY ONE," I said to Deirdre that afternoon, and promptly sneezed. "Escaping Dust Duty."

"Took myself out for a bite, too," Deirdre said, rubbing it in.

"Must be nice not to have a narky little lunch in the back room, like some I know." I skimmed over my pile of receipts, then sneaked a look at the computer.

"Ooh, poor you—but I called round at Liz's office, like you asked me to."

"Well, what do you think of her? Won't she be a great fourth for Saturday night?"

"Deirdre!" Polly prompted from the front counter. "I'll need a bit of help here."

"In a minute, Mam," Deirdre called back. "Liz is a crack, all right. Kept me in stitches with her crap-husband jokes. No wonder you like her."

"What's that supposed to mean?"

"Honestly, Ash, you're always saying you don't want a husband. Here's one of Liz's bits—there's this old couple in their sixties, been married forever, and a magic genie appears."

"Deirdre, we've better things to do." As in, me composing a return e-mail to Ben. "Like chatting up the customers out front, like Polly asked."

"In a sec—anyway, the genie gives them each one wish. The wife says, 'Grand! I've always wanted a cruise around the world.' Lo and behold, they're on a cruise ship on their way to the

Bahamas. The husband takes a good look at the old girl and says, 'For my wish, I want a wife who's thirty years younger...'"

"Really, I've got tons of work to—"

"Wait, here it is: the husband suddenly turns ninety years old!"

I had to laugh. "All right, all right," I said when I finally caught my breath, "That's great, but truth is, I've got to e-mail Ben."

"I *knew* it," Deirdre said, and reached over my head to click the e-mail program.

"I...em, really think I should write this one on my own." Seeing Deirdre's face fall, I added, "But I'll give you a shout if I need advice."

"You know where to find me," Deirdre said, luckily not sounding insulted.

Oh, I do. I sighed, clicked on "Reply," then went for it.

TO: Ben Carpenter

SUBJECT: Galway

Hi Ben,

Galway's always lovely. My granny's a dear, and it's a treat to get away from the city crowds and petrol fumes and all that. Kevin even got to play with the O'Donnell dogs between rainstorms.

I PAUSED to admire my efforts so far—a bit prim to start, then segueing nicely into friendly without gushing. I resumed typing, *Regarding your PS—*

"Ash!" Deirdre hissed from the front. "Get out here."

"I'm busy—"

"Sam's here."

Shite. My fingers froze, and before I knew it, I'd typed a line of *SSSSSSSSSSSS.* "Be right there," I said and smoothed my hair, wishing I'd some cover-up for the circles under my eyes, then headed out front.

I saw Sam before he saw me. Busy brushing imaginary lint off his coat, Sam was impeccably groomed, as usual. At least "as usual" for the last year. When we first met, he'd dressed in jeans, with rather endearing floppy hair, like Hugh Grant in *Notting Hill.* I'd been touched, not turned off, by the scuffs on his shoes, and his eagerness for me had been heady.

Once he'd gotten a job at a posh bank, though, things were... different. "Sam's making a great salary," I'd told Maggie and Deirdre with pride. "And he'll be up for a promotion in three months." But it wasn't long before his success revealed a downside.

All his spare money went for clothes. As his puppylike fondness for me had waned, he'd adopted this *attitude.* As in, *I have money and know how to look good, girls like me, and finally I'm cool.*

Jaysus, I wanted to say. *You're only cool if you're not trying, and if you don't know that by now I'm not going to tell you.*

"Sam," I said, waiting for that little leap in my middle I always felt. Except this time, the leap was more of a squiggle. "What can I do for you?"

He looked slightly taken aback at my businesslike tone. "Just wanted to say hallo, see how you're getting on." He tried on a tentative smile/self-conscious hair-smoothing combo.

Meaning you want to get back together for real? After Sam's hiatus deal, I'd wondered if I should play hard to get. You know, like all the dating-advice articles said. But suddenly I felt like I could do it without pretending. "I'm great."

"Really?" He sounded surprised.

"I've some new plans for the future," I said. *Did I ever.* "And Kevin's speech is enormously better these days." *Take that, will you.* Sam had always been distressed by my son's stutter—and not out of worry for Kevin's well-being either, I was sure. But because it made him look bad.

For a moment, Sam looked like his underpants had got too tight. "That's...grand."

"Speaking of plans," and I threw in a pleasant smile, "I've some *strategies* to work on in back." Another plus about being honest was that you didn't have to stand there looking like an eejit while you tried to think up excuses. I turned on my heel.

"Wait—I'll ring you," he said, actually sounding quite keen for it.

I couldn't help it; my heart warmed a little. "Talk soon, then," I said, then hurried back to the computer.

"Woo, aren't you a cool one," Deirdre said admiringly a few moments later. "I think he wants you back."

"You think so?" I asked absently, and pulled up my half-finished note to Ben. "But I've really got to concentrate on this e-mail." Quite inspired, I began typing...

P.S...

... Regarding your PS about the boyfriend bit, sorry about Kevin mentioning it—must be terribly embarrassing for you. I don't think he minds too awfully that Sam isn't coming round for the time being—though Sam is perfectly nice, they never quite hit it off. I think it's more that Kevin is like any other little boy, who needs a man in his life.

Sincerely, [You always have to wonder when people use, "Sincerely," if they're being anything *but* sincere, but in this case, I was really trying.]

Aislin

PS Regarding your previous PS, you mentioned that your girlfriend isn't the jealous sort. What sort is she?

HI AISLIN,

Courtney's great. She runs marathons, likes the Seattle theater and art scene. People tell her she looks like Jennifer Aniston. She's going to be up for a VP spot before the end of the year.

About Kevin needing a guy around, I definitely see your point. If it works for you, I'd like to take him out for ice cream. And you too, of course. How about Saturday?

Take care,

BEN

PS To avoid confusion on Kevin's part, are you with Sam or not?

I read Ben's e-mail with mixed feelings. Upside: he seemed genuinely interested in Kevin's welfare. Downside: Ben's girlfriend was a bloody paragon. I was ready to get a bit depressed about Perfect Courtney, when in came another e-mail. From an entirely unexpected source.

FROM: Anne Carpenter
   SUBJECT: Hello from Annie
   Dear Aislin,
   I was real surprised to get your message. I'm not much for writing but Ben got me on the e-mail last weekend. See, he bought a computer and got it mailed it right to my house, then he had some expert from St. Cloud drive over and set everything up and show me how to do things. So I thought, shoot, Ben went to all that trouble, I should write Aislin. I can't type worth a darn, and I had to call the expert back six times to help

me figure out how to send the e-mails, but I think I got the hang of it now.

Ben said he said saw you, and that you're real good and have a little boy. I keep hoping Ben'll give me some grandkids but so far nothing. I haven't met his girlfriend. She seems okay but she works a lot. They broke up a couple times cause they're both so busy with their jobs but then they got back together. He said she's real outdoorsy. Around here, that means a person likes dogs and horses, but I guess she likes to jog all day and climb rocks for fun. Doesn't sound too fun to me but it takes all kinds. And some kind of exercise called Pee-lotties. She sounds like she should eat more with all that exercise, but Ben says one time he'd cooked for her, and she pulled the skin off the fried chicken, then before he could open the ice cream she made him throw it out, and it was that expensive kind that only comes in pints. I never heard of such a thing, throwing out good food, but like I said, takes all kinds. Maybe it's good they don't have kids yet if she's going to make them go hungry and since she works weekends they'd never see her.

I always wondered how things went for you after Ben got deployed with the Navy and you and your folks moved away so I'm real glad you're good.

Sincerely,

Annie Carpenter

PS. I asked Ben if you still had those blue eyes that look pert-near like Liz Taylor's but he didn't say.

I read Annie's e-mail twice, a bit misty-eyed. And not just because Perfect Bloody Courtney wasn't so perfect after all. Annie reminded me a lot of Polly, only without the fairy thing. Or the nagging thing. In fact, I got so inspired I wrote her back straightaway.

At first, I was a bit nervous about what to say—after all, she was my son's granny, only she didn't know it, and I was so afraid I'd let it out and not realize it. But I focused on chatting her up about when Ben and I were kids, you know, safe stuff, and no snarky questions about Perfect Courtney either, which I was quite proud of.

The funny thing about Annie's e-mail was that it told me I was totally on the right track. Obviously, Ben was a devoted son, without overdoing it, so I just knew he'd be an equally brilliant father. Also, without overdoing it. And since Annie might hear about Sam, I'd want to give Ben the full, open, honest, aboveboard story.

Hi Ben,

Sam and I see each other occasionally, but we're not officially together.

[By that, I tried to imply we're not having sex. Hopefully Ben will think I'm a fantastic mother who sacrifices her personal life for her child.]

And yes, Saturday would be fine.

Then, PS Have you noticed that the most interesting parts of letters can be in a PS?

HONESTY REALLY IS THE BEST POLICY

"Sam, that's Mam's old boyfriend, never t-took us to McDonald's."

The following Saturday, when Ben took us out for a bite, it was clear Kevin's rapport with Ben hadn't been a one-off. "Says he hadn't enough money," Kevin went on, "but Deirdre said he just bought a new c-car." He took a huge bite of his Big Mac.

A new car? I swallowed an oversized spoonful of ice cream. Wincing, I rubbed the cold-induced ache in my forehead. Hadn't Sam made a big deal about saving money?

"You okay?" Ben asked me. I nodded, though I wasn't, then he said to Kevin, "Is that so."

"He hasn't t-taken us for a ride yet," Kevin was saying. "He doesn't call round anymo—"

"Aren't you good with the talk today," I broke in. How will a man think you're a desirable commodity—as in, a great mother —if even a crap guy doesn't care? I'd been sure this outing would be a great way to facilitate my Think Organic Plan, as in Ben and Kevin getting to know each other. But I hadn't counted on my quiet little boy turning into such a fount of information. "I'm sure Ben's not interested."

"Actually, I am," said Ben. Eyes intent on Kevin, he hadn't touched his French fries in ages.

"Deirdre c-calls him Mr. SOS," Kevin continued. "But she said the letters don't stand for Sam O' Sullivan."

Wouldn't you know, I walked right into it. "What's 'SOS,' then?"

"She t-told me it means 'Help.' But don't b-bother asking him for any, she says."

"I think that's enough about Sa—"

"Says he only looks out for the main ch-chance. What's a main chance?"

Oh my God, Kevin was really on a roll—but hardly stuttering! Again! "Really, Kevin," I said mildly, but felt my face burn.

Ben's lips twitched. "I think it's when someone is mostly interested in—"

"And B-Bill says he's a fairy."

"Kevin..."

"Maggie's husband?" Eyes dancing, Ben was studiously avoiding mine. "You mean, the magical kind we talked about last week, cousins to leprechauns?"

"No, the other k-kind," Kevin said, "that has flowers on his shirts—"

"Kevin!" This had gone far enough. "Sam does not have flowers on his—"

"And varnishes his nails," Kevin finished.

"He wears fingernail polish?" Ben asked.

I couldn't look at him. "It's time we got back to the flat—the girls will be round soon for Girl's Night. And by the way, Sam gets his nails buffed," I pointed out, trying not to sound snippy. "Lots of men do." Privately, I thought it was over the top, but Sam said the bank liked a posh appearance.

"Sure they do," Ben said, winking at Kevin.

Seeing my son's eyes shining, I sort of lost my appetite, if that was possible. I told myself who could eat, when you're so happy about your son's rather miraculous cure from stammering.

But who was I fooling? This "Think Organic" thing was working better than I'd ever counted on. Which could only mean, the Honesty Clock was nearing midnight.

THE MINUTE I let the three of us into the flat, in the spirit of their new Fellowship of The Guys, Kevin dragged Ben off to show him his favorite toys. I was still trying to get my bearings when Deirdre called round for Girls' Night. "Ben's here?"

"I ended up inviting him for the evening," I whispered. "So he can get better acquainted with Kevin. You know. Intuitively."

"He doesn't know Liz's coming, does he?" Deirdre kept her voice low. "Might be a bit awkward."

"I'll explain it somehow. But where's Maggie?"

"She says she's too tired to come—she's even sent the kids over to Mam's."

"Must be all that extra shagging," I guessed. "Wearing her out."

"I accused her of staying home to have it off with Bill, *again*, but she's just sent him round to the chemist for a pregnancy test."

"Not letting any grass grow under her feet, is she?"

"Not that one," Deirdre said, giggling, then she sobered. "It's going to be weird though, having Ben here, we girls knowing about Kevin, and him not knowing—"

"Shhhh—here he comes!" I smiled weakly at Ben as he joined us, then another knock sounded at the door.

"Liz!" I said brightly. "Oh—and the kiddies." Her eldest, Josh, made a beeline for Ben, while Emily, her blue-eyed toddler, said, "'Lo," then glued her cheek to her mother's shoulder, furiously sucking her thumb.

Liz looked miserable. "I'm so sorry about the kids—I

couldn't find a sitter. And Dan insisted he had to work. I could just kill him."

"It's fine," I said, and touched Emily's curls. "Hallo there, gorgeous." I actually had to wrestle a bit with the urge to hold her. I'd never been very keen on other babies—I was over-whelmed enough with Kevin—so I wondered if I was evolving. Or, perish the thought, having Ben close by had set off a previously unsuspected nesting instinct.

I directed Kevin to take the kids to his room, then faced Ben's quizzical look with an airy, "Ben, Liz is...joining us."

"I can see that," he said, eyebrows raised. "Uh... what...how?"

Liz began, "I know this looks strange—"

"But it's really not," I jumped in, and hastened to recount our meeting at the shop, naturally, leaving out the way Liz had taken one look at Kevin and Knew All. "And I'm a great one for inviting my favorite customers home," I joked.

"Whew," he said. "Here I was thinking Dan sicced his wife on me, to find out why I'm not burning the office midnight oil with him."

"Dan doesn't believe in weekends anymore," Liz said with a short laugh.

Ben grinned. "But I do." He looked right at me.

As for me—okay, okay, you dragged it out of me—I looked right back.

WE GIRLS QUICKLY NOMINATED Ben as the designated pizza picker-upper. While he was out, I brought Liz into the kitchen. "I know I promised you lots of lovely cheap wine, but with Ben and all the kids here..."

"Not to worry," Liz said. "We wouldn't want any alcohol-induced loose lips."

"I rather hate to put you in this position," I said, a bit

anxiously. "With Ben being your friend, but I really am going to tell him soon." *Definitely.*

Two hours later, I'm happy to say the conversation hadn't even come *close* to the danger zone. The two boys were sleeping in Kevin's room, while Emily dozed on Ben's shoulder. "Amazing what a little carbo-loading will do." Ben smoothed his hand over the baby's jumper.

I yanked my eyes from his hand—and my thoughts from wondering how it would feel on *my* back—telling myself my lethargy was *not* due to mild lust. Like Emily, I'd obviously over-done it on the pizza. "What did everyone think of the film?"

"Fun," Liz said, sprawled on the end of the couch. "Great *craic,* as you would say."

I pulled the tape from the player. "It's one of my all-time personal favorites."

"*You've Got Mail.*" Deirdre groaned. "God help us."

"Oh, who are you kidding," I said. "You watched it. You even laughed."

"I was being supportive," Deirdre shot back, then said to the others, "There's nothing Ash likes better than a Meg Ryan film with no sex."

"No true," I defended myself. "There's sex in this one—Meg and what's-his-name…"

"Frank," said Liz. "Greg Kinnear."

"Right—she's in bed, and Frank kisses her."

"Yeah, on the cheek," Deirdre pointed out. "But he's not in the bed himself."

"Well, there's…" I disregarded Ben's amused look, "there's *Sleepless in Seattle*—another one of my top ten films. Remember, Meg is sleeping with Bill Pullman."

"Uh-uh, Aislin," Liz put in. "They never actually have sex. He's busy with his allergies."

"But we could hardly play a sexy movie, with the kids round," I said.

"There *are* naughty bits in *You've Got Mail*," Deirdre pointed out. "That lesbo stuff, with Tom Hanks' stepmother having it off with Nanny Maureen. And his dad was a regular rotter."

"Don't forget Tom was living with that other girl while he was after Meg," Ben put in.

"Parker Posey." A Girls' Chat with Ben here wasn't as awkward as I'd anticipated. "Rather a gobshite-ish thing to do, wasn't it? Even if she was a pain in the—"

"With some men, it's chasing women. With others, it's some other... addiction," Liz said. "Once you're married, you find out there's always something."

"As the token male, can I object?" Ben asked.

"I will too," I said. "I'd like to keep the few illusions I have left about marriage."

"Why?" Deirdre said. "You always say you don't see the point of getting married."

I succumbed to temptation, and nibbled on one of Deirdre's leftover pizza crusts. "My parents weren't exactly the poster kids for marriage. Not like yours."

"What about you, Ben?" Deirdre asked. "Since we've an informal poll going."

"Mine don't count," he said with a shuttered look. "My mom's been a widow forever."

"Oh...sorry." Deirdre said quickly. "I didn't mean to—"

"Don't worry about it," he said. "He wasn't much of a dad."

"Neither is Ash's," Deirdre began, then Liz broke in, "No families or marriages are perfect."

Obviously, we should have stuck to films. "Even if *I* don't think marriage is so great," and I crunched through a second crust, "*some* people need to be married. Or society will fall apart."

"Is that why you're getting married, Ben?" Deirdre's flirtatious smile was back.

"You are?" Liz asked. "Since when? I can't believe you didn't tell me—"

"Actually, nothing's settled." Ben's smile looked sickly.

I had to wonder if that meant he wasn't keen on marrying the Perfect Courtney too soon—which of course would work out best for Kevin. *But what about us?* asked my Inner Single Girl, who isn't quite as resigned as I am to a sexual deprivation.

Before we could pin Ben down, Deirdre volunteered, "Nothing's settled with Ash and her boyfriend either."

I sent her a dirty look, which she carefully avoided, the wretch. "Maybe we're a bit on and off and all that, but I suppose we'll move in together if it's meant to be."

"And not make it legal? What about Kevin?" Ben gave me a straight look.

Which my motherly guilt didn't care for. "If you're not sure if the fellow is the One," I shot back, "you know, with the capital 'O,' why muck things up with a permanent commitment?"

He was quiet for a moment. "Good point." He shifted Emily off his shoulder, then checked his watch. "I'd better go."

"Me, too," Liz said, not sounding too happy about it. While I held a sleeping Emily, Liz extricated her son from his nest of blankets in Kevin's bedroom, then Ben ferried Josh to the car.

"What a darling Ben is," Deirdre said, as I somewhat regretfully surrendered the baby to Liz. "He's going to make what's her name—"

"Courtney," I inserted with just the right amount of friendly disinterest.

"Yeah—a great husband."

"I hope not," Liz said. "He could do better. A hell of a lot better." Fortunately, before my Inner Single Girl could ask, *Like who?* Liz gave me a quick goodbye hug. "I had the absolutely best time."

"Wasn't bad at all, considering the potential complications." Deirdre giggled, then hugged me too. "Maggie said she'd come round if the test was positive," she whispered as Ben returned, "so it must have been a false alarm."

I waved both girls off, feeling understandably elated about the success of our first Girls' and Boy Night. With all the goodbye hugs going round—and to make up for being a bit sharp with Ben, I decided it was the most natural thing in the world to give him a brief hug too.

Bad Idea. I was instantly enveloped by Ben's lovely man-smell. And the smooth skin of his neck that I'd once kissed was only inches from my face. His touch on my back set off more memories, and his shoulders felt so strong and solid under my hands I had to force myself to let go of him.

Sending him off with a forced smile, I quickly closed the door, my knees trembling. Clearly, I hadn't left my stint as a Natural Woman strictly in the past. Now that she'd wormed her way back into my life, I had to admit the rest: *If I tell myself that hugging Ben Carpenter is the same as hugging a girlfriend, my new honesty-is-best policy has just gotten shagged.*

THE PERFECT OPPORTUNITY

*A*t O'Fagan's pub, Liz and Deirdre leaned in close. I unfolded an e-mail print-out, and carefully set it on the scarred wood table.

FROM: Ben Carpenter
SUBJECT: Galway
Hi Aislin,
I'm going to Galway City this weekend on business. In case you're visiting your grandma, would you and Kevin like to hitch a ride?
See you,
Ben

"THERE YOU GO," said Liz, divvying up the last of her chips among us. Liz had turned out to be the perfect addition to our Girls' circle, especially now that Maggie the Shag Queen was unavailable more times than not. "The perfect opportunity to tell him."

"And a ride in a lovely car," commented the ever-practical Deirdre.

I hid my trembling hands under the table. "I can hardly talk to him with Kevin around."

"Oh, really, Ash." Deirdre pointed a chip at me. "Of course we meant that your granny could mind Kevin while the pair of you chat."

I'd already rung Granny, to tell her Kevin and I were catching a ride with a friend. And that Kevin would probably burble on about said friend all weekend, but I'd explain everything later. Granny was no slouch, of course, but I couldn't worry about what she was thinking *too*.

"Deirdre's right," Liz said, taking a bite of her cheese sandwich. "You've got to tell Ben soon. I mean, *soon*—I'm terrified I'll suddenly space and let it out accidentally. And it's just getting more and more bizarre that he doesn't know what's going on, since he and Kevin get along so well."

"And since he fancies you," Deirdre added.

Rattled, I stuffed the paper back into my rucksack. "Go on. His e-mail wasn't exactly teeming with undying passion."

"You wish it were?" Deirdre asked.

I ignored her. "Anyway," I said with false brightness, "we don't always have to talk about my problems, do we?"

"I don't have any problems," Deirdre pointed out.

"And mine aren't the least bit interesting," said Liz. "Not like yours."

I rubbed my finger into some water drops on the table. "But I'm just not ready to tell—"

"No excuses," Deirdre said. "Every day you don't talk to him is another day you risk really mucking things up."

"And according to Dan, when Ben's backed into a corner," Liz said, "watch out."

Deirdre eyes widened. "I don't believe it—he's a lovely guy."

"Believe it," I said, then clamped my mouth shut. Change

focus, if not subject. "Before I do anything, I need to find out how long Ben's going to be in Ireland. Liz, has he said—"

"Whatever his plans are," Liz said gently, "they don't change anything."

"Liz is sooo right, Ash." Deirdre finished off her pint. "You were the one who rang Ben's mam, and here he is."

"It'll take some doing, finding the right moment, the right way to say it, and all that." I gave them a pleading look.

"Whatever, Ash. You've got to finish what you started."

"That's right," Liz agreed. "Once you're in Galway, get him alone, and 'fess up. You'll feel one hundred percent better."

HURLEY'S PUB in the village of Ballydara hadn't changed in twenty years. The two old fellas in wool caps, already ancient the first time I'd come in here with Granny, were still in the same corner, still talking in Irish. The same Guinness adverts were on the wall, though why they hadn't curled up their toes by now was a mystery. By way of new décor, Pat Hurley had added photographs of the World Cup finals, from the nineties. Practically yesterday, from the Irish point of view, but then, we've always been great ones for living off past glories.

Whatever the drawbacks, Hurley's seemed like the safest place for The Conversation. I'd chosen the booth the furthest away from the bar, and if Ben thought I was making a play for him, it couldn't be helped. Although that would be a definite long shot: I'd been frozen with nerves since we got to Galway, and consequently hardly spoken to Ben when he took Kevin and me out yesterday.

"So." Ben folded his hands on the table. "You wanted to talk to me?"

"I...em, wanted to thank you for taking us to the seashore. It was a treat, watching Kevin tromp round to show us shells and rocks and..." Ben's distant look made this hard going. Rather like one of those religious pilgrimages, where you climb Croagh Patrick on your hands and knees, and you're halfway dead by the time you reach the top. "...He's quite keen on slimy beach creatures," I finished gamely.

"You thanked me yesterday," Ben said. "What counts is that Kevin had a good time."

I guess that meant I didn't. Count, that is. But I couldn't blame Ben for that either. After our lovely outing, I hadn't asked him in to meet Granny, just grabbed Kevin and fled. Ben's face had gone stiff, but what could I do?

Just as I was trying to formulate the perfect, the most absolutely stunning opening gambit that would change Kevin's and my life forever, Pat Hurley materialized at our booth. "Well, if it isn't our Yank—em, Ben, is it? Will that be a pint for you and Aislin? If I take a good look round the place, I can probably find a menu."

Pat had a rather minimalist approach to service. "No menus, thanks," I said. "I'll have a Coke, please."

"Make it two," Ben said.

Pat gave us a strange look that said, *Are you mad, when you could have a nice pint?* "And a packet of crisps," I added. As Pat walked away, scratching his head, I asked, "Are you and Pat... mates or something?" Not a very auspicious beginning, but a girl has to start somewhere.

"I've, uh, passed through Ballydara village a few times," Ben said.

That should have tipped me off, but like I said, I was distracted. "So." I leaned my chin in my palm, hoping my *I simply find you fascinating* look would give me an advantage when push came to shove. "You've finished all your business in Galway City?"

"Uh...for now. I'm not sure I mentioned it, but Dan and I are setting up an office there." Ben avoided my eyes.

"Oh. That's strange," I said. "Liz didn't mention relocating here."

"They're not—I'll be running the new office."

"You'll be living in Galway?" I almost slumped in relief. *Now I won't* really *have to share Kevin*, I thought fiercely. Then I hardly understood myself. Wasn't it what I wanted? To have his daddy's help? Either way, Kevin and me in Dublin and Ben in Galway City simplified things. "That's great—really great!" My relief showed a bit more than it should, because Ben's mouth tightened. I hurriedly tacked on, "I mean, it sounds like a...a wonderful career opportunity."

"Missing me already, huh?"

"Sorry?"

"Just kidding—and yes, it should be." Ben's smile didn't seem to reach his eyes. "In fact, moving here means no more city flats for me—I'm ready to close on a house, here in the West."

"A house?" Wait a minute. Houses meant stability. *Looong*-term commitment. If Ben was going to live in Ireland for the next few years, my life was getting rather...messy all of a sudden. What had happened to my initial lovely daydream, about the devoted Yank dad coming to Ireland to visit three times a year? "You've bought a house? Where is it?"

Just then, Pat came over and set the Cokes and crisps in front of us. "Anything else?"

I shook my head, which now seemed to have a whole cart-load of stuff to get itself around. "We're fine." *And please, get the hell out of here.*

Ben said, "It's not too far away—"

"A grand little place," Pat confirmed.

"Really." *Where is it, where is it, where is it?* I opened the crisps, hoping the salt would settle me down.

"Needs a bit of work, though," Pat went on. "But you know, my brother Bernard could install a new bath for you inside a year or two."

"I'll take one of his business cards," Ben told him. When Pat finally moved away, he lifted an eyebrow at me. "Two years for a bathroom?"

"Irish time." I bit into a crisp, feeling calmer already. "So, you've a place and you'll be fixing it up—it must mean you're to stay in Ireland for a long while." *Okay, I think I can put a good spin on this...* "And did you say it's a country home?" I took a big, healthy sip of Coke.

"Yes—it's Ballydara Lodge."

"The Lod—" I choked, and started coughing. Ben jumped out of the booth to pat me hard between my shoulder blades. As I caught my breath, he began smoothing slow, easy circles on my back. Can't say I remember that being part of choking therapy, but I was in no position to argue. "Ballydara Lodge?" I croaked, my eyes still watering. "Down the road a bit?"

Ben left off what was turning into a pleasant massage, and returned to his seat. "You know it?"

"The whole district does. It's a lovely place. Lovely," I repeated, and felt my chest heave. "Quick trip to the Ladies," I gasped, and slid out of the booth.

Once I was alone, I managed to control the hyperventilation thing, thank Jesus, then I stared into the speckled mirror. But my reflection offered no guidance whatsoever. I suddenly had to reframe all my preconceptions for Kevin having a daddy, and quite frankly, I wasn't taking it well. I stood there a long time, wanting a good cry, really, but Ballydara was enough of a fish-bowl without having a breakdown at Hurley's pub.

As I slipped back into the booth, Ben said, "Everything okay?"

"Just had to...freshen my make-up." I lifted my glass for a more careful sip.

Ben peered at my face. "I can't see you've got much make-up on to fix."

"Yes, well..." I gave him what I hoped was a mysterious smile

121

—lucky for me, he was the polite sort, so could hardly ask what the hell I'd got up to in the loo—then realized there was something a bit fishy going on here. The...coincidence of Ben living in Ballydara. If the man had stalking tendencies, it would be better to know sooner rather than later. "Why'd you choose Ballydara?" I asked carefully. "I'm sure there's lots of great houses around Galway City."

Ben looked uneasy. Even...embarrassed. At least the shoe was on the other foot for a change. "Well...after Dan and I came up with this plan for me to work out of Galway City, I was happy to get out of Dublin, away from the big city. I wanted a place where I could settle down."

"That doesn't explain why Ballydara," I said, an edge in my voice.

Ben shrugged. "Uh, well..." He cracked one of his knuckles, then looked straight at me. "Okay. I remember my mom mentioning Ballydara years ago, seeing the address on the letters from your grandma. I've felt so rootless since I left home and went into the Navy. So when I looked around for a place, I had no idea if your grandma still lived there, or even if she was still alive. But I...well, I wanted something familiar. Where I had a connection, however small. So, yeah. I picked Ballydara deliberately."

Ben's gaze was challenging, as if he was daring me to make more of it. To tell the truth, I'd enough on my plate, and even if I'd been in the back of Ben's mind all this time, I didn't want to face it. Besides, his explanation didn't sound any more bizarre than my own situation, hanging round with the father of my child, whom I was deceiving every minute we spent together.

I bit my lip, casting about for a new starting spot. "What does your girlfriend think of living in the country? I'd have guessed she's a city girl."

"Actually," Ben said, "we haven't discussed it."

"You bought a house without telling her?" This was so fascinating I almost forgot my mission.

"Well," Ben said slowly, "I'm not really sure where we're headed."

"You did say that night at my house, that you were thinking of getting married," I reminded him, for the pleasure of seeing him color.

He didn't disappoint me. "Well, yeah," Ben said, and cleared his throat, "but on the other hand, we've never—" he broke off.

"Never...what?" I couldn't help it. "Really, you don't have to tell me," I added politely, not meaning a word of it.

"Well, like...shared anything." Ben seemed surprised—apparently this insight was entirely new to him. "And we've never come close to moving in together. All I've ever kept at her condo was a toothbrush and a few CD's. And some...uh, guy stuff."

I took that to mean condoms. "Some fellows travel light," I said. *Wouldn't leaving a pregnant girl behind be proof of that?*

"She didn't encourage me to bring any more," Ben said.

"Maybe you didn't really *want* to keep anything else at her place," I said before I could stop myself. Well, if Ben wasn't going to think of these relationship things, I defended myself, someone has to.

"I suppose we've still got some bugs to work out," he admitted. "But I see your point—Courtney and I should clear the air."

*Speaking of clearing the air...*It sounded so loud in my head I was sure I'd said it. But no—here's what eejit nonsense came out: "A heart-to-heart can be daunting, but once you start, it's not so bad." *So, then, why don't you get on with it?*

"I guess I should do it ASAP," Ben said.

Ben was actually such a good sport about unsolicited advice, I couldn't help but enter into the spirit of the thing, before I dropped my bomb. "It's hard, though, isn't it?" I said, oozing sympathy. "When you're so far away from each other..." I gathered my courage—I'd have rather had a dental procedure administered by a particularly inept dentist, than say what needed to be said. "But on the subject of heart-to-hearts... there's something I should tell..."

Ben wasn't listening. He seemed fascinated with his Coke bubbles. Finally, he looked back up at me "Well, uh... I won't be far away from Courtney for long." He scrubbed the tips of his fingers through his hair. "I'm going to Seattle. Next week."

THE TALK THAT WASN'T

*I*t wasn't my fault. It really wasn't. Hadn't I been all set to begin The Talk, when Wham! The man's off to see the girlfriend!

I pretended to sleep most of the way back to Dublin—the only way I could recover from the cumulative shock of our conversation at Hurley's pub:

1) Learning the incontrovertible evidence—buying a house —of Ben's intention of staying in Ireland. So I'd no longer any excuses for not telling the man he's a father.

2) Discovering Ben was to be a neighbor of Granny's—so I'd absolutely no way to avoid telling him he's not just a father, but *Kevin's* father.

3) Now he was off to see Perfect Courtney, so I had to put off The Talk until he was back!

All right, I confess. Back at Hurley's, I'd nearly fainted from relief. Because Ben's announcement had provided a lovely magnanimous rationale to delay telling him. With Ben set to make big decisions about his girlfriend, it wouldn't be fair to lay fatherhood on him now. He deserved the chance to sort out his relationship first.

So. New Plan...

Actually, I was having a hard time concentrating on the future. Sitting next to Ben in a dark car, with Kevin fast asleep—making it all too easy to pretend we were alone—was causing old memories to bubble up to the surface.

Like traipsing down country roads with Ben round Eagle Prairie, Minnesota, only I'd be snugged up as close to him as I could manage, and his hand resting on my knee. On the inside. Until we'd find some deserted spot, and Ben would cut the engine—and his hand would no longer be resting. And no longer on my knee...

I yanked my unruly thoughts back to the present, embarrassed. Not so much for having sexual fantasies starring Ben Carpenter—I mean, I may not be a sexual dynamo, but I'm not dead from the neck down either—but having them when he was probably having *his* about his girlfriend. Even if she hadn't the decency to give him a bloody drawer at her place.

"Guess I won't be seeing much of you and Kevin," Ben said suddenly.

We were already entering the outskirts of Dublin. "Sorry?"

"After I move to Galway." Ben's voice was clipped.

"Oh. Yeah." If I'd Told All back at the pub, I could have said, *Actually, my seeing you depends. On how often you plan to see Kevin.* "It won't feel...quite right, you being gone from Dublin," I couldn't help saying wistfully.

"But back at Hurley's," Ben said, a little sharply, "you sounded pleased that I'd be running the Galway office."

I had, hadn't I. But I didn't want Ben to think I didn't...like him. And not just to keep him sweet about Kevin. "I was... worried about Liz," I improvised. "I thought you meant Dan would be relocating to Galway. On his own."

"Without Liz and the kids? What are you talking about?"

"Well, she sounded a bit tense about Dan the other night." I'd the feeling she might have sounded even tenser if we'd given her the opportunity.

"Oh, that," Ben said. "Dan said Emily's teeth are coming in, and he and Liz aren't getting much sleep. You know, the joys of parenthood."

I do know. And soon, so will you. But if you want to think every-thing's hunky-dory with your friends, who am I to stop you.

Firmly pushing aside thoughts of all the hunky-dory things Ben and I had got up to in cars seven years ago, I concentrated on figuring out a whole new scenario for telling Ben. That is, after he got back from the States. Then, I could ascertain where the girlfriend would fit into the scheme of things, so Ben and I could settle into the limited, v-e-r-y platonic friendship proper for people committed to others.

With such a fabulous plan, I was in great form when we arrived at the flat. Before I could wake Kevin, Ben touched my arm. "Let me take him."

"Mammy?" Kevin said sleepily as Ben lifted him out of the car.

"Ben's got you, but I'm right here."

As Kevin clutched him round the neck. Ben said softly, "You can go back to sleep, buddy." He sounded so paternal I dropped my keys, but I somehow got us inside the flat, and led Ben down the hall. He gently laid Kevin on his bed. "Shall we put him in his PJ's?"

"We shouldn't want to wake him," I whispered back. I felt a lump in my throat as we got Kevin's shoes off and covered him up, and my smugness about my plan evaporated.

There's something about the innocence of children that forces you to be honest. Suddenly, this seemed so wrong, our being parents together, and Ben not knowing it. Now I felt small and mean, for being glad Ben was moving away.

All right, so I was a hopeless mammy, but I could still kiss my son goodnight. "There you are, all tucked up," I murmured. "'Night, now—I love you."

I said it every night. But with Ben here, I felt exposed and raw with my love. And my secret.

Ben touched Kevin's shoulder. "Goodnight, sport." He seemed to hesitate, then he kissed Kevin's forehead too.

"'Night, Mammy," Kevin mumbled. "'Night, Ben." Tired sigh. "I love you."

Ben froze. For the space of one moment, I saw a vulnerability in him I'd never seen in my father's face, or Sam's. Or any man's. His Adam's apple moved. "I love you too," he said, his voice raspy, then he left the room without looking at me.

Oh, God. Ben. Loved. Kevin.

Why hadn't I seen this coming? Why, why, WHY?

I rushed after Ben. Plans, Pro and Con lists, timing, Ben and his girlfriend—whatever—it was all bollocks, wasn't it? When I caught up with him, I could see the shattered look on him, but I'd no experience with a man's emotions. "K-kids are never so loveable as when they're asleep." Weak joke. But it was the best I could do.

"Yeah." His voice cracked a little.

"And…and it was lovely of you to carry Kevin in." All these words that came from the word *love*… "He's getting a bit heavy for—"

"You know what, Aislin? "My dad never told me he loved me. I never told Courtney I loved her either. But with Kevin, it was easy." Ben's eyes were red around the edges.

They say the eyes are windows to the soul. Well, Ben's windows were wide open, and I could see right into them, straight through to a love and hunger I wanted to look away from, but couldn't. Maybe that love was new and uncertain, but there all the same.

Needing something to hang on to, I grabbed his hand. *Tell him. Now. Now. Now.* "Ben—"

"Why did you keep him?" He gripped my hand so hard it hurt.

"What?" *Don't sidetrack me now, I'm doing the right thing—*

"Why'd you keep Kevin? Christ, you were nineteen. You had college, your whole life in front of you."

"I...I—"

"You could have gotten rid of him, or given him up for adoption, but you didn't. Why?"

You know how your throat aches, when you're trying not to cry? Well, mine was hurting, from my face down to my ribcage. I'd seen into Ben's soul. But I realized no way was I ready to let him into mine.

Not tonight. "It seemed like...the right thing." Feeling horribly unprepared for this, for Being Real with Ben, I tried to disengage my hand.

Ben wouldn't let go. But he looked like he didn't realize it. "That's no answer."

I wanted to shake him. *What the bloody hell do you know about it? Being too young, confused, and immature to be a mother, but having a baby anyway?* Then after I was done shaking him, I wanted to throw myself in his arms.

You won't believe this. I can hardly believe it myself. Because that's exactly what I did.

Fortunately, Ben chose that exact moment to pull me close. So we collided nicely. "I shouldn't have said that," he whispered against my neck.

I couldn't speak. I burrowed into his chest, like a baby seeking comfort. *I'm sorry too...*

Ben's arms were tight around me. As he kissed my hair, hard, wanting swept over me. I didn't dare move or even look at him, because if I did, I'd kiss him, and I wouldn't be able to stop.

Somewhere in my maelstrom of emotions, I found my voice. "Have a safe trip."

"I'll call you when I get back," he said, still holding me.

"I'd...like that." *Let go of him. He belongs to somebody else. Let. Go.*

But I couldn't. You know when you're so tired or ill or otherwise so out of it you can't move? The alarm clock's screaming, the toilet's overflowing, or the house is on fire, but your muscles will not obey? That's exactly how I felt, too choked with remorse and desire to wiggle a finger. But after a few eons, I managed to push myself from Ben. Also managed a fake laugh. But come on. Under the circumstances and all that. "Or I can ring you."

"I'll probably beat you to it," Ben said, not laughing himself. He opened the door, touched my face, then left the flat.

I had a passing urge to pound my fists on the door, but I was too emotionally depleted to give it a go. Instead, I touched my cheek, still feeling the brush of his hand. Tears trickled through my fingers.

Oh, Ben, I mourned. *The past is catching up with us.*

WHAT ABOUT COURTNEY?

*B*etween the opposite sex, there are hugs. And there are *hugs*. Maybe the one with Ben wasn't quite the sort where the two lovers see each other across a field of daisies, then run full-on into each other's arms, but it was bloody close.

The next morning, though, I decided I'd over-dramatized the experience—Ben *was* with Courtney, after all. So we were either growing into *really* good friends, or I was on the long, dangerous road of being torn between two fellows. Not good.

When I got to the shop, Deirdre took one look at me. "You didn't tell him."

I shook my head unhappily. "The...timing was all wrong." Deirdre rolled her eyes, and blessedly left me alone to rearrange the bottom shelf in Fairy Central.

By Thursday, though, Deirdre's patience appeared to be running thin. Sam had been ringing for me all week, and when I asked her to take yet another message, she gave me a dirty look. "I don't get you, Ash."

I don't get me either. I frowned, trying to make sense of the ledger, but the numbers looked like a jumble of squiggles and lines. I didn't like to put my lack of concentration down to the fact that Ben had left Dublin last night. But if the shoe fits...

"Ash." I jerked my head up as Deirdre wiggled her fingers in front of me. "You've been staring at that page for twenty minutes."

"You've been counting?"

"Come on—you've been a zombie all week. Even *I* can tell the accounts are a bloody disaster." Deirdre was in one of her rare super-organized modes, which only made me feel more incompetent.

I scoured my mind for an excuse—I wasn't ready to share the whole attraction-to-Ben dilemma with Deirdre just yet. "I realize I'm not all here—"

"You're on bloody Mars," Deirdre said.

"Yes, well—but not getting The Talk over with, I'm rather dreading having to deal with it when Ben gets back."

"And you've had no e-mails from him all week."

So Deirdre had noticed too. "Ah, no," I said glumly. I'd e-mailed Annie Carpenter, what with her being Kevin's gran but not knowing it, only I hadn't heard back from her either.

"Go on, and take a break. Ring Liz, have a bit of a chat."

"But then I'll have to explain to her, how I didn't tell..."

Deirdre waved her hand. "I saved you the trouble."

"Oh." I didn't know whether to kiss Deirdre for taking the pressure off, or smack her for interfering. Which about summed up our entire association since we were kids. But, I reminded myself, if Deirdre hadn't been looking out for me, I'd have never found out about Sam's car. "Well, thanks, then."

"And if you're worried that I'll mind your time off, worry no more. I'm leaving early to meet Adrian—we're making plans for Saturday night."

No Girls' Night then. My already up-and-down spirits felt like they were experiencing heavy turbulence. If they'd been on an aircraft, they'd have been splattered with food, drink, and the odd air hostess. Still, a chat with Liz would be therapeutic. I'd just picked up the phone when the shop's bell rang.

"Say, Ash," Deirdre murmured, "Hold on—you've a visitor."

It was Ben, he'd cancelled/postponed his flight, he wanted to see me! I turned, jubilant, only to see a slighter, more dapper fellow enter the shop.

"Sam!" After thinking of Ben all week, and comparing Sam to Ben—which was unfair, since Sam couldn't help it if he was four inches shorter, had added some extra flesh round his middle lately, and most importantly, didn't send me funny e-mails—I forced a wide smile. "What a lovely surprise."

He blinked. Had my smile been too warm? Apparently not. "You haven't rung," was the first thing out of his mouth.

I felt guilty about that too. Ready to apologize, I thought, *Hello! You* are *a free woman.* "It's been a frantic week." Yes, I've been frantically thinking of how to handle the Ben thing.

He launched into some rather laborious chit-chat, to which I didn't pay much attention, until he said, "Let's meet at O'Fagan's Saturday. I'm not doing anything."

A few weeks ago, my heart would have surged for joy. While today, I was only mildly tempted. Could it be I was waiting for something a little more inviting? For instance: *Are you free?* Or, *Can I pick you up in my shiny new car I haven't mentioned and take you to dinner?*

Fat chance. It would be pub grub, and I'd probably pay for my own. "Sorry, I've plans." I pivoted round. "Will you excuse me?" I said over my shoulder. "I've a phone call to make."

LUCKILY, Liz was in her office. "All the partners are out." She sounded relaxed. "Mari's doing her nails, and I'm reading a novel in between phone calls."

"Liz, I—" I hated to put her on the spot, but, well...not enough *not* to quiz her about Ben. "I understand Deirdre let it out that my Big Talk was a non-starter—but...had you a reason for not telling me Ben was off to see Courtney? She'll have something to say about his being a daddy."

"Oh, Aislin." Liz sounded genuinely distressed. "I forgot all about it. Things at home have been...oh, never mind that. Anyway, I got the idea she hasn't been on Ben's radar screen much."

"She'll be on his radar, right enough, if they have it off while he's in Seattle, which they're probably doing as we speak," I blurted. Then winced. "Oh, Jaysus, I can't believe I said that."

"Too early," Liz said, laughter in her voice. "It's only mid-afternoon there, sweetie."

"Maybe they've missed each other so much they're at it morning, noon, and night."

"I don't think so," Liz said. "I got the impression Courtney's too busy for getting it on, except at politically correct times."

"I'll bet she's making an exception, if she hasn't had sex for months." Was it too much to ask, I queried the Powers That Be, that she'd get her period the minute Ben arrives, one of those awful ones with mega-cramps that last a week and a half? "That means in just a few hours, they'll be at it right enough."

Liz was silent. Which meant I was right. "Maybe," I said, brightening a bit, "I should wake up at dawn tomorrow, and ring him. It should be about eleven p.m. by then, Seattle time, when they're in the middle of...of..."

"Doing the deed?"

"I know, I'm awful—" I couldn't help giggling. "It's not that I mind or anything—them having sex..." Oh, dear. There I was again, fecking up my new honesty policy.

"Oh, really?" Liz was giggling too.

"It's just that once Ben knows about Kevin, I'm all for him being a little more invested in his life here."

"Makes sense," Liz agreed, though I wondered if she was secretly laughing at me.

"Now that he and I are friends," I went on, the bollocks factor increasing by the minute, "I want whatever will make him happy."

"Me too," Liz said. "So let's hope for a little coitus interruptus, hmmm?"

We both sniggered. "I hate to correct you," I said, "but that's *Courtney* interruptus."

THE SURPRISE SNOG(S)

I sat on the lid of the loo, thumbing through *Marie Claire*, one eye on Kevin's enthusiastic tub-splashing. Amazing, how much productive reading you can get done at times like these.

"Mammy, am I late yet?"

"No, you're not meant to be at Maggie's for another half hour, love." Another splatter, and water lapped over the edge of the tub. "Mind the water, Kevin." I glanced over "New Products for Difficult Hair," and restrained myself from looking in the mirror. Steam turned my hair to pure frizz.

"When's Ben coming back?"

"Next week, I think." Actually I hadn't asked him. I didn't want to know, in case he got back to Dublin and didn't ring or e-mail me for a fortnight.

"Why do I have a bath before I see Chris? 'Cause we're just gonna sleep on the floor, and the blankets sort of stink."

I turned a page. "Because it's the proper thing to do." I might not be the best of mammies, but my child will at least bathe regularly if I've anything to say about it. "And don't forget to scrub behind your ears." I looked up from the magazine and grinned at him. "You don't want to go for a sleepover and smell all narky, do you?"

"I s'pose not," Kevin said, and stuck soapy fingers in his ears.

I turned to a mini-poll on sex. Apparently women under-reported what they got up to between the sheets. I suppose if I didn't make up with Sam pretty soon, I was going to forget what it's like altogether.

Out of some self-torture impulse, I slipped into my bedroom and pulled last month's *Cosmo* from my To Be Read pile—the one in my knickers' drawer—that Deirdre had passed along. Back in the bath, I thumbed through it, feeling inadequate. None of the girls in *Cosmo* fudged about sex, they were all proud to say they're having it off like rabbits, with bizarre sex toys—

"Mam, I've soap in my eyes!"

I tossed the magazine aside, and turned on the tap. "Right, there you go, rinse it out—"

The minor crisis averted, I dove back into *Cosmo*. "The New Sexual Position that will Drive Him Wild." I slapped the magazine closed. When you're going to be all alone on Saturday night, who needs that restless longing, that makes you wish that you could be in bed with your fellow. And also makes you wish that the actual *act* lived up to everything you read about—

"Mammy, someone's here."

Then I heard the knock. "That'll be Maggie and Chris to fetch you."

Kevin scrambled out of the tub. "Mam, I gotta get dressed!"

I grabbed the nearest towel, swiped him front and back, then wrapped it round him toga style. "I'll get the door, while you pick up your shirt and knickers and toss them in the hamper."

"But Mam—"

"No arguments, mind, if you're going to the Tobin's."

But when I neared the door, all was silent. No knocking. I opened the door anyway, the evening sunshine—a Dublin miracle, sunshine in June—dazzling my eyes. As I blinked the spots away, a man wearing sunglasses was going down the walk. "Ben!"

He pivoted at a flattering speed. "You *are* home." Removing his glasses, he said, "First time I've needed these since I moved to Ireland. You in the middle of anything?"

"Not at all," I said quickly. "Come in." I could feel myself turning three shades of red—my Courtney interruptus comment, then all the sex bits I'd just read made me feel a bit squirmy. "You'd a good trip?"

As he came inside, I wondered if I dared reprise our friendly/casual first hug—not our more recent desperate/emotional clutch. Well, then. Friendly clasp, I reminded myself. Not misplaced lustful grab...I'd my arms half lifted when Ben palmed my shoulders and kissed me.

Oh my God. What is this? We're friends, I shouldn't, but it feels so good...Unable to help myself, I kissed him back just as he broke away, looking shocked.

"Jeez, I'm sorry—I don't know where that came from—"

I choked back a gasp. *I* knew where the kiss came from. Bloody *Cosmo.* "Right. Have a seat." How do I handle this?

He looked exhausted. And embarrassed—I couldn't hold him responsible. So it had to be me.

"Maybe I shouldn't stay," he said, still not looking at me. "I took the red-eye from Seattle last night, there a long layover in New York, then an emergency landing for an ill passenger. I hardly know what day it is."

I get it. You kissed me because you've entered that woozy stage of beyond fatigue and into hallucinating. Not very flattering. "It's Saturday, and a perfectly respectable seven-thirty." My hopes dashed in a funny way—I wasn't thinking I wanted to shag Ben, was I?—I told myself to straighten up. "Now, sit down before you fall down."

Before he reached the couch, the bathroom door banged.

"Ben!" I turned at the same time Ben did, as towel-clad Kevin shot past me and leaped into Ben's arms. "I missed you!"

"I missed you too, buddy." Ben shifted Kevin into one arm, wearing a pleased, goofy grin as Kevin told him all about tonight's sleepover.

And my son's uncomplicated joy had to mean he hadn't seen the kiss, thank God. Ben and I had enough hurdles between us already. Especially now that I'd discovered his mouth felt as good as it had seven years ago, if not better.

Had Courtney revved up his sexual engines? I wondered resentfully, just as another knock sounded at the door. "Kevin, that's got to be Maggie and Chris." I reached for the knob. "Time to jump off Ben and get dressed."

Kevin wriggled out of Ben's arms. "Come on, Ben," he said, and ran down the hall.

"I must owe you at least three sleepovers, Maggie," I said, opening the door. "Oh—Sam!"

Oh, Jaysus. It never rains but it pours. Or was it a Perfect Storm? I stepped back, sensing Ben had stopped mid-stride on his way to the bedroom.

Sam took advantage of my open-mouthed shock. Sliding inside the flat, he took the door from my lifeless fingers, closed it, then pulled me into his arms and kissed me.

His rather masterful embrace—and the fact he'd just had a breath mint—surprised me into acquiescence. Then into kissing him back. I needed to know if Sam and I had some chemistry left—although a part of my brain said, *push him away, Ben's getting an eyeful...* What the hell, I decided. Let him.

"Ahem!" Male throat clearing at two o'clock. Figuring Ben had seen enough, I pushed myself out of Sam's arms with only a slightly discomfited laugh, quite upbeat all of a sudden. Although I hadn't seen any stars or anything—being rather uptight with Ben looking on, of course—Sam's kiss was significant. The mint meant he'd planned to kiss me. And the bit of desperation in him meant he really did want me back.

Knowing you're wanted is always a boost—surely better than being a sexual substitute for Ben's vastly superior girlfriend. "Sam, I've a friend here." I smoothed my hair as Ben approached. "This is Ben Carpenter."

The two men looked wary, then to my mixed gratification and dismay, gave each other what appeared to be one of those Alpha-male, bone-crunching handshakes. Sam managed to extricate his hand first.

"Nice meeting you," said Ben, and shoved his hands in his pockets.

"Hallo," said Sam, and flexed his hand. Although they didn't move, they seemed to be figuratively circling each other, sizing up the other. Sure this was a novel thing. Two guys acting territorial over me—even if only one had even a smidgen of a right to. "You're a Yank," Sam added, almost accusingly.

"You got a problem with that?" Ben asked, his tone jovial. But his eyes were sort of... hard.

"Ben's an old...family friend," I said weakly. Ben looked at me, surprised. I'd thrown in the "family" bit for more credibility, now that Sam and I were...must be...back together. It wouldn't be right for me to entertain other men in my flat.

Just then, Kevin ran back into the front room in his underpants. "Kevin, go on with you and get decent!" It seemed too intimate, having your sometime boyfriend, your son's father who hadn't a clue, and your son in knickers, in one room at the same time.

"S-s-sam?" A flash of anxiety showed in Kevin's face, then he immediately dismissed the new visitor, and grabbed Ben's hand. "Come on, Ben!"

"Just a minute, sport," Ben said. Kevin tugged again, but Ben stayed where he was.

I hadn't imagined it—Ben's eyes were like flints. Situation

rapidly escalating out of control...emergency measures needed. "Kevin Moore, get to your room this minute!"

Before I could move, Sam's eyes narrowed on Kevin, then Ben. "Jay-sus Christ," he said, "You're—"

"Not staying long," I broke in gaily. "Show me your new car?" With a rigor mortis-like grip, I pulled Sam outside, slamming the door behind me.

As we stepped down the walk, Sam yanked his arm away. "What the feck is Kevin's *dad* doing here?" he hissed. "I thought he was out of the picture! And what's between you anyway?"

"What the hell gives you the right to ask me that?" I snapped, then remembered the tightrope I was walking. *Sam had Connected the Dots. Must be kept away from Ben.* "Nothing's between us. Really."

"You call a kid 'nothing?' And what gives him the right to hang about here?"

"Look," and I aimed for a more conciliatory tone, "Ben just came back from the States, popped in for a short visit. And Maggie'll be here any minute for a Girl's Night," I lied.

That would get Sam out of here pronto. He hated Girl's Nights, since he knew he'd get no sex that night. Not that there was an icicle's chance in Hades that he would *this* particular night.

"So get rid of him," Sam said, still looking rather fierce. His jealousy was actually a bit of an ego boost. But not enough of one to take orders from him.

"I will, but when I'm good and ready," I said tartly. "You were the one who put our relationship on hold. And I'll remind you I've never asked you to explain your past, so I've certainly no obligation to explain mine." I must say, going on the offense was rather liberating.

"You've been avoiding me," he said, more moderately. "I thought we could..." His voice trailed away, and he shuffled his Italian-shod feet.

You thought you could just call round and I'd get rid of Kevin and have it off with you? "Does this mean our 'hiatus' is over?" I asked playfully, to hide my resentment.

"Yes," he said eagerly. "Cancel with Maggie, get rid of this Ben dude, and after Kevin goes to sleep we can—"

"Sorry," I said. "Tonight's just not on." I was too confused to contemplate anything physical with him. Much less consider our future relationship.

And come to think of it, I was still a bit disoriented with the shock of being kissed by two guys in the space of three minutes. With a vague promise of getting together soon, I sent Sam off in the lovely car I hadn't even noticed, and went back inside. Despite my carouselling emotions, though, things had never been more clear. Tonight Was The Night.

For The Talk.

TRUTH OR CONSEQUENCES

*O*nce inside, I realized I'd been gone with Sam long enough for not just another kiss, but a full-out snog session, but Ben was already down the hall, with Kevin. I took a quavery breath. I could live with it, that Ben had kissed me from a horny, missing-Perfect-Courtney, jet-lag reflex. Now that Sam and I had sorted things out, and I was taken again, I could get on with what was really important: Kevin and Ben.

I could hear them in the bedroom, Ben sounding amazingly fatherly. "Now that you've got your jammies on, let's finish drying your hair." Then, "Hey, how about this!"

"What?" Kevin asked.

"Your hair grows in two little whorls instead of one—just like mine." Despite my jumpy insides, I thought, how sweet. For Ben to notice a little detail like that. As I tiptoed down the hall to peek inside the bedroom, Ben added, "My mom always told me that having two was real special, that not many people have 'em."

"Awesome," Kevin breathed, his eyes shining. Incredible, that my Think Organic was working! Having seen Kevin's funny hair thing, Ben wouldn't even be shocked when I told him..."I've something to show you," Kevin added. "It's really super."

"What's that, sport?" Ben rustled around for Kevin's slippers.

"It's a photograph, in my drawer."

I got a funny feeling. I was spying, that was it. I should let the guys have their privacy.

"See?" Kevin flashed the small square in front of Ben. "It's a pit'cher of you."

A picture of Ben. Since when did I have a photo of Ben? Perplexed, I slowly backed away into the hallway.

"No, it's a picture of..." Ben's voice trailed away. "Where'd you get this?"

"Mam's jewelry b-box at Granny's house. From when she was little."

God help us—*that* photo! I froze, my heart pounding like an army brigade marching through my chest. *Move!* I uged. Burst into the bedroom, tell Ben before he can see Kevin has his eyes...his chin...his lopsided grin...But my feet refused to obey. And there wasn't a word from Ben. Which could only mean...

He'd guessed.

Feck. Feck! The shock sent tremors through me...then I realized I was off the hook! The Universe had managed the lot for me! The relief was like a lovely sunburst inside me—I wouldn't need to confess after all! I could run in now, we'd have a big group hug, I'd explain everything, then we'd ring Annie...

"Ben?" I heard worry in Kevin's voice. "What's the m-matter? You look s-sorta funny."

Ben didn't answer.

"Are ya sick?" Still nothing from Ben. "I'm g-gonna get Mammy," Kevin said, his voice small and scared. Somehow I pushed myself away from the wall as Kevin flew out of the room, crashing right into me. "Mam! Somethin's wrong with Ben!"

I started to shake. I had to get Kevin away from here. Now.

From some previously unknown Mammy Power, I dredged up a gay smile. "Ready? Off you go to Maggie's now!"

"But Ben—s-somethin's wrong—I think he's gonna throw up."

"Jet lag," I lied. "You get a jiggly tummy from the airplane."

Then my chest clenched, until I could hardly catch a breath, but the same Mammy Power helped me choke out a blithe, "Don't worry, I'll look after him. Maggie and the kids are waiting!" Knees wobbling, I whisked Kevin down the hall and through the front door before he could protest. Then, gasping as my lungs went into suspended animation, I turned round to Face The Music.

And The Music, brow thunderous, his face an interesting shade of green, was heading straight for me.

TIMING IS EVERYTHING

a white line round his mouth, Ben dangled a small photo in front of me. "Look familiar?"

My chest heaved. I cupped my hands over my mouth, but I only gasped harder.

"Jesus H. Christ," Ben muttered. "You have any paper bags?"

I could only suck mouthfuls of air, as Ben watched me with those flint-hard eyes. After another long, humiliating series of gasps, I felt the heaving subside and lowered my hands. "I'm sorry," I whispered.

"You're sorry. Sorry you don't have paper bags?" Ben shoved the photo in his shirt pocket.

"I d-do," I cleared the wheeze from my throat. "But I didn't mean for you to—"

"Sorry I saw my old school picture?" His voice rose. "Big of you!"

I flinched. "I'm sorry," I said again. *I'm sorry, sorry, oh my God, am I ever...*

"You're sorry I got you pregnant?" He was yelling now, and I fought the urge to cover my ears. "Or you're sorry I came to your..." effing... "store?" There was more, along the lines of, *or you're sorry I effing came over tonight or sorry I effing found out or really really sorry I'm Kevin's effing father?* Each accusation hit me like bullets of guilt and regret.

I must say, though, Navy men had a way with the Anglo-Saxon-ese. I drew myself up, despite my churning stomach. "If you would just leave off the 'fecking this and that' before the whole block hears you, we'll talk like two civilized—"

"You'd like us to be civilized? You should've thought of that before you lied to me—"

"But that's why I tried to contact you," I said, stung. "I was going to tell you."

His hard eyes made me feel like he was the pin and me the poor sod of a butterfly. "That's really big of you too. After seven years, you were going to tell me. Why?"

What had seemed so reasonable before now seemed petty, inadequate. I couldn't answer.

"Oh, I get it. Money. I saw the photo—you don't even need an paternity test."

He reached for his back pocket, and jerked out his wallet. "You want cash? Here's a start." As I watched, aghast, Ben wrenched out a wad of American dollars and flung them down. The bills fluttered gaily to the floor around our feet. "There's plenty, all my unspent travel money. I'll get more—"

"Please—don't..." Tears filled my eyes. "That's not why I...I never meant to—I mean, I did need some money but it's not—" Remembering the list I'd made, I stumbled to the drawer I'd slipped it into a fortnight ago, trying not to step on the money.

My hands shook as I extracted the bit of paper and showed Ben. "See?"

He only glanced at it. "This is total bull—you should've told me as soon as you found out you were pregnant!" Ben grabbed the paper from me, tore it in half, and threw those pieces too. They landed next to a crisp fifty-dollar bill.

His contempt vaporized my contrition. "I could have told

you? You've a bloody nerve." Uneasiness flashed over his face. "That's right, you remember it too—ripping up your Navy address so I couldn't write you—"

"That's bull too." Ben's jaw looked made of granite. "You could have gone to my mom, but instead, you just kept your secret all this time, and made a complete fool of me!"

"That's not true—"

"Oh, yeah? You must have laughed yourself fu...freaking *silly* after everything I said before I left for Seattle last week."

The night Kevin told Ben *I love you*... When Ben's naked emotion had been too...too visceral for me.

"No, I would never laugh..." Ben looked even more skeptical. "It's true," I said, "I did put off telling you, but I thought we were friends, that you'd understand—"

"Friends? You're some friend all right. Lying and cheating from the get-go."

Lying and cheating. Like my father...Suddenly, I was done being sorry. "Let's get this straight," I spat. "Did you ever ask me straight out if you'd fathered Kevin?"

"That's beside the point. You knew I thought Kevin's dad was that weaselly intern—the short guy, with the red hair."

"*That's beside the point*," I mimicked. "But did I ever say right out that no, you didn't?"

"It doesn't mat—"

"So *I'm* meant to set you straight on what you're too bloody blind to see for yourself?"

"You can't pin this on me. Lies of omission are still lies," Ben said stubbornly. "And you've lied to Kevin too."

That *really* hurt. "You'll keep Kevin out of it! If I didn't tell, it's because the timing had to be right."

"It's all in the timing, huh? Like back in Eagle Prairie—you were a great friend, then, weren't you? Keeping our so-called friendship a big secret, then kicking me out of—" He broke off.

"For all I know, you were using me to—" He didn't finish that either.

"Me! Me, using <u>you</u>?" Was Ben thinking I'd wanted to make Kelly the Intern jealous? When at the time, I'd pretty well forgotten he existed?

His brows lowered, until they nearly tangled in his eyelashes. "That's right," he pounced. "Using me!"

"How do I know you weren't using me?" Ben looked surprised. "For one last fling before you were stuck on board ship with no sex!"

"You weren't a fling." Before I could get all starry-eyed at his admission, Ben was off again. "Don't trying sticking the blame on me! You made a fool of me, and you're still doing it!"

I took an incensed breath. "It's all about you, is it? When it was me who got pregnant?" He opened his mouth, then closed it again. "Me who had her life turned upside down after your bloody stupid condom didn't work?"

Ha. I'd got him there. Finally he said, "Nobody said condoms are foolproof."

"Too right they're not. And you, joking that night, that you'd had it in your wallet like forever! So you were using some narky decrepit condom, so even if we'd split up, it never occurred to you to ring me, see if everything was all right? Oh, but I forgot." I managed an ironic laugh. "It's all about you—even though it's been Kevin who hasn't had a daddy."

Uh oh. "Daddy" was the red flag in front of the bull. Ben's eyes shot sparks. "You're right. You're goddamn right. It *is* about Kevin. He has a daddy now. And this daddy is going to see his kid." He stepped toward the door.

Wait a minute. Situation out of hand... Panicked, I grabbed his arm. "Ben—"

Ben shook me off. "I'm his father. He's half mine."

"You can't slam into Maggie's and blurt this out to Kevin just like that, for bloody's sake!" I tensed, ready to tackle Ben if I needed to.

"Goddamn it, what do you take me for?"

"A crazed, bloody-minded bollocks..." *No*, said my rational side, *just a daddy who wants his boy...*

"Call me names if it makes you feel better. But here's what this *bollocks* is going to do: slam into my lawyer's office and have him draw up a petition for sharing custody." He kicked at the nearest bills. "And don't worry, there'll be plenty in it for you. Lots of child support."

It scorched my pride, seeing him abuse a pile of cash that had to be half my monthly salary. "I've changed my mind. I don't want your fecking child support."

"Too bad. You're getting it. Just like I'm going to get shared custody of Kevin and I don't give a flying...crap how much it costs."

I saw a red mist. "You can't. He's mine. Mine!"

"Too bad, he's mine too. Money talks—and it talks damn loud, I can tell you."

"You've no legal claim to him, and no proof, and if you think you can get one *speck* of *my* son's hair or spit for a DNA test you're a bigger bollocks than I—"

"What do you mean, 'no proof.'" He slapped his pocket, eyes blazing. "I'll just show my picture to the judge!"

I wanted to pummel him like I'd never wanted to—or actually had—hit anyone. "You...you bloody gobshite! Good job I found out what a bastard you were before I—" Argh!

Furious at myself, for the close call, I gave him a double-barreled shot of pure spite. "I'm sure the courts will want to know what a bloody awful temper you have, throwing things and swearing at your child's mother." I paused for greater effect, then, "You're not fit to be a father."

Ben's face paled. I saw a stark hurt in him. For a moment, I wanted to cry out, *I didn't mean it...* Then fury shot back to his eyes.

"And I'm sure the courts will want to know what a cheat and liar *my* child's mother is. What a great example she sets for *my* son. So you'll be hearing from *my* lawyer."

Three "my's" in a row were three too many. I flung the door open. "Go on, take yourself off—and don't hold your breath to see Kevin! Because I'll be getting a barring order to make sure you won't!"

Ben strode away without so much as a backward look. He wrenched the door of his Micra open, leaped in, then peeled away, tires shrieking.

And that awful thought that had flashed into my head a moment ago sprang back. ...*Good job I found out what a bastard you are before I fell for you again.*

Infuriated at myself, at Ben, at the world, I slammed the door so hard the flat shook on its foundations. I pounded on the door for good measure. *You're history*, I raged. *I'm never going to set eyes on you again.*

Then it hit me. Seeing Ben would be unavoidable—if he took me to court. Fear—the honest-to-God sort, like a knife slicing through your insides—diluted the adrenaline racing through me. I stumbled back from the door, tears choking my throat. Oh, Jesus, what would I do?

Footsteps, then a scratch at the door. "Aislin?"

"Maggie!"

As I swung the door back open, Maggie's eyes widened. "Aislin, love, what on earth—"

"He's trying to take K-K-Kevin, I'll need a solicit-t-t—" I blubbered. "And m-m-mon—Oh, Jaysus, Maggie—" I threw myself, sobbing, into her arms. "My life is over."

THE SURPRISE E-MAIL

$\mathcal{O}$ ne way to make sure you're still alive and kicking is if you're still getting e-mails. Monday morning, feeling like Death—not warmed over, but cold and congealing on a plate—I opened my Inbox:

FROM LIZ:

Had a really interesting e-mail today. First, I'm busy dumping all my spam, including something from a Kurt, who has to be selling a home refi or Viagra, so I send that puppy to the Delete folder. Then I get one from my mom, who says, "Do you remember your college friend, Kurt? I ran into him at Whole Foods and he asked for your e-mail..."

Then, Gaaah! Of course—it's *Kurt*! Who lived in the university ceramics studio with me almost 24/7! So I jump into the Delete folder, and he says he's back in Seattle, opening a gallery in Belltown this summer, and he and some Shawnna woman just broke up after eight years, then he asks, do you have any work you'd like to sell? Omigod, is that amazing? I haven't touched a potter's wheel since I met Dan. But it's great to know someone in this world appreciates my talents for something other than reading "Goodnight, Moon" six times in a row without putting a gun to my head.

Liz

I TRIED to be happy for her, but I had to wonder. When you're married, should you *really* be this happy to hear from an old friend? An old *boyfriend*? But I was too listless and sorry for myself to quiz Liz about her love life, much less spill about Saturday's debacle. The only reply I could muster was, Are you going to e-mail him back?

Two seconds later, Liz's e-mail popped into my Inbox: You bet your ass I am. Yee-ha!

Nothing from Ben of course. Not that I wanted to hear from him, the bad-tempered gobshite.

Then another e-mail came in, one I didn't know how to answer at all:

FROM: Anne Carpenter
SUBJECT: Hello again
Dear Aislin,

I was sure happy to get your last e-mail. Now that I got the hang of it myself, I've been e-mailing all over the place. I send Ben one every few days, and I wrote to my sister in Dubuque. I've been thinking of going all out and e-mailing Ben's friend Liz, to ask her to find him a girlfriend who eats, ha, ha.

Ben's real excited about his new house. I guess he's still a country boy at heart. He promised to send pictures. Imagine that, you can send photos right through the air.

Hearing from you sure took me back. Like when you and Ben two were kids, the two of you sitting together, you reading a storybook and I could see Ben had such a crush on you he couldn't take his eyes off you, though he wasn't more than ten or so. My friend Marge teases me about who do I think I am, e-mailing the Congressman's daughter and all but I always said Aislin Moore is no snob.

Speaking of that, I always meant to tell you something. I didn't try to write you after you left town 7 years ago cause Ben said we weren't your kind of people. I always say that you're as good as anyone else, when you work hard and get a real good job like Ben. He's a good boy. He sends me money every month, and though I tell him it's too much, he says he doesn't want me to worry about money ever again.

I hope your little boy is good too.

Sincerely,

Annie

PS Ben came for a little visit last week, and I told him I got an e-mail from you. When I said you were like a daughter to me way back when, he said well, wouldn't that make her my sister? Then he just laughed and laughed til I said, be quiet, it's not that funny.

SINGIN' IN THE RAIN

I kissed Granny and Kevin goodbye, then joined Deirdre on the stoop and peered at the thickening clouds. "Think it'll rain?"

"Duh," Deirdre said as we started down Rosehill's drive. "In Galway?"

"Let's hoof it, then." Racing to Hurley's pub fit right in with my latest tactic, which was running away from my problems as fast as I could.

"What's the rush?" Deirdre protested. "I'm making my big escape from my granny and Aunt Bridie before they drive me round the bend. Even if I've got out of that parish do tonight, I'll need a couple of pints to get me through tomorrow."

I jostled her affectionately. "You're grand to come up to Galway with me for the weekend." My smile faded. "But the sooner we get back to Granny's the better—Kevin's been clingy all week."

"Can't say I blame him," Deirdre said as we turned onto the road. "Hasn't everything been a bit... weird for him?"

"Why should it be?" I intercepted Deirdre's skeptical look.

"Okay, I've been sort of…edgy lately," a bit like a guillotine, I admit, "but I've tried to keep it to myself."

"Well, you haven't succeeded," Deirdre said frankly. "After that big duke-out with Ben—kids pick up the vibes, you know. Gods knows what Kevin makes of that mess in your flat."

"I told him it was a game." I kicked a tussock of grass. "I just haven't got around to explaining the details." Putting a good face on for Kevin had been hard enough—my brooding and crying had been in private. But yesterday, after hearing from Ben, my anxiety flew off the charts.

First, his no-salutation e-mail: We need to talk. You pick the time and the place.

Yeah, sure, lots of warm fuzzies there. I deleted it immediately. Next, a message on my answering machine. "Just making sure you got my e-mail," he'd said in an expressionless voice. "Call me when it's convenient."

I'll tell you what's convenient—a lay-low at Granny's until my nerves settle. I hadn't mentioned Ben's messages to Deirdre—she'd only tell me to get on with it and ring him. "At least there's some good to come of it—you know, the showdown with Ben," I said fake-cheerily.

Deirdre wrinkled her brow. "You won't have to screw up your courage to tell him about Kevin, 'cause he already knows?"

"Well, yes, but—"

"Support checks in your future?"

"No," I said impatiently. "Well, yes, but I meant Sam. He's really interested, and we're seeing each other again." I felt a sprinkle on my nose.

"Sam. Of course, he'll be all for you having more mon—ah, never mind."

I stopped in the middle of the road. "More money, did you say?" I felt another raindrop. "You're implying he's greedy?"

"If it quacks like a duck, it usually is one," Deirdre returned.

"That's a fine thing to say," I began, indignant. "There's a gazillion reasons why Sam's a decent catch. In fact, a great catch." I'd even made a list last night.

Before I could tick off the first item, Deirdre jerked my arm. "Ah, don't get your knickers in a big 'oul snarl. Especially if we're going to get caught in a bit of weather."

"My knickers aren't snarled in the least," I said with dignity.

"Well, then, if it makes you happy, it's great the pair of you went out this week, and that you're making a commitment..."

Were we? Even if he'd taken me to dinner, without so much as a hint that I should stand for the tip. And even if I'd kissed him, and put a lot into it. Alhough our brief snog seemed to be missing some of the old magic—well, what little there'd been, anyway. "Perhaps," I ventured, "calling it a 'commitment' may be a bit premature."

"But while you were in the loo, your gran—well, she didn't say it in so many words, but I got the idea she's concerned you're taking Sam back for the wrong reasons."

I didn't ask what those were—I'd read the self-help books, thank you very much: Girls raised without fathers are desperate for a man's attention, so they often settled for unhappy relationships, instead of being okay solo. Which was ridiculous. I was like any normal girl, wanting a guy...right? "Just what I need, to have you and Granny analyzing me," I said crossly.

"Well," Deirdre said, stepping over a rut, "Your granny let out that you no sooner arrived at Rosehill, than you announced, 'Looks like I have a boyfriend again.' Doesn't it strike you that you didn't say, 'I'm back with the man I love?'"

As if Sam could ever be the love of my life, I almost said. But...I wasn't settling, it was a rational decision, to be with Sam...wasn't it?

"And my granny and aunt Bridie are clucking like mad over the fact that you still haven't rung your dad when he's not feeling well," Deirdre continued relentlessly. "I get that you don't like him much, but he can't be that bad, can he?"

"I've told you before he never abused or mistreated me," I mumbled. But saying anything more would hurt too much. Before Deirdre would ask the inevitable, *So, then, what'd he do?* I complained, "Don't I need all the O'Donnell family on me too, about my lack of filial respect."

"If not us, who?" Deirdre chortled, and gave me Polly-like elbow in the ribs.

"Ha, ha," I said. "But back to Sam—I haven't *really* taken him back, if you know what I mean."

"No sex then," Deirdre guessed, then the raindrops came faster. "Shite—let's get a move on. Anyway, better keep it that way—so your mind will be clear for sorting things out with... you know who."

Just thinking of Ben sent a chill through me, far more than the prospect of walking another half mile in the rain. I ducked my head to avoid the worst of it, and noticed a car approaching from the village. With a familiar color and silhouette.

No. It couldn't be... "Come on," I said. "Let's duck near the hedgerow, and avoid a spray."

Instead, the car slowed down to a crawl. "Let's hope it's somebody we know or their cousin ten times removed and they'll offer us a ride to Hurley's," Deirdre muttered as a Micra pulled up besides us.

The window slid open and I looked into the vehicle's interior. My heart did a belly flop.

"Need a lift?" Ben asked.

"Do we ever," Deirdre said, grinning. As he leaned over to open the passenger side door, she clambered inside. "Ash?"

"No, thanks," I said shortly. "I need the exercise." I stumbled over a rock, ruining my dignified getaway, then I caught myself and started up again.

I heard the shift of gears, then Ben drove in reverse alongside me. "Come on," Deirdre called over the whine of the engine. "You're getting awfully wet."

"I'm fine," I said, my stride a bit wobbly. "It's a warm summer rain—well, for Galway."

"Really, Ash, don't be an eejit. It's coming up to a real downpour."

I plodded forward. Either way you look at it, I was fecked. The car stopped and Ben cut the engine. I jerked up my head as he climbed out of the car.

"If you won't let me give you a ride, I'll walk with you."

"Be my guest, get yourself wet," I snapped as Ben matched my steps. Then I clamped my mouth shut. Actually, he wouldn't be the one to suffer—he had on one of those posh rain-proof jackets, that wannabe hikers wore to shop on Grafton Street.

I, on the other hand, could feel the rain penetrate my jumper. A lorry rumbled slowly past us, and several minutes later, a tractor from the other direction. I walked on, determined not to give in and talk to him.

Another long silence, then Ben said, "I told Deirdre that if I couldn't talk you into a ride by the next signpost, she should take the wheel and follow us into the village."

I was dying to continue the silent treatment, but the temptation of sarcastic repartee was too great. "Deirdre's an awful driver, even worse than I am, but hey, go ahead, let her crash your gears to pieces. I don't care."

"It'll be worth it, if you'll let me give you a ride."

"Ah, yes, I forgot—you've pots of money. If you don't want to fix your car, you can just buy a new one, right?" Rain trickled into my hair. And sarcasm didn't relieve my feelings—I wanted to scream and cry and hit him all at the same time.

He didn't answer. The silence edged on the interminable... until he touched my arm. "Aislin."

I whirled to face him. "Don't *touch* me. Don't even talk to me. You need a fecking anger-management programme or something."

We stared at each other through the sheet of rain. "You're

right," he said. He reached inside his jacket, seemed to hesitate, then pulled out a fat envelope and showed it to me.

My heart in my throat, I saw, "Feeney & O'Shea, Solicitors." Fat raindrops plopped onto the paper, blurring the neat type. I wanted to grab the envelope, and fling it into the mud alongside the road. But before I could move, Ben ripped the envelope in half.

I refused to show my surprise. "I'd no intention of reading it anyway."

He looked wry as he stuffed the envelope halves back into his pocket. "I'd throw this into the ditch, to follow my new mode of expressing myself, but then I'd be littering."

Oh, but he had a bloody nerve, joking about flinging stuff round my flat. "Sure, you can rip up and stomp on your papers until the end of time, but your solicitor will have ten more copies in his office."

"Not if I've instructed him to pile them into the shredder." Ben's eyes were trained on my face. "I know I have a lot to answer for, but Kevin's well-being is what's important here." He swiped the water running down his face. "Now, will you get in the car?"

THE CONVERSATION

*A*fter climbing into the Micra, I was too wet to argue when Ben didn't turn the car around, but headed toward Rosehill. Shivering convulsively with wet clothes and anxiety, I slumped in the back seat and let Deirdre's chatter fill the undeniably narky atmosphere.

When Ben arrived at Granny's, however, Deirdre had the door open before Ben could stop the car. "See ya," she said brightly.

"Deirdre—!" *Please don't leave me alone with him.* But too late —she'd sprinted into her granny's house and disappeared inside. Bollocks. So here we were, stuck in a car together.

The silence was deafening, until Ben said, "Well...?"

"I suppose you've got to come inside," I said grudgingly. Granny would have my head if I sent Ben away without introducing him. Once I'd let us into Rosehill, though, I could tell the cottage was empty. Still no buffer between Ben and me. Double-triple bollocks.

"My granny and Kevin must've caught a ride to the parish— some sort of party." I felt ridiculous in my sodden jumper. "So you can go on—I mean, you'll want to go home and dry off."

Instead, Ben sauntered into the front room, then looked at me. "That's…hospitable of you," he said with the faintest of smiles, his big shoulders square beneath his depressingly hardly-damp jacket. "But I was hoping I could borrow a towel for my hair."

I resented it, him controlling the situation, while my insides felt like they were being squeezed by a giant fist. Just as I was tempted to say, *A towel? Only if you'll gag yourself with it*, his face turned serious. "We can't avoid talking forev—"

"All bloody right." Jaysus, might as well get it over with. Fetching a tea towel from the kitchen, I thrust it at Ben, then stumbled up the narrow stairwell. And remembered I had a bit of a clothes issue right now. Shite, shite, shite!

Rustling round Granny's closet, I couldn't help thinking about Ben and me raging at each other last week, over who'd been using who seven years ago. I would never admit that my attraction to him had involved a bit of rebellion. Even now, I hardly know how to explain it…that at the time I was done being a nineteen-year-old virgin. And since you only get one shot at giving up your virginity, I certainly wasn't going to use *my* shot with Kelly Keenan. But I couldn't—not then, and not now—remind Ben of how much I'd cared.

Moments later, I headed downstairs, my confidence shot to pieces. Ben gazed at my tropical-print sack dress and bare feet.

"Fetching."

"My clothes are in the wash," I said. "This is Granny's—all she has that'll fit me."

He appeared to be stifling a smile. "A Hawaiian mu-mu? I imagined her more of a Irish woolens and tweed kind of grandma."

"You imagined wrong." That's it—take the offensive. "So," I tilted my chin aggressively. "You think you're going to take Kevin away from me?"

"Of course not," he said, but his trace of cockiness disappeared. "Why do you think I ripped up the legal papers?"

"To prove you're not a gobshite? It doesn't mean a thing, after everything you said last week."

His jaw firmed. He opened his mouth, closed it, then finally, "I'm sorry."

I waited, but when no further expressions of his extreme guilt and utter contrition, along with the possibility of self-flagellation seemed forthcoming, I said, "You're... sorry. For what?"

"Okay, I overreacted—"

"Oh, you're sorry for your bit of giving out? But what's a little yelling, swearing, throwing between fr—" We were no longer friends. And probably would never be again. My mouth trembled. I could take a bit of disillusionment. But not losing Ben's friendship entirely.

"I *am* sorry, Aislin." He turned away. "For...everything. That night, I was tired, the Seattle visit had been weird, but that's no excuse...The way I acted was...like I said, there's no excuse."

Ben went to the mantle, apparently intent on the neatly arranged photographs. "When you didn't return my messages, I came to Galway, hoping..." then he faced me again, "No, determined to track you down, so we could find out if we could do better than—" He dug the soggy envelope pieces out of his pocket. "Than this." He tossed them onto the side table.

"Throwing down the gauntlet, are we? Or offering peace?"

Ben's eyes were steady. "I think we can figure out Kevin's visits ourselves, without going to court." He rubbed his fingers through his damp hair, a gesture I recognized—meaning he was upset. It was like being a lover, knowing some secret parts of him.

Well, we *were* lovers. Wait—no, we weren't. Once doesn't count...

He went on, "You never did get that restraining order, did you."

"I...well, I..." He'd obviously guessed I'd threatened him out of desperation—which meant he knew secret parts of me too. I blushed. No, no—not *those* parts. Although he did do a bit of investigating ages ago...but this was no time to remember *that*—

"I don't want to involve the law any more than you do," Ben said earnestly.

"Then you shouldn't have started that row. Did you think that you could waltz in here and pretend you hadn't been ready to throttle me just a week ago?"

"'Throttle' is a little strong, isn't it?"

"Not from my perspective. You have a bloody vile temper."

A muscle moved in Ben's jaw. "I...know. But look, let's not start throwing blame around. I don't want to make trouble for you. Or make your life miserable either."

That's big of you, I wanted to spit, but I didn't want to veer too far off our road to semi-reconciliation—even if it was no more than a weed-choked footpath. "I'll say this once. I don't intend to let you, or any man, control me." Ever again. "I'll make *my* own decisions, about *my* son. Got that?"

He nodded. "I really want to do what's best for Kevin. And... something else."

"Which is?"

"I want—" Ben looked if he intended to say something else, then slipped off his jacket and set it over the nearest chair. "I want the real story."

"About what?" I stalled.

He gave me a who-do-you-think-you're-kidding look. "About why you didn't tell me about Kevin before. And let's not pick fights over this too. I just need the truth."

TRUE CONFESSIONS

I sat down carefully, feeling breakable all of a sudden. "You say that like you don't think you're going to get it."

"To be honest, I still don't trust you."

Ouch. "If you came to extend an olive branch," I said, "throwing insults at me is a strange way to do it."

"Can you blame me?" He began to pace the room. "After you kept our son a secret?"

"You're still calling me a liar?" Maddening—that I could be *sooo* furious with the man, but couldn't help admiring his big shoulders, the way his trim hips...no. Forget it. "Even though I'd every intention of telling you?"

"So you say."

"I do say! I realized Kevin *did* need a father, and I finally mustered the nerve to contact you, and all I get is grief?" My voice spiraled upward. "And I'm the villain? What was my crime?"

"You..." He stopped, looking uncertain. "You let me see Kevin, talk to him, without telling me who he was. I call that deceiving me. What do you call it?"

"I *let* you see—" I clenched my fists. "I call it you coming to my flat uninvited one night, and seeing Kevin for yourself, before I'd had the chance to figure out how I'd tell you. The whole prospect wasn't easy, with the way you acted seven years ago—"

"Yeah—let's not forget *that*. I knew it was stupid, to go out with a little princess like you, but when I realized you didn't give a shit about me—"

"That's the most bloody nonsensical thing I've ever heard! Of course I...I mean, do you think I'd snog with you and not lo—" Aarrgh! What was I saying? "I kept Kevin, didn't I?"

Oh, no. Wrong thing to point out.

His eyes sharpened on me. "Why? I asked you that before... why *did* you keep him?"

Offense, take the offense... "How would I know you'd be keen on fatherhood? You were big on going to college, and being successful."

"Still, I should've been told," Ben gritted. "Every child needs a father."

I didn't. Did I? Beside the point. "If I didn't tell you about Kevin all this time, it's because I thought he and I were getting on all right." Sort of. At least, until recently.

A shadow crossed Ben's face. "That's what my mom used to say after my dad died. 'We're doing okay, aren't we?' I always said yes, but I knew the score—empty cupboards days before payday, a car with bald tires that barely ran. And forget sports— no money for Little League, or Pee-wee football—"

"Pee-wee what?"

He looked past me, like he wasn't even seeing me. "Like I said, it was hard."

I hardened my heart against the vulnerability in his face. "You'll forgive me if I'm not overly concerned about sport, as I'm supporting the pair of us on a shop assistant's pay."

Ben's gaze snapped back to me. "Why...too proud to ask Daddy for help?"

I stared at him open-mouthed. "My fath—have you gone completely bats?"

"Oh, come on. Your dad's loaded, powerful—what do you know about going without?"

I gaped at him. "You are so full of bollocks..." then it dawned on me. "Didn't you ever hear about my father? I mean, your mother told you, didn't she?"

"Tell me what? Did he pass on?" He looked mortified. "God, I didn't mean to—"

"No, he's still around." I snapped my mouth closed before I let anything else out.

"Around?" Ben's face smoothed, then he glanced at the mantle. "That must be your dad in those photos."

"Yes. Could we get back to Kevin?" I asked shortly.

Apparently not. "Who's the woman with him? Not your mom."

"Sister," I said. "He and Grace are... pals." I tried a more blithe tone. "You know, two of a kind. Unlike my parents—they divorced ages ago."

"I'm sorry. I hadn't heard."

"You mother—why didn't she tell you about the divorce?" I couldn't help asking. "God knows the local newspapers lapped up anything on my father."

"Mom was never big on gossip—she said you could never keep a maid's job if you talked about your employers." He was quiet for a moment. "Deirdre implied that you and your dad had...problems."

"I wouldn't say that," I lied. "But I've never, and *will* never, take money from him."

Ben held his hands out. "I did it again, didn't I? Shot my mouth off. I'm...sorry. Again."

I looked at him suspiciously. "You're apologizing so I'll be easy on you about Kevin?"

"Of course not," he said, then surprising me, he grinned. That crooked, endearing smile I'd seen on my son all his life. "Well, I can hardly make a case for myself—to start being Kevin's dad—if I keep offending you." His smile faded. "But Aislin, we've got to work something out."

I stuck my chin out. "Like what?"

"Like tell Kevin. As soon as we can. Then figure out the visitation."

I dropped onto the couch. Feeling cold terror return at the thought of some hideous custody agreement, I wrapped my arms around my middle. "You'll understand, I'm sure, if I'm not keen on having my son ripped from me." I tightened my arms, scrunching my breasts—which reminded me that I hadn't a bra on.

"I want to spend time with Kevin. Not 'rip him from you.'"

"But being shuttled between two homes will be dreadful for him," I said. "It's dreadful for any child."

"Aren't you being overly dramatic?" Ben asked. "In the States, kids of divorced parents do it all the time. They adjust fine."

"This isn't the States," I flared. "And we've just got the divorce referendum in Ireland from the mid-nineties, so it *is* a big deal." I knew plenty about shared custody from the papers, and women I talked to. "The back-and-forth bus rides, the young ones trying to keep track which weekend they're meant to spend with the father, with the girlfr—" I broke off, embarrassed.

Ben looked sympathetic. "If you're concerned about girl-friends being involved in raising Kev—"

"Or stepmammies," I put in. Beating round the bush was pretty silly at this point.

"I see your point, but in this case, you've got nothing to worry about."

"What about Courtney?"

Ben's expression was enigmatic. "She's not in the...she's not in Ireland now, is she?"

"What about later?" I asked resentfully.

"Maybe I'm the one who should be concerned about my son being raised by someone I don't know, like this Sam guy." Ben glanced at my mouth. "He is still around, I take it?"

I colored. He wasn't going to let me forget that he'd seen Sam kissing me, was he? And all of a sudden my "I guess Sam and I are together" assumption I'd come up with seemed rather...nebulous.

Of course we're together, I reassured myself stoutly. "I don't see myself *marrying* Sam, but at least Kevin knows him."

"So he's not the Boston Strangler, but there's the risk he could take my son out for facials after they get their nails done."

"Not funny," I said. Unable to resist the jab, I added, "Sam's quite easygoing. Doesn't throw things, or give out at people. Not like some I could name."

"I'm never going to live down my little...incident, am I?" Ben looked genuinely discouraged. "But I really do want to be a good father. So...can we tell him tomorrow?"

Against my will, I felt my empathy roused. "I don't have much choice, do I." Uncrossing my arms, I looked down at my lap. "With all this talk of visiting, I can't help worrying. Kevin's so little still."

Ben dropped to the couch beside me. "I'll make sure he's safe."

I could feel the heat from his body. *I can't believe I'm having sexual thoughts about him again, when we're meant to be deciding Kevin's future.* "I'm...sure you will," I said in a strangled voice. I meant it. Hadn't he been good to my little boy even when he'd thought...Kelly—I could hardly remember his name sometimes —was Kevin's daddy?

"You're the mother of my son—I don't want you to hate me."

"I don't," I managed.

"I realize visiting isn't a perfect solution. It's just really hard, you know, to find out I got a girl pregnant, had a child out there. I always thought I'd do things the right way."

I looked up from my lap, and found him closer than I'd thought, a somber expression on his face. "I didn't know you were so retro," I said. "No one cares about that out-of-wedlock stuff."

"Call me old-fashioned," he said, still serious. "I just wish Kevin wasn't in this position."

"'This position' being illegit?" I said flippantly. "One-third of all births in Ireland are these days. What's the big deal, really?"

"The big deal is that these kids often don't have a father around." Ben touched my arm. "You really think the kids with absent fathers won't grow up longing for a dad, the kind they can count on?"

I turned away from him, as pain hit me. I knew all about that longing. So did Kevin.

"I feel like I'm letting down my own son, not being around—not living with him."

"Well," I said brightly, not thinking, "we could always get married."

"Married?"

God help us! Horror filled me. *Did I really say that? Jaysus, I don't want to marry Ben, I don't want to marry anyone!* I suddenly felt tension coiled around his whole body. "It's a joke!" I said quickly. "One of those marriages of convenience—like in novels, or...or films." The trouble was, every marriage of convenience story I'd ever read or seen included the couple always having sex. Good sex. Great sex.

"Hey, that's not a bad idea." He chuckled.

"But out of the question, of course." I worked up a lovely fake chuckle myself. "Unless your Courtney would go along with it."

Ben only shifted his body. Closer. "Your joke must mean I'm forgiven, at least a little?"

"A little," I said grudgingly. Then remembering how contrite he'd been just now, I glanced at him. "Let's just put it behind us."

"Works for me," he said, his eyes trained on my face. "This, uh, means a lot to me."

"Me, too." I smiled, suddenly, ridiculously happy we were back on good terms. Visions of Technicolor daddy-visits danced in my head...Then Ben slid his hand off my arm. To my waist.

Ummm...I couldn't help relaxing. Strange, because when I was with Sam, this was usually the point that unless I'd had a glass of wine or something, I always got sort of...uptight. With the unfortunate urge to back away from him and say, *Sorry, but it's my period again.* I'd secretly concluded that I simply wasn't much for the whole business...

But here I was, a serious cuddle looming, and thinking wouldn't it be nice if Ben moved his hand, just a little, and touched my breast? And finished that lovely kiss he gave me last week?

Mother of God! Was I daft? The man obviously hadn't gotten enough sex when he was visiting Courtney! Still, you'll notice I wasn't pushing him away...

"Trouble is, Aislin," and Ben's laugh sounded more genuine this time, "if I was married to someone, I could never go for that 'in-name-only' stuff."

"You'd want mad, crazy, wild sex, would you?"

"You got it," Ben murmured wickedly. "The kind that would make me never want to be with another woman."

"So you're the faithful sort?" An unfamiliar warmth invaded my body. I didn't dare look down, but something told me that if I were to shift my hips toward him, and he toward mine, I'd feel a very interesting bulge. I felt the thrill go right down to my—oh, yesss... "I didn't think they existed anymore."

"I said I was old-fashioned." Ben curved his hand around my ribcage.

"Old fashioned," I repeated, to escape the undertow of lust overtaking me. But all I could think about was his hand. *Yes, go up. No, down. Oh, God, both...* Had I been all wrong about the whole "I'm not a great one for sex" thing...?

"And by the way," he said in my ear, just as there was a rumble on the stoop, "there is no Courtney."

THE CONVERSATION, PART 2

J have a decidedly short memory—or else lust had
tinkered with my brain chemistry. Here I was, your
typical single mammy who often felt overwhelmed with motherhood. But ever since the night Ben and I had The Mother of
All Rows, the thought of actually sharing Kevin—and with the
only fellow who'd ever pushed my sexual buttons, mind—scared
the bejeezus out of me.

However, your granny and child walking in on your imminent snog, and you without a bra on, has a way of making you
forget every sexual thought that ever dared to enter your head.
Except for that inconvenient haze of semi-desire that settles
down on your couch and turns on your telly, determined to
stick around until you forcibly kick it out.

I mean, talk about a close call: another minute on Granny's
couch, and Ben would have had his hands all over me. And I'd
have let him.

But back to my point: Although my sexual thrill would have
to go back where it came from, our discussion had been useful.
For one thing, we'd bonded a bit. I felt a rush of emotion seeing

Kevin run straight into his father's arms, and Ben's hard kiss on his hair.

For another, I was spared any awkward confessions to Granny. Her first good look at Ben was with him holding Kevin, their faces side-by-side. "This is my best friend ever, Granny," Kevin announced. "He's called Ben Carpenter."

Granny's sharp blue eyes briefly skewered me, then she turned a dazzling smile on Ben. "Ben, is it? I've been wanting to meet you."

"Mrs. Moore—nice to—"

"That'll be 'Granny' to you, young man." She kissed Ben's cheek. "Since you're Aislin's and Kevin's very good *friend*."

Dealing with Granny had been a cakewalk, really. Later, in private, we covered the lot: Granny: *Fine young man, he'll make a good daddy, etc.* Me: nod and smile idiotically. Granny: *And he's taking you and Kevin back to Dublin so the pair of you can talk to the boy?* Me: Idiotic smile disappears. Granny: Pats my hand. *Glad to hear it.* Tacks on a decidedly ungrandmotherly, *If you don't make a clean breast of it at the first opportunity, I'll tell Kevin myself.*

So, then—one Conversation down, one to go. I'd no way to weasel out of revealing Ben's real identity to my son.

THE NEXT DAY, the Galway-to-Dublin trip seemed to last about ten minutes. As I was letting us inside the flat, I was a St. Elmo's fireball of nerves. Takeaway dinner, then talk? I fretted. Talk first? The one bright spot was knowing that Kevin would be absolutely *ecstatic*.

However, I'd conveniently forgotten the scene waiting in the front room. Ben stepped over the threshold and dropped Kevin's holdall. "What the hell—?"

The cash he'd flung at me last week was still strewn every-where: under the coffee table, in the crate of toys in the corner, on top of the lampshade, under the easy chair, and between the sofa cushions.

I gave him an ironic look. "It's our favorite new game, isn't it Kevin?"

As Ben stared, Kevin raced around the room, picking up bills. "Mammy and I made it up," he chortled, and tossed a handful of money into the air. "It's called 'Throw the Money.'" Grinning, he collected another wad of cash and pitched it too.

"That's enough for now, love." Despite my apprehension, I couldn't help enjoying the stupefied look on Ben's face. "We can play more later. Go wash while I ring for pizza."

As Kevin tripped out of the room, Ben cleared his throat. "You never…"

"Picked it up? No. I do have *some* pride."

He crossed the room in a flash, and plucked the phone out of my hand. "Aislin—"

"You want pizza later?"

"No…I mean yes—" He set the handset in its cradle, then touched my shoulder. "I really am such a bastard."

I guess I'd wrung whatever enjoyment there was to be had from this, and smiled at him. "Were. Unless, of course, you refuse to clean up the lot."

Watching Ben crawling round the room was gratifying, but regretfully momentary. Because as he picked up the last bill, he said, "Okay, let's get it over with—I'll get Kevin."

I saw his hands were trembling. I could identify—my entire body was quaking. But though my stomachache reminded me a bit of *The Matrix*, when that scary Goth girl extracts that alien whatever from poor Keanu Reeve's navel, I plunged right in.

"You know I love you more than anything in the whole world," I said to Kevin, as the three of us settled on the couch.

Kevin's eyes widened. Probably because this was how I prefaced any bit of bad news. My mouth so dry I had to peel my tongue off the roof of it, I tried again. "You remember about how mammies and daddies get together and make babies?"

Kevin squirmed. "Mammy, I don't wanna talk about *that*—"

"Of course," I said hastily. I wasn't keen to revisit *that* either, not with Ben here. "So, then, before you were born, the man—the dad who helped make you—had to...go away. So he didn't know about you."

Kevin bobbed his head. "I wished he didn't go away. I wished he knew about me."

Ben patted Kevin's knee, looking a lot like the morning after a *very* rough night before.

"Well, yes." I stroked Kevin's hair. "I've felt very bad you didn't have a daddy about. But now you will."

Kevin's brows pulled together, then his eyes lit up. "Are you g-gonna mar—" He tugged on my jumper. I leaned close, and his whisper tickled my ear. "Can you marry Ben? Can he be my d-dad then?"

Perfect opening! "Well, yes!" I whispered back. "I mean, no. I mean—" I straightened back up, clasping my hands across my waist like a cheery schoolmarm. "We've no need to whisper, love. It's all right if Ben hears."

Although he looked not only helpless, but maybe a little sick at this point. *Well, get used to it, if you're going into the parenthood business.* "You see, we're not going to get married, but—"

"Oh." Kevin's face fell. "You're g-gonna marry Sam."

"No, I'm not." My stomach twisted. "But if you'll let me say the rest—"

"Good. 'Cos I like Ben heaps better."

"That's grand, darling!" I said, love and exasperation swirling in me, "but that's just it. Ben is your, em...your d-d-dad." I held my breath.

Kevin's eyes widened until the whites shone around the iris, then he gave Ben a fearful look.

"That's right," Ben said, calm as the Buddha, though a muscle twitched in his jaw. "I'm your real dad."

I COULD FEEL a smile start to break through, delight singing through me...The worst is over, now it's a happy-ever-after... But wait a minute—

Kevin's face crumpled. "He's m-my-my d-d-d-d—"

As I reached for him, he moved as if to burrow into my arms, then wrenched away and tore down the hall.

I leaped to my feet as his bedroom door slammed. "Kevin!"

Ben caught my arm. "Aislin, give him a minute."

I wanted to smack him. *What the hell do you know about it? I'm his bloody mother!* Instead, I collapsed back on the couch. I was actually too upset to cry. "Oh, God, what have I done?" I wailed. "Did you hear him stutter? I thought—I was so sure he'd be happy—no, *delirious.*"

"So was I." Ben looked crushed.

Worst-case scenarios hit me thick and fast, like in old films when newspaper headlines swirl in black space: *Kevin Has Total Stuttering Relapse...*then, *Kevin Fails at School...*and finally, *Kevin Turns into Premature Juvenile Delinquent...* I pressed my hand to the knot in my middle. "What if he hates me? What if he never forgives me? Like I'll never forgive my—"

Ben pulled me close, shocking the heedless words back inside me. Our embrace was clumsy and lopsided—my shoulder dug into his breastbone, my ear crunched against his jaw—but I was comforted. Until I felt him shaking.

So Ben was hurting too. I managed to hook my arm round him and give him a squeeze. Just as it dawned on me that this was feeling too good, that I should be suffering more, Kevin's doorknob rattled.

I broke away as Kevin skidded into the front room. His face

red with tears, he stared down at the floor, and swiped his runny nose on his sleeve.

I clutched the cushions to hold off one of those needy mammy hugs. "How're you doing?"

Kevin shrugged, and scuffed the toe of one battered trainer against the other. "I d-dunno."

"Are you..." Hard to ask, but no way out of it, "Are you sad about—you know, Ben being your daddy?"

He flashed a look at Ben, then shook his head.

Ben and I exchanged a perplexed look. "You're not sad about it?" Ben asked.

Kevin slid another glance at Ben with a half-embarrassed, half-hopeful expression. "Ben is really and truly my real, real d-dad?"

The innocence, the utter purity in Kevin's eyes was breaking my heart. "Ben is really and truly your dad."

"Then how come he..."

I knew what Kevin was asking. "You mean, why he wasn't with you...us...all this time?"

Kevin nodded.

I swallowed hard. "Ben didn't know he was your dad," I said matter-of-factly. Though I heard that narky, accusing voice inside, *And whose fault was that, I'd like to know?* "But now that he does know, he'd like to see you at the weekends." I gave Ben a seems-like-a-good-time-to-take-the-floor look.

He stretched out a hand. "Come here, uh...son."

Kevin obeyed, looking apprehensive again. Ben took him by the shoulders, looking into his face earnestly. "It's okay, then, that I'll be your dad?"

"It's g-grand altogether," Kevin said with a sweet, shy smile, and I suddenly understood why a mother bear will literally tear someone limb from limb for so much as touching her cub. I looked at Ben murderously. *If you ever hurt my son I will kill you.*

Ben didn't see it. A vulnerable look flashed across his face, which rather took the wind out of my homicidal sails. "Then why were you so upset?"

Kevin gazed into his father's eyes. "I…em, I felt so strange inside my whole self."

"Strange how?" Ben smiled encouragingly.

So this is what it's about, I told myself—sharing your child. Letting him confide in his father. Lovely, right? So why did I want to bawl?

"Well, I d-didn't know what to do, 'cept cry. And all the b-boys at school say only b-b-babies cry. Sure I thought you wouldn't want a big 'oul baby for your b-boy. So I had to run away before you saw."

Ben pulled Kevin into his lap, a lovely fuchsia round his eyes. "Uh, did you know it's all right for boys *and* grown-ups to cry?"

"Ah, sure. I seen Mammy cry lots."

I choked up even more.

"No, I mean grown-up men," Ben explained. "They cry too, sometimes."

"Really?" said Kevin. "I thought grown-up fellas don't cry ever."

"Well, they do, once in a while," Ben told him. "Their throat hurts, and tears come into their eyes. That's what happened to me, when I found out I was your dad." Kevin looked amazed. "Just like you," Ben said, "I felt strange, but so happy inside, that I…sort of…cried."

"You were happy?" Kevin wore a serious expression.

Here it was—the tipping point, the make-or-break daddy moment. I couldn't breathe.

"I *am* happy," Ben said. "So happy to have you for my son I could bust!"

An immense pleasure burst from Kevin's face, like sunlight. "Awesome!"

Overwhelmed by another needy urge, I sort of wilted into

the couch, watching in painful delight as my son and his father really, truly fell in love.

"You don't want to make a regular habit of crying, I guess," Ben said, and by now his nose was brick red, "but when a really big thing, or a sad thing, or a happy thing happens, sometimes you just have to let it all hang out."

"Well, I'm really happy," Kevin said, and I swear I saw real stars in his eyes. "I'm the happiest ever, ever, ever!"

"Glad to hear it," Ben said, his eyes damp, and suddenly the pair of them were clutching each other, grinning like fools. "Think you can call me 'Dad' one of these days?"

"Yeah!" Kevin gave Ben a shy kiss on the cheek. "I'm all done cryin' now!"

It was the kiss that did it. Tears choking my throat, I realized, that for the first time, I was the outsider with Kevin.

Had I just made the biggest mistake of my life?

"THE LAP DANCE"

I would be the perfect custodial mammy, I just knew it.

After Ben and I had The Talk with Kevin, I'd given myself a good scolding. Really, my fears about where-will-I-fit-in-now, and that I'd given Kevin someone he'd love more than me were *so* unworthy. I would be sharing my child as a mature, emotionally-evolved adult. You know, respectful of my child's father, and maintaining a friendly yet impersonal relationship best suited to enhance said child's emotional development. In fact, I decided it was rather lovely, being parents together, having Ben tuck Kevin up, and Kevin call him "Daddy."

So here we were, Kevin's official Mam-and-Dad. I flopped on the couch, too emotionally drained to deal with pizza cleanup. "That'll be in the record books for the quickest bedtime yet."

Ben collapsed next to me. "Oh, yeah?"

"Definitely. No two-hour bath, endless stories, drinks of water, where's my Spidey torch, please open the door more, I've got to go to the loo again, and by the way can I have the new Harry Potter action figure..."

SUSAN COLLEEN BROWNE

All right, I was babbling. And unsure of myself. First of all, I looked dead scary, with my eyes all swollen, and I swear the stress had frizzed my hair. Ben still had pink round his eyes, but on a man, a near-cry is like gray hair—strangely dignified.

"Actually, Kevin managed to work that one in." Ben settled himself more comfortably. And slightly closer?

Suddenly being alone with Ben brought me back to the almost-snog at Granny's. *Let's not go there*, I told my on-again, off-again, mostly on-again-when-Ben-was-around libido. "Still," I pointed out, "You've had the easy part so far—the hugs and 'I'm so happy's,' being on best behavior and all that."

"What else can I look forward to?" Ben leaned back, clasping his hands behind his head. "Besides comforting my son's mother in an emotional moment."

I colored. The aftermath had been...interesting. Me: Watching Kevin and Ben embrace, promptly burst into tears. Ben: Pulls me into lap. Adds comforting pats. Me: Swear I feel him get aroused. Become very flustered and jump up. However, crying stops instantaneously.

"Glad you asked," I said, trying to keep the conversation and my mind on my six-year impersonation as a mother. "There's when your child has a meltdown in public, or when you're running late and you discover your child hasn't any clean clothes. *Real* good times are cleaning up sick in the middle of the night." Ben didn't seem put off. I sank deeper into the couch. "But you know, if your idea of an exciting evening is like tonight, staying in with takeaway, some telly, then tucking your child up, you won't do too badly."

"I thought it was good family time for us," Ben said, smiling.

But we're not a family, I thought, stricken. Then it hit me like a blinding flash: In a way, Ben *was* family now. Especially with the impending weekend rendezvous and holiday visits. As for future child support...well, it wouldn't be right, to accept money from Ben, then act like he was some anonymous man on the street.

Speaking of money... I clambered off the couch and dragged myself to the shelf where Ben had set the bills he'd picked up. "This is yours."

Ben surprised me by pulling me onto his knee, then he took the money and set it on the coffee table. "No, it's not. It's yours and Kev—"

"I'm not going to take it," I said emphatically, trying not to make a big deal out of this sure-to-be-fleeting cuddle.

Ben looked embarrassed. "Because the bills are marked with 'money Ben once threw at me?'"

"No," I said. He had a point, but I could be big about this. "If you want, use it to start a fund for...I don't know. University or something." A bit ironic, really. Ben making sure Kevin would go to university, while getting me pregnant meant I'd had to give it up. "Any money I take from you will be under a support agreement or whatever they call it."

"But Aisl—"

"No." I got the inspired thought: by staying on his knee, I'd show him I could reject his money, but not him. "I won't be one of those mammies jockeying for a handout every time the father calls round." In fact, I'd always be understanding about visits and last minute plans and unavoidable fatherly tardiness.

"I wasn't worried—I know you'll do the right thing," Ben said.

With that somewhat misplaced vote of confidence, I was suddenly struck by the unwelcome vision of Kevin-less Christmases and Easters, and me sitting alone in a dark flat with a frozen dinner...What if Kevin decided he loved Ben better? Or God help us, wanted to live with his father full time? Feeling more tears behind my eyes, I couldn't help a sniff.

Ben peered in my face. "You okay?"

"Ah, sure," I said, and sniffed again. "But the future is so full of unknowns."

"It doesn't have to be." Ben patted my back again. "I promise you, we're going to make this work."

Easy for him to say. But with my vow of perfect parent still fresh in my mind, I said, "If you've your diary with you, we can fix the first visiting time—"

"Jeez, Aislin, let's not worry about visits now. I mean, we just got through this big emotional moment. I'm still trying to get my head around having a son." His arms tightened, and before I knew it, I'd sort of slid down his knee and into his lap.

Oh, God. This *really* wasn't a good idea. But wiggling round to get out of his lap would just get me into deeper trouble. "Kevin's living proof, all right," and I couldn't help grinning, "that we made..." *A baby*. I gulped. "That we're parents."

Talk about déjà vu. Sitting in Ben's lap, years ago, I'd first discovered the delights of serious snogging. Just as I wondered if he was remembering too, his clasp changed to something more... intimate. Nothing improper, but his hands moved a teensy bit: Hand One from back to waist, Hand Two from knee to thigh.

"You know," he murmured, "this is starting to feel a little familiar."

So he did remember. "Oh?" I said. "It's slipped my mind, actually." As if.

As if I could ever forget that almost everything I'd learned about kissing, I'd learned with Ben. And about ninety percent of it, sitting in his lap.

There was the French-kissing part, the wandering hands part, the clothes pulled awry part, which, involving my full cooperation, lead to my first... "Mmmm..." I breathed, as the memory lit a fire inside me. Then realizing what I was about, I scrambled off Ben's lap before I was overwhelmed by the temptation to...you know. "It's getting late."

You'd think I wouldn't need reminding, that you can get pregnant doing it just once, and with protection too.

"Uh...right." Ben rose slowly. "If it fits with your schedule," he said formally, a set look on his face, "I'd like to see Kevin next Saturday."

"Lovely," said I. This was no time speculate on the source of that look. "We'll work out the details later." I got Ben out the door before I could change my mind about the lap-sitting bit.

For now, dealing with the new visits seemed easier than the fact that I'd seriously contemplated a protracted snog with Ben. And me back with Sam! Had I gone mad? Even if Ben was the one who'd started the whole lap thing?

However, another burning question: was he just out for some recreational shagging, when he already had a girlfriend? Then I remembered something else. That he'd said yesterday.

There is no Courtney.

YOU'VE GOT MAIL, PART 2

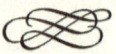

*W*here do you go to find out about a guy's
girlfriend? To his *girl* friend, of course.

At work Monday, I volunteered to clean the back room. And
while dusting the computer, it seemed only efficient to catch up
on e-mail while I was at it.

TO: Liz McCarthy

SUBJECT: Saw Ben on the weekend

Hi Liz,

If it seems like I've been avoiding you—well, all right, I *have*
been avoiding you. Ben and I had a real donnybrook the
weekend before last—he found out about Kevin before I could
fit in the Big Talk—and I didn't know how to tell you. I thought
if I kept quiet, Ben could give you his side—only fair for him to
get first crack right?

But—we had a chance to settle things regarding Kevin. Ben
was nicely remorseful, which ideally, will give me an upper
hand with all Kevin-related matters, but that remains to be seen.
Ben's actually going to have Kevin overnight this weekend, let's

have a Girls' Night! My place.

Hugs,

A.

P.S. Ben implied there's something up with Courtney...any chance you're in the loop?

FROM: Liz McCarthy

SUBJECT: Donnybrook

Hi Aislin,

I don't know what's going on with Courtney. After Ben got back from Seattle, he acted really strange for a few days. I thought it was because of her until he confessed what happened between you two. But I'm glad it all worked out and he's out of the doghouse with you.

You wouldn't believe what Kurt wrote me this week—that the assistant he hired last week turned out to be a disaster, and if I lived in Seattle, he'd recruit me in a minute. Who knows if he really means it, but between my boring job and Dan pretty much being the Invisible Man around our house—and when he's home, he's complaining about Ben having personal life, so he's not available to put in the 18-hour days Dan practically demands—the offer has a certain charm.

Can't wait to see you and Deirdre this Saturday!

Hugs,

Liz

FROM: Ben Carpenter

SUBJECT: My mom

Hi Aislin,

I called Mom Sunday night, after we told Kevin. She took the news about having a grandson pretty well, all things considered. First, she didn't say anything for about ten minutes. Then I thought she was going to do the verbal equivalent of whomping me upside the head, but then she said she'd had a few suspicions, which surprised the hell out of me.

Anyway, she cheered right up when I proposed that we bring Kevin out to see her this summer or something. You okay with that?

Ben

GIRLS' NIGHT PLUS

"*D*id you know it's a proven fact women eat more when men aren't around?" I said to Deirdre and Liz, then crammed a fistful of popcorn into my mouth.

"Duh," said Deirdre, and pressed the rewind button on my video player. "Ever notice how much we eat when we watch a film with sex in it?"

Trust Deirdre to bring up sex at the most inopportune moments—meaning, when I didn't want to talk about it. But she'd an excellent point. When you're in the mood but haven't a prayer of a bedmate, a Saturday night eat-fest was a good way to get your mind off sex.

And forget that your child was having his first solo visit with his father.

"It's the old 'reach for your plate instead of your mate' thing." Liz took a healthy slurp of wine. "One thing I've learned is when you're married to a workaholic, you can't let yourself get too worked up with a sexy flick."

The film was bad enough, reminding me of the old thrills with Ben—the effect on my libido was sort of like trying to suppress your hiccoughs, then having a particularly violent one burp up despite your best efforts. But having a sex-themed Girls' chat was even worse. I tried to think of the un-sexiest activity possible—shop dusting—but boom! there I was, thinking of our almost-snog at Granny's again.

I practically dove into the popcorn bowl head first. "I must say, it's lovely to have Kevin all taken care of." Then Liz's gaze zeroed in on me.

"I'd have thought it would be sort of traumatic for you, Kevin's first visit away."

"Oh, no," I lied. After deciding I'd be the perfect, under-standing custodial parent, I couldn't let on about the lump that came to my throat, watching Kevin's jaunty little stride to Ben's car, without so much as a backward look. "Seems silly now—I was so dreading telling Ben about being a daddy, I forgot to look at the upside—almost guilt-free time off."

"Before, Ash always felt horrible, going out," Deirdre said. "Some nights I'd have to drag her out of her flat."

"Well, I did feel I was neglecting my son," I admitted. "Palming him onto Maggie's Bill—who has been a saint, by the way—never felt right."

"St. Bill is rather a misnomer these days," Deirdre said disgustedly.

"Why?" asked Liz, and drained her wineglass.

Deirdre pulled a face. "You wouldn't want Kevin sleeping over these days, with the pair of them still having it off like rabbits every night."

Didn't I know it—the headboard usually commenced its steady rocking against the wall promptly at half ten. Thank God they were fast. "Maggie says she and Bill are more in love than ever—they're spending Saturday nights having romantic suppers, with wine and candlelight, the whole caboodle."

"At least *Maggie's* having fun." Liz poured herself another glass of wine.

"I've no worries about Kevin hearing things at Ben's he shouldn't," I said, "since the girlfriend isn't on the scene. Yet."

I realized I'd been finding ways to bring up Ben all evening. Only because I'm apprehensive about the "There is no Courtney" mystery, I told myself. I mean, wasn't it a bit of cheek to ask Ben about her, even if I'd the excuse of being Kevin's mother? But I was determined to get a reading on the situation when Ben brought Kevin home tomorrow.

"As long as nobody's married, the visits should go without a hitch," Liz put in. "It's after the 'better or worse' part, when your husband treats looking after the children as 'babysitting.'"

"Now that *is* cheek," I agreed.

"Damn right." Liz took a slug of wine. "These guys must think fathering a child happens through... through..."

"Immaculate conception?" said Deirdre.

"Exactly!" Liz gesticulated wildly with her glass—good job it was only half-full.

"Sure, men can be such sprogs," I said loyally. "But you know, Irish guys are probably behind the eight ball compared to Yanks, when it comes to pitching in round the house."

"Still, it's like you created the little darlings all on your own, so he just needs to 'help.'" Liz looked mulish. "You wouldn't believe the pressure I had to put on Dan so I could go out tonight. You're lucky, Aislin, that Ben's your friend, *and* good daddy material."

"Well, after a few fireworks." I'd given Liz a quick rundown —a sanitized version, if you must know—about my fight with Ben. The discovery that Ben could still turn me on was still classified information.

"Marriage can be so complicated," Liz added. "It's like you've got to negotiate a Geneva Convention to get your husband to do the damn dishes once a month, or pick up a gallon of milk. Not like...oh, never mind." An inscrutable smile curved her lips.

Deirdre sat up. "You've something to dish?"

"I don't know if I should." A giggle.

"You're being coy," I said. Had to be the drink. "But since you're the only one here who's married, give us a bit of insight, won't you? It'll be a public service."

"If you tell us something worth our while, I will too," Deirdre said.

"What?" I forgot about Ben for the moment. "You and Adrian finally did it?"

Deirdre's smile was a bit audacious. "I'll tell all—but Liz goes first. You have to divulge something sexy too, Ash."

I blanched. I hadn't quite settled down from my recent lascivious thoughts of Ben. So I certainly wasn't going to share them.

Lucky for me, though, Liz was in a confiding mood. She took another gulp of wine, then flopped back on the couch. "Oh, you've read it a zillion times in women's magazines. The sex is always great before you're married, but once you tie the knot, it's all downhill."

"Not for Maggie and Bill, mind," Deirdre pointed out.

"Well, they're the exception," Liz said. "When I met Dan, he seemed like Mr. Personality compared to a lot of the bores I'd dated in college. We had this really great sex every day—you know, hanging from chandeliers kind of stuff—and twice on Sunday."

I could feel myself turning red. "There *is* such a thing as Too Much Information."

"Not for me," Deirdre said, and turned back to Liz. "So...now?"

"Well, it's just..." her voice trailed away. "Average." Long pause. "Or not happening. Period."

I sent her a sympathetic look. Quantities of great sex—or even mediocre sex—had never happened to me. But that's not to say I wouldn't have liked to give it a go. "Hasn't Dan's new business, and the move to Ireland, been rather, em... absorbing?

Give it some time."

"Whatever." Liz laughed, but with a definite edge. "Meanwhile, I've met someone."

Deirdre's jaw dropped. "You?"

"You're having an affair?" I felt sick. Too much popcorn, obviously. Or I was a lot less liberated than I'd thought. "But Dan...the kids—"

"God, of course not," Liz said emphatically. "What kind of person do you think I am?"

"Well, not the adulterous kind," I said, feeling better.

"Well, I haven't really *met* someone." Liz sounded a bit strange. "Remember I told you about Kurt, my college friend? He was actually a...boyfriend, if you must know."

"Oh, we must," said Deirdre.

"Well, we've been eee-mailing," she squealed the word, "each other."

"One of the bores you mentioned?" I was so relieved I had to have more popcorn.

"Actually...Kurt wasn't boring." Liz giggled, and topped off her glass. "We were fellow angst-ridden artists. He was amazingly talented, but la-*zy*. I'd drag him out of bed to art fairs and craft shows, and his stuff really took off."

"So, why didn't you marry him?" I asked. "Since you had the whole meeting-of-minds thing."

"He didn't want...kids, and he smoked too much...dope." Liz's speech was starting to sound a bit slurred. "I'm sure he's improved, though, if he has a succesh... successful ...gallery. It'd be great to be friends again."

"You know what they say," Deirdre said darkly. "It always starts innocently, but ends with the Fallen Woman sobbing to the divorce court judge."

"Me, a fallen...woman?" Liz scoffed. "That...that would be the day."

"'But we were just friends, yer honor,'" Deirdre interrupted in a despairing falsetto, "'please don't take my kiddies away!'"

"Oh, honeshtly," Liz complained. "I'm too...tired to have an aff...affair. And Kurt lives halfway around the...world."

"What about e-mail sex?" Deirdre teased.

You wouldn't. I pressed my lips together to keep from saying it.

Liz didn't deny it. Bad sign. Then she yawned. Bored with the idea? Or was the wine simply taking effect? "For that, I'd have to sh-send him a photo." She looked glum. Also a bad sign. "Whish I'm not about to do, with the size of my butt. Sho...So," she corrected, "there's nothing to worry about." She stood up suddenly, and swayed a little. "God, I think I'm tip...uh, tipsy. You two are a rotten influensh."

"Oh, why not tie one on, if you feel like it," I offered, to jolly another giggle out of Liz. "You can stay the night if you need to."

"You're shwee...sweet." Liz belched delicately. "I'll see how I feel. Though I'd love to see Dan's face, telling him I'm shtay—staying over. He'd have the kids all morning too."

"Maybe you should stay here on principle," Deirdre said. "But you know, single girls hoping to snag a fella are always going to roll their eyes when married ones who've got their man—like you, Liz—start giving out about it."

"While Dan may not be Mr. Perfect," I said diplomatically, "he sounds like a good sort. Reliable."

"Reliable," Liz repeated. She lifted up her wineglass, and peered morosely through the liquid. "Do you really think it's universal, that shingles, I mean singles, and marrieds want to trade lives?"

"Not necessarily," I said. "But it's a bit like the old joke about the entire male sex," I sloshed some more wine into my glass—and Liz's too. A bit more drink might cheer her up. "They spend nine months in the womb, trying to sort how to get out, then the rest of their lives trying to get back in."

"Isn't that the truth." Deirdre grinned. "Now, with Adrian

and me—whoops, we were meant to hear your sexy story first, Ash."

"I don't have one," I muttered, pretending to study the remains of the popcorn bowl. "We've eaten all the buttery kernels, haven't we?"

"What about you and...and..." Liz gulped her wine. "Sam?"

I stiffened. I'd trouble remembering that Sam and I had actually had sex. With each other, I mean. "We're still on the back burner, while Ben and I work things out with Kevin's visits."

"Oh, come on," said Deirdre. "If you've nothing recent to share, you must have something in the not-to-distant past. You and Sam have been together for...what, well over a year?"

"Off and on," I confirmed.

"Still," Deirdre persisted, "you must have something halfway interesting to tell."

"Not a thing," I evaded, then thought, *hell, what've I got to lose.* "Well, it's not the least bit romantic."

"So, stop pissing us about and tell us."

"Don't say I didn't warn you." I couldn't help giggling. "With Sam, I was always too busy getting the birth control lined up, to get all that carried away. Pills didn't work for me, so it was condoms, foams, diaphragms, you name it, I used it."

"Eeuww," Deirdre and Liz groaned. "That's not sexy at all," Deirdre added.

"I spent more time in the loo organizing the whole business than I did in bed with him," I went on. "Sometimes, I'd mysteriously have two periods a month, which he never noticed. Plus, he was often in a big rush, so I'd want to ask, 'where's the fire?'"

Deirdre giggled. "Reminds me of another old joke, about the oul' Irish pair—Paddy's notion of foreplay is rolling on top of Bridget, and saying, 'Brace yourself.'"

"So why'd you bother, Aislin?" Liz wanted to know. "If the shex...sex was boring."

"I suppose he was good company." After a fashion. And I was

lonely. But really, how did a girl answer this one? *Sam was better than nobody...*

"Then how about you and Ben goin' for it?" Liz persisted. "If you had shex...sex with him once, you could do it again."

"Don't be fecking ridiculous," I sputtered. "Not in a million years." I took a deep breath. "Our goal is being responsible parents to our son," I said in what I hoped was a lofty tone. "Not confuse our child with illicit goings on."

"Then how 'bout a quickie every once in a while?" Liz grinned.

"I'm not the least bit attracted to Ben," I hedged, and dug back into the popcorn bowl. *I'm a lot attracted to him.*

"Well, maybe if you tell that to yourself enough times, you'll make it true." Deirdre laughed again. "But Ash, I'm warning you —sometime I'm going to worm a sexy story out of you." She hiccoughed. "Speaking of illicit goings on, Adrian and me were —" Someone knocked at the door.

Liz blinked. "Did we order...um, takeout and forget about it?"

Mystified, I heaved myself off the couch. "Food on the way? I'd remember *that*. And if it was our Maggie or Polly, they'd call out from the stoop." I frowned at my friends' expectant, if slightly inebriated, faces, then said through the door, "Who is it?"

JUST FRIENDS

I'm not the sort who needs to be hit over the head. I hope. So, finding Ben on the stoop, his jaw tight, with a thoroughly unconscious and tear-stained-faced Kevin draped over his shoulder, the story seemed clear: Visit Number One had not been a resounding success.

While the girls exchanged an apprehensive look, I decided bundling Kevin off to bed would be a handy diversion. Even if Ben and I almost cracked heads when we kissed our son goodnight. We tiptoed back to the front room to find Deirdre and Liz struggling into their shoes.

I gave them a pleading look. "You don't have to go." What with the sex chat with the girls, and me a bit worse for drink, I wasn't sure I could trust myself to be alone with Ben. At least not so soon after our lap dance last week.

"With Kevin's upset... I mean, I'll bet you've loads to talk about," Deirdre said.

"Loadsh," Liz repeated.

Ben looked nonplussed. "You're not drunk, are you, Liz?"

"A little," she said, and stuck her chin out. "You got a problem with that?"

"Not at all," Ben said quickly. "Moms should be able to go out, have some fun—"

"I should hope so!" I said, a bit aggressive. But in my defense, seeing the way Kevin had obviously fallen apart did not bode well for my Perfect Custodial Mammy persona.

"I've invited Liz to crash at our place," broke in Deirdre. "Mammy loves company. Even drunks. She'll make Liz look at fairy catalogues over breakfast, and be happy as a pig in a mud wallow."

"Thanksh a lot," Liz said. "Love the pig analogy."

Deirdre headed for the door. "Just pray you won't have a head on you in the morning, or the fairy pics will scare the shite right out of you. Now, mind the steps."

Liz gave me a big, wine-scented hug, and on her way out, she threw her arms around Ben. If you can believe it, I actually felt a tiny pinch of jealousy. "You're a great guy, Ben," said Liz. "Alwaysh believe that."

He said, "Uh...thanks," then Deirdre stumbled against his chest and reached up to kiss his cheek. I felt another pinch. Definitely had to be the drink.

"See ya later, Ben." Deirdre kissed him again, and commenced patting him on the back. "We'll do another Girls'-n-Boy's Night soon."

"Uh, that would be great," Ben said, as Deirdre kept patting him as if she didn't know how to stop. Finally, I said sharply, "Deirdre, get on with it, will you?"

Deirdre finally released him and opened the door. "Give 'im a goodnight kiss too, Ash."

"A lil' smooch," Liz added. The corner of Ben's mouth twitched.

The pair of them were going to hear from me later. "Ben's not leaving yet."

"Oh...yeah," Deirdre frowned. "Well, then, plenty of time for a shag, hmmm?"

"Deirdre!" I hissed, and saw Ben's grin.

"Well, off to see Mammy," Deirdre said, and pushed Liz through the door.

Ben and I watched them stumble to the O'Donnell's stoop, then I locked the door. "Sorry about that. They're a bit scuttered." I quailed, wondering what Ben would make of the girls' comments. What if he thought we'd discussed his potential as my boy toy?

But he only said, "I see that—how about you?"

"Perfectly, almost sober." I stuck out my chin. "I've the wits to see your visit didn't go exactly as planned."

Ben sort of slumped. "Don't hold back with the 'I told you so's or anything."

"And why should I?" I felt entirely justified in giving out at Ben. Because when we'd had a private moment earlier, I'd requested a short visit, instead of a sleepover. But Ben only said blithely, "Kevin'll be fine."

Now, my heart wrenched a bit, thinking of my little boy, homesick and wanting me. "I'm just his mother, how would I know what's best for him? I mean, he'd just found out you're his daddy, and with the unfamiliar flat—"

"Okay, I might have rushed Kevin—"

I picked up the empty wine glasses. "Might have?"

"Okay, I did rush things," Ben admitted. "But it gave you the chance to party with your girlfriends."

"'Party?' So I'm a bad mother?" The glasses tinged as I dropped them into the popcorn bowl. "You've changed your tune already?"

"No!" Ben's jaw clenched. "Do you have to take everything I'm saying and smack me in the face with it?"

"I'm not smacking—"

"Well, if you want to rub it in, it's true. I came at this whole weekend feeling possessive about my kid, and regretting I'd missed a huge chunk of Kevin's life. So, when our first visit fell apart, how do you think it felt?"

My satisfaction shriveled. I was glad Ben loved our son. I mean, wouldn't it be awful for Kevin if he didn't? "I... I can't blame you for being disappointed."

Ben rubbed his fingers in his hair. "With me moving to Galway soon, I wanted to see as much as him as I could."

My contrition, always reliable when I've done wrong, plummeted into shame. "I'd forgotten...about your move." I set down the bowl. "And that Kevin doesn't know about it."

"After tonight's fiasco, maybe he won't mind that I'll be living on the other side of the country." He pressed a thumb and index finger against his eyes. "Oh, hell—I'd better go."

Ben snarling at me over our son was one thing. His hurt was another. I fumbled for his hand and pulled us to the couch. "If you're tired, you're welcome to sleep here tonight. I mean, *here*." I hastily patted the couch cushions. Ben's woebegone expression reminded me so much of Kevin I was actually feeling a bit motherly toward him.

"Only if you think it'll be okay with Kevin." Ben stared down between his knees, looking sadder than ever.

I slung my arm across his shoulders. "Don't take it so hard. You'll have noticed how much better Kevin's stuttering is since he met you."

"Yeah, but tonight, seeing him trying not to cry..."

I squeezed his shoulder. "Kids will cry. And do a million other things you don't expect. You'll learn to roll with it."

"I...uh, how do you do that?"

"Practice." I tried to sound light, but thinking of my hit-and-miss mammy skills brought a bit of a pinch. "Actually, you figure it out as you go, because you don't have any other choice." My mouth trembled. "I'm not saying that to make you feel guilty —it's just the way things are." Realizing how close we were, I let go of Ben and inched away from him.

Funny, how that motherly shoulder clutch had been so, well…friendly, and lacking in sexual tension. Because as soon as I moved away from Ben, the Sexual Tension blindsided me. I sensed that Ben was looking at my mouth, but I had to keep my face averted, or we'd be in a lip-lock. Not appropriate, was it, after such a serious parental discussion? He seized my hand. "You have choices now," he whispered, then he kissed my forehead.

The gesture, so tender and supportive, was my undoing. I gazed at him, all gratitude and warm fuzzies, ready to give into whatever was between us. Until he said, "You have me."

A BUZZER WENT off inside my head: *Reality check, reality check. Nuke the fuzzies.* I stiffened. "I don't think—"

"You do have me," he insisted, and tightened his clasp on me. "We're in this together—raising Kevin."

"But I don't have you!" I jumped up. "Courtney does."

"No, she doesn't."

"She does too!"

"Does not."

"Stop it!" I yelled. "She's not in Ireland, so she doesn't count?"

"That's not what I mean," Ben said, then he gripped my waist and pulled me back down to the couch. "It's over."

My mouth dropped open. "You've split up?"

"That's right," Ben said in a clipped voice.

I waited, then narrowed my eyes at him. "Well…?"

"Well, what?" Ben hedged.

"That's all you've got to say?" Drat. I'd gone back to acting like his mammy. "What I mean is, if there's a chance you'll get back together, Kevin *will* be affected—"

"Not gonna happen," Ben said.

"Oh. Mutual agreement, then?"

"Mutu—uh…yeah. The thing is, our goals weren't the same."

I snorted. "You *are* having me on, aren't you?"

Ben hunched his shoulders. "If you want the ego-killing truth…"

"I do." All right, I'm shameless.

"Turns out there was a Roger involved."

"A Roger," I echoed.

"Yeah—lives right in Seattle, and easily pulls in seven figures. Also involved was a big diamond ring. Very big."

"Ooohh. And here you'd gone out to America to propose and everything."

Ben frowned. "Uh…right. But it's…okay."

"Is it really?" I squeezed his arm.

"I had to face the fact that we just weren't all that compatible," Ben said. "And if I don't know the first thing about raising kids, she knows even less. Kevin deserves better."

I diplomatically refrained from your basic mother-bear response: *You bet your arse he does.* "You should've told me before." Searching Ben's face, I had one of those rare flashes of insight into the Male Psyche. "I suppose you didn't like admitting she broke it off with you."

"Uh…yeah."

Ben's status changed instantly. Previous: Geographically Separated From Girlfriend. Current: Dumped and Dejected.

The former meant hands-off, while the latter—although a sexual hands-off policy was still in place, mind—opened up vistas of good times and friendship. Hadn't I always wanted a man friend, the sort you always encounter in novels? A relationship that involved a teensy amount of sexual tension, so you still felt like a woman, yet you got oodles of manly emotional support.

"That was really sweet of you." I smiled at Ben. "Saying that Kevin deserves better."

"I meant it," Ben said in a croaky voice.

He was clearly overcome by emotion. I put my arm round him again. "You said I have you—well, you have me too. And now that you're free, there's nothing between us."

Ben looked a bit startled. If I hadn't had drink in me, I'd have realized what I was implying. "And nothing between our friendship," I added dreamily, quite taken by this girl/guy pals thing. I conveniently ignored my sizzling nerve endings. "That's really what's best for Kevin. Our staying friends."

JUST FRIENDS...RIIIGHT

*a*s the days passed, my platonic friendship with Ben was going even better than I'd imagined. That our trifling, surface sexual attraction had blossomed into a definite under-current didn't concern me. After all, a bit of a spark was only natural, right?

Because Ben and I were both unattached, weren't we? And we'd certainly had a hot thing going in the past, hadn't we? And what was a bit of attraction, anyway, between true friends?

But why am I asking all sorts of rhetorical questions when I know the answers already?

I'll also confess I toyed with the idea of hooking up with Sam —that it would be healthy to burn off a bit of sexual steam. Which would result in a more "pure" friendship with Ben. But I quickly dismissed it. For one thing, it sounded like a chemistry experiment, and I'd never been a great one for science. Besides, I just didn't want to have sex with Sam.

The thing is, if Ben got the occasional flirty-look on him, it could be put down to him being On The Rebound. Such fellows were prone to unconsciously hit on anyone, even a friend, and were not to be taken seriously. As for me, what girl didn't enjoy a bit of flirting with an entirely presentable man? So we could joke and tease and hug with impunity.

Case in point: our third weekend together, the second at his flat.

"Fixing dinner with someone who doesn't count fat grams or carbs is a hell of a lot more fun than the starvation rations Courtney and I used to rustle up," Ben said, and pulled a carton of cream from the refrigerator for tonight's pudding. "If she found whipped cream on the premises, there'd be hell to pay."

"Don't you know, it's not polite to run down an ex in mixed company," I said primly. Kevin was in the loo, so I could tease as much as I liked. "But if you don't have an egg beater or something for the cream," I added daringly, "I will have to punish you."

Ben produced a hand blender. "Guess I'll miss a spanking tonight."

"And I was so looking forward to it." I giggled.

"There's always a next time." Ben said, grinning, and brandished the small bottle of vanilla we'd bought for the cream. As I poured the cream in a bowl and threw in a couple of spoons of sugar, he looked at me doubtfully. "You're whipping it all? I'm not sure what I'll do with the leftovers."

"Use your imagination," I said before I could stop myself, then gave him a sultry glance as I turned on the blender. Really, I was behaving quite badly, but I hadn't had this much fun with a man since...well, since Ben. "But I forgot, you and Courtney broke up, right?"

"Very funny," Ben said. "But she wouldn't go for whipped cream *on* her any more than *in* her." He ran his finger around the rim of the vanilla bottle, and before I knew what he was about, he dabbed some on my neck.

"Eeek!" I almost lost my grip on the blender. "Vanilla goes in the bowl, not on me."

"Mom used to say it's the best all-natural cologne there is," he said. He turned red, then as Kevin tumbled back into the kitchen, he shoved his hands into his pockets .

I was blushing too—though why the pair of us should get all flustered about a perfectly innocent remark about his mam, when we'd gone a bit over the top with the whipped cream jokes, I'm not sure. But there's something about a man who's sweet about his mother.

We're talking about the sort who cherishes his mother, but doesn't live with her, eat dinner with her every Sunday, or avoid staying over at his girlfriend's because the mother will know he's having sex. Maggie and Deirdre told me about those fellows.

Anyway, as soon as dinner was over, Kevin asked, "What'll we do next, Daddy?"

"How about cards?"

"How about bed?" I countered.

"Sounds like a good idea," Ben said, and winked at me.

"Ha, ha," I said, and blushed again. "For *Kevin*."

"Oh, come on, just a few hands," Ben cajoled, and before I could protest, he rustled up a deck of cards. "How about poker? It's a good educational game. Teaches math skills."

"Really, Ben, he should—"

"And instead of poker chips, I've got a secret weapon." Ben pulled out a sack of foil-wrapped somethings.

"Ooh, gourmet chocolate?" You'd think I hadn't had two servings of pudding—with extra whipped cream, mind—ten minutes ago.

"Yep—brought them back from Seattle last month."

"And raspberry truffle flavor?" I rubbed my hands together. "Kevin, love, your bedtime's just been postponed."

"Yaaay!" Kevin's ear-to-ear grin made my heart lurch. To think, I'd doubted contacting Ben! "Me and Mam'll do anything for chocolate."

"You've come to the right place, kid." Ben gave Kevin a one-armed squeeze, then shuffled and dealt. "It's you and me, against your mom."

As Ben explained the rudiments of the game to Kevin—me pretending to listen attentively—I got a bit choked up, seeing the radiance on my little boy's face. I hid my face behind my cards—until I noticed I had a bloody good hand.

"You do know how to play?" Ben asked.

"Oh...yes." I stared sadly at my cards. "Deirdre and I used to play with our grannies." Sigh.

"Well, crummy hand, then?" Ben asked.

Bigger sigh. "I can't help wondering what'll folk think of us, teaching our son to gamble." Ordinarily, I was the nice sort of mother who let her son win, but when Ben revealed himself to be a reckless card player, wildly betting his and Kevin's chocolates, what can I say? I bluffed shamelessly, and won the hand. And ten more after that.

I glowed in triumph as Ben tossed his cards down next to my admittedly substantial pile of chocolate wrappers—I'd needed the sustenance for clear-headed betting. He scooped up his paltry remaining chocolates and passed them to Kevin. "Guard them well from you-know-who."

"You think I'd steal my own son's chocolates?" I said, indignant. But before I could work up a head of steam, Ben initiated a mock battle with chocolate wrapper weaponry, then hoisted Kevin on his back for a mad gallop around the front room.

Then, as Kevin, Ben and I did the washing up, Ben took a break to steal one of my chocolates, and I had to defend my hard-won winnings with towel-snap. Which of course set off a three way towel-snapping skirmish.

What Ben had in brute strength, I made up for in finesse. And while Kevin's first attempts were a bit flaccid, he showed great promise as a towel warrior. In fact, he managed to snap his daddy in the bum. Daddy pretended to keel over from the force of it. Then ruined the effect by laughing in the middle of his death-throes.

Seeing Kevin's ear-to-ear grin, my heart swelled, like it would burst through my chest. Even the memory of wishing that my father would play with me, but he never did, could dull this bliss. Bringing Ben into our lives had to be the best decision I'd ever made, full stop.

In the interests of full disclosure, I'll admit that I occasionally wondered if I was playing with fire, to allow this sparky man-woman thing. Especially now that our weekends together were a regular thing. But I had the answer to that too. *Naaah.*

WHAT WOULD BRIDGET
(JONES) DO?

eirdre and I sat in Granny's front room in Galway, sorting through a box of jumble from one of Bridie O'Donnell's parish sale safaris. As potential stock for the shop, the box's contents left much to be desired, but as Granny—cycling madly on her exercise bike—pointed out, if you wanted to find diamonds, you had to chip away at masses of useless rock in the bowels of the earth.

"Here's a prospect," Deirdre said. She pulled out a decent-looking copy of *Bridget Jones' Diary* and waved it in the air.

"I'd like..." huff, puff... "...a look at it first," Granny said, slowing down.

"Granny, really," I began, but before I could stop her, Deirdre jumped up and passed the book to Granny, who promptly cracked it open.

Deirdre plopped back on the floor. "Speaking of wild weekends—"

"How would you know?" I interrupted. "You haven't read the book."

"Actually, the last time a copy came through the shop, I

looked at the juicy parts," Deirdre said. "Almost made me want to read the lot. But I was talking about *your* wild weekends."

"There's no such thing," I said. "Anyway, do you mind? My granny's in the room."

"I was talking about you and Ben sleeping on each other's couches—isn't it a bit...weird?"

"Not at all." I quickly dug into the box again, hiding my face. I'd wondered if I'd let last weekend's flirtation get out of hand. I could still feel Ben's touch on my neck with the vanilla, and couldn't help wondering how those fingers would feel on the rest of me. And had to remind myself that Kevin needed a daddy more than I needed a lover. "The sleepovers are no big deal—I think we're quite mature about it."

Deirdre lowered her voice. "I meant, since the pair of you have a...past."

"I heard that, Deirdre." Granny stopped pedaling altogether and turned a page.

Pulling an Austen paperback from the box, I said, "Actually, we're great friends now."

It was true. We e-mailed each other every day from work, then he'd ring Kevin in the evenings. I'd get on the line—only at Ben's request, mind, as I wasn't *really* trying to horn in on my son's relationship—to ostensibly chat about Kevin. But before long we'd be on about work, or what funny things had happened that day.

"What does Sam think of all this?"

Who? I wondered automatically, then caught myself. "He hasn't much to say about it." Sam's name occasionally came up with Ben, but surprisingly, it wasn't that awkward.

One topic that never quite surfaced, however, was what had happened seven years ago. If it was my doing, or Ben's, who knew. But then, it was ancient history and all that. Dismissing Sam, I added, "Ben and I are even planning to take Kevin to see Ben's mammy."

At least, it *seemed* like a lovely idea. I had to give Annie credit, for not hitting Ben with the guilt—and through association, me —that she'd missed the first six years of her only grandson's life. The only problem: I swore I'd never go back to Minnesota. The next time Ben brought up the idea, I'd suggested having Annie visit us here. Since travel was awfully hard on young children.

"All three of you, going to America? You and Ben *have* come a long way since your big row last month." Deirdre pulled out a hot-pink lamp, shaped like a giant seashell. "What do you think, Ash?"

"Hmmm…possibilities. Your mam will love it."

"I meant about your fight."

I pretended to study the seashell lamp with great interest. "That's *so* over. On our weekends, Sunday mornings, I laugh at his bed hair, and he pretends to freak out when he sees me without make-up, which Kevin thinks is hugely funny." I kept last weekend's vampy behavior to myself.

Deirdre put the lamp into the keeper pile. "Good, clean fun, is it?"

Granny chuckled. "Sure, Aislin's a good girl."

Not that good. "Oh, Granny, really—"

"Certainly compared to this Bridget. She's a wild one."

I rolled my eyes at Deirdre. "Here's a nice Austen novel, Granny," I coaxed. "We won't need it at the shop, since we've tons of her already. You haven't read *Pride and Prejudice* in years, have you?"

"Nice try, love, but I'm really keen on Bridget," Granny said, turning a page. "There's no end to the trouble she gets up to."

I pressed my lips together to keep from laughing, and dug back into the box. "Kevin doesn't seem to get homesick, being with Ben all day, as long as I'm nearby at bedtime. Tonight starts the real test, though, with our week's visit at the Lodge."

"I'll perish of boredom, with you out of the shop so long," Deirdre sighed.

"Ah, sure you will." I grinned. "You'll be so busy buying new nail varnish with the extra money you'll earn, you won't even miss me. While I will be slaving away, fixing up Kevin's new bedroom, unpacking his things…" And trying to be on my best behavior.

Deirdre picked up a chipped teacup and grimaced at it. "I guess he'll really be officially settling in with his dad."

I felt a shiver of apprehension. Sharing Kevin on weekends was grand, but Tuesday, Ben and I were meeting with a solicitor. To be truthful, the prospect of being legally committed to Kevin's visits really gave me the willies.

To get my mind off it, I focused on seeing Ben soon, and getting my first good look at Ballydara Lodge. It did not escape my notice that the man I was beginning to fancy far more than was good for me, was also the same fellow who could really muck up my life with my son.

Because once Kevin was ready, I'd be spending my weekends alone.

"You've put that mildewy Dickens in your keeper pile, child," Granny observed.

Not much gets past Granny. I wondered if she realized that I, who should be used to my terminal ambivalence, was driving myself mad. Did I want to be a solo mammy 24/7, or to have a lovely break, provided by my son's lovely father? And did I actually want that lovely father for myself, or was I simply exercising my hibernating-for-seven-years feminine power? And What Would Bridget Do?

A shame there wasn't a sort of internal Stairmaster to help you firm up your flabby selfhood.

Avoiding Granny's keen gaze, I moved the Dickens to my Not Fit For Anything But The Bin pile. "What's with Liz these days? It seems forever since I've talked to her."

"Her last e-mail mentioned she'd lost three more pounds,"

Deirdre said, "though Dan's been giving her grief about her diet. But she said she didn't give a feck what he thought about it."

Liz's marriage appeared to be heading downhill before our very eyes. But not wanting to go there, I steered Deirdre to weighing the relative merits of indulging in wine versus chocolate, and which one we'd give up under duress.

As a knock came at the door, I glanced at my watch. Too early for Ben, but I jumped up anyway.

Deirdre beat me to the door. "That'll be Aunt Bridie to fetch me for tea, and we're not half finished," she said resignedly. "Why she just doesn't ring, I'll never know…" As she swung the door open, her back stiffened. "What are *you* doing here?"

THE DILEMMA

I craned my neck to see our visitor. Sam! Heading for the door, I promptly tripped over my keeper pile. What in Jesus' name was he doing in Galway? I pasted on a sickly smile. "Come in."

Deirdre looked a bit strange. "I've got to run, save Bridie the trip—"

"Don't even *think* about leaving me," I muttered. Could Deirdre have something to do with Sam's presence? I sent her one of those if-looks-could-kill stares—which actually must have had some effect, since she didn't move.

"Well, Sam, you've come a long way," I said with false heartiness. "You remember my granny?"

"Mrs. Moore," he said almost sullenly. Funny, my gran never asking Sam to call her Granny, given her warm reception for Ben. Or kissing him either. His face was only nominally warmer as he nodded at Deirdre.

An uncomfortable silence descended on the cottage. "Everything's all right, isn't it?" I ventured.

"And how would you know, the way you've—" he broke off. "Look, could we go outside or something?"

I've no secrets from Deirdre and Granny, I wanted to say, like in the cheesy dramas on telly. But Sam and I were due for a showdown.

Stepping out to the stoop, I closed the door behind me, Sam practically breathing down my neck. As I collected myself—after all, my thoughts had been on the Ben Carpenter track for weeks—I gave him a once-over. He was sporting not only a different haircut, but a new European-look outfit. Unfortunately, neither suited him.

"This must be important," I said tartly. Sam had come to Galway on my behalf all of twice in over a year.

"I'd say it is," Sam said heatedly. "I haven't seen you for weeks."

Now *you decide you can't live without me?* "I said I'd be busy, that there'd be quite a big adjustment period, with Kevin getting used to his fath—"

"It's one thing to postpone going out, or spending time at my place, but you don't ring me back. And when I call at the shop you're always out. Or maybe you're not out after all—" he stopped.

Because I'm hiding in the back room, I finished for him. *You're not as thick as you look.*

Put on the spot, I had one of those blinding flashes of illumination: the thought of dating Sam, even with no sex—meaning inventing new excuses to keep avoiding it—made me feel... queasy. I'd rather have a platonic thing with Ben, I realized, than have the greatest sex in the world with the man in front of me.

However, I tried to sound fair, since he'd motored all the way to Galway. "It was just weeks ago you said you needed a...a time-out." I'd be bloody damned before I'd repeat the word *hiatus.* "Now that *I* need a break, it's time for you to be understanding too."

"Is it a break you want," Sam said, two spots of color on each cheek, "or to live high on the hog with that Yank?"

"Kevin's dad? Where'd you get an idea like that? Ben's comfortable, but not—"

"Rich? Maybe he doesn't need to be, what with your inheritance—he's probably keen to get a share of it."

My jaw went slack so fast my cheeks hurt. "My *inheritance?* You're hallucinating."

"Don't play dumb," Sam almost snarled. I recoiled in surprise. He *never* gave out at me. "I know all about the money—heard about it weeks ago."

Weeks ago? About the time that Sam got strangely attentive? And heard it from whom?

"That's why you wanted to get back together?" I asked dangerously. "With me and my pots of imaginary cash?"

"Don't lie to me!" His fists were actually clenched. "Deirdre told me the lot—that your dad came into some money, wanted to give it to you."

Deirdre told me. I flung open the door without answering, and stomped back inside the cottage. "Get in here," I hissed at Sam. Then I turned a glare on Deirdre, who was practically cowering against the far wall. "Have you any suspicion why he's come to see me?"

"Well, Ash, I could hazard a gue—"

"Don't give out at Deirdre," Sam interjected. "It's only fair that I know—"

"Ah, shut up, the pair of you." I turned to the only sane person in the room. "Granny, would you know anything about this fairy story—my father getting an inheritance?"

Granny didn't blink. "I do, child. His uncle Barry left him a tidy sum. John wants you to have it."

"Me?" It took me a minute to get my head round the idea. "Barry must've been a real nutter, trusting my father with money," I pointed out. "Maybe his nest egg was a figment of the poor man's imagination?"

But as Granny looked at me steadily, I knew *she* knew what

she was talking about. Holy Jaysus. "Don't tell me," I scoffed, to hide my shock, "my father has already bought this year's Rolex and thought he'd share the bit left over."

"Your father's present lifestyle might surprise you," Granny said.

"What surprises me is how he can muck up his entire life, and still have an endless supply of misguided souls willing to support him."

"Whatever you think, Aislin, John has managed on his own this long," Granny said evenly. "He's not depending on Barry's money."

"But he'll need it for the country club, a new car, his Armani suits," I said bitterly. "Why would he give it away?"

"Because it's the right thing," Sam put in. "Any decent father would do the same."

"Be quiet," I said without looking at him. "Granny?"

"Because he loves you, child, and he wants to make amends," Granny said, her thin fingers clutching the handlebars of her bike. "If you're wondering why I confided in Bridie O'Donnell, I was a bit worried, having a big cheque in the cottage. I knew it wouldn't be easy to tell you."

I tried to make allowances for Granny's age, but failed altogether. "For God's sakes, Granny, you might as well sashayed through the village with a bullhorn, as tell Bridie."

"She'd promised to keep it to herself," Granny said. "And now that you know, I can start persuading you to take it."

"I'll never take anything from him. Ever!"

"All right," Granny said calmly, surprising me. She clambered off the bike, settled into her favorite chair, then opened *Bridget Jones* again.

I glanced at Sam's tense features. Probably on pins and needles, to see if I'd accept the money after all, I thought cynically, before making his next move. But I'd Deirdre to deal with first. "So," I rounded on her, "your aunt couldn't keep her mouth shut, and told you."

"Yes," Deirdre said miserably. "But then, she tells me everything."

"Then you told him." I jerked my head toward Sam. "And gobshite that he is, he discovered he was in love with me after all."

"Apparently," Deirdre said. "But Ash, I only told Sam about the money to rub it in, that you'd taken a fancy to Ben—"

"I do not fancy Ben—we're friends, damn it! And leave him out of it!"

"And I thought," Deirdre went on, undeterred, "serve Sam right for dumping you, the money-grubbing bollocks."

While part of me was enjoying the shock on Sam's face, I didn't know who I was angrier with—Gobshite Sam, now inching toward the door, or Loose Lips Deirdre. Or Granny, come to that, who had the nerve to serenely read about that English madwoman Bridget. And barely hiding her smile.

"Sam," I said suddenly, "go back where you came from. I don't love you, it's—we—are through. You'll want to find someone else to help you bankroll your new car and your fancy clothes. Which by the way," I couldn't help one last dig, "look a shade too gay for a straight guy."

Deirdre hooted, but sobered as I gave her a flinty stare. "As for you," I said as Sam let himself out without another word, "you'd better go back to your granny's. We're officially not speaking."

"But Ash—"

"Out." Although Deirdre and I rarely had even minor rows, I steeled my heart. "Maybe I'll talk to you again when I'm back in Dublin next Monday week. Or not."

Without a word, Deirdre followed Sam out the door. At a loss, I gave Granny a woebegone stare.

"All I've got to say," murmured my grandmother without

looking up, "is that no one denies your father hurt you. But isn't it time to...what's the expression?" She turned a page. "Get over yourself."

I calmly walked to the kitchen table, seated myself, then, as if my head were made of bone china, set it down on my folded arms. And burst into tears.

Granny gave me two minutes of blubbering, then she set *Bridget* down to stroke my hair. "There, now, love. Sam wasn't for you."

"It's not that." I sniffed mightily and willed my tears away. Ben was expected momentarily, to take me to the Lodge, and I wasn't keen for him to see me blotchy-faced and puffy-eyed. "I'm just a bit overwhelmed by...everything," I admitted. I rose to splash cold water on my face.

"Understandable," said Granny. "An unexpected inheritance will do that to you. But should you have taken it out on poor Deirdre?"

I dabbed my eyes with a towel. "But she interfered, went behind my back."

"Only because she cares," Granny said.

Having your granny as your conscience means you can never get away with acting badly. Still, I wasn't ready to forgive Deirdre's perfidy. "Granny," I went to her and took her hand, "Ben isn't to know about the money." It would be too horribly depressing to suspect him of warming up to me, because I was rolling in cash.

"I'm sure it wouldn't affect his feelings for you," Granny said.

"Sorry?" I dropped Granny's hand.

"You heard me, child. And don't think I've no eyes in my head, because I do," Granny said, and put the kettle on.

We'd no sooner made tea than Deirdre actually had the

bloody cheek to show up at the cottage again. I swung the door open and gave her a baleful look. "What?"

Granny had the temerity to smile at the traitor. "Tea for you, love?"

"Sorry, Granny," Deirdre said pleasantly, then returned my glare. "I've come for my box of jumble."

"Fine." I threw the items back in that we'd carefully parceled out into piles. Lifting the box with a slight grunt, I pushed it into Deirdre's arms.

Deirdre balanced the box on one hip, then thrust a crumpled piece of paper at me. "Since we're not talking," she said sarcastically. "But you'll want to know this." Before I could answer, she turned and left.

Too curious not to at least get a look, I straightened the paper and squinted at Deirdre's careless scrawl:

Your dad's check is for...

I blinked as the figure danced before my eyes. "Mother of God!"

"Everything all right, child?" Granny looked concerned.

"Nothing for you to worry about," I said, and flung the paper into the bin. "Ben should be here any minute."

Seething, I took a gulp of tea and burned my tongue. Shite! If my father thought he could buy my forgiveness, I thought righteously, well, too bad. It wasn't for sale.

THE MUDDLE

*B*en turned up a narrow, curving drive bordered with old chestnut trees and yellow woodbine. As Kevin craned his neck behind us for a good look at his new home away from home, I tried on a deep, cleansing breath and decided there's nothing like distracting yourself with picturesque surroundings when you've been hit with two major Life U-Turns:

#1: Broke up with longtime boyfriend. I should be feeling very sorry for myself but having trouble doing so.

#2: Am suddenly rich. Relatively speaking, that is. Problem: no way will I take money.

Both developments only added to my ongoing worry about Liz's marital woes. But I firmly shoved my troubles to the back of my mind as I glimpsed Ben's two-story manor house.

"Oh...my," I breathed. Ballydara Lodge was your average Irish tourist fantasy—sort of an upgraded version of John Wayne's cottage in *The Quiet Man*. And call me shallow, but I loved it. The rambling garden was filled with rhododendrons, with wild fuchsia in midsummer bloom. It was just untidy enough to suit my rather disorganized approach to life, *and* be a lovely playground for Kevin.

When we got inside, I half expected to find Maureen O'Hara poking at a peat fire, but let's face it, the polished wood floors, modern kitchen, and huge windows were quite an improvement over the charms of a Hollywood-ized Irish cottage.

Kevin raced up to his new room as Ben showed me around. I ooohed and aaahed at the appropriate moments, and when he muttered something about only three bedrooms, and the bathroom needed remodeling, I vigorously pooh-poohed it.

"The house is absolutely grand." God knows, it was going to be dreadfully hard to go back to North Dublin and my small flat. Not to mention being surrounded by O'Donnell women, who took up enormous amounts of psychic space.

Then, remembering my fight with Deirdre, I realized it would be horribly hard working with *and* living next door to someone you're no longer speaking to.

So here I was, still upset about Deirdre, and out of the blue Ben said, "I know this sounds crazy, but...what if you and Kevin moved? Out here, I mean."

"Sorry?" Did Ben just say he wanted us to move house? To Galway?

"Well, once I get settled here, the visiting routine will be pretty tough. If you and Kevin lived in Galway, I could see him every weekend, and maybe the middle of the week too."

I was so shocked that I could only think, *and I could see you.* "But...my job..."

"It's a lot to ask." Ben pushed his hands into his trouser pockets. "Especially since you've been great about disrupting your life so I can be with Kevin. And okay, maybe it's too soon. But I got to thinking, the school's close by, your grandma's out here, and Deirdre visits all the time."

Part of me wanted to be annoyed about his presuming I'd

turn my life around on his behalf, but the other part of me felt…
well, rather tender about his desire to be a hands-on dad.

"I think Kevin's adjusting pretty well to being with me, too."
Ben was starting to babble, and I felt rather tender about that
too. "I've got a few contacts here, to help you find a new job."

"But the shop…" I didn't want him thinking I'd no life at all
to give up. "The pay is terrible, and Polly doesn't know the first
thing about managing a business, but she's been good to me.
And my job, well…" It was hard to admit. "It's the only one I've
ever had."

"I'm sure you could find an equally bad job around here."
Ben turned a cajoling grin on me.

"But…there's Liz. I'd feel like I was deserting her."

"She's got her family," Ben said. "And you can visit on the
weekends I have Kevin. So…will you think about it?"

I didn't know what to say—and Ben's proposal was important enough for me to want to say the right thing. Then I realized he hadn't brought up what Sam might have to say about my
moving. I felt too off-balance to mention Sam myself. And my
being unattached too could change the whole chemistry
between Ben and me. Which, after last weekend, could veer
over to the volatile side without a lot of encouragement.

I mumbled something about seeing what Kevin had got up
to, and turned toward the stairs. Then promptly stumbled on
the first step. "Bollocks," I muttered, catching myself.

Ben neatly caught my elbows from behind. "You okay?"

With his touch, I felt a new burbling in the hormonal depart-
ment. "I've this blasted trick ankle," I said, without turning
around. "From dancing. It gives way under me at the most
inconvenient moments."

"I wasn't inconvenienced at all," Ben said, and let go of me.

·   ·   ·

I CURLED up on Ben's lovely new leather couch that night, trying to get into *The 7 Habits of Highly Effective People* I'd found on his bookshelf, but found it heavy going. Possibly due to jumping up every other minute to fetch one of the chocolates I'd stashed in my handbag after last weekend's poker game. And after what just happened, I needed chocolate therapy in the worst way.

"How c-come when Daddy visits us, he sleeps on the c-couch?" Kevin asked, as Ben and I tucked him up a little while ago. "And not in your b-bed with you, like Maggie and Bill?"

Well, it wasn't the most embarrassing question he'd ever asked, though Ben's ears were suddenly an interesting shade of maroon. "Because we're not married," I said with amazing equanimity, if I do say so myself.

"But Ted, on our road, his mammy's not married, and she's b-boyfriends sleeping in her bed all the time."

Poor Nan. Her flat was a regular fella turnstile. "Well, yes," I said, as Ben pulled up a chair for storytime, his lips twitching, "some people who aren't married still sleep in the same bed, but..." I wasn't sure where to go with this. Possibly because where Ben and I were concerned, the idea was looking more and more attractive.

I looked at Ben's bare arms, the dark hair on them perfect—not too hairy—and caught the scent of his aftershave. I was suddenly, terribly conscious of his closeness. Will you get your mind back on your son, I scolded myself. "But with Nan, I'm thinking she hopes one of her fellows might marry her someday."

Kevin looked thoughtful. "If you sleep with Dad, maybe he'll marry you."

Sweet Jesus! I almost squeaked. "But I don't want him to mar —I mean, we're friends, so we've...no plans to get married."

" 'Cos you have a boyfriend already." Kevin nodded wisely, then looked at Ben. "Dad, you won't get c-cross with my mam, like Sam did, 'cause she doesn't let you snuggle in her bed?"

Ben coughed. My cheeks afire, I plumped Kevin's pillow, waiting for Ben's answer. Which didn't come. Because he doesn't want to sleep in my bed anyway?

"But your daddy and I don't want to snuggle, or get married, because we're friends, like we told you," I said to fill the silence. "Now, under the covers."

"But can't friends get married, same as anyone?"

I'd been a mother long enough to know kids picked up mixed signals better than a sophisticated telecommunications system. Kevin had obviously sensed my conflicted attitude toward Ben—be distant/be friends/be open to cheap sex à la Nan. So if I was sincere about trying to be a good mammy, it was time to clear up the confusion.

"Sure they can, but they usually don't," I said, my voice strangled, and sped out of the room.

So here I was, lolling on Ben's couch, in no fit state for major decision-making. Especially with my life-altering muddles to solve: money and moving. I sighed, and retrieved two more chocolates to help me focus.

The problem was, when I managed to stop thinking of Ben, all I could see was the enormous sum Deirdre had written, flashing like neon in front of my eyes. I abandoned *The 7 Habits* altogether, unwrapped the second chocolate, then wrapped it back up, suddenly queasy.

What to do about the Check?

There was an ironic, almost bizarre thing about me and money, particularly recently. Needing more money for Kevin's speech therapy, I'd contacted Ben. If I'd waited just a few weeks, and was willing to accept my father's gift, I would've have had all the funds necessary. But because of Ben, Kevin's need for therapy had dramatically declined, therefore saving money all round for everyone.

Confused yet? So then, the situation was still ironic: I didn't need my father's money, because Ben was turning out to be a grand friend who would also pay child support. Although how one managed the friend issue and the child support—not to mention the sexual attraction to said friend—without mucking everything up was as yet undetermined...

I concluded this was no time to think about The Check.

Which only left Sam. Since being friends with Ben beat sex with Sam any day, I didn't dare wreck that friendship, despite the delicious flare of warmth in my...well, all over, really, being close to Ben.

Which of course incited memories of the pair of us snogging like mad. I tore the sweet wrapper off again and in my agitation, practically swallowed the chocolate whole. Way back, I hadn't realized how patient Ben had been with me. If he *had* rushed me, we could have gotten to the Main Event, as it were, a lot sooner. And maybe I would've turned out to be better at the whole sex business.

But just because I wasn't good at it, didn't mean I wouldn't miss parts of it. Like the snuggle afterward. Having a man's arm about you, knowing that even if it was just for a moment, he was yours, utterly, was certainly something you wouldn't find in bed by yourself...

So...what if. What if I decided to live in Galway? See Ben a lot? Say, several times a week? When the sexual attraction seemed to rise exponentially every time I saw him? And here I was, already missing the sex I wasn't getting, and hadn't really liked.

If that's not muddled, I don't know what was.

THE CHILDBIRTH STORY

*A*fter running upstairs to get ready for bed, I was back on Ben's couch. Dressed in my unsexiest sleepwear, a burqua-like cotton affair, I propped my feet on the coffee table, trying to give *The 7 Habits* another go. Thinking strategically, I had a blanket, sheet and pillow laid out next to me, in case Kevin got up for the loo/drink of water/more embarrassing questions. So he'd have no doubts where his mother was sleeping tonight.

"Kevin's finally asleep."

I looked up from my book. Ben's face still looked a bit flushed—rather endearing, I thought. But I reminded myself of my new mission: tamping down my attraction. "You've discovered instant fatherhood is no walk in the park?"

"Yeah." Ben plopped on the couch, a safe distance away. "So...how do you like the book?"

"Twenty pages in, and I'm still not effective." I tossed the book aside. "But then, I'd already concluded I'm not and never will be."

"Come on." Ben crossed his hands on his stomach. "You're effective at being a mom."

"You think so?" I asked. "Kids Kevin's age like to think their parents have all the answers." My Madonna-like—as in the saint, not the celebrity—serenity surprised me. "We might as well keep the fantasy going as long as we can."

"I liked our united front just now," Ben said. "In fact, I'm going to make it clear ours is a strictly non-adversarial relationship, when we see the lawyer."

I winced. I'd forgotten about the bloody lawyer. "Oh...right."

Ben shifted to face me. "Aislin, we're only settling the visits and the child support."

Which reminded me of my father's check. "What if I decided I don't need the child sup—"

"You're going to get it, regardless," he said firmly. "Our son's going to have a normal life."

"He's had a normal life," I said defensively, "just not with a lot of money."

"That came out wrong," Ben said. "But I don't intend to let you and Kevin—"

"I know, I know, you want to do the decent thing," I almost snapped. Then I felt terrible, for taking my conflicted feelings about my father and his money out on Ben. I managed an apologetic smile. "Really, I'll be glad of a bit of financial help for Kevin. Nan, a neighbor down the road, hasn't got a euro from her kids' daddies."

Ben's gaze turned intense. "I'm glad *my* kid's mom never went that route—shacking up with guys. But I'm sure you had...offers."

The suddenly personal turn of the conversation took me aback. "Not exactly," I muttered. "In fact, not one."

"You?" The surprise in Ben's voice was, I confess, highly gratifying.

"Single moms don't exactly have the freedom to go trolling after fellows," I explained. "Add the complication of finding one who's keen on kids—well, Sam wasn't. I mean, isn't."

"Oh," Ben said in a neutral tone. I wondered if I'd been too confiding. Then he stretched his arm along the top of the sofa. "You can tell me to mind my own business, but us being friends and all—what about the...guys before Sam?"

I swallowed hard. "There weren't any."

Ben released a whoosh of air. "You're kidding, right?"

I shook my head.

"You mean, all this time, you've had one boyfriend?" His eyes sparkled.

"Boring, isn't it?" I stretched my legs, still modestly covered by the hideous nightshirt. "Only two fellows my whole life, and you and I being a..." A what? Had we reached the point where our past history wasn't such a loaded subject?

"Youthful indiscretion?" Ben laughed, but I saw the tension in his shoulders.

I'd always thought of our encounter as My Terrible Mistake, but I couldn't be that tactless to Ben. "Maybe one of those 'time out of time' things," I ventured. "Or ships that pass, et cetera."

Ben seemed to relax a bit, then he leaned forward, resting his forearms on his knees. "I feel pretty rotten I wasn't... there for you. When you had Kevin."

I could feel a blush start on my face, then zooming through my whole body. So... what if Ben had accompanied me into the delivery room? The fellows on telly and in films always managed—after the requisite comic mishaps—to help deliver their babies with great aplomb. But something told me that Ben —or any other dad—would have likely run screaming out of hospital.

So in case Ben had some romantic notion of childbirth being little more than an aerobic exercise on your back with grunting, I decided friends don't let friends stay ignorant. "You'll be glad you missed it. Kevin's birth was quite...difficult."

Ben didn't look at me, only hunched his shoulders. "How's that?"

"If you want to gory details…"

"Sure. Bring 'em on," Ben said, but now his head was almost between his knees.

"Don't say I didn't warn you. Breech birth, twenty-two hour labor, and forceps delivery," I said relentlessly. "Stitches you wouldn't believe, and I lost so much blood the doctor thought I'd need a transfusion—shall I go on?"

Ben had turned a pale green. But now that I'd started, he could bloody well hear the lot. "Let's see, a week in hospital with a catheter and a fever, I couldn't breastfeed, and to compound the misery, after we went home to my parents', Kevin had projectile vomiting all night long. For weeks."

"Uhhh," emanated from Ben's direction. "Is projectile vomiting sort of what it sounds like?"

"It's exactly what it sounds like," I said. "So, a boyfriend was my last priority." Especially since sex didn't so much as cross my mind for the next year. Or two. "Are you sorry you asked?"

Ben straightened up so fast I thought he'd snap his back. "I needed to hear this," he said fiercely. "That I'd basically left you on your own."

Really, I hadn't intended to give him a guilt complex. "Actually my family helped—Granny, with the birth, and my mother with, well…"

Scratch Mother. I couldn't say, *she wasn't the sort to help deliver babies. Though she could manage a five-minute cuddle—that is, before cocktail hour.*

"Your dad?" Ben's voice had gone all quiet.

I normally didn't let bitterness get the better of me, but right now, *everything* was getting the better of me. "My father's idea of help was to hire a very overbearing nanny. Jaysus—like I wasn't qualified to take care of my own child."

"Maybe he was trying to be a good guy, thought it was the right thing—"

"He's *not* a good guy, and he knows *nothing* about the right thing," I said between my teeth. "And I don't want to talk about him."

Ben frowned. We both had to be thinking the same thing. *If you didn't want to talk about him, why'd you say anything?*

I didn't know, only that sometimes, when you open the floodgates, you get a lot more water than you planned. So, bringing up my father set off a trickle of hurt, that turned into a torrent. The same way his bloody check reminded me of the way he'd taken over my life. "I took Kevin," I sniffed, "and came back home. I didn't want some nanny telling me how I was doing everything wrong."

Ben scooted closer and touched my arm. "I'm sure you didn't..."

To my disgust, I started to cry. "I w-wanted to be a good mother," I sobbed, "not blithely hand my child over to someone else to look after, like my parents did me."

"Come here." Ben put his arm round me and pulled me close. I didn't—couldn't—resist. "God, I've been a jerk. You've been through hell, all because of me."

"No more than a lot of m-mammys," I choked, then thought of my gory childbirth again. I bawled harder.

"Hey, come on," Ben said helplessly. "You *are* a great mom, and from now on, I'm going to be there for you and Kevin."

Still, I couldn't stop crying.

Ben patted my shoulder. "Mom always said, the more you cry, the less you pee."

I tried to laugh, because by now I should be dry as the Sahara. But it only came out as another sob. "I'm sorry," I wept, "really, I don't know what's the matter with me..."

Ben's arm tightened. "Maybe it's all the curve balls coming at you lately. Me showing up in Ireland, Kevin getting a dad...and all that."

I wondered if he meant asking us to move to Galway. I sniffed, taking one of those spasmodic, air-sucking breaths that are comical when someone else does it, but feels really pathetic when it's you. With all this blubbering, I'd really mucked up my potential as Ben's mature woman friend. "I don't want you thinking my crying is a cheap ploy for sympathy."

"Sympathy for what?"

"Ah, you know." I swiped my sleeve under my nose. "'Poor girl,' Polly O'Donnell would say. 'Poor single mam.' She's always acted like it's a fate worse than death."

"It...uh, meant a lot to me," and Ben patted my shoulder, "you telling me all this."

Since I'd actually let on I'd stitches on my bum, what harm could there be, sharing one more confidence? After all the gruesome childbirth stuff, there was no way Ben could escape being my friend now—and there'd be no more secrets between us.

Except for the one Ben would never hear.

"There's something else you should know." I tucked my head under Ben's chin, to avoid his eyes. "I split with Sam today. For good."

FULL DISCLOSURE

*B*en loosened his arm immediately. "I'm sure the break-up was hard." Only I'd have preferred him to say, *It's what I've been waiting for*, with passion vibrating through his manly voice. Then sweeping me into his embrace. "Can't blame you for being upset."

Ben was clearly turning on the Just Friends spigot. So I shifted away from him to let him know I'd got the message. "Sam showed up at Granny's unexpectedly today, and I just knew it was over." I knew men didn't really like deconstructing relationships, but too bad. If Ben was going to be my friend, he could bloody well put up with it. "God knows why I'm crying. I didn't really love him—I basically discovered he...wasn't the man I thought he was."

"He wasn't the man I thought he was either, with those girly-looking shoes he was wearing the night I met him," Ben joked.

I relaxed. Making fun of the guy you'd the guts to finally dump will do that to a girl. "If we're talking manliness, there's the manicure-metrosexual issue." Then my witticisms got away from me. "I never even had good se—" *God help us, tell me I didn't really say that...*

"Good sex with him?"

I *had* said it. "Just ignore me, I'm an eejit, don't know what I'm saying..."

"Uh, don't worry about it." Ben's voice sounded far away. No wonder, since I tried to pretend I'd just left the room. No, make that left County Galway entirely. "A lot of people don't have great sex," he added.

"Sure, but no orgasms either?" I blurted. Ben's whole body jerked. "Omigod!" I clapped my hands over my mouth, my spine prickling with horror. What in the feck had gotten into me? "Sorry, sorry—must be rogue hormones or something—I didn't mean to say that—"

"No problem," Ben cleared his throat. "To be honest, uh, sex with Courtney was...uh, nothing to write home about either."

My mortification eased a bit, and I lowered my hands. "How...so?"

"You really want to hear this?"

God yes, like I've never wanted anything in my whole life. "If you want to tell me," I said in my best gal-friend voice. "It's only fair, since I told you about Kevin's birth." There's nothing like hearing someone else's sexual humiliations to help you forget your own.

"Well, here goes." Ben leaned back, and let his arm sort of fall onto my shoulders. Obviously, he'd lost track of it. "I don't want to put all the blame on Courtney, but she preferred quickies. Because she liked to save her energy for exercise."

"Very dedicated of her," I said.

"And she was so big on her workouts, she was often too tired for sex."

This was even better than I'd hoped.

"And if one of us worked late, which was a lot of nights, there was no sex either, so she could be sharp for work in the morning."

"I hate to point this out," I said, rather enjoying myself, "But it rather *does* sound like Courtney's fault."

Ben laughed ruefully. "Obviously, we put so much energy into other things we didn't save any for each other." He grinned down at me, and suddenly I felt more comfortable talking to him than anyone in my whole life. "But back to you...you're telling me you didn't experience the, uh... ultimate?"

I can only blame my candor on first telling Ben about the stitches on my bum. Once you've confessed that, you can talk about anything. "Well, no," I said. "Not even close."

Ben didn't say anything, but his hand dangled over my upper arm, his fingers lightly brushing my bulky nightshirt.

To fill the silence, I said, "It's no wonder I'm falling apart, then? Breaking up with Sam, I haven't any prospect of even bad sex now." I had to laugh. "That's what you get for being my friend—I've never told my no-orgasm secret to anyone."

Ben's fingers stilled. He suddenly stared at me, like he'd never seen me before. Probably because he was grossed out, with my pink eyes and swollen nose, and wearing a fecking tent... "Actually," he finally said, his voice low, "I think you're the sexiest woman I've ever met."

Whoever made the first move, I don't know, but suddenly we were snogging, open-mouthed, lip-sucking, you name it, *kissing*. And in a tangle of arms and legs we stretched out on the couch.

YOU MAKE ME FEEL (LIKE A
NATURAL WOMAN)

*B*en stroked me on top of my nightshirt, then beneath, his thumbs sliding over my knickers, while he murmured sweet and über-sexy nothings against my mouth.

I ran my hands under his shirt too, stroking his bare chest, and before I knew it, I was rubbing his jeans. His...fly, to be precise. I tensed when Ben slid his fingers under my knickers, though—a rather desperate thigh clench, if you must know. But he must've sensed my hesitation—we were *that* attuned, so In Perfect Sexual Synch with each other—and moved his hand away to caress the insides of my thighs. Which made my Inner Natural Woman wish he'd get back under my knickers.

So when Ben pulled up my nightshirt to get to my bare skin, I wiggled cooperatively to help him. He kissed my breasts, his mouth lingering everywhere I wanted it, then he trailed his lips over my ribcage, down my tummy, past my navel, and onto forbidden territory.

I was in the red-hot zone by now. I pulled Ben closer, but somehow, "But I can't..." came out.

"You can, because I'm going to make you feel so good..." He

slid his hands under my bum, lifting me, and suddenly his mouth was *there*, I mean, right *there*, deliciously warm even through my knickers, and a thrill shot through me, a shivery, shimmering bolt of delight.

Woozy and lust-addled, I knew I was just seconds away from, you know, *It!* I would finally discover what all the fuss was about! Only I got so turned on I shifted away to lower Ben's fly and tear at my knickers. Ben fumbled with something in his pocket, but I was so mindless with wanting his mouth and hands all over me, I didn't care. As he slid inside me, I could feel wild sparks pulsating all over me, rising from my toes to my thighs. The sensations spiraled higher and higher, and I could feel a cry in my throat, ready to burst out. As Ben groaned, then collapsed on top of me, still hard, I knew *It* could still happen. I pulled him closer...

THEN I REMEMBERED KEVIN UPSTAIRS.

What if he heard us? What if my little boy came down and *saw* the pair of us half-naked and writhing together? Before I knew it, some weird Conscience/Mother-Guilt/Sex-Hating Mutant suddenly took control of me. And it...well, *I* shocked myself.

I pushed at Ben's shoulders. "Let me up."

He nuzzled my neck, then moved inside me. "I want to take care of you first."

"No." Ben and me, sex, had to be just *wrong*. When he pressed his body closer, I grabbed his hips, pushing him away. "No!" Then, though I've no idea where I got the strength, I somehow jackknifed Ben straight off me.

He clutched my thighs instinctively, and I shoved at him again. He fell off the couch, smacking his head and elbow into the coffee table before he hit the floor.

"Shit!" He rubbed his head, looking bewildered. "What happened? Did I hurt you?"

"No." *And I don't know what happened.* Wanting to cry again, I yanked my nightshirt down. Jaysus, I really was a wreck. Here I'd had it off with the man who was my friend. Confidant. Co-parent. Then pushed him away like he was a one-night stand.

"What'd I do?" Ben sort of staggered to his feet, pulling up his jeans. "I thought you wanted it as much as I did."

To ward off tears, I forced a casual tone. "Sure it was a lovely shag, but now it's done—"

"A shag?" His eyes suddenly blazed. "That's all you wanted?"

I remembered the condom he'd conveniently had in his pocket. He'd probably brought it back from Courtney's place. "Maybe that's all *you* wanted. You came prepared for it."

"I wanted to *make love* to you. That's why I went to Seattle to break up with Courtney."

To break up with Courtney? For me? I was ready to say something conciliatory, then he said, "But I guess after your break-up, you were just in the mood for a little casual, rebound sex." He jerked his fly closed.

Sam. I'd forgotten about him. What a slutty thing to do, break up with one guy, and hours later, sleep with another. And while I was at it, completely ruin the closeness Ben and I had shared. And I'd no clue how to make this right.

"Have you got some grudge you're holding against me? Maybe you're still mad about our fight at your flat?" Ben fisted his big hands. "Or that I got you pregnant in the first place?"

I could only shake my head. I was so confused, so wretched I couldn't look at him anymore. In fact, I pretty well checked out of the situation entirely.

Look, I know I rushed you... I thought he said, and I think I came up with some shite like, *It doesn't matter...* Despite my misery, I told myself, *Just reach for him, he's Kevin's dad, just kiss him and make it better.* Instead, all I could do was pretend I wasn't really here. I turned away, and curled myself into a ball, tucking my knees inside my shirt. As his silent, accusing stare bore into my back, and I roused myself enough to whisper, "I'm awfully sorry." In my side vision I saw Ben turn on his heel.

"So am I," he said, and headed for the stairs. He took them three at a time.

THE AFTERMATH

*A*fter a sleepless night, I faced the morning with a fresh vow: grow up and get with the program. I was part of this visit so Kevin could get to know his dad. Not so I could have my ego—as well as my secret parts—massaged by a good-looking fellow. I couldn't muck everything up by putting our child on the sidelines.

Left to my own devices, I moped round the Lodge, making sure to do it in the places Ben wasn't. Not at all difficult, because he was avoiding me as studiously as I was him. But when the three of us turned up in the kitchen—and Ben and I couldn't dash away from each other because of Kevin—he acted like I wasn't there. After several horrible minutes, he picked up his coffee mug and downed the contents like he was in a pint-chugging contest, then said to Kevin, "How about a trip to the store?"

Kevin gave Ben an uncertain look—you'll recall my previous observation about kids picking up signals—and asked, "Can we buy Mam a Cadbury's?"

"You betcha, buddy." Ben grinned, which seemed genuine, and ruffled his hair.

"That'd be grand," I said, faking a brilliant smile that nobody noticed. As Ben grabbed his car keys, the thought of joining Granny for Mass suddenly held the appeal of a holiday in the Bahamas. But I'd sooner have been boiled in oil than ask Ben for a ride.

To make matters worse, I was meant to stay here at the Lodge all week. How would I endure Ben's and my alternating Silent Treatment/Putting On A Good Face for Kevin?

Not that I could really blame Ben. I hadn't meant to kiss him, then have it off with him, and fatally muck up our friendship. *And* our parental relationship. And I certainly hadn't meant to shove him away and make him crack his head on the table. And I still felt so muddled about the sex thing I couldn't quite remember how or even *if* I'd explained myself. So I had that to look forward to.

And no Deirdre to help me figure it out. Clearly, time for a list.

Option #1: Swallow oversized lump of pride and ring the O'Donnell's. Then perform penitence on bended knee to Deirdre, apologize, and hope for the best.

Problem: Even if Deirdre had managed to escape going to Mass herself, I was afraid that if she forgave me, I'd blurt out that Ben's and my friendship was now deader than the proverbial doornail. Then I'd have to explain our misbegotten shag. No can do.

Option #2: Ring Liz. By what she'd dropped about her marriage, Liz might understand about relationships gone awry.

Problem: I couldn't dish to her about Ben. On the friends scale, of say, between one and ten, Liz and Ben would be an eight, or at least a good solid seven, given the family ties and length of the friendship. While Liz and I were probably more like a five. I suddenly felt very friendless. And alone.

Option #3: Go for time-honored standby—the refrigerator. I'd seen half a dozen potatoes, and a slice of ham, so I could

SUSAN COLLEEN BROWNE

cobble together a halfway decent Sunday dinner, *and* make a few points with Kevin.

Problem: I risked Ben thinking I was trying to play wifey, despite my rather underwhelming performance on the couch last night.

Option #4: Take bath. To help me relax.

Problem: How can I ever relax again? After succumbing to Natural Woman urges…

I squeaked aloud and slammed the fridge shut. *Oh, just bloody pull yourself together! Peel the damn potatoes, draw the bathwater while the pot comes to boil, then let the lot simmer while you hide out in the bath.*

The potatoes now on the stove, I scooted up to the bathroom, assessing the "amenities" with a jaundiced eye. The tub was a claw-footed, old-fashioned affair, miles bigger than mine in Dublin. I had a vivid, if fleeting, fantasy of a certain man in it with me, then shoved the vision away as ruthlessly as I'd done to Ben last night.

This being his bathroom, though, I couldn't help thinking a person with any pretensions to modesty would feel a bit… exposed here. There was only an ancient clear-ish plastic shower curtain suspended from a ceiling ring between the bather and the outside world. I looked closer and wrinkled my nose. The undersized curtain was dotted with mildew too. Question: don't men notice these things? If I'd still been friends with Ben, I could have marched him to the village and stood over him until he bought a new one, but now, I was stuck with it. And this was no time to be a prima donna. I turned on the taps.

The bath was almost full when I heard the phone. Deirdre and salvation? I turned the water down to a trickle, and raced downstairs, but by the time I reached for the phone, Ben's answering machine had kicked on.

And it wasn't Deirdre.

THE MESSAGE

"*I*'m calling for Aislin," an ultra-decisive voice said. A seldom heard one, but familiar all the same. My sister Grace.

I tried to make myself pick up, but I could only stand there, frozen.

"I got this number from our grandmother—I understand your cell wasn't working. Dad's been out of the hospital for over a week now. He hasn't complained about not hearing from you, but inquiring minds, including mine, would like to know why you haven't been in touch. It's none of my affair if you have… issues. But it seems the least you could do. I mean, Dad could have died from this thing."

This thing? What thing? Grace left a number to call, but I could only stare at the blinking red dot on the machine. Was my father in hospital what Granny had been trying to tell me, aside from the money? Only she'd put it, "under the weather?"

With shaking hands, I deleted the message, so Ben wouldn't hear it. And wouldn't start wondering just how dysfunctional my family relationships were.

For instance, that I'd never really gotten to know Grace, my only sibling. And that back when I was little, whatever childish longing I had for my elegant teenage sister had faded away once I moved in with Granny.

Then there was my mother. Her drinking meant I didn't really want to talk to her, then my turning up pregnant meant she didn't really want to talk to me. When she'd sobered up and turned her life around, our habit of not talking didn't change much.

And my father? Let's just say it's easier to adore the idea of a father, and a long-distance one at that, rather than the actual flesh-and-blood fellow who turned human frailties into an art form. Still, I could hear Grace again: *Dad could have died from this thing.* But did my father really deserve to be ignored, cut out of my life, *and* completely cut off from Kevin?

Cut out, cut off... "The fecking bath!" I stumbled up to the bathroom, and got to the taps just in time. Staring at the steaming tub, I was almost too dispirited to bother. But I could hardly waste all that hot water. So I pulled off my clothes, my arms and legs as heavy as lead, and slid into the tub.

What was I meant to do now? And exactly *who* was I meant to be? Besides a rotten shag, a distant sister, a disappointing daughter, an inadequate mother... Resenting my father for years had defined me, and now I was like a shell, empty inside, with nothing holding me together.

Dad could have died from this thing.

My sister's voice still haunting me, I lay, limp, in the hot water for what seemed like hours. And with nothing to read, since I'd forgotten to bring up the *7 Habits*. Not that I could have made head nor tail of it anyway, in my present funk.

I roused myself sufficiently to wash, and as I finished, the bar of soap slipped off the tub edge into the water. Instead of fishing it out, I pulled the plug, and lay in the still-warm water while it drained. But whatever dubious enjoyment there was to be had from my last few moments of peace was overcome by daughterly angst.

By shunning my father all these years, had I really thought I was being independent? I recalled the news stories in the months following his indictment: *Charges dropped against Rep. Moore.* Soon after, *Moore resigns from Congress*, with a subhead, *Now cleared, plans to adopt child.* And finally, *Rep. Moore and wife to divorce...* Some journalist had missed a wonderful opportunity to do an epilogue of my father's public life: *Adoption falls through; former congressman's ex-wife enters rehab clinic.*

Maybe I'd rejected him to pay him back for hurting me. Which made me the worst sort of self-delusional gobshite, with too much pride to forgive and forget. So had I not just hurt darling Granny's feelings, but possibly cheated my son out of a grandparent?

And worse, a father? Somehow, everything circled back to Ben. My chin wobbled, and my eyes filled with tears, but I dashed them away. I could *not* turn into a paralyzed wreck, when I'd so many decisions to make. Though I could forget the moving house dilemma. I couldn't imagine Ben wanting me to live in the district now—or even the entire West of Ireland.

It was almost a relief when a rumbling sounded downstairs. The shoppers had returned. And I didn't even care if they'd remembered to buy chocolate. Meaning I was in a very bad way indeed.

There was a rat-tat-tat of footsteps, then Kevin burst into the bathroom. "Mam! The pot's boiling over! Daddy's still out at the car, and water's spittin' all over the place!"

"Jaysus!" I leaped up, and promptly slipped on the bar of soap I'd left in the tub. I grabbed the shower curtain to catch my fall, but the bloody thing tore out of its rings. "Eeeek!"

I crashed back into the water in a stunningly graceless reverse-belly flop, then my ankle turned under me as bathwater sloshed all over the floor. "Shite, shite!"

As my entire foot flamed, Ben came in the house, but I'd offended him horribly. *And Dad could have died from this thing.* Suddenly I couldn't bear it, couldn't bear anything. I erupted into frantic sobs.

"Mammy, why you crying?"

"Oh, God," I wept. "I'm the worst bitch, I mean, witch, in the world." *And a terrible mother who shags a friend then swears in front of her child.* "This is just what I get," I sobbed. "I'm a fecking disaster area." I sobbed. "If I'd only cracked my head—"

"You hurt your head?"

"—And knocked myself out, I could at least forget my problems for a bit!"

"Mammy, is it bad?"

As Kevin's anxiety finally registered, I clutched the shower curtain to my breasts, gesturing wildly. "Go downstairs, tell Daddy to turn off the stove!"

He flew out the door. "Daddy," he yelled. "Mammy's knocked up bad!"

The warning was only seven years late. If only I hadn't been crying so hard, I would've fallen down laughing. Although I'd still be trapped naked in the bathtub.

Seconds later, Ben strode into the steamy room, Kevin trotting behind. "Should we ring Granny?"

I flapped a hand at them. "Get out of here!" The last of the water slurped down the drain, and with it, my modesty—the mildewy curtain was the only thing between my naked body and Ben. I pulled my knees to my breasts, in a vain attempt at strategic concealment, and cried harder.

"You're injured?" Ben knelt at the tub, and gently tried to pry the shower curtain from my iron-fisted hold. "Where?"

"Oh, just go away!" Mortified beyond belief, I pushed at him with one hand, tightening my hold on the curtain with the other. "I've sprained my blasted bloody ankle!" I blubbered, as my ankle *and* my heart throbbed. "I won't be able to walk, and the kitchen's a bloody mess, and..." *And everyone bloody hates me and I deserve it...* I couldn't stop crying.

"The stove's taken care of. Come on, let's get you out of here." Ben reached for me.

"Leave me alone!" Without looking at him, I was amazingly on target as I slapped at his hands.

"Look, I...will you just stop crying, for God's sake, so we can get a look at that ankle?"

"I won't stop crying!"

"Aislin, if you'll just..."

"No!" I sensed Ben's exasperation growing. Too bloody bad. "I'll cry if I like—"

"It's not going to get any better with you sitting here—"

"—How I like, and when I like, and if you think—"

"Shut-up!"

I broke off mid-sob and stared at him. "What'd you say?"

"You heard me. Just shut up."

Kevin piped in, "Should we ring the doctor?"

Ben shook his head, his eyes boring into mine. "Son, you go on downstairs now."

As if I'd let him stay here with me alone, *and* naked? "The pair of you, just g-get out of here!" I hiccoughed.

"What's the matter, Mam? Dad's tryin' to help."

"I'm handling it, son," Ben said in a new, Take No Prisoners dad's voice. How he'd acquired it so fast I'd no idea. "Go downstairs."

Kevin went, and I sat frozen, until Ben tried to move the curtain. "No, wait!" I made a last-ditch effort to push his hands away. "Don't touch me!"

"If you know what's good for you, you'll be quiet."

I couldn't believe he was ordering me around like this. "You've a nerve—"

"We've got to see if you need an X-ray." He once again had

the bloody cheek to ignore my flailing hands and pulled the curtain from my feet.

I gave him the dirtiest of dirty looks. "I can fecking examine at my own ankle—I've had first aid training!"

As I groped round my ankle, Ben got up and fetched an oversized bath towel from the rack. "I don't care if you're a goddamned orthopedic surgeon," he said with maddening calm. "But since I don't see any bones sticking out, we can probably delay going to the emergency room."

"I'm *not* going to hospital," I said hotly. "I know what a sprained ankle feels like, and this is sprained! And I don't need you to play doctor either!"

"And I was so looking forward to it," Ben jibed, then shook the towel out and handed it to me. "Just keep in mind that if you want to get out of this bathtub, it's me, or nobody."

I'd barely time to fasten the towel round me, as he ruthlessly yanked on the curtain and slid it away from me beneath the towel. He wrapped one arm around my back and another beneath my thighs, and hauled me out of the tub.

Seeing the sweat beading his face, I stopped wriggling and glowered at him. Jaysus, if being heaved from the tub like a sack of cement wasn't bad enough, if he dropped me I'd wind up sprawled naked on the floor.

As my bare thighs slipped against his forearm, I couldn't believe this was happening to me. It was somewhere between the most humiliating moment of my life, and the sexiest interlude I'd ever experienced. That is, if we'd been alone in the house and I could forget I'd already ruined things with Ben. And if my fecking ankle didn't feel like a hot iron was stabbing it.

And if Ben was swashbuckling me down the hall to his bedroom, like heroes did in films. In real life, though, guys staggered a bit. Mr. Masterful gasped audibly as he shifted my weight, then once in his room, he dropped me onto his bed so abruptly my teeth rattled.

As I grabbed at the towel, to keep all the critical bits covered up, I saw my ankle was turning an ominous red—then caught Ben glancing at my thighs.

Oh. Boy. I could actually take control of the situation. Brushing my knuckles under my nose, I looked at him resentfully. "Okay, you've had your bit of fun," I said, despite the invisible knife in my foot. "I have to get dressed."

"So we'll get you dressed. Then we'll take care of the ankle."

"*I'll* get me dressed," I correctly loftily. "Then *I'll* take care of my ankle."

Ben lifted one Sean Connery-ish eyebrow. "With what?"

"Well," and my loftiness took a bit of a nosedive, "my clean clothes are in the chest you cleared out for us, in Kevin's room."

"I'm not going to rifle through your stuff." He rummaged through his own drawers, pulled out a shirt and tossed it in my direction, then presented his back to me. "I won't look."

"It's a bit late for you to pretend to be a gentleman now." I groused just for the hell of it, now that the immediate crisis seemed to be over. Once I'd struggled into the shirt, I slid the towel off beneath it and draped it over my thighs, then tried to rotate my ankle. "Ehhh!"

Ben turned around. "Hurts?" He did look sympathetic, to his credit.

"I think I..." It was hard to ask, after my ridiculous tears/protests/brattiness just now, but there I was. Stuck. "Might I have an icepack?"

"Good idea," Ben said, and sped out the door.

Mr. Masterful had just morphed into Mr. Looking For Any Excuse To Leave.

Good. Because I'm ecstatic *to have you out of my hair.* Then I realized arguing with Ben had taken my mind off my father. Suddenly I wanted Ben back, so we could fight some more, and I could obliterate Grace's echo: *Dad could have died from this thing.*

THE APOLOGY

*A*fter an eternity—though a quick peek at the bedside
clock indicated less than eight minutes—Kevin came
in. "Here's the ice Daddy got for you."

"Very nice of him, I'm sure," I managed. If there was one rule
I'd stick to—despite the provocation—it was no badmouthing
your child's father. Kevin helped arrange the ice-filled towel
around the swelling, kissed my cheek with his baby soft lips—
making me feel more of an inadequate mother than usual—then
promptly escaped. To more entertaining company, naturally.
And I was alone again with my thoughts, none of them
welcome.

My throbbing ankle exacerbated the conflicts swirling
endlessly round my brain. Before long, a pair of clichéd alter
egos, Good Person/Angel and Cowardly Person/Devil, had
materialized on either side of me, and settled into easy chairs.
Sort of like the relatives you can't stand who come to visit every
Sunday and infiltrate your front room like viruses.

Good Person: You've got to go see him. Any Normal
Daughter would. Don't forget, he could have *died*.

Cowardly Person: But I can't afford it.

GP: Yes, you can. You've that fat check waiting for you at Granny's.

CP: But I haven't decided to take it.

GP: Even to pay for visiting your ailing parent?

CP: I *can't* visit him, because I'm stuck here with a sprained ankle, and no condition to travel to the States.

But you could ring him. Or write him a letter.

I can't. I'm not ready.

Then you could at least ring Granny, ask her forgiveness for cutting her off every time she mentions him, then inquire after his health.

Does he really deserve my concern, or is it the pain talking? And enough about my father, anyway! What in the holy hell will I do about Ben?

After a good two hours of this, I took one of the bed pillows and flung it across the room. "Jaysus, I've gone completely bats," I said aloud, and pressed my index fingers to my temples. I took a deep breath. "One thing at a time." If I wasn't ready to deal with my father, the least I could do was make amends to Ben.

If he ever came in here, that is.

I'd a million reasons to apologize to him, not the least of which was a biggie: he was Kevin's father. A good one. He'd welcomed us into his home. And because last night, I *had* led him on. Even if I'd never meant to, even if the feel of his mouth, his hands, his body had taken me places I hadn't visited—or even dreamt about—for years.

I was having a hard time concentrating on my apology, what with reliving the details of our shag, complicated by lying in Ben's bed, and coupled—bad verb choice—with being half-naked. Not having any knickers on will do that to a girl. I was contemplating hobbling to the other room for a pair when I heard a soft rap.

Kevin wouldn't bother to knock. "Come in," I called, and Ben entered with a bowl of ice and a tall glass of... "Is that a Coke, or are my eyes deceiving me?"

"It is," Ben confirmed. He set the glass on the nightstand, and the bowl next to me.

"Bless you, my son." Perhaps a lame joke could ease things between us. "You must have read my mind." *Jesus, I hope not.* "The ice is helping already," I added hastily. Taking care not to dislodge the towel on my lap, I replaced the ice on my ankle.

"No problem," Ben said. He stuffed his hands in his trouser pockets and looked down at me, his face impassive. "Look Aislin, we've got to—"

"Sorry, I've been a—" I said at the same time.

A pregnant pause, then, "You first," we said, again in unison.

This was shagging ridiculous. I forced myself to meet Ben's eyes. "I'm terribly sorry for that whole bit in the bath. I had some bad new—" Did I really want to bring my father into it? "I mean...there's something I didn't tell you..."

"Yes?" But he didn't really look interested.

"Besides breaking up with Sam yesterday, I had an argument with Deirdre." I fidgeted with Ben's shirttails. "But that's no reason for bawling and yelling and the rest. I was a proper eejit."

His expression didn't change. "Yeah, well, that's understandable."

Really. He understood why I'd been such a cow? Or he guessed I was grasping at any reason to act badly and get away with it?

"And there's the other thing," I blurted, before I lost my nerve. "Last night."

Ben's eyes flickered. "It's not a problem."

Apparently he was already over our interlude. Still, I should apologize for the lot. "I shouldn't have let things go so far...I'm so sorry I...ah...I—"

Ben actually *laughed.* Laughed! "Don't they say changing her mind is a woman's prerogative?"

"I suppose 'they' do," I said, resentful. "Even if it's dead sexist."

Ben shrugged. "You had every right to cut it short. But you can't blame a guy for wanting the whole deal, huh?"

I gaped at him. Here I was horribly conflicted about being attracted to him, and he was being flippant? Even more depressing, he was acting like I wasn't worth the trouble. "I suppose not," I said past the lump of mixed emotions in my throat. "Still, it was wrong of me..."

"Why?" Ben was still smiling.

Sure, fine for him to smile, when I was dangling in the wind, exposed. But we needed to get Last Night out in the open so I could put the whole fecking disaster behind me. "For one thing, we recently broke up with people—we're both on the rebound. We've no business having it off with anyone, and certainly not with each other."

"You're absolutely right." Ben rocked back on his heels. "And don't forget, we shouldn't be having sex, since we're friends. You're always reminding me what great friends we are."

I frowned. Was he being sarcastic? After last night, I'd figured our friendship was so much flotsam on the shore. "I didn't think we wanted to be the sort of friends who...who give each other stopgap sex until someone we really want to be with comes along."

"Well, it's tempting, but—"

"*Tempting?*" Outrage flooded through me.

"The thing is," Ben went on, still with that maddening casualness, "I don't think stopgap sex really works out in the real world." He picked up the bowl. "Someone always seems to end up getting hur...messed up. Anyway, I'm not big on the 'friends with benefits' thing."

"Well, we're agreed on that," I said, determined to finish this bloody conversation if it killed me. "If we ever got involved, and we couldn't make a go, where would that leave Kevin?"

When he didn't answer, I felt a new sting in my nose and eyes. "I'll take a bit of a nap now."

Ben's jaw firmed. "Before you do, I think it's important to set out a few parameters for Kevin before we see the lawyer. We've only got two days to nail something down."

"Oh. Right." I'd momentarily forgotten about the dreaded lawyer, and suddenly my ankle ached worse than before. "I'm crushed," I said, stalling, and faked a fairly credible laugh, though I really wanted to cry. "You didn't come upstairs for the pleasure of my company?"

"You wanted me to?" He didn't smile.

Yes...no...Bollocks, I don't know. But I'm not ready to talk about officially sharing Kevin. "Really, my ankle...it's a bit hard to concentrate on legal things."

"But we can't put this off." Ben crossed his arms. "Besides, like I said, we only need a few preliminaries. So...visits. I think every other weekend is standard."

Dread tightened my chest, especially with him standing over me with a face like the wrath of God. But I wasn't about to ask him to sit on the bed. *Here, get comfy while you break my heart.* "I suppose it is."

"How about holidays? And summer vacation?"

Wait, let me get used to weekends without him first... "Really, Ben, I—"

"Daddy!" came an imperious call from downstairs.

Ben glanced at the doorway, then back at me. "We'd better make this fast—how about Kevin stays with me for half the major holidays."

"Half." I almost bit the syllable in two, and started to shake. *I'm finally getting what I deserve, for not cherishing Kevin enough—*

"Great. And one month in the summer—"

"Don't forget about bank holidays." Now I was tearful *and* queasy. "Really, can't we do this tomorrow?"

"Oh, yeah, bank holidays," Ben said. "I'll make a list of them, and we can divide—"

"Or we can each take one of Kevin's arms and pull," I snapped. "Once he's split in two, we'll each have equal share."

Ben gave me a sharp look. "Aislin…"

"Daaa-deee! Where are ya?"

Ben strode to the doorway. "Be down in a sec," he called, then came back to the foot of the bed. "Looks like this isn't the best time."

"That's perceptive of you." I sniffed.

"I'll bring up a calendar so you can mull the dates over."

"Is that a suggestion, or an order?"

He sighed. "Look, getting Kevin's visits down on paper is one of those necessary evils, so why are you getting upset?"

"I'm not up—"

"DAAAD! You promised you'd be right back!"

"I'd better get downstairs," Ben said, not meeting my eyes. "We can talk this out tomorrow."

"Can't wait," I muttered as he vanished through the door, and throttled the impulse to throw my ice at him. *I can't wait to give you the legal right to take my son away.*

THE SNAPPY DECISION

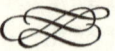

I stared at the bedroom ceiling. Day Two. Midafternoon.

Going Mad.

This had to be the loneliest, most frustrating, crawl-out-of-your-own-skin day of my life. In between wrestling with what had to be my Worst, Most Unsolvable Dilemmas Ever, I'd iced my ankle, tried to read *7 Habits*, then flung it across the room. Instantly regretting I'd disrespected my host's book, I crawled off the bed and hopped over to retrieve it.

I decided not to ring Granny. First, I was no closer to dealing with my father than I'd been before. Second, Granny would somehow divine the sprained ankle—she always knew when something was wrong—and I didn't want to worry her.

Earlier, I'd tested my ankle with a few tentative steps. Swiftly concluding it was a long way from healed, I iced it some more—courtesy of my son again, as Ben hadn't come round since yesterday except at my request. I'd heard the phone ring numerous times all day, but depressingly, the calls seemed connected with Ben's business.

Isn't that how it always happens. Lying on my back, I craned my neck to glare at my icepack, then dropped my head back on the pillow. Just when you're practically going batty with your worries twirling round and round like someone's put your brain in a salad spinner, and dying to talk to someone...*anyone* —save for estranged family members—no one will ring you.

The absolute worst part of being laid up was being totally dependent on someone you've sexually rejected. Prime example: having that someone help you to the loo.

Especially having him put his arm round you when you hadn't any knickers on, which you hadn't bothered with, since it was a bloody struggle to simultaneously balance on one foot and yank up your knickers with one hand. Although he could only be aware of your knicker-less state if he'd X-ray vision.

What was really driving me round the bend was that except for Kevin's two-minute visits, I'd endured the last twenty-four hours in solitary confinement. To sum up my day: *Kevin and Ben are having a jolly time kicking footballs, playing cards, and watching videos, while I contemplate my navel and the utter unfairness of life.*

HOWEVER, my prospects brightened considerably by three o'clock, when I was able to complete a three-minute hobble round the room. Hearing Ben's rap on the door, I leaped toward the bed. In case he wanted to talk about the bloody parent agreement again and I might need to put him off again with my "ankle hurts" excuse. "Come in," I called, and pulled the covers over my legs.

My fears were realized when Ben had a legal-size yellow tablet and the dreaded calendar under his arm. He stopped next to the bed. "How's the ankle doing?"

"A teensy bit better," I acknowledged.

"I promised Kevin we'd play ball if he could entertain himself for a half an hour. So...a great time to sketch out our visiting arrangements."

"I've been doing some thinking," I said. "We can do without the legal business, can't we? I mean, it's no problem, you can have Kevin two weekends a month—you can mark the calendar right now. As for holi—"

"Aislin," he said heavily. "That's not good enough."

"Why not? I'm not going to renege, I—"

"The lawyer, Feeney, made it clear that only an idiot wouldn't get something down on paper." Ben perched on the bed.

I quickly made room for him. I could be magnanimous, since I could tell he didn't relish telling me this. "Well, couldn't we just write something up ourselves?"

Ben shook his head. "Feeney told me one horror story after another, about mothers cutting off access to the kids, even leaving the country." He set the calendar on my knees. "The fathers couldn't do a thing about it, because they didn't have an agreement filed with the courts."

"Oh, so my promise isn't good enough?" I felt my chest constrict. "Being Kevin's father doesn't give you the right to force me—"

"Aislin—I hate to put it this way, but you've got to get real about this custody stuff."

"I am real," I blustered. "I mean, we can be perfectly amicable —we're friends." Hadn't he said so just yesterday, here in this room, despite evidence to the contrary? "So it's totally realistic to handle it ourselves."

Strangely—since I thought we were arguing—Ben took my hand and looked at it. "If you don't want to deal with a legal agreement, then why don't you live he—" He broke off and met my eyes.

"Live here?" I snatched my hand away. Who was insulting who now? "So you can keep your eye on me?" As if my father's illness, Granny's hurt, and this bloody custody business wasn't enough, Ben was twisting the screws. A sob caught me unawares, and I grabbed Ben's calendar and threw it away like a Frisbee. "So I can't sneak off with Kevin?"

"Goddamn it, Aislin, that's not what I'm saying." Ben reached for me again.

"Don't touch me!" I dashed furious tears away. "Now it all comes out, that you don't trust me—no wonder you're so keen on your bloody parenting agreem—"

"Damn it all!" Ben jumped off the bed. "Do you always have to take things the wrong way? Okay, so asking you to move in with me was a really bad idea. You don't have to rub it in."

My tears dried instantly. Mother of God. *You mean—you want us to move in together, like a couple?* I almost had the words out when the sound of banging on the front door echoed up the stairs. Oh, great—visitors!

"Jeez," Ben muttered. "Does she think she's got to pound the door down?"

"Who?" I asked. The only people I knew who banged on the door like that were the O'Donnell's, but old Nora and Bridie would have no reason to be here, and Deirdre had gone off me —maybe for good. Besides, she was in Dublin.

Ben strode to the doorway without answering. "Kevin, can you get that?"

"You betcha, Daddy," Kevin called up the stairs. The door squeaked on its hinges, then a female voice murmured something.

"It is Deirdre!" I was caught between delight and horror. Just what I needed, for Deirdre to see me lounging on Ben's bed. On his unmade bed. "How did you know she'd call round?"

"She phoned a while ago." Ben's voice was edgy. "I didn't think she'd get here so fast."

"Thanks a lot, for letting me know," I said with only a minimum of sarcasm.

"Deirdre wanted to surprise you."

"Well, it worked." I suddenly smiled, unbelievably relieved to

SUSAN COLLEEN BROWNE

drop the argument with Ben for now. I smoothed my hair, only to discover it was blossoming into a serious case of bed hair, and God only knew what Deirdre would have to say about *that*. I yanked off the covers and set the ice pack on the bedside table, just as Deirdre's voice floated up from the hall. "You're saying your mam's in *Daddy's* room?"

No time to lose. I swung my legs to the side of the bed.

"What the hell do you think you're doing?" Ben was at my side like a shot.

"It's obvious—I'm getting up." I heaved myself onto one foot, balancing carefully. "And not a moment too soon. Didn't you hear Deirdre?"

Ben grabbed me round the waist. "Get off that foot—I'll take you downstairs."

"You will not—Jaysus, you barely got me down the hall from the bath. I've no wish to add a broken neck to my sprained ankle."

"That...that was an isolated incident!" Ben practically bellowed. "You don't think I can carry a...what, measly hundred and twenty pounds?"

"What *are* the pair of you up to?" Deirdre's laughter wafted up the stairs.

Her laughing perked me up further. The best thing about Deirdre is that she never carries a grudge. "Don't go anywhere —I'll be right down!" I yelled. Then to Ben, "And I'd be bloody grateful if you'd leave off screeching in my ear." As I retrieved yesterday's bath towel—crucial for protecting one's modesty— my balance wavered.

Ben's hold tightened. "Aislin, will you just—"

"If you want to make yourself useful," and I fixed the towel round my waist, "you'll let me lean on you. We'll be downstairs in no time." I took a sort of step-limp, which made my ankle throb more than I expected. I sucked air through my teeth until the pain subsided, then took another tentative step.

Ben clutched my waist more firmly. "Aislin, this is really stupid, you could re-injure—"

"Be quiet and let me concentrate." Rather nice, to be ordering Ben about for a change.

"Not breaking any speed records up there, are we?" Deirdre laughed again.

"Just hang on," I called again. "Don't you dare leave!"

"Mammy's sprained her ankle," Kevin was saying. "Daddy's helpin' her."

"Sprained ankle, hmmm?" Deirdre said loudly. I heard footfalls on the stairs. "That's what they're calling it?"

"Ha, ha," said I, and with Ben's support, I managed to limp halfway to the bedroom door. "This is taking forever. And Deirdre's going to keep the jokes coming." I took another halting step.

"To hell with this," Ben said suddenly, and swung me into his arms.

I clutched him to keep from falling. "I told you, you're not to carry me downstairs!" But I couldn't help noticing that being in Ben's arms certainly took my mind off my aching foot. And he didn't seem to be straining quite like yesterday.

"And I'm telling you to be quiet and let me do my job." Ben shouldered through the doorway, and we met Deirdre on the landing.

She grinned at us. "Hope you lot are decent."

Ben stopped. "Anything for you, Deirdre." He shifted me more firmly in his arms.

"You haven't gone off me then?" I asked her, then felt the towel creep up my thighs.

"As if," Deirdre said, then allowed, "All right, I couldn't stand you for about ten minutes yesterday, but I got over it."

"I'm so sorry—I was horrible."

"Me, too." Deirdre giggled. "But you were worse."

"You really are a brat." I laughed in relief. "You can put me down now," I whispered in Ben's ear. He didn't move. Granted, I didn't feel up to arguing with him, but being held by him wasn't half bad. "What brings you here?" I asked Deirdre.

"Just wanted to say 'hi' and 'let's make up else I'll be terribly depressed' before I head back to Dublin, of course. I've Aunt Bridie's car—she's lent it to me for the week."

My throat choked up a bit. "Silly—I meant you being here, on a Monday."

"Did you forget? Bank holiday."

I felt Ben's arms tighten all of a sudden—those infamous bank holidays meant more visits to argue over. I realized how bizarre this was, carrying on a conversation while ensconced cozily in the arms of the man you're fighting with. But I could hardly invite Deirdre into his room for a chat. "Shall we go downstairs?"

Deirdre ignored me. "That's some getup you're wearing," she said jovially. She peered into Ben's room and her grin widened.

"I didn't feel well enough to get dressed," I said with great dignity, as my towel hiked higher up my legs.

"But well enough to..." Deirdre let her voice trail away suggestively.

"Ha—aren't you a Laugh-A-Minute Machine today," I said. "But if you're done making jokes, you can go down first. Ben and I will follow you."

When Deirdre didn't move, Ben shifted me in his arms again. "Anytime in this century would be great, Deirdre," he said patiently.

She gave me another impudent once-over, then her gaze sharpened. "What'd you say happened to your leg?"

"I really did sprain my ankle, you little beast," I said, laughing.

"No there, on your thigh."

I stretched my neck to peer at my leg, and abruptly stopped laughing. A half moon of small bruises ringed my thigh. Fingermarks. From Ben's reflex-clutch when I pushed him off me. "Ah...I fell, on one of Kevin's toys." I said quickly. "When I sprained my ankle."

"Kevin said it happened in the bath."

"Ah. Well, he left some Legos in the..." I stopped. Lie or 'fess up? But if you have to lie, shouldn't you go for one closest to the truth? "Actually, Ben and I were...it's funny really..." Deirdre would think it was hilarious, especially after my emphatic denials about being attracted to Ben, so I tried on, "The other night, we were playing around, you know, a bit of wrestling, and..."

Ben's arms turned into iron, then he put me down so fast I had to hop madly to keep from falling over. As I clutched him, he actually lifted the towel to glance at my leg, then our eyes locked.

Ben wore a look of pure horror. His face turned red, then white. I wanted to say, All right, so it's not that funny, but it's my fault...

"God, I'm sorry, I didn't mean to—" Ben broke off, his face losing more color.

"What'd I say?" Deidre asked.

I dragged my gaze from Ben's to find Deirdre looking embarrassed. And she didn't embarrass easily. "Nothing, really, it's just that—"

"Oh, Jaysus, I've really put my foot in it," Deirdre said uncertainly. "But really, Ben, you're not to worry. Aislin's got that tender Irish skin, bruises like mad. She's the flipping *Princess and the Pea* all over again."

"I'm sure she is," Ben said, and removed my hand from his arm. "I'll check on Kevin."

As I stood, wobbling, Ben scurried downstairs as if the banshees were after him. Stranded, I turned to Deirdre. "That wasn't exactly helpful."

Deirdre gave me an apprehensive look. "I won't ask you what happened, but..."

"I told you, Ben and I were only joking about, and you know how it goes..." God, I sounded lame. "I really don't know why Ben's so bothered."

"Fellas—who can figure," Deirdre said loyally, then she chewed her lip. "Though Dad's always said I've a bigger mouth sometimes than Mam and Aunt Bridie both. I'd better go."

Don't leave, I wanted to plead. *Ben and I will just start fighting again...* Suddenly, I couldn't take any more wildly see-sawing/brain-spinning emotions. The prospect of more legal wrangling with Ben, having to depend on him and have his hands on me, no matter how lovely those hands felt when we weren't getting along, *and* the lawyer's meeting tomorrow was just too much.

All I wanted was the safety and predictability of Deirdre, Polly, and the shop. So I made the snappiest of snappy decisions.

"Deirdre," I said, limping toward Kevin's room, "could you help with a bit of packing? Kevin and I are going back with you. To Dublin."

THE DEPARTURE

*O*kay, so I'd a bit of lawyer-phobia.

The funny thing was, I trusted Ben, even if he didn't trust me. But I knew what people were capable of, using love as an excuse. All you need is money and/or power, which in most cases is one and the same, and a halfway decent solicitor. I'd neither. And highly unlikely to get even one of the three anytime soon.

I was so relieved at scuttling the lawyer meeting, I could feel my ankle almost spontaneously heal. I'd just limped into Ben's spare room, where Kevin and I had our things, Deirdre right behind me, when she said, "Ash, wait."

"What? You don't think I should go back to Dublin?"

"Well," Deirdre said, a frown marring her pretty features, "I didn't want to say anything, but there's another reason I called round—it's Liz."

My momentary annoyance forgotten, I clutched a handful of knickers. "Is she all right?"

"She rang me at my granny's today, sounding a bit depressed. To jolly her up, I asked if she'd any new bad-husband jokes. But she didn't laugh, just rang off with hardly a goodbye."

Deirdre wasn't the most perceptive girl on the planet, so Liz must've been quite low. "Did you ring her back, try to find out what's bothering her?"

"I was going to, but she rang again a few minutes later, so chipper I knew she was completely faking it." Deirdre piled Kevin's things into his holdall. "She said she hasn't been anywhere outside of Dublin since coming to Ireland, and she wanted to see Ben's new place, so she's coming to Galway this Friday for the weekend, and did I know any B&B's."

"Seems awfully sudden," I said. "I don't remember her saying she'd a holiday coming up."

"That's exactly what I said." Deirdre mashed a pile of clothes into my case. "But she said she needed a break from work before she committed hari-kari from boredom, and she couldn't wait to see you."

"Oh. But I'll be in Dublin this weekend..." Hearing Liz's story reminded me that I wasn't the only person with a few problems. "If she's having troubles, she should have rung me—"

"I wondered at that myself," said Deirdre. "But before I could say anything, she said something to the effect that she didn't want to intrude, since you and Ben were sure to be dead close to a shag."

Feeling mournful, I couldn't even muster a sarcastic *ha, ha*. I hastily shoved the rest of my things into my case, slammed it shut. Deirdre must've seen something in my face, because without even being asked, she picked up my case and Kevin's holdall. Steeling myself for Ben's displeasure, we trooped down the stairs.

KEVIN MET me at the foot of the stairs. "Dad 'n me are g-gonna play football! But he said he's got to remember where he put the ball first."

Where was Ben? Then peering into the front room, I glimpsed Ben on the couch, his head in his hands. Sure he wasn't trying out ESP to help him find the missing ball? "That's lovely," I said, now steeling myself first for Kevin's disappointment, "but—"

"Why d'you have our c-cases?" Kevin's little mouth turned down.

"We're going back to Dub—"

"But I don't wanna go!"

Kevin rarely whined. My motherly patience was in short supply, with my ankle starting to throb, and still having Ben to deal with. But I somehow managed a conciliatory, "I realize that, love, but we—"

"But Daddy said we'd stay all week!" He burst into tears.

I curved my hand over his small head, but he recoiled from me—my own son, not wanting his mammy to touch him!—and ran straight to Ben.

Ben jerked his head up, then jumped to his feet as Kevin threw his arms round him with such force Ben rocked on his heels. As dread filled me, Ben picked my wailing son up and came toward me. "Are we going somewhere?"

Deirdre gave him a guilty look. "Em, Dublin," she said over Kevin's sobs.

Ben's gaze bore into me like a dentist's drill. "You've forgotten about our appointment tomorrow?"

"Actually, no." I tried to balance myself with the toe of my injured foot, but I was still awfully wobbly. "But it'll be easier to get round in my own flat. And I'm...em, needed at work."

"We thought Mam could muddle through without her for a few days," Deirdre said, bless her loyal soul, "but she..."

Her voice trailed away as Ben set Kevin down. "How about Deirdre gets you a cookie." It wasn't a question, and everyone in the room knew it.

Kevin sniffed hard, but took Deirdre's outstretched hand. "I wanna stay with you, Daddy."

Ben squeezed Kevin's shoulders, then gave him a gentle push toward the kitchen. "I want you to stay too, but I'm sure your mom will bring you back soon."

Deirdre scurried away with my son, as Ben turned a glare on me. "Won't she?" I opened my mouth, but being so great at breaking promises, I didn't see the point of making any new ones.

I could hear more tears in the kitchen, and another outburst, "I don't want a cookie!" Then Deirdre's voice, low and soothing. I seemed to be the only person round who'd no idea how to handle my own son.

Clutching the banister for support, I said, "I'm really sorry, that I have to go—"

"No problem," Ben bit out. "This wasn't working out anyway."

"Our staying here?"

"No, *you* staying here."

It was a slap in the face—but one entirely deserved. "I promise, I'll bring Kevin back—"

"Whenever," Ben said rudely. "See you," he added, with hardly a glance at me, as Deirdre and Kevin returned. When she picked up the two cases, the fact that Ben unchivalrously let her without doing it himself, showed just how furious he was. "Kevin, I'll wait in the car," said Deirdre, "while you say your goodbyes to your dad."

"Me too," I seconded, relieved to leave the scene of the crime, and I began limping to the front door. Just as I was about to pick up my handbag on the entryway table, Deirdre said, "No, Ash, you're not to carry anything. Kevin will bring it out."

"Okay," I said heavily. Any other time, I would be sensitive to the fact that a single mam shouldn't have her son carry her handbag. But if Ben didn't object, I wasn't going to.

Deirdre turned back at the door. "Remember, Kevin, about your very important job, bringing Mammy's bag."

Deirdre and I traversed the few feet to her aunt's car in silence. She bundled the cases into the boot, then settled behind the front wheel. Wondering how to make this up to Kevin, I leaned against the car, and watched him with Ben through the open door.

Ben crouched and drew Kevin into his arms. As Kevin snuffled against his shoulder, I could hear Ben say, "You be good, now, and I'll see you next week."

Kevin clutched him tighter. "I don't want to see you next week—I want to see you now!"

"I know, son," Ben said, setting Kevin down gently. "But the week's going to go by real fast, and you'll be back." He pressed my bag into Kevin's hands. "Be a good boy."

I could see Kevin trying not to cry, then he pulled on Ben's sleeve. As I watched, Ben leaned down, and Kevin cupped his hands around Ben's ear.

Ben drew away, then quickly shut the door, with Kevin still inside. "Look there," I said to Deirdre. "He's pulled Kevin back into the house."

"Mother of God," Deirdre said. "Will you let the man say his goodbyes in private?"

Seething a bit, because I knew she was right, I opened the car door and climbed in next to her. Moments later, the door opened just enough for Kevin to squeeze through. He dragged his feet to the car, handed me my handbag, then clambered into the back seat, not looking at me.

So. My life had entered an entirely new phase: Total Crap. I was on the outs with my son, and poor Liz needed my support —support I felt entirely unequipped to provide. To add to my problems, she'd take one look at me and know I'd mucked things up with her friend.

And with Ben, who'd been so keen for us to move house to

Galway, and whose horizontal mamba with me just days ago seemed so promising, was so disgusted with me he couldn't make himself wave goodbye his son.

ANOTHER U-TURN

I slunk down in my seat, feeling so rotten I hadn't the strength to sit upright.

"You *do* know what you're doing, right, Ash?"

"Going to Dublin?" With great effort, I yanked my thoughts from the memory of Ben's furious look. And his almost-parting shot: *this wasn't working out anyway.* "I'm sure Granny will understand I didn't have time to ring her goodbye."

Not to mention ringing to inquire after my father, who could have *died*, since I hadn't heard anything since my sister's message.

"Your granny always understands every stupid thing you do," Deirdre retorted. "I meant running out on a certain someone—"

"Shhh," I hissed, and jerked my head toward Kevin, sulking in the back seat. Not that I blamed my son. If I were him, I wouldn't talk to me either. "I know, it looks bad…"

"Really," Deirdre said snidely. "Let's see—this *person* is great to your kid and wants to pay child support, *and* he looks after you when you're laid up. All you've got to do is see the solicitor. Instead, you leave him in the lurch."

"That about sums it up," I muttered. "But you forgot, I've let a certain other person down too," and I nudged my head toward Kevin again. "Ben has every right to be furious with me."

"Well, I imagine he is," Deirdre said in a conversational tone. "But there's one other thing."

"Which is?" I asked without much curiosity.

"Well, Ben may not be as forgiving as yours truly," Deirdre said. She turned onto the Galway road and gunned the engine.

I forgot my misery long enough to touch Deirdre's arm. "What would I do without you?"

"Probably muck up your life even worse than you already are," Deirdre said frankly.

"Thanks—I needed that." My voice was glum. "So, your point with Ben?"

"What if he's so angry, he really turns the screws on you as regarding custody?"

"Ben wouldn't do that." Would he? "He said so, weeks ago."

"That was before you pissed him about like you did this weekend," Deirdre said, low. "And likely before he'd come to love Kevin."

I glanced into the back seat, and saw Kevin had dropped off to sleep. "You think Ben's really keen on him?"

"Mad about him," Deirdre confirmed, and my heart lightened. "But I don't know why that should make you too happy," she added.

"Why not? Ben's turned out to be a lovely father."

"Sure, that's a plus, but what if Ben decides to fight for Kevin?"

My stomach lurched. "I can't believe..." Then my mind played over all the scenes of Ben and Kevin playing together, reading, exchanging simpatico father-son looks. Was there such a thing as Ben growing too fond of Kevin? And come to think of it, the look he'd sent me when I came downstairs could freeze oxygen at twenty paces. "I'd see him in hell first."

"Fighting words, Ash," Deirdre said, "but if Ben takes you to court, you're too broke to do a thing about it—unless you take your dad's money."

I looked blindly out the window. Money or no money, how long could I keep avoiding my father? A cloud of indecision settled on me, nearly paralyzing me. And how long could I keep hurting Granny in the process?

"You're upset with me for pointing that out?"

I shook my head. "You're so good to me—especially today, giving us this lift. I'll never give out at you again."

"Good," Deirdre said cheerfully. "Because, whatever you decide about the check, it's in your handbag. As we speak."

I opened and closed my mouth like a fish. "W-w-what?"

"If you want to know if I did it, the answer's yes. But don't bite my head off—it was your granny's idea."

Just two days ago, hadn't Granny been terribly anxious? *I was worried, having that big check in the house...*

I saw a lay-by ahead, and suddenly my paralysis cracked. Wasn't it time to do the decent thing for a change? "Pull over, there," I directed.

"What for? There's no latte kiosk, no toilet—"

"Please," I said desperately.

Deirdre slowed down. "Well, if you put it like that..."

I took a deep breath. Deirdre," I said in a small voice, "I hate to do this to you, but could you turn around?"

THE EPIPHANY

"*Y*ou didn't seem surprised, when Kevin and I walked in," I said to Granny. She jabbed a fork into the steak she was browning and turned it over. "Well, child, nothing you do really surprises me."

An hour after I'd waved Deirdre off and crept into Granny's house with a still yawning Kevin, I was chopping salad vegetables. Primed for the easy fib, *We left Ben's because he'd an unexpected work commitment*, I decided to go with honesty. And not just because my son might be listening. "Things got a bit tense at Ben's," I began.

"Sorry to hear it, love." Nothing if not tactful, is Granny. Sometimes I wondered how different my life would have been if she'd shaken a bit more sense into me. But right now, I was in no condition to regret her sparing the rod and spoiling me.

I chopped in silence, my tension building. I wished Kevin would abandon his Lego project, get underfoot and plead for his tea. But when I peeked over at him, he seemed entirely absorbed in building something…that looked a lot like the Lodge.

I couldn't hold in my guilt and all-around bad feelings any longer. "Why we're really here..."

"Things weren't tense at Ben's, then?" Granny flashed a smile, reminding me of my father so strongly I felt a stab.

"No, they were, but what I'm trying to say is, I...em, got a message from Grace. About my father."

A clatter came from the stove. Granny had dropped her fork in the hot pan.

"I'll get it," I said quickly. Seeing the distressed color on her cheeks, I took her elbow and sat her down at the kitchen table. I turned off the stove, fished out the fork, then sat across from her. "You didn't tell me he'd been ill."

Granny folded her hands together. They were trembling. When had my grandmother's hands gotten so veined, the fingers knotted? "An aneurism in the abdominal aorta," she said. "It nearly ruptured, I understand. There was surgery, and several days in hospital."

I blanched. "It...it sounds awfully serious."

Granny launched into a description of the malady, the details of which escaped me, because the gist was, yes, my father could have died. It's funny, that I hadn't really thought of Granny being my father's mammy—I mean, her having the same tender, maternal feelings for a grown man, as she'd had when he was small.

And here I called myself a mother! I thought of Kevin, ill, in hospital...sure, wouldn't I be just as frantic fifty years from now? My eyes stung. "He was in a bad way?" I whispered. "You should have said something,"

I didn't want to worry you, child."

"Worry me—!" My guilt-o-meter went off the charts. "*I'm* the one who should be protecting *you* from fretting!"

"You'd enough on your plate, with Kevin adjusting to his daddy, and Ben and you...ah, a full plate, yes."

Actually, my plate couldn't be emptier at the moment. "If I'd known, you could have shared the worry."

It hadn't been so long ago that I was convinced my father's comings and goings—Washington D.C., courthouse, possibly prison, even hospital—were of absolutely no interest to me. When had that changed? When he veered uncomfortably close to the mortuary?

Granny's shoulders drooped. How was it, those shoulders seemed a lot frailer than they had two days ago? Even her vivid hair looked dull. "I didn't want to go on at you, though Bridie and Nora told me I was indulging you—again."

"I hate to admit it, but for once they might be right," I said. "Maybe you should have pressured me to do the right thing, ring him...something." *You're blaming Granny now? That's really scraping the bottom of the barrel.*

"I was never good at laying down the law," Granny said.

"And I've always been rather shameless about twisting you round my finger," I pointed out gently.

"And wasn't John was the same way? Beguiling as the devil himself."

"I can believe that." I suppose my father's charm—infrequently turned my way it may have been—was the reason I'd gone out with Kelly the Intern when I wasn't the least bit interested.

"And wasn't our John full of schemes," Granny said, a faraway look on her face. "At age six, he'd be down at the pub, sweeping the floors for tips, and at eleven, running the football pools."

"Life in the fast lane, even then?"

"Oh, to be sure. He couldn't wait to go to university, then make pots of money."

Feeling my bitterness return, I jumped up to finish the vegetables. "He'd lots of grand plans."

Wearing a reminiscent smile, Granny didn't notice my mood

change. "Ah, sure—his law degree, marrying into the Hennessys…"

I whacked the knife through a carrot. So, he hadn't married Mother, he'd married her family. Was it any wonder the woman went the martini route?

"Then politics," Granny went on. "Nothing seemed to get in his way. Until his last scheme, when he pushed his Irish luck too far—"

"Bollocks!" I'd sliced into my finger. I dropped the knife, ran to the sink, and turned on the taps. "Maybe he deserved—shite!" Cold water hit my cut. "Deserved everything he got." I pressed on the wound.

"I shouldn't think John deserved to lose you—or his only grandchild," Granny said sadly. "The only one he's likely to have —with Grace apparently not interested in kiddies."

"And why not?" I shut off the tap. "He didn't trouble himself much with me—that is, until Kevin came along. He managed to muck up that too."

"You'll know he was just a boy when his father died—if Sean had lived, maybe John would have been a better father. Isn't that how it works?"

"Not always." I grabbed a dishtowel to press on my cut. "Ben lost his father too, but he's a good daddy."

Granny's pinched look relaxed a bit. "You've realized how lucky you are, then?"

"I…I…" *I am lucky, aren't I?*

"Sure, John has learned his lessons." Granny was matter-of-fact. "A shame, though, that it took him so long."

I found my voice again. "You're saying he's changed? If he has, why is he using money to try to get to me?"

Then it struck me: *Because money is the only currency he knows.*

Why hadn't I seen it before? Before I'd got accustomed to this epiphany, a second one swooped in and hit me between the eyes: the money wasn't as important as the freedom it represented. Maybe it was a way for me to make a good life for myself and Kevin.

John Moore hadn't been a perfect father. But how long could I hold it against him?

"I'm afraid the supper's gone cold," Granny said, and returned to the stove.

I watched Granny, remorse heavy in my chest. I'd been thoughtless, and selfish. I wanted to climb onto her lap like I had when I was little, and cry on her shoulder, but you know, this time I'd have to live with feeling like shite personified. I fumbled the salad together.

As the meat began to sizzle again, Granny said, "You'll know John still lives in that little cottage by the lake?"

I almost dropped the bowl. "That narky little..." The place we'd moved to after losing the Eagle Prairie manse, the cabin he'd been so sure we'd leave before Kevin's first birthday. I'd always thought he would've found a way to resume his old life. What didn't add up here?

Then it came to me. "With the money he gave me, he could get a much nicer place," I said faintly.

Edith smiled at me over her shoulder. "Didn't I say he's changed? He's never stopped asking about you, love."

"Oh, right." The tears in my eyes were twenty years old—inside, I felt about Kevin's age. "Grace was always his favorite."

"Darling, that's not true—"

"It is," I insisted, and for once, let myself feel the hurt of it. "I'm an afterthought—it's Kevin he misses. Kevin he wishes never left America."

"You're wrong, love. When I saw him in Chicago this spring, he wanted to fly back with me to see you, but he wasn't feeling quite himself. So we thought it better to wait a bit."

He'd wanted to see me, but instead, he'd gotten ill, and was all alone except for Grace's infrequent attentions. As if I would win any Good Daughter prizes myself.

"Tell me, love, why did you contact Ben after so long?"

I shot a glance at Granny. She wasn't one for probing questions. "You know why," I said, surprised. "So Kevin could have a father."

"Well, then." Granny speared the meat and set it on a platter. "I've never understood why you think Kevin needs a daddy but you don't."

A tear rolled down my cheek. I caught it just before it ran into the salad. "Sure, you took your time," I blubbered with a watery smile, "to point that out."

Granny grinned at me, looking more like her old Maureen O'Hara-ish self. "You weren't ready to hear it."

THE TROUBLE with country life is it gives you too much quiet—except for Nora and Bridie's "Coronation Street" blaring next door—for thinking. When you stare out the window, and start pondering all sorts of elevated Deep Thoughts, you find there's nowhere to run. From your mistakes, or from the changes you've conveniently ignored for years.

Before my eyes, Granny was doing the unthinkable. Getting old. Older, I corrected myself. Still, how much time would we have together? I glanced back at her, cuddling with Kevin. *Oh, Granny, all these years, I've taken you for granted...*

And with my father in America, and Grace giving every impression that her Irish relations were on her list of People Not To Bother With, Kevin and I were all Granny had too. And to think, there was one simple thing I could do to make her happy...

Following an intuition—or mad impulse, take your pick—I didn't understand, I suddenly lunged to the kitchen jumble drawer. A fine place to keep passports, wasn't it, with all the identity theft going round these days?

As I caught Granny's eyes on me, I winked at her, and held the passports up. "Just in case I need them sometime."

And how wise of me, I couldn't help thinking as I stuck our passports in the inside pocket of my handbag, to have kept them here at Rosehill all these years, instead of the flat.

Kevin jumped off the couch and threw his arms round me. "Have you any more chocolates?" After I'd dragged him out of his dad's house, apparently all was forgiven—in that amazing way children do.

I ran my fingers through his hair, then rifled through my bag. "Ah ha! Two left. One for Granny, and one for...hmmm... who could it be?"

"Me!" Kevin scrambled back to the couch to share the sweets. I wouldn't win many more prizes for Best Mammy than I have for Best Daughter, I thought, but I had the chance to do much better for my son than my parents ever did for me. *Which means not taking Ben's love for Kevin for granted, like I've taken Granny's...*

The phone rang. It had to be Ben! I leaped toward it—didn't it always work that way, just when you were thinking so hard of a certain person, they always rang?

It wasn't Ben. "Liz!" Didn't it always work that way? When you'd totally been ignoring someone special to you, and feeling guilty and ashamed for not ringing them, they rang you first? *Liz, I've missed you, I've been meaning to ring for ages,* I was ready to blurt, but before I could get the words out, Liz said, "I realize it's last minute..."

I heard something awful in her voice. Bracing myself, I said, "What is it, love?"

"I'm coming to Galway tomorrow, instead of this weekend." She took a long, spasmodic breath. "And I need a favor. A big one."

THE DONNYBROOK

*L*ocation: Outside Ballydara Lodge.

Day/Time: Tuesday afternoon, misbegotten Date with Destiny—re: solicitor—imminent.

Status report: No car in drive. No answer at door.

Conclusion: Ben was visiting bloody "Feeney & O'Shea, Solicitors" without me.

Still feeling very low, to think that not only was my life a fecking mess, but so was poor Liz's, I skulked back to Granny's seldom-used Ford.

I crashed the gears attempting a two-point turn—which worked out to be more like six—then thumped and jerked Granny's poor abused car onto the road. As I hit a pothole, the scrapbook on the passenger's seat bounced, then slid onto the floor.

Really, how could I blame Ben for meeting Feeney on his own? I'd been a complete eejit, so consequently lost the opportunity to create a fair visiting agreement. Nothing left for me but to approach Ben, proverbial hat in hand, and lay out my Most Important To-do List Ever.

Item #1: Sit down calmly with Ben, let him know about Liz leaving Dan.

#2: While we're still experiencing mutual sorrow at friends' predicament, mention need to visit father.

#3: Pull out Granny's scrapbook I dug out of the closet earlier this morning. But since rather despicable to go for pity angle, and because scrapbook too awful to look at again, use #3 only as absolute last resort.

With my plans firmly in mind, since one is all too apt to forget details when one's life has turned to shite, I coasted through Ballydara village. Then, struck by a sudden inspiration, at the edge of town, I made a spectacularly inept U-turn and headed for the pub. While I was still mobile phone-less, I could try ringing Ben one more time from Hurley's.

I must say, though, when you've a friend going through hell, it helps take your mind off your own little problems. Last night, on the phone, Liz started bawling. *Dan found the e-mails from Kurt. I admit, I didn't try to hide them, I was hoping he'd see he was ruining our marriage with his long hours, but he accused me of having an affair, and I said unfaithful husbands spend more time at home than you do, then I threatened to quit my job and he said how will we pay our mortgage and I said I didn't care, you were the one who wanted this big house, and I'm taking the kids to see Mom and all he had to say was good riddance...*

Well, at least Ben hadn't said that to me, even if he'd wanted to.

As I limped into Hurley's, the place was filling with the leisure-class regulars, along with two sports-mad fellas watching football, whom I swear had been in the same stools the last time Ben and I were in here. "Aislin." Pat Hurley was polishing a glass with a suspiciously gray-tinged towel. "We've not seen you for a bit."

"Right...hallo." *I've been too busy fecking up my life.* "I'll have a

Coke and…a large order of chips." I always say, in the absence of chocolate, something fried will kick your brain cells into gear. "Might I use your phone?"

"Ah, sure." Pat reached under the counter and brought out the heavy black rotary phone that had been an antique when his dad ran the pub, then set down the glass he'd been polishing in front of me. "Himself is—"

"I'll just take the can," I said hastily, then dialed Ben's mobile number. As the ring tones sounded, I got a strange feeling, like someone was drilling holes into my back. I wondered if the sensation related to my anxiety about Liz—as in, how could I be supportive for her when I hadn't a clue how to do it for myself…Then the line picked up. "Ben Carpenter."

"Ben?" I tried to summon my nerve to confront him, but trouble is, I'd used it all up walking out of the Lodge yesterday. "Em, could we get together for a brief chat today?"

"Why?"

Hardly encouraging. "Well, there's something I need to ask you… Could we meet at the Lodge? Or anyplace convenient," I added quickly.

"How about twenty feet from where you're standing?"

I frowned, the holes-in-back sensation stronger than ever, then whirled around. All thoughts of Liz whooshed out of my brain as I met the glowering eyes of none other than Himself, slouched in a back booth.

And here I'd been bracing myself to face Ben over a measly phone call. Thanking Pat, I rang off, then picked up my Coke, and threaded my way through the tables.

I pasted on a sickly smile. "Fancy meeting you here." He didn't say anything, just stared at me, so I sat down. After several moments, I couldn't take it any longer. "You've taken a vow of silence?"

"No. What are you doing here?"

I lifted my Coke. "Isn't it obvious?" I said, trying on a winning smile.

"I mean, why aren't you in Dublin?" His tone hardly encouraged cozy confidences.

My smile petered out. "I...em, changed my mind."

"You do a lot of that, don't you?"

I shifted uncomfortably. "I suppose I have...lately. I realize it's been inconvenient, but..." I took a big gulp of Coke for courage.

"No inconvenience," Ben said, his casual pose at odds with the hard glint in his eyes. "Feel free to go, do, be whoever you want. And if it affects anyone else's life? Hey, don't lose sleep over it." His mobile chimed, but he ignored it.

"I decided to stay with Granny, since she's feeling a bit...off." Can you blame her, with a granddaughter like me?

"At least you're considerate to your *grandma*."

How I longed to snap out a scathing retort! But! Open Dialogue was required here. I took another fortifying gulp of Coke, the can rattling against my teeth, and quickly set it down before I chipped another tooth. "Before we...get started, what did you mean yesterday?"

"When...?"

"When you said my staying at the Lodge...wasn't working out."

"Isn't it obvious? You and me, being parents."

I blanched. Worse than I'd thought. "You...still want to be Kevin's dad, don't you?" His mobile rang again, and he ignored it again. "Don't you?" I asked again.

"Yes...but not with you."

That hurt. Not as in *ouch*. More like a big tear in my heart. "Well." Voice quavers. Clear throat to minimize pathetic factor. "I...see. But there's something I need to do—something really important—and I hope you'll understand."

"Which is?" Ben sounded bored.

My heart tore a bit more. But I forged on, "I'm going to Minnesota to see my father."

Ben's eyes flashed, the sharp edge of them making me recoil. Then he looked away, and didn't say anything for like, *eons*.

"Well?"

"Why tell me?" He said finally, sounding bored again. "You don't need my permission."

I clenched my fists until my nails dug into my palms. "I'm telling you because I'm taking Kevin with me."

Ben's jaw turned to granite. "The hell you are."

Grrrr. Hang on to conciliatory spirit by its fingernails. But fail miserably: "He's my son," I spat. "I can take him where I please!"

"He's my son too, and you can't take him out of the country unless I say so!"

Biting back a childish, *Can too!* I stared into Ben's eyes, wondering when they'd turned so hard, then threw back more Coke to buy some time.

The fizz burned down my throat. Stifling a good choke, I said carefully, "I don't see how a short visit to America could—"

"No way," Ben snapped. "Absolutely no way."

Ah, feck conciliation. "You've no legal agreement yet! And who the hell are you to forbid Kevin to—"

"I'll tell you who I am," Ben said through his teeth. "I'm the guy you stiffed so you wouldn't have to sign a parenting agreement. And I'm the guy who can trust you about as far as the next table!"

"That's a snide thing to say!" Even if he had a point. And if I wasn't mistaken, people at nearby tables were taking an unwonted interest in our conversation. "Really, I can explain—"

"Explain?" Ben's eyes ignited into flames. He shot out of the booth and leaned over me. "Why don't you start with the freaking ninety-thousand dollars in your purse!"

My mouth dropped open. Simultaneously, the hum of voices in the pub went silent.

Someone finally said, "Did you hear that?"

"How many euros is ninety-thousand?" said another.

I pushed my drink aside with trembling hands. "I can't believe you'd snoop in my bag," I whispered.

"I can't believe you think I'd stoop that low!" Ben didn't bother to lower his voice.

"Looks like our man's ready to ring her neck," someone commented.

"He's a good lad, wouldn't harm a flea." Mrs. Murphy, from the shop, advised from two booths away.

Ben leaned closer. "Just how long did you think you could keep a secret like that?"

"With Deirdre involved, I'm lucky it lasted two days." As I tried to pull myself together, I was uncomfortably aware of all eyes on the premises trained on us, even the telly-watchers. "All I can say, Deirdre better have a bloody good explanation for letting it out."

"It wasn't Deirdre—Kevin showed me the check. So you've been caught red-handed!"

"Red-handed!" I sputtered. "You act like I've committed a crime, when the money was completely unexpected—"

"It's just like before—when you kept me in the dark about Kevin. But this time, the check's just one more nail in the coffin of me wanting anything to do with you!"

A fellow at the bar elbowed his mate. "Now he wants nothing to do with her."

I deserved shunning because my communication skills wouldn't win any prizes? "It's just money." I faked my most reasonable tone. "Not a great sum, either, relatively speaking." I gave a pointed look around us. "And would you mind sitting down? You're making a scene—"

"You think I give a flying f—care? When you've got this

secret deal worked out with Daddy? Just what else have you been up to with him behind my back?"

My phony patience snapped. Before I could stop myself, I scrambled out of the booth and stood toe-to-toe with Ben. "Feck's sake! There've been no 'secret' deals. We don't even speak! Like I told you, the money was a surprise—"

"You expect me to believe that?"

"That's telling her, Benjy!" said Pat's brother Bernard, the erstwhile plumber.

"Yes I do, because it's true—"

"With you, truth is always relative. In fact, I don't know how I've lasted this long, being around you—Aislin Moore, the queen of mixed signals! You want Kevin to have a father, but you don't tell me about my son. You agree to stay at my house, then you run off. You want me to share responsibility for Kevin, then you blow off a parenting agreement—"

"But I—"

"*Then*," Ben ignored me, "you kiss me like there's no tomorrow, then you shove me away!"

"Did you hear that," said one of the fellows at the bar. "Kissed him like there was no tomorrow!"

"I didn't mean to—"

"And now, your new, late-breaking story—you say you've got nothing to do with your dad," Ben snarled, "then you're taking his money! And this isn't the first time you've been in cahoots with Daddy, remember!"

"Jaysus, I'd rather watch the pair of them than telly any day," said another onlooker.

As I glared at Ben, a shocking thought hit me: We're close enough to kiss...again...With that, I didn't know if I was more infuriated with him or myself. "Cahoots? What the bloody hell are you talking about now?"

"I'm talking about seven years ago, when we—"

'That's it!" I poked one index finger into Ben's chest. I'd be double-triple damned before I'd willingly entertain Hurley's customers another minute. "Outside. You and me."

"You got it!" Ben slapped his hands on the table.

"Shaggit," Pat said, forgetting himself. "Just when things were getting interesting."

THE DESPERATE MEASURE

In times like these, a dignified exit is always desirable. Instead, I was forced to hobble after Ben, through a gauntlet of amateur relationship counselors. "Don't hit him too hard, Aislin." "You stick to your guns, love." "You can sweeten him up later, dearie, if you know what I mean." "Ninety-thousand'll make a lovely bathroom," said Bernard Hurley.

I rolled my eyes with that one and slammed the door behind me.

I found Ben leaning against his Micra, a stiff wind whistling through the car park. Taking advantage of the white noise, I launched the next volley. "Where were we? Ah, yes—you were running through your list of 'what trumped-up ancient history can I still throw in Aislin's face.' Isn't it about time you got over it?"

"Got over it! Get over you dumping me two seconds after we make lo—"

"Oh, come on," I said, vastly satisfied by the outrage in Ben's voice. I'd been on the defensive bloody long enough. "If it makes you feel better, give out at me all you like." *It should up my chances for you letting me take Kevin to America...*

"It doesn't make me feel better, goddamn it!" His bloody mobile rang, again. He visibly gritted his teeth, yanked the phone out of his pocket to check the display, then jammed it back in.

"Could have fooled me," I said. "But let's have it, don't hold back now—"

"All right, maybe I haven't gotten over all the crap you pulled on me—"

"Jaysus, I was nineteen, a bit immature—"

"Immature's one thing, but jerking people around is another. See, I'm having just a little trouble with the part about me being good enough to sleep with, but not date openly."

I felt my bravado slipping away. "But I never planned to..." *Sleep with you...Fall in love with you...*Or let's not forget, *have your baby...*

"I'm also having trouble with the part about you throwing me out the back door that night, when your parents came home." He cranked up the volume another notch. "Then we come to the part when your dad asked, 'who's here?' And you told Daddy, 'no one—just the han—'" He broke off. For a second, he seemed to go pale.

I felt sick. "You...heard that?"

His chest heaved, then he threw another flaming look at me. "So why would I go along with pretending you and I would stay in touch?"

"So you ripped up your Navy address," I said faintly.

"Since you didn't tell me you'd gotten pregnant, in hindsight, I can only draw the obvious conclusion: a little princess like you didn't want some drunken dirt-farmer's kid to be the father of your child." He thrust his hand in front of me, his fingers splayed. "Last time I looked, I'd gotten all the manure out from under my fingernails!"

I stared at Ben, his accusation reverberating through me, and saw something for the first time: that behind his anger was the hurt of years. A whole world of it.

My mind time-traveled backwards, like a video in rewind. I saw my past with crystalline clarity. I saw Ben...

The son of our maid, who'd lost his father...A boy who'd been too quiet. Too careful.

Not my fault...

The young man I'd rejected without meaning to, whose retaliation had been minor compared to my thoughtless self-preservation.

Okay, that was sort of my fault...

The father of my son, whose needs I'd discounted, whose feelings I'd been careless with. Over and over.

All my fault, you mourn.

So it is here, in the weedy car park of a country pub, that you discover that someone else's pain matters more than your own. And you know what that means, don't you?

But I can't go there. Not now. Somehow I got out, "That's not how it was."

Ben suddenly looked tired. "Then how was it?"

Guilt and regret swirled round me like a whirlpool. But I couldn't let myself get sucked in. Because if Ben thought I was worthless now, if I blurted out what I'd almost done years ago, he'd reject me forever.

My eyes stung. And if my son found out...

I felt my insides shred, imagining Kevin's hurt—and losing the confidence he'd gained since Ben had come along. For that alone, I couldn't let Ben think that he didn't matter to me—now, or back then.

I swallowed round the tears clogging my throat. "Whatever you think of me, I'm not a snob. Jaysus, what've I to be snobby about?"

Ben looked away. "Your dad was the big-shot congressman.

291

My dad was the drunk who couldn't keep a job, and even hit my mom."

There it was again. More pain than I could begin to assuage. I remembered him back at the Lodge yesterday, his head in his hands after he'd seen my bruises. Resisting the urge to throw my arms round him and blubber, *it's all right, it's all right*, I said, "My mother liked the drink too, so I...know how it is."

"Do you? And was *she* the family breadwinner who let down the family every time they turned around? The reason my mom had to suck up to rich people and clean their houses?"

Pity clutched at me. Now I really wanted to weep. "Well, no," I said carefully. But this was no time to get into a dust-up about which of us had the most dysfunctional childhood. Praying for some way to mend the rift between us, I came up with one possible remedy. "Don't go anywhere—I've something to show you."

I began hobbling toward Granny's Escort, then noticed Ben right behind me. "There's no need to trail me."

"Who's to say you're not going to get into your car and peel out of here?"

"I doubt Granny's car would peel anywhere," I said, determined not to take offense. Ben was hurting—and I was going to make it better. I opened the door, pulled out Granny's scrapbook, then pushed it into his midsection.

"Oomph," Ben grunted, clutching the album. "What am I supposed to do with this?"

"Whatever you want to." I felt another weepfest come on, at the thought of looking at the scrapbook again, but there was no getting out of it. "I want to prove that I don't think I'm better than you—and that you can trust me. Because I'll trust you—with this."

I held my breath as Ben opened the Moore's Hall of Shame book, and scanned several pages of my father's accolades. "Like

I said, your dad was a big shot all right." He started to close it. "Are you trying to rub it in?"

I grabbed the cover, and flipped the scrapbook back open. "Keep reading."

Ben turned two more pages, then, "Jesus H. Christ—what is this?"

"It's showing you the perfect family I come from." As penance, I made myself look at the page, bad news, all of it, and caught a glimpse of my father's indictment. "It's all here. My father, the liar and cheat who trashed his grand political career *and* his family."

In silence, Ben turned more pages. Finally, "Aislin—I didn't know—Mom never said..."

Fair's fair—now Ben was pitying *me*. "You'll see, I hope, that I never expected money from him, and I've no intention of accepting it. But Granny wants me to see him."

Ben was silent for what seemed long enough to gather dust. "Maybe I've misread the situation," he finally said, his voice stiff. Then he turned to the last set of clippings.

A thought zinged out of nowhere. Was I forgetting something?

"What's all this about your father adopting a—"

Bloody hell! I slammed the scrapbook shut, pinching his fingers in the process, and yanked on it. "We'll look at the rest another time, shall we?"

But Ben didn't relinquish his hold. "You've got another brother or sister somewhere?"

"No! Really, I'll fill you later, but right now—" I practically wrenched the book from his hands, tearing frantically through my mental how-to-change-the-subject files, then...ah ha!

Liz!

"Wouldn't you know, I've got to run." I flung the scrapbook into Granny's car. "I forgot that Liz's coming to Galway—unexpectedly. In fact, I'm going to meet her at Granny's."

"Is she all right? She's been acting a little…strange, lately."

"I thought so too," I said, to prepare Ben for the shocking news I'd have to tell. "I thought it was her…diet—that she wasn't getting enough fats or something. But it turns out that she…she and Dan are—"

Ben's mobile chimed, and this time he jerked the phone out. "It's Dan. He's called me at least six times today."

"You'd better take it," I said, a bit ominously.

Ben took one look at me, then put the phone to his ear. "Dan —what's going on?" He lost color. "Are you out of your goddamn mind?"

I must say, it was a relief not to be on the receiving end of Ben's fury.

"Jesus, you are one misguided son-of-a—Liz's the best thing that ever happened to you!"

Though we'd never met, I was plenty furious with Liz's husband. But now I almost felt sorry for him. Obviously, Dan was explaining their blowout not being his fault, but Ben just as obviously, wasn't buying it. "You're nuts, Liz'd never do that— she's *friends* with a guy, because you're too damn busy for her."

Pause. "I get it now," Ben yelled back. "You didn't walk, she's leaving you! Jesus, you've let your marriage go to hell! And you're kidding yourself—she wouldn't leave unless her back was to the wall. You've lost her, you're going to lose your kids, and all you can do is argue about who goddamn left who? I'm going to goddamn hurl!"

Holy St. Joe, when you're upset, you're almost eloquent, I thought admiringly.

"You have lost your goddamn demented mind! You want to trash your marriage? Be my guest. But if you don't do something drastic to get your family back, you and I are through. So get out of my face before I really do puke all over you—"

Dan must've been explaining something again. "Then call her, you dumbshit!"

294

Another long pause. "It's not too late, you can always—" Ben stopped and met my eyes. I was the first to look away. "There's one thing you can do—get your sorry ass out here as fast as you can…it's up to you."

Ben rang off, then stared at the phone in his hand like it was Enemy Number One. "I don't believe this. Liz and Dan. My best friends."

"Liz hasn't been happy here," I ventured, in case Ben got the idea to go off on her too.

"And that she's taking the kids to the States." Ben sighed heavily, and pocketed his mobile. "I didn't see it. Dan was acting really stressed out, but I thought it was because he was taking on more projects than we could handle."

Strange, wasn't it? How fast we'd segued from our Unhappy Past, to Liz and Dan's Unhappy Present. But it was actually a nice change to feel sad for Liz, instead of for Ben and me. "I'm to give her a ride to Shannon airport tonight."

I hadn't asked Liz if she'd explored every avenue to saving her marriage, like all the relationship gurus counseled. But then, I doubt you could find anyone less qualified than I to give advice about relationships.

Ben scrubbed his fingers on his hair. "Shannon airport," he repeated.

"Liz is meeting me at Granny's." I slammed the Escort's passenger door, pulled out my keys and limped to the driver's side. Thinking what Liz must have been going through, while I was oblivious, I put too much pressure on my bad ankle, and stumbled.

"Wait a sec." Ben grabbed my elbow, then he swooped me into his arms and sprinted toward his car.

It was like flying. With a sexual thrill thrown it. For one glorious moment, I forgot to feel like shite. "Ben…!"

"No time." Ben panted. "We've got to talk Liz out of leaving!"

He set me down next to the door, unlocked and opened it. "Get in."

"But there's Granny's car," I objected. "Let's leave the keys with Pat. He'll find someone to drop it off at Rosehill."

Ben gave her a strange look. "Someone you don't even know? What if they try to steal—" he broke off. "Oh. I get it. Everybody trusts each other around here." He plucked the keys from my hand and ran inside.

I was still trying to climb into the Micra with one working foot when Ben returned. "Here," he said, and without ceremony, thumped me into the seat. Two seconds later, he had the driver's side unlocked and was leaping behind the wheel.

"Now this," he said, "is peeling out."

As gravel clinked around the rear wheels, a cloud of dust rose from Hurley's car park. Ordinarily, it would be horribly awkward to be joyriding round the countryside with someone you've just had a huge fight with, but there was nothing like someone else's break-up to take the pressure off. "We'll be at your grandma's in two minutes."

"Unless the Guards get you," I reminded him, my father's Life of Crime still fresh in my memory. Even if he hadn't been convicted, the result was the same. A wrecking ball in the wall of your life.

Speaking of wrecks, I remembered Ben and I weren't even close to working out our conflicts. "Now that you know all about my father being a right loser, and that there's no way we're planning anything underhanded, will you reconsider Kevin's visit?"

Ben's face grew stern. My fingers itched to smooth away his worry lines. I'd actually moved my hand when he said, "No." The kind of "no" with finality written all over it.

I clenched my fingers. *Things can't get much worse if I ask him...* "Well, then, is there any way I can get you to change your mind about...what you said yesterday?"

"Which was...?"

"About us being parents...together."

"What's the point?" He stared through the windscreen. "We've proved we can't be friends. And we'd never make it as a couple. So nothing's changed."

"I get it—you still can't trust me." I couldn't even be bitter. "You're thinking, like father, like daughter? I guess now I'm the one who's not good enough for *you*."

Tears of self-pity blurred my eyesight, but I couldn't miss the way his hands tightened on the steering wheel. "Look, Aislin. We just don't..." He took a deep breath. "Love each other. Without that, it could never work."

I stared blindly out of the window. *We don't love each other.*

Well, Ben, you're half right.

How's that for timing? I asked myself bleakly. Just when I've mucked up our relationship past any repair, I've gone and fallen for him.

Truly, madly, deeply.

THE SHANNON CHA-CHA

"*A*re you absolutely sure you want to do this?" I asked Liz for the third time.

In the greenish light of the airport Ladies, Liz washed her hands, looking, quite frankly, haggard. She'd been about as chatty as a corpse too, on the journey to County Clare.

At Granny's, Ben and I hadn't been able to dissuade her from leaving straightaway. But as he said to me privately, "Knowing Dan, the chances of him racing across Ireland to save their marriage are pretty nil."

He and Granny had been trying to buck up everyone's spirits, but jollying up confused-looking kids and providing biscuits-and-tea therapy will only get you so far. While Granny handed more biscuits to Kevin and Josh through the open windows of Liz's minivan, Ben helped Liz strap Emily into her carseat. "Anything else I can do?" He had a helpless note in his voice.

"Well, a truckload of Prozac sounds pretty good about now," Liz said shortly, "but I think we're good to go."

Feeling pretty helpless myself, I asked him, "You want to come? Kevin adores airports, he'd love it if you'd share in the fun." I rather nobly didn't mention not wanting to drive with a sore ankle.

Ben shook his head, not meeting my eyes. "I don't want to... see her leave."

"Ah...right." I clambered in, and suddenly there was Ben grasping on my elbow, helping me. I'd have liked to take it as a hopeful sign for the future, but then he backed away, like I was carrying the Bubonic plague.

I summoned up a smile for Granny, standing next to the minivan. "See you soon."

She met my eyes, her gaze troubled, then glanced at Ben's averted face. "Well, child, maybe you'll take a holiday yourself, one of these days."

"I hope so," I said, and waited for Ben to add, *Aislin and I will be taking Kevin to see my mom soon*, but all he did was shut the car door in grim silence.

"No reason not too," said Granny, with determined gaiety. "A bit of cash and your passports, you can go where ever you fancy."

Ben turned his head, as if in slow-mo, to stare blankly at Granny. This Liz thing had clearly hit him harder than I thought, because the last thing I saw as we drove away was the black frown on his face.

NOW AT SHANNON AIRPORT, we were killing time in the loo after discovering that Liz's flight was delayed. So we'd hours to go even before they went through security. I sighed. It was going to be a long night.

I cast a quick glance at Kevin and Josh, sulking next to the door at the ignominy of being dragged into the Ladies for safety, then smiled down at the angelic Emily, asleep in her pushchair. "The delayed flight," I said low, "could be a sign. That you really need to think about this. I mean, being a single mammy can get...dreary at times."

Liz's eyes grew pink. "I could contemplate leaving Dan for the next week—no, the next year—but it wouldn't change anything." She emitted a great, long sniff. "He didn't even call the kids one last time this afternoon. I've had it with him."

"If ending your marriage makes you cry..." I ventured.

"The only reason I'm crying," and Liz wrestled rather violently with some tissues, "Is that I'll be getting divorced and never have sex again." She didn't appear to notice the startled looks of the other occupants of the loo.

"Boys," I said quickly, "I think we're all set." Before they got too restive—or before Liz grew more indiscreet—I herded them out the door. She followed listlessly with the baby. Back in the terminal, I settled the boys in a quiet corner to play with Josh's GameBoy so Liz and I could stroll with Emily in the immediate area.

I picked up where we left off. "You'll meet someone, surely?"

"No, I won't," Liz said with finality. "I'll be working and raising the kids and spending Saturday nights with Mom and never go anywhere."

Though I *hated* to remind Liz at a time like this, I said, "Well, if sex was so awful with Dan, maybe you won't miss it at all."

"It wasn't that bad," Liz said morosely. "For a Mr. Reliable."

I checked the boys, then gave her a skeptical look. "But that night, at my flat, you said it was—"

"I know what I said, but I was sort of...exaggerating. It's just that we hadn't done it in so long—"

"Wait—I'm no sex therapist," I broke in, hoping to forestall more Too Much Information.

"I'd almost forgotten, he does this thing with his—"

"Liz!" I said desperately. "When did you say your flight leaves?"

Liz wasn't listening. "What was missing was the...spark. I

kept turning down sex because the orgasms just felt sort of... empty. You know what I mean?"

"I'm afraid I don't," I said frankly. The mini-explosions I'd felt with Ben when we'd snogged years ago probably didn't count. "The proverbial mind-blowing...spark and I never really hooked up."

"Really?" Liz's eyes went wide. "I can understand Sam, but... not even with Ben?"

I gave a quick glance round the terminal. Not too many people about this time of night, and plenty of background noise...

"When we conceived Kevin," I said, blushing, "it was my first time, and...and..." I wished I'd never started this. Especially since I had to pretend my second escapade with Ben had never happened. But wasn't this sharing bit a good cause, applying first aid to Liz's marriage with the tried-and-true-Misery Loves Company? "It was rather... awful."

"You're kidding, right?"

"I wish I was." I reached for the pushchair. "Let me give this a go."

"Gladly." Liz relinquished the chair. "Well, come on, spill the rest..."

"Well, we were in the middle of snogging, and though I was mad about Ben, I didn't really plan for...you know, *it* to happen."

"When you're a kid, you never do." Liz commented, sounding cheerier already.

The truth was painful. But humiliating myself may as well be good for something. "So then..." I checked the boys again. "Ben was going off to the ship the next day, and my parents were gone for the evening. And I *thought* I was ready..."

Liz looked fascinated. "What happened?"

I hesitated. Don't stop now, we've got Liz's self-esteem picked up off the floor... "Things were rather rushed, and... awkward, since I didn't know what I was doing."

"Nobody does," said Liz.

"Well, this sounds like bollocks too, but the bathroom taps were leaking, and the drip, drip, drip was driving me batty. And before the feelings could really take hold, the spark, you know—it was over."

Liz patted my arm. "No big deal—it's like that for most people their first time. You and Ben just had the bad luck of it being your only time."

"Riiiight," I said uneasily. "There was hope, when Ben started to..." I squeezed my eyes shut for a second, remembering he'd just about revved me up... "but then, my parents came home, and here Ben was still in my room. So I..." Even after seven years, it was hard not to still feel ashamed of myself. "I got in a bit of a panic. I rushed him down the back stairs," actually almost threw him, "and pushed him out the door. When my father asked who'd been in the house just now, I said...I said it was only the...the handyman, fixing the tap."

Liz pulled an awful face. "Tell me Ben didn't hear that." When I didn't...couldn't answer, Liz added, "Did he?"

I nodded miserably. "Let's just say our goodbyes weren't too fond." No way could I tell Liz about the depths of Ben's hurt. "And now...well, I didn't want to add to your troubles, but...he and I...our friendship...is over."

"Oh." Liz sort of drooped. "I was so sure you and Ben were starting something—I mean, the attraction was obvious..."

I shook my head. "That's a no-go too. He wants to be Kevin's daddy, but that's it."

I waited for Liz's certain-to-be-encouraging advice: *Ben still cares, or he wouldn't have bothered to get in touch in the first place... Ben adores Kevin, he can't help but have feelings for you...*

But nothing. Liz only looked more downcast. I sighed again. "We'd better turn round here." I maneuvered the pushchair round a pink-cheeked older couple. As we started back toward the boys, I glimpsed a tall man striding—actually, race-walking

—through the terminal, a bearded, bear-like fellow huffing and puffing behind him.

As they came closer, the man's features grew clearer. He looked a lot like…

Oh. My. God.

I stopped walking and pressed my hand to my somersaulting stomach. It was! It was Ben! He'd discovered he loved me after all, couldn't wait another instant to tell me, and came all this way to save our relationship!

A lightness filled me, love expanding into my whole being…

Wait a minute… Dan had to be the huffer and puffer with him. Dan had to be into relationship-saving too! "Jaysus, would you look who's just come?" I elbowed Liz none-too-gently. "Isn't that your husband?"

It was a dream come true—the pair of them had finally got their priorities straight! Liz and I were headed for Happily Ever After Land… "Let's go say hallo!"

As I quickened my pace, the scene unfolded before me, like watching a film:

Liz stops in her tracks, hope shining in her face.

The fellows find the boys, each sweeping a son into their arms, the picture of Perfect Daddies.

Over Kevin's head, Ben looks round the terminal—naturally, for me! HEA imminent!

Then, Liz's romantic script goes all wrong. Dan falls into chair, Josh in his lap, seemingly uninterested in terminal-searching or wife-chasing.

"Look at him," Liz said, looking crushed. "Sitting there like a lump. He didn't come after me, that's for sure."

As I tried to reorient the storyline, Ben spotted me. He tipped Kevin out of his arms and into the chair next to Dan, his eyes fixed on me with laser-intensity. In fact, fixed with what could only and charitably be called Absolute Fury.

Suddenly, my own HEA was in mortal danger. He looked

SUSAN COLLEEN BROWNE

angrier I'd ever seen him. Prepared to meet my doom, I handed off the pushchair to Liz as Ben plowed toward me.

I felt exposed—nowhere to run or hide—but damn and blast him, I hadn't done anything wrong—at least not this time! He stopped right in front of me, his Wrath-of-God face as wrath-like as I'd ever seen it, and jabbed his finger at me. "What the *hell* do you think you're doing?"

"Helping a friend, if it's all the same to you," I said with spirit, to cover the Twilight Zone-ish, why-are-you-yelling-at-me feeling. "As you bloody well know."

Ben didn't even look at Liz, just stabbed his finger at me again. "You and me. In private."

"And hello to you too," Liz mumbled. She steered the pushchair around him, and plodded toward Dan, then crumpled into the chair next to him.

I met Ben's eyes squarely. "You know, she's a bit down. You could've at least faked a greeting."

"Who's got time for that when—Jesus Christ, you and I have had our problems, but I never thought you'd do this!"

"Do what?" I was really confused now.

When Ben grabbed my bag, I couldn't seem to move until he'd nipped it off my arm, opened it, and was rooting around in it. "Did you really think you'd get away with it?"

"Wha—?" I jerked my head back as Ben thrust two passports at me, an inch from the end of my nose. "If the plane hadn't been delayed, my son would've been halfway across the Atlantic by now!"

So that was it—Ben wasn't here to declare his love. He thought I'd betrayed him yet again. The poofy-loving sensation in me collapsed, until I was dizzy with hurt.

Instead, I gritted my teeth, straightened my spine. "You," and I smacked his hand—the passports dropped on the floor but I couldn't bother with that now—"have a fecking, monster nerve. You thought I would actually..." I had to keep my anger alive

304

and kicking, or I'd dissolve into a puddle of pain, "...take Kevin to see my father, when you'd expressly not given your permission?"

"Your grandma mentioned you packed your passports in your purse last night—how stupid do you think I am!"

"You—you...gobshi...you eej—" I didn't have the strength to even swear at him. "You wouldn't know the truth if it fell on you!"

The faintest glimmer of uncertainty appeared in Ben's eyes. "But...you've done everything you can to avoid a parenting agreement."

"Still, you thought I'd sneak off, without luggage, without so much as a clean pair of knickers? You really do think I'm the lowest of the low." *Good job I found that out before I fell even harder for you than I already have.*

"You were so gung-ho on seeing your fath—"

"Yes, *sometime*, but not tonight, for bloody's sake!"

Ben stared at me, and the aggression in his face slowly morphed into shame. "Wait a minute...I may have gotten this all wrong..."

I refused to feel sorry for him. "No, you've *really* got it all wrong."

Ben slowly picked up the passports. "Jesus, Aislin, I'm sor—"

"Shut up. I'm talking now. I'm not sure how I feel about my father, but he'd been ill. I thought, sometime soon, I could give him his bloody check back in person. For once, I wanted to at least try to do the right thing."

When he opened his mouth again, I grabbed my handbag back. "I said, shut up! I know our friendship is over, but friends or not, I'd never do a back-stabbing thing like that to you. Ever."

Ignoring Ben's stricken look, I stepped around him and headed for my dozing son. Unfortunately, that also meant hanging about with the McCarthys, who were surrounded by a cloud of marital depression, and not-even-thinly-veiled hostility.

"Lovely to meet you," I said to Dan, who mumbled something similar by way of reply, but Jesus, they were a sorry bunch. Liz sagged in the chair next to her husband, Emily sagged, sleeping, in her pushchair. Likewise, Josh sagged, asleep as well, on Dan's lap, while Dan looked about as sad as a person could look without actively crying.

As I collapsed next to Kevin, I knew I'd bottomed out not only as an inadequate mammy, but an awful one. Because my poor child was stuck asleep in an airport in the middle of the night while his parents argued in public like tinkers, but I was too shattered to care.

BREAKING UP IS HARD TO DO

*B*en, slumped in the chair on the other side of Dan, was as trapped as I was. But when Liz muttered to Dan, "Don't feel like you have to wait here with us," I knew their silent treatment was preferable to the pair of them actually speaking.

Escape, I thought, and started to rise as Dan stuck out his bearded chin. "And where else would I go?"

"In case you need to find a wireless hotspot or something." Before I could get to my feet, Liz grasped my arm. "Don't go."

I slumped back into the chair, unable to miss Dan's wounded look. "You're really going to do this, then?"

"No, I drove all the way across Ireland for the hell of it," Liz snapped at him.

I hunched my shoulders, trying my best to close my ears. And to think, marriage counselors had to hear this sort of thing all day long. So, as Liz's Ever-Supportive Friend, I was privy to the gory details of their marriage-busting fight. There was the usual, money, in-laws, *money and* in-laws—Liz spending too many euros on phone calls to Seattle—and work of course. Dan: *You* know *I'm dead keen to make a big success of MacCar.* Liz: *For*

307

you, the kids and I are work, the office is playing. Well, at least they weren't arguing about sex. Then a major breakthrough...

"Ben thinks I'm an fecking eejit," Dan confessed. "Don't you, boyo?"

"That's right," Ben muttered. "But then, I know all about being an idiot."

A flare of hope hit me—not that Ben had changed his mind, but that maybe this fight would eventually conclude and I could leave. Until Dan said, "Ben said he was through with me if I didn't—"

"Ben!" Liz hissed. "Are you asking me back because *Ben* told you to?" She jumped up, and for a minute I thought she was going to hit Dan with her handbag, even with Josh on his lap. "I won't sit here and be insulted..." Then Emily whimpered in her sleep. Liz abruptly slumped back in the chair.

I've concluded that babies always sense when something's wrong—but you're usually too distracted by their crying or throwing up or other proven method of getting attention to see things from their point of view. "It's all right, honeybunch," Liz whispered. She stroked Emily's limp little hand, and I knew she'd forgotten all about the lot of us. "You don't want Mommy to sacrifice her self-respect, do you?"

Then Dan was on a new tack. How he'd been Googling something, and gotten inspired. This sounded more promising, but Liz pounced on him. "Isn't our leaving enough inspiration? Think of all the work you can get done."

Dan persevered. "I looked up 'marriage,' and I found this grand quote from Simone Signoret."

"The French actress?" Liz said sarcastically. "Great. Wisdom from someone who makes a living pretending to be other people."

Dan wore the sort of dogged, half-dead expression you'd see on people doing the last mile of a marathon. "'It is threads, hundreds of tiny threads,' he began, "which sew...'"

"I don't have time for this," said Liz. Just then, their flight announcement crackled over the PA system. She began pushing herself out of her chair. "We're out of here."

My relationship with Ben was in shreds, but maybe... "Liz." I reached across Kevin and touched her arm. "Don't you be an eejit too—let him finish."

Liz pressed her lips together, then hung her head. "But it's easier," she whispered. "Being angry, leaving."

From some unknown fount of wisdom, I said, "Do you really want the easy way out?"

Liz didn't answer, only clenched her handbag. So apparently, this reconciliation was in my inadequate hands. I prompted, "Dan, you were saying?"

The poor man looked terrified, but he went on, " '... hundreds of tiny threads, which sew people together through the years. That's what makes a marriage last...'"

I thought we were on the upside of this, until he finished, "'more than passion or sex.'"

I saw Liz's knuckles turn white. "Thanks for reminding me," she said, "of what a lousy sex life we have. We *had*."

I scrambled out of my chair, not up for the sex stuff at all. Ben jumped up and dashed away too. Okay, so neither of us was therapist material. "Don't leave me," Liz beseeched, but all I said was, "This is between the pair of you. While Ben hovered near a closed-up shop, I took shelter behind the nearest kiosk. But have you ever noticed when you're trying so hard not to eaves-drop, suddenly your hearing becomes superhuman?

Don't you see? Dan was pleading. *We've lots of threads. Should we really rip 'em all out? But I can't go on—the way we were,* says Liz. Dan comes back with, *I'm a right bollocks, but if you'll give us another chance, I can change...*

Then, if you can believe it, they actually started talking. About selling the house, getting a smaller one. Next, maybe Liz finding a job she liked better...Then there was a protracted silence. A makeup kiss? I peeked round the corner of the kiosk, for a progress check, but Dan only wore a pained look.

"What if I...adjusted my...goals for the business? Not work... so many hours."

"You could really do that?" Liz asked.

"I think so," Dan sounded determined. "If it's all right with you, Benjy," he said louder. Ben took two cautious steps toward them. "Change the business plan a bit," Dan explained. "More free time, less money."

"Anything for the cause," Ben said, with a half smile.

I could see Liz's hand resting on Dan's arm. I thought we were home free until I heard the dreaded word: *Counseling*.

Dan made a predictable protest; there was more backing and forthing, then he said, "I tore an awful lot of threads, didn't I?" Liz gave him such an incredulous look, I realized this was incredibly insightful of him. Then she said, "You've left something out."

The silence seemed to extend to the next century. Finally, "I'm sorry, Lizzie."

Liz's mouth trembled, relief blooming on her tired face, and Dan looked like he'd just got a stay of execution. He leaned toward her, nearly squishing Josh, a kiss clearly in the works, but Liz drew back. "Not until after we've seen the counselor," she said primly. And actually smiled at Dan teasingly.

Since I'd facilitated this reconciliation, didn't I have the privilege of a final bit of advice? Unable to help myself, I scuttled back to Liz. "I've heard dating your estranged spouse does wonders for a marriage."

Only Liz got the last word. "But I'm not putting out until we're going steady."

THE TRUTH WILL OUT

*T*here's something about watching two people fall *back* into love that helps you forget your own life is a shagging train wreck. Especially when your Troubled Couple wears the kind of glow that could light up the entire airport terminal.

Ben and Dan also worked in a bit of male re-bonding. Ben: "Looks like you pulled it off, you lucky bastard." Handshake, lots of throat-clearing. Dan: "Easy for you to say. You're not the one seeing the shrink."

With the fellows thus occupied, of course I had to hug Liz. "Looks like your flight will have three empty seats."

"Apparently driving hundreds of miles and wasting a fortune on plane tickets really paid off." Liz giggled as we broke apart. "And don't forget our luggage gets an all-expenses-paid trip to New York."

"It's fantastic, you and Dan staying together," I told her. "Deirdre and I would've been lost without you. But where's the passionate make-up kiss?"

A secret smile curved Liz's lips. "Don't think I wasn't tempted. But Dan and I never were into the tempestuous stuff.

I'll leave the big dramas to you. And—" She cut her eyes toward Ben.

My smile faded. "I'm done with dramas. And Ben and me—we're done too."

"What about your long drive back to Galway—"

"Now there's a good time for you." I gave a short laugh.

"I meant, could be a great opportunity for making up," Liz suggested, looking even glowier.

"Sorry, Liz." Clearly, the lovesick, rosy-spectacled state of her had her believing in the impossible. "It's too late for sorting out anything with Ben." *We've hurt each other too much.*

Liz gave me one of those wise/married-woman looks. "If you hadn't told me to hear Dan out, I'd be on that plane right now. And my kids would be without a father." As she slung her holdall over the pushchair handles, Dan joined her, holding a sleepy Josh in one arm. "Think about it." With a final wave, the McCarthys trooped of the terminal, trailing a hint of forgiveness in their wake.

As Ben and I awkwardly stood over our sleeping son, I wondered, what next? Lighting into Ben over the passport misunderstanding no longer seemed important. Like I'd told Liz, it...*we* were so over. All that remained was to rouse Kevin and get the hell out of this airport.

Kevin murmured in his sleep, his little chest rising and falling, his lashes making half-moon shadows on his cheeks. I reached for my handbag, thinking, *might as well get this over with*, when Ben leaned down and kissed him. I froze, transfixed by the love in his face, then gazed round the airport like I'd never been here before.

Being here at Shannon, with *Ben*, when I'd had such an epiphany about daddies the last time I'd come here, had to be more than a coincidence. It had to be a *sign*.

My eyes stung. Had I gone through so much to give Kevin a daddy, just to cut Ben out of my heart and my life alto-

gether? Even if he never returned my love, it was in everyone's best interest if we cleared the air and he could get on
with being Kevin's father. And if he was affected by the
McCarthy reconciliation even half as much as I was, I might
not find a better time to… "I've something to tell you," I made
myself say.

Ben didn't speak.

Whoever said silence is golden was full of shite. Still, I forced
out, "I've made so many mistakes about…*everything*, I've lost
count." I wrapped my arms round myself, in dire need of some
hugs right now, but my own were the only ones available. "But I
thought if you could somehow trust me again, we could share
raising Kevin."

He looked bleak. "I don't know—"

"Let me finish." I had to get this out fast. "If you truly believe,
though, that our being friends is hopeless, we'll do exactly as
you wanted—you'll be Kevin's daddy, and have nothing to do
with me."

Not so long ago, I could have burrowed into his arms, but
those days were gone. "I never told you the *real* reason I wanted
Kevin to know his daddy." I was desperate for Ben to say something halfway encouraging—even a look would do—but all I got
was his jaw clenching.

"I've shuttled Granny to the airport over the years," I began.
"Call me sentimental, but I can't keep my eyes away from the
reuniting families. Especially the kids and fathers. When they
catch sight of each other, the children start running, the dads
open their arms wide. And suddenly, the whole place rings with
'Daddy, Daddy!'"

Ben's nose turned pink, giving me the courage to finish. "I…I
knew I had to try, to give Kevin a chance to feel that same joy.
I…can't think why I left it off my silly list." I managed not to say,
that you ripped up.

"Aislin, the passpor—"

"It's all right." I said gently. "Anyone might've thought the same."

Another muscle shifted in his jaw. "If...uh... you ever go on a trip with Kevin, I'll make sure to meet you at the airport."

Nice of Ben to say it, but I didn't see that happening. He'd made it plain how he felt about my taking Kevin anywhere. I glanced at our son, still dozing peacefully. "It's funny—well, sort of," I said. "You thinking you weren't good enough for me."

Ben rubbed a hand down his face. "Maybe we should... reassess that sometime."

"How about now?" I took a quavery breath. "Because I'm the one who's not...good enough for you."

"I hope you don't mean some garbage like you didn't finish college, or that you work in a shop." Ben gave me a straight look.

"You left out that my dad's sort of a criminal." I hugged myself tighter, and shivered. "But I need to tell you the real reason I didn't want to see your solicitor."

Ben suddenly slung off his jacket and draped it over my shoulders. It wasn't his arms round me, but it was close.

"Aislin, I don't need to be hit over the head. You felt cornered, and I can't blame you. I was pressuring you pretty hard."

I clutched the jacket together with a shaking hand. "Actually, you *can* blame me." Strange, that it was only this afternoon when I realized how I felt about Ben. Hadn't I always loved him? Unfortunately, what I had to say would destroy the slightest chance he could love me back.

"I didn't want to involve a solicitor in Kevin's visits because I'd already had a run-in with child custody. When I..." I swallowed. Sometimes, time doesn't heal all wounds—just rubs salt in them. "I..."

"Christ, what is it?"

I whispered, "When I almost let my father adopt Kevin."

Ben opened his mouth, but no sound came out.

"S-s-s-so..." My teeth chattered. "N-now you know what a horrible mother I am. G-g-good job we never went beyond our one-off at the Lodge, isn't it? Because I'd rather be alone, than be with someone who's got to think—quite rightly—that I'm beneath contempt."

Ben just stood there, looking like he was in some kind of trance, until I couldn't stand it any more. "You *are* thinking it, aren't you?"

He whirled around, saying, "Be right back," over his shoulder, and strode away.

My knees wobbled, and I dropped into the chair next to Kevin. I'd disgusted Ben so much he had to find a loo so he could puke, that was it. I stared at my knees, wondering how I'd endure the trip back to Granny's with him.

I lost track of the time, only dimly aware of another scratchy "call for boarding" announcement, then suddenly Ben was in front of me, grasping my elbows. "Come on—you're on Liz's flight to the U.S." He pulled me to my feet, and waved two boarding passes at me.

I gaped at him. "Have you gone mad?"

Ben stuck my handbag into the crook of my arm, then carefully lifted Kevin. "Hey, there, buddy," he said softly as Kevin roused, "you're about to have an adventure."

"Oh, good," Kevin murmured.

I wanted to cry, seeing my little boy nestling his head so trustingly against Ben's neck, but I was *way* too upset. "Didn't you hear me?" I hissed. "I told you, I almost gave..." I cut my eyes toward Kevin, "...away!"

"Yeah, I heard you," Ben said. "You're still going."

"I just can't run off like this—" Could it be *another* sign? Liz and the kids not getting on the flight to New York—making room on the plane? *No, no, and no...* "But I...I haven't done a Pro and Con list," I almost wailed.

SUSAN COLLEEN BROWNE

"Look." Ben gave me a gentle push. "I'll never have the chance to make things up with my dad, but it's not too late for you."

"I…we can't go—we've no clothes!" I sputtered.

"So find a mall," said Ben.

"But my job—Polly—"

"I'll call Deirdre."

"But I can't leave my granny—"

"I'll go see her, tell her you're off to see your dad." He handed me our passports, that he'd picked off the floor. "Think how happy she'll be, huh? Then she and I will take another look at her scrapbook."

My bewildered mind skimmed over the word "scrapbook," then promptly forgot about it. I felt like I was on one of those airport conveyor belts, borne along by the force of Ben's plan. "He might be gone from home—out of town—"

"You said he'd been ill—he'll be home," Ben said, then suddenly, we were at the check-in. He could go no further. He set a sleepy Kevin down and pulled out his wallet.

"B-b-but my father," and I made a desperate, last minute appeal to Ben's sanity, and couldn't worry about Kevin hearing, "almost *stole* him! How can you trust him?"

"Your tickets include a connection to the Twin Cities, and here's some cash for a rental car. And hotel, if you need it." Ben stuck a wad of money into my hand. "Have I forgotten anything?"

"Your wits!"

For want of a better place for it, I stuffed the cash in my bag, while Ben gave me a faint grin. Then he leaned down to kiss Kevin on the top of his head. "Be good, son. See you soon."

He straightened, and met my eyes. "I can trust him. Because I trust you."

Now you tell me? A flood of confused emotions rolled over me, too many to sort out. I could only stand there staring at him, my feet seemingly permanently attached to the floor. Then I remembered Ben's jacket, and slipped it off my shoulders.

Ben caught it and slung it over my arm. "You might need it."

I willed him to kiss me, at least touch me. Or at a rock-bottom minimum, let me know why he thought he had to prove his trust with this hair-brained trip. But he only said, "Get going, before you miss your plane."

In a daze, I somehow got Kevin and myself through security, boarding the plane, flight preparations and takeoff. Blessedly—since making conversation with a six-year-old was the last thing I could handle right now—Kevin dropped off again within minutes, wrapped in his daddy's jacket.

As we flew against time, deeper into the night, I still couldn't fall asleep. Because as soon as I gave up trying to decipher Ben's feelings, I was gripped by the ordeal in front of me.

Jaysus. I've gone and done it now. And no getting out of it. I really will *have to face my father.*

THE SURPRISE VISIT

*P*ut together the Minneapolis-St. Paul morning rush hour, a jet-lagged, really bad driver from abroad—and God help us, fighting the urge to drive on the other side of the road—traffic that seemed to have quadrupled since the last time said driver had gone this way, *and* a travel-hyped child whining for crisps and a Cadbury's for breakfast, and you have a recipe for disaster.

So perhaps the most reliable indicator that this trip was indeed a sign, was that we managed to make it to the suburb of Wayzata in one piece. A glimpse of Lake Minnetonka prompted me to the proper turns, then I crept past summer homes that once belonged to Minnesota's old-time filthy rich grain/railroad/mining magnates. I passed the last estate, and moments later, pulled in front of a converted caretaker's cottage.

For a moment, all I could do was stare at the place. Could you have found any house with more unhappy occupants? There was my father, in the middle of a court trial, his career smashed to smithereens, my mother, upping the martini—not to mention Valium—quota weekly, and myself, a trapped young mother without a clue about how to raise a child. At least Kevin had been too young to realize how miserable he should be.

Have you forgotten? asked a small voice inside me. *Your father doted on him. And even babies know when they are loved. Do you?*

My heart was pounding so hard I thought it would burst out of my chest. Suppose my father slammed the door in my face?

Surely he wouldn't. Not to Kevin. Clutching my boy's small hand, I marched up the walk and knocked. *If there is a God*, I thought, *my father will be gone from home, and we can go to our motel and put this off a bit longer.*

But no. I heard footsteps—and if that wasn't a sign I didn't know what was. It was all I could do not to flee to the car.

The knob turned. As morning sunlight flooded the doorway, I saw a man's silvery hair, and my eyes went blurry. I blinked, and my father's face swam into focus.

I didn't move as a vast hurt sprinted through me, love and resentment all muddled together.

He looked the same. The same chiseled features, same Bill Clinton haircut, same Ralph Lauren polo shirt. The same piercing blue eyes.

But yet... My father seemed very pale beneath his tan, his shoulders stooped, and he held himself stiffly. *The surgery*, I remembered. And actually, he was vastly different. His eyes... they were the most changed of all.

"Aislin?"

"It's me...Da—yes, it's me." I donned my full-body emotional armor. All right, so he'd been ill, but that didn't mean I was going to slobber all over him. "I've brought Kevin to see you," I enunciated carefully. "Your *grandson*."

Wisely, my father knew better than to give me one of his flyby kisses. I sensed him bending over with difficulty, to say hello to Kevin. I only half heard my son's shy reply, and discovered my old longing for my father's approval was still there, duking it out with wishing he'd fall off the edge of the earth.

Kevin was saying, "I don't know any granddads. My friends're mostly dead."

"Do I look dead to you, kiddo?" said my father, in a jokey Chicago accent. Slowly straightening, he held out his arm, and I saw a frayed spot on his sleeve. "Whadaya say? Pinch my arm and find out."

Great. I was dying here, and he was going for the laugh.

Kevin took a tentative step toward him. "My mam says it's not nice to pinch people."

My father glanced at me. "I'll bet she'll say it's okay, just this once."

I glared back. He might spread his bloody charm on Kevin, but it wouldn't work with me! "So then, Kevin, give your granddad a proper pinch. So you know for certain he's no ghost."

Kevin slowly reached out, and pinched my father quickly on the forearm, then yanked his hand back. "I guess...you're really alive."

My father opened the door wider. "Now that you know the place isn't haunted, why not come in?"

Evidently Kevin wasn't as charmed as I'd thought. His faint grin disappeared. "I'm tired now, Mam. I wanna to go home."

"We're both knackered—we can't stay long," I said to my father coolly. Part of me wanted to hurt him for not immediately dropping to his knees and begging my forgiveness. Which of course he couldn't do, what with the surgery. If he had, it would've been so completely out of character, I'd have known the fairies had spirited my real father away and left this guy in his place. "We're headed to Eagle Prairie, to see Annie Carpenter," I lied.

"Annie Carpenter..." my father frowned. "Our...old housekeeper?"

"The very one," I said evenly. "And Kevin's granny."

"Kevin's gr…" his voice trailed away. "Oh."

Kevin said, "I didn't know we were—"

"Hush," I said under my breath. "Later."

I saw my father's shoulders droop even more. "Before you go, how about some breakfast? If you haven't eaten already?"

No way, no how… Before I could refuse, Kevin piped up, "Do you have egg?"

"I sure do. And ham *and* toast. So, will you stay?"

"Okay," Kevin said, and without consulting me, I'll have you know. "For a bit."

I gave in to the proverbial inevitable and followed them inside meekly—If truth be known, I was bloody famished—wondering where this take-charge little man-child had come from. Then it hit me. *His* dad.

Speaking of fathers, there was something else different about mine: the hint of supplication in his voice. A good thing, since I'd no intention of letting him bulldoze me anymore.

As my father began preparing the food, I looked round the room, bad memories oozing out of the woodwork like wraiths. Wasn't this the kitchen table where he'd read the paper, mouth tight with the stories on his trial? And there, the counter where Mother had made a midnight vodka safari, and slipped, banging her head on the edge?

I pushed the images away before I was tempted to run from the house. Although there was no way I could leave, because Kevin and his granddad were actually getting on like two old mates. I watched, unbelieving, as my father, whom I'd never seen even pick up a dishtowel, produce a very passable—and only a few courses short of a full Irish—breakfast. "You came just in time," he said, filling three plates. "I was about to head out to the golf course, try a little putting."

"I suppose you're still a bigshot round the Woodhill Country Club." I baited him deliberately. "And on the tennis courts."

"Not at all," he said. "I play at the public links in Orono. I stopped playing tennis *and* bigshot a long time ago."

That shut me up. And reminded me that my manners had gone missing. But I wasn't up for "let's catch up on the last four years" with this man, even if he was my father. Apparently not too upset to eat, though, I scarfed down the meal, and listened to him entertain Kevin. God, you'd think the man chatted up six-year-olds for a living.

As Kevin took his last bite, I stood up. "We're off for a bit of a sleep." Actually, I needed to find a place that sold knickers—I couldn't tell him we'd no clothes with us.

My father's expression changed. "There's room here, if you want to rest...or stay the night."

"No," I said baldly. I was afraid to fall asleep in this house. No—more like I was afraid to wake up here. What if I opened my eyes, and everything was back to the way it had been before?

"When do you leave for Eagle Prairie?"

"Tomorrow," I said, making it up as we went along. "But we..." I heard myself adding, "...could stop in before we leave."

My father escorted us to the door. "I'd like that. For breakfast again?" The hope in his voice shamed me further.

"Let's make it an early lunch." Which would cut a few hours off our visit—okay, so I was no saint. "Say, half eleven?"

"I'll be waiting," he said. Before I could lead Kevin down the steps, my father rested a surprisingly tender hand on my son's hair, then leaned down and kissed his forehead. "You used to call me Poppa."

THE BIG STRETCH

"I have a dad now," Kevin told my father the next day.

I watched my father out of the corner of my eye, not sure what to make of him. A good night's sleep, a long shower, and new pair of knickers went a long way toward my feeling like a new woman, but what was I to do with the new, improved John Moore?

"A stepfather?" he asked me. "Are you married now, Aislin?"

"She and Daddy aren't married," Kevin cut in, "but they like each other."

Oh, Lord. What those pesky mouths of babes get up to. And how Kevin had concluded *that* was a bloody mystery, when Ben and I had practically done nothing but argue since we laid eyes on each other again. My father looked at me with a question in his eyes.

"Annie's son—Kevin's father—turned up in Ireland a few months back," I explained stiffly. "And we're to share...custody."

"A boy needs his father," said my dad.

"Right," I said, hating to agree with him. "Which led to us coming to Minnesota, to have Kevin meet his American granny. He and his dad will want to visit her from time to time."

"I'd say so," my dad said, and set out a plate of sandwiches.

The familiar Midwestern vernacular tugged at my heart. I felt guilty all over again, for letting him think he'd nothing to do with the pair of us coming all the way from Ireland.

"It's a lucky thing, for Kevin to have his father around," said my dad, pouring three glasses of milk, and not a magnum of Champagne for him in sight. "Is he...a good man?"

I recalled suddenly, painfully, that my dad had hardly known his own father. The remembering softened me a little more. "He is," I said without hesitation, and missing Ben was a sharp twinge.

"Ah," my dad only said.

I realized the calculating edge to him was gone entirely. Floored, I struggled with a whole new perception of my father. Years of anger still curled up inside me, like a knot. But seeing my dad's humor and patience with Kevin, I wondered, *can I really let the past go? And simply live for the present?*

Or will I hold my grudge until it's pried from my cold, dead hands?

THAT AFTERNOON, we played tourists round the lake. My dad insisted on buying us ice creams, over my objections—I still had Ben's cash, after all—then indulgently watched us eat.

"You've gone off sweets, then?" I said, then could have bitten my tongue off. "Because of the, ah, aneurism?"

My dad nodded. "Your granny mentioned I'd had surgery?"

"Actually, Grace rang me."

He looked chagrined. "She fusses too much."

"Everyone deserves to be fussed over once in a while," I told him. *Even you.*

"Do they?" He didn't meet my eyes. When Kevin trotted ahead of us, he said, low, "I've let down a lot of people."

Will wonders never cease. "You mean...your constituents?"

"Your mother," he said, still not looking at me. "And you."

"What about Kevin?" I asked boldly.

My dad watched Kevin with a bittersweet pride. "I thought I was doing what was best for him. But I lost him anyway—like the rest."

As I tried to absorb *this* revelation—my dad almost apologizing—I thought, *here's an opening, you might never have another*...But I was mute.

When the silence stretched on, he glanced at me uneasily. "Your granny says you're happy in Ireland—you enjoy your work?"

"That's stretching it a bit—I might look for a new job," I said, not realizing until this minute that I needed to stretch *myself*. "I might even move to Galway."

I didn't know where that came from either. Maybe...just maybe, I no longer needed my life to be quite so *safe*. "We'll be closer to Granny—and to Kevin's dad. And yourself?"

I wasn't all that curious about my dad's life, but I'd had about all the self-epiphanies I could take for one afternoon.

"Golf can keep a fellow only so busy," he said, and pushed his hands in his pockets.

Pulled out of my self-absorption, I noticed a few worn spots on his trousers. And that the Clintonian hair was overdue for a trim. "What else do you do, then?"

"There's not much work for an ex-congressman who's been disbarred," my dad briefly. "Once in a while, some old pals send me a little under-the-table consulting work."

"I hope it pays more than my job," I joked, wanting to ease the pain in him.

He shrugged. "Keeps me in green fees."

I almost dropped my handbag. My father's check—I'd forgotten all about it. An impulse I hardly understood made me open my bag, reach inside...then I stopped myself. My dad had lost everything—except maybe his pride.

And why doesn't that make me feel better? Still, I shied away from having it out with him. I simply hadn't the courage.

So, then, I scoffed to myself. Your idea of Stretching Yourself is looking for a new job? What about trying the Really Big Risks on for size?

AFTER DINNER, Kevin fell asleep watching telly. I didn't mention Eagle Prairie, and my dad didn't ask. As the evening shadows lengthened, I made noises about going back to the motel, but I couldn't bring myself to move. The tension inside me, to have come all this way and not have the guts to confront my dad, spiraled higher and higher.

He got up to peer at Kevin. "I'll just move him to my bed—if it's all right with you."

That hint of humility froze my instinctive refusal, but as my dad started to bend over Kevin, I recalled his medical condition. "I'll do it."

His lack of protest told me a *lot*. He led us to the bigger bedroom, where I set Kevin on a threadbare, and familiar, duvet. Once we were back in the front room, me on the couch again, my dad in the armchair, I felt a clutch of anxiety eating at my middle. What now? Bedtime was still hours away...but how would I last that long, with all the emotional landmines between us?

The hum of a car engine, and the flash of headlights was a welcome distraction. "You're expecting someone?"

My dad shook his head. You don't get visitors, I surmised, and the knowledge added to the day's hurts. As the car passed the house I picked up the remote.

Commencing channel surfing—not very polite, but it was how I'd whiled away the empty hours in this house before—I felt worse than ever. Here we'd so much to talk about, and I was pretending to watch telly. Deep in my couch-spud mode, I disregarded a second vehicle passing by, but when a third approached from the original direction, I set down the remote. "Is it a regular motorway out there?"

"Probably summer tourists who've lost their way," my dad said. When the car parked in front of the cottage, he slowly rose. "They might need directions."

Sure enough—footsteps crunched on the gravel drive, then the stoop, and my dad had the door open before the visitor could knock. He really must be lonesome...

Then, as I heard a familiar voice, I bolted upright. "Sir."

THE SECOND CHANCE

"*B*en!" I gasped, and switched off the telly.

"Kevin's father, I presume," my dad said. I stood, dazed, as the men shook hands with the usual manly introductions: "Ben Carpenter." "John Moore." "Sir." "Call me John." Ben was barely across the threshold when he said, "Aislin and I have some unfinished business. If you don't mind." Pause. "Sir."

"Th-that couldn't wait until I got back?" I asked faintly.

"I didn't know how long you'd be gone." Ben said. But I sensed something uncertain, unsaid: *Or if you'd be back at all.* He faced my dad squarely. "I have some unfinished business with you too, sir." No small talk for this pair, evidently, even if they'd just met. "About my son."

"You went to see Granny," I said before my dad could answer. And the scrapbook...

"I said I would." He looked at my dad again. "Some people might say what happened with you and Aislin is old news or whatever, but I think you still have some explaining to do."

My dad didn't pretend to misunderstand. "Because I tried to adopt Kevin."

I could only stand there, shut out as my father and my once-lover went at it. *Mano à mano*. Jaysus, I never thought I'd see the day.

"That's right," Ben told him. "Trying to force Aislin to go along with it, you wronged her. And me."

"I realize that," said my dad.

I took a sharp breath. I *really* thought I'd never see the day.

"It was your idea to keep her pregnancy a secret from me, right?" When my dad nodded, Ben prompted, "I'd like a 'Yes' or 'no.' Sir."

"Yes."

"And talked her into keeping the baby?"

"That right," my dad admitted. "I'm not particularly proud of how I handled it."

"With good reason," Ben said. "Aislin should've been able to decide for herself. But I'm willing to hear your side."

I froze. Unlike *me*.

I've always been slow learner, and slower still to take the bull by the horns. But if ever there was a time for it, it was now. "Ben," I said, "I appreciate your sticking up for me, but...isn't this *my* life we're talking about?"

I INSTANTLY REALIZED I couldn't quite go it alone, and reached for Ben's hand. "Well." I stuck my chin out at my dad. "Let's have it."

My dad took his time. When he finally spoke, he wore a wobbly sort of dignity. "It's true, I did my best to persuade you to keep Kevin—"

"More like hounded me into it." Suddenly, so angry I could hardly see in front of me, I let him have it with both barrels. "I hated that you made *my* baby into *your* photo op, so you could get on the jury's good side. I hated that you hired that horrible nanny, so I couldn't learn how to be a proper mother." I clutched Ben harder. "And I hated that I got turned into Mother's nursemaid."

The memories were painful: getting my mother sobered up, dressed, and to the courthouse on time, where she sat, listing to one side of her seat.

"But that wasn't the last straw," I went on inexorably, my voice ragged. "It was when the trial was over, and you were free. You'd the adoption papers ready the same day—meaning you'd been planning it for a long time. How could you do it, Dad? How could you hurt me like that?"

He didn't answer. In the silence, Ben gently wrested his hand from mine—which I'd been clenching in a death grip. "I need something in my car," he said.

"Don't leave." *I need you.*

Ben shook his head. "This is between you two now." He let himself out.

I felt horribly shaky with Ben gone, but the longer he was gone, the stronger I felt.

My dad had a hunted look. "When I first came to America, and saw how it was here, I got a...what to call it? A grand notion. It wasn't exactly rational, but I wanted to...*be* somebody. Somebody *big*. Wanted to start a...a dynasty, like the Kennedy's."

How pathetic, I wanted to say, but I couldn't. Because it wasn't. "So, you were Irish, and made some money." I tried to sound sarcastic, but I failed at that too. "Not a bad start."

"You've heard what Ireland was like forty years ago. But here, in America, I could see my sons going to top universities, then heading for politics."

"Girls can be in politics too," I said sharply.

"But you and Grace weren't interested," my dad reminded me.

"So, you should have kept trying 'til you got a child who was," I snapped.

"Actually, I did," he said, which really took the wind out of my sails. Took the sails too.

My mouth trembled. "Wh…what do you mean?"

"Your mother and I had hoped for a big family, but…she had three miscarriages."

Three miscarriages. The reason she started drinking?

There was a long silence. "The third was stillborn," he said finally. "It almost killed her."

"When I was six years of age?" Dear God. All this time I'd carried round the childish paranoia that I'd been sent off with Granny because I was somehow…unlovable.

He nodded. "Still, I refused to believe that my dynasty wasn't meant to be. Instead of looking after your mother, and finding a new dream, I threw myself into the money and power game."

By the time I came back to America, for university, he'd been at the top of his career, surrounded by a parade of interns. How jealous I'd been, that they had a place in his life, and I didn't. No wonder I went out with that Kelly guy.

"The best players know how to bend the rules, but as you know, by the time Kevin was born, I'd bent too many past bearing. But he gave me a whole new lease on life. I was sure he was my second chance."

"But Kevin wasn't *your* chance." I grit my teeth. "He was *mine*. Not your personal wind-up, groom-for-your-ambition toy."

"He was more than that," my dad said, and his voice softened. "You're thinking I only wanted Kevin in court so I could look good?"

"Well, what else?" I folded my arms.

"Having him there…was a comfort," my dad said, looking a bit paler than he had before. "He made me remember that I should've done better by you and Grace. And…and made me remember…" Another long pause.

"Remember what?"

"The…the last baby. Who didn't make it."

SUSAN COLLEEN BROWNE

My belligerence crumbled. Almost timidly, I asked, "Was it by any chance...a boy?"

My dad didn't answer, only looked at me, and the heart I'd hardened so resolutely cracked open. Tears flooded my throat. "Dad...I'm sorry." *For both of us...*

Funny, that the Irish had a reputation for being famous talkers. When it comes to family secrets, their lips are all but soldered together. But my dad wasn't off the hook—yet. "But Jaysus, Dad—how fair would that have been for Kevin, being a replacement for the baby?"

He rubbed his forehead. "All I knew was that I could start my dynasty after all. Part of me knew it wasn't a healthy obsession, as unhealthy as your mother's drinking, but..." His voice trailed away.

Mother had taught me all I cared to know about addictions. And that you can't break your vice of choice until... "But you couldn't let it go...until you hit bottom," I concluded, feeling sort of wise.

My dad leaned against the wall, like he was having a hard time staying upright. "I'd avoided prison, but I was left with nothing. No dream. No profession." He looked like someone in an old photo—the colors faded, features blurred. "And no family."

"But there was Grace," I reminded him. For the first time, I felt better about my sister not forsaking the man entirely.

"I thank God for her. But I lost everyone else," Dad said, grief and regret in each word. "Kevin." Pause. "You."

That one syllable told me everything Granny had been trying to convey for months. The tight knot of anger inside me, that had slowly eased over the day, suddenly dissolved. "I think...I think you've found us."

"There's something I never got a chance to tell you," Dad said. As if an Irishman confiding his innermost secrets wasn't traumatic enough—for the teller *and* the hearer—there was more? "I'd always thought you were just like your mother—biddable, easily dominated. But when you stood up to me, took Kevin and left, I realized you were—"

"Stronger than you thought?" I put in.

"That's it." My dad pushed himself away from the wall. "A cold comfort, but I realized I did have a legacy. You were a fighter. Just like me."

"Oh." I sniffed hard. "It's just taken me a bit of time to jump into the ring."

DAD and I were looking at each other sort of uncertainly—and me thinking it was too soon to try on a hug but not knowing where else to go with my feelings—when Ben poked his head in the door. "Okay to come back inside?"

"Everything's...fine." I resolutely blinked away my tears.

"Great," said Ben. He looked from my dad to me, and back again, as if assessing the damage. "I've got to find somewhere to stay, before I totally forget what sleeping is like."

A proper sleep sounded pretty good to me too. But it seemed rather cold-hearted, to leave for our motel just after Dad had just spilled his guts. And come to think of it, a bit of mine were littering the floor too. I thought quickly. "Dad, have you any extra sheets? If Kevin can bunk with you, perhaps Ben could have the couch."

"Okay with you, John?" Ben didn't demur. I guess he could sense the emotional muck hanging round the place himself.

As we organized the bedding, Ben wrestling with the sofa hide-a-bed, my dad pretending he was helping, our busyness was like the last bit of anesthetic before it wears off and everything hurts like bloody hell. After finger-brushing my teeth, I'd just stepped out of the bathroom when Ben and my dad trod softly past me, stopping in the doorway of my dad's room.

"Just wanted to get a quick peek at Kevin before I turn in," Ben said to him.

I tiptoed into the hallway, and saw the tenderness on my dad's face as he gazed at Kevin. "I hope you'll bring him to see me every once in a while."

"You bet," Ben said, and cleared his throat. "Or you can come visit us."

Us? Before I could ponder *that*, Dad said, "I'd appreciate it, son."

Son? I thought my ears were deceiving me, until Dad carefully slung an arm around Ben's shoulders, and gave him a rather feeble pat on the back.

I backed into my old bedroom, realizing, in a bittersweet kind of way, that sometimes you have to just butt out and be gracious about it. And that father-son bonding wasn't limited to blood relations.

I looked about the plain little room, a small desk with bills and things scattered on it in the space Kevin's cot used to occupy. For the first time ever in this house, I knew an easy peace. And no trace of the spooks I'd felt haunting the place earlier.

I edged toward the desk to peer at some of the papers. Looking for more insights about my dad? I almost laughed at myself. Maybe just plain snoopy. But my smile faded when I got a closer look. There were bills all right. Hospital bills. And big ones—the likes of which I'd never seen.

A brief rap on the open door made me jump back from the desk. "I'm turning in," Dad said. "How about you?" His smile told me how much our staying meant to him. "I found an old nightgown of your mother's."

"Grand," I said, choking up a bit as he handed it to me. Of all the bittersweet experiences this weekend, my dad still having one of Mother's nighties had to be the saddest. "Guess I'm still a bit jet-lagged...I'll see you in the morning, Dad."

I met his eyes, remembering the forced jauntiness I'd seen in him today, and prayed that despair would never conquer him. "I'm…really glad we came."

"I am too," he said, and pink bloomed around his eyes. "Well, good night, Petunia."

My childhood name. I bit my lip hard as I watched him disappear inside his bedroom. I'd done so well, not blubbering all day despite the provocation—reconciliations being a tear-inducing business. I knew if I released one sob, I'd fill the cottage with an operatic wailing and gnashing of teeth. "I love you, Dad," I whispered. Maybe tomorrow, I thought, I'll say it aloud.

BACK TO THE FUTURE

*H*earing the various creaks from the hide-a-bed, I held on as long as I could, then stumbled my way to the front room. "Ben?" I whispered. "I couldn't sleep."

As my eyes adjusted to the dark, I saw him sit up. "I don't think ten minutes counts as insomnia," he said, laughter in his voice.

"Well," I persisted, "could I sit with you a bit?"

The sofa-bed creaked ominously. "If you're having trouble sleeping, you've come to the wrong place," he complained. "This has to be the most hellaciously uncomfortable bed—using the term loosely—I've had the privilege of sleeping in, and that includes my Navy berthing."

By now I could make his features out. I sat down before he could say no, the questions in my heart tumbling over each other. *Does your being here mean you've forgiven me?* Or even, *Do you love me? Or is there a chance you might in the future?* But I had to finish off the confession I'd started at Shannon Airport. "I just wanted to…talk."

Ben yawned. "I thought you and your dad had pretty much covered everything."

"Well...he's starred as the villain in the story," I said, feeling anything but sexy in my mother's nightie. "But you see...I've had a supporting role too."

A sudden breeze off the lake fluttered the curtains, and I shivered. From nerves or cold, who knew, but what the hell. "Could I climb in with you? I'm freezing."

Ben hesitated, then pulled the covers back. I crept in to lie on my side facing him. "What I wanted to say..." You'd think I'd be used to difficult air-clearing by now, but my throat tightened round the final details. "I told you before, I'll never win any prizes for best mammy..."

"Come on, Aislin, you were just a kid—"

"It doesn't matter. When my dad's money ran out, and the nanny was redundant, I realized how hard it was to be a mother, and the temptation..." My voice broke. "I'm shamed to say it, but I was seriously—overwhelmingly—tempted give Kevin up. But it wasn't until tonight that it...dawned on me..."

Ben touched my hand. Feeling the understanding in that touch, I said, "I thought I'd hated my father for trying to make me give up Kevin. But...it was myself I hated."

"But you didn't give him up," Ben squeezed my hand. "You hung in there, made it work. And he's a great kid. So no more of this 'I hate myself' stuff. Okay?"

"Okay," I said shakily. When he tugged on my hand, I took that as an invitation to nestle my head on his shoulder. I'd never felt safer.

We shifted and adjusted and he got his arm round me. "Before I forget," he said, "Deirdre wanted me to pass something along."

"Mmmm?" I was *waaay* too comfy to think about Deirdre.

"She saw a great job for you in the Situations Vacant." Ben tucked my head under his chin. "They need someone," he yawned again, "with a background in Irish cultural activities."

"I guess step dancing counts," I said dreamily. "But if you

flew thousands of miles to tell me that, I'm afraid you've wasted the trip," I smiled in the dark. "My job hunt will start—and stop —in Galway."

Ben's chin moved slightly. He had to be smiling too. "What d'you know—the job *is* in Galway."

The girl formerly known as Aislin would have leaped up, run to ring Deirdre, get all the particulars, and e-mail a letter of interest straight off. But right now, all that mattered to me was being here. In Ben's arms—well, almost. If the job *was* meant to be, it would stay vacant until I returned to Ireland.

"Anything else?" I asked, resting my forehead against his neck.

"I've got a message...from your grandma." Ben spoke slowly —two days without sleep will do that to a guy. "She's forgiven you for hiding the scrapbook at Rosehill. But after you showed me the scrapbook, I sorta half-guessed the adoption stuff. When I got back to her place after I put you and Kevin on the plane, she filled me in."

"I've given up trying to pull one over on Granny," I said, feeling I could have happily melted into Ben.

"But...before I drop off, there's...uh, something else I wanted to tell you." Ben sounded even sleepier, if that was possible. "Since I won't last much longer."

"Something else you flew thousands of miles to pass along to me?"

"That's right. It, uh, came to me," and a new significance came into his voice, "...that seven years ago, I totally overreacted to, uh..."

I braced myself.

"...You calling me the handyman."

I ducked my head, shame replacing my melty feeling. "I'm so sorry...really, I never meant to...to hurt you. I was just afraid—"

"The thing is, if I'd had half the guts I should've had, I would have marched back to face your dad, and told him how I felt about his daughter."

I held my breath, forgetting to feel horrible. *Well, how* do *you feel?*

"I'm seven years late, but I needed to finally face your dad myself. Prove that I'm, well, worthy."

"There's no one more worthy." I couldn't help touching his face, then I quickly pulled my hand back.

Ben captured my hand and kissed it. "After all the times I've blown up at you? I don't have any excuse, except that...oh, hell. It's always been easier for me to get upset. Instead of...you know, dealing."

"A man thing," I said. "Jaysus, you lot all do it."

"It seemed more politically correct to yell, than—okay, let's be honest here—haul you off to bed."

"Oh." Shivers of delight crept along my skin. "Since we're into confessions in a big way..." Wait...This was *the* Make or Break Relationship Moment. I had to do this properly.

"Could we get out of bed?"

"No," Ben said. "I'm too tired to move."

"Just for a minute," I coaxed. I pulled the covers back, and made Ben sit on the edge of the bed. Then I crawled into his lap and put my arms round his neck. "Is this...okay?"

"Could be better," Ben said. "We could be lying down."

"We will," I promised, but I was keen to see where this Meg March/John Brooke lap dance would go. "But what I was going to say...at the Lodge, after we...you know, did it, then argued so horribly, I thought things would never be right between us again. I was dreading a future with nothing but cold little e-mails between us for the next twelve years."

"What are you saying?"

I took a deep breath. "I've missed being your friend."

"I don't want you for my damn friend," Ben growled. "If you

339

haven't figured it out by now, I want you to be my lover. Permanently."

Pure joy flooded me. *Me, too,* I tried to say but couldn't, because Ben kissed me. It was every bit as good as the snogging we'd done before. Better even.

"I, uh..." Ben seemed to have trouble catching his breath, "decided I'd be optimistic, and stopped at a drugstore. Since I'm no longer carrying narky decrepit old condoms in my wallet."

I laughed against his mouth, then rolled closer to him, trying to figure out if there was any chance in hell to have it off with him without a cacophony of hide-a-bed squeaks, when a spring popped inside the mattress and bumped my stomach. "Oh, bollocks."

Ben sighed. "It's killing me to say this, but let's wait until we're alone—not with your dad down the hall."

"Could we..." I blushed, but well, all the magazines say you have to ask for what you want in bed. "Sometime soon, could we do a re-enactment of that bit you tried on, when we were on your couch?" I'd daydreamed non-stop about his mouth traveling down my tummy to my... "The next time, I'm planning for us to...you know, finish. Everything."

"You can bet on it," Ben said, trailing his hand across my breasts, and down my side. "Not making love to you, right now, is the hardest thing I've ever—"

"No, this is the hardest thing." I giggled, and let my hand creep toward his fly.

"Hey." Ben caught my wandering hand. "If you touch me again, I won't be responsible."

We proceeded to torture each other by lying down close, then describing what we were going to do the minute we were *really* alone, until my nascent jet-lag kicked in. "I didn't know you could fall asleep..." I mumbled, feeling like I couldn't stay awake even if my eyes were propped open. "...And still have a perfectly decent—using the term loosely—conversation."

"I'm living proof," Ben slurred. "I've been sleeping for the last half hour."

"I've one more thing to say," I managed sleepily. "I suppose if I can forgive my dad...I can forgive anyone."

Ben's whole body tensed up. "Even...me?"

"No," I said, and curved my arm round him. "Me."

EPILOGUE

You've Got Mail…Again

TO: Deirdre O'Donnell
SUBJECT: Minnesota travels

Hi Deirdre,

Well, you won't believe it, but I'm in Eagle Prairie now, to visit Ben's mammy. Thought of sending you a postcard, but I knew I'd get to Ireland before it did. Anyway, as you seemed keen for me to see my dad, I wanted you to know we've made up, and we'll probably get on great altogether from now on.

In case you're wondering whatever happened to that giant check my dad gave me, I'd like to tell you we're stopping in New York on our way back to Ireland, for a shopping spree, and I'd be bringing back quantities of Jimmy Choos and Prada hand-bags. But no. I did a sneaky thing, which I'm quite proud of. I stole an armful of my dad's medical bills to pay off. He'd never let me do it otherwise. If I've any money left over, I'll buy you a sponge bag from Target.

And before I forget, I need your advice. Think I should keep my own name, or go with Aislin Carpenter? That's right, Ben and I are mad for each other and making it legal. Any chance you're up for a gig as a wedding planner?

Love,

Ash

TO: Liz McCarthy

SUBJECT: Reconciliation

Hi Liz,

Well, I've just discovered for myself that making up feels tons better than breaking up. And now that I've given Kevin a daddy and a granddad in practically one fell swoop, I'm feeling positively virtuous! Well, maybe not entirely, but more on that later. Ben and my dad seem to have become grand pals overnight—Dad actually hugged him when we said goodbye. I've never seen the like before.

I hope your own making up is going great guns, and that Dan won't be out in the cold much longer. Speaking of which—in a roundabout sort of way—Ben's mam insisted on taking Kevin for a bit and shooed Ben and me out the door. We moseyed over to the local graveyard, where Ben had a good long chat with his dad. Apparently they had a few things to clear up, and weren't going to let a little thing like one of them being dead get in the way.

I tactfully skipped off to admire gravestones, which are practically fresh from the quarry compared to the ones in Ireland. Then we toured the town—and discovered my old house is now a B&B! So of course, I had to go inside for a look. Ben wasn't too keen, but upon discovering my old room wasn't let, I talked him into checking us in. Can you say "hourly rates"? Just kidding, but all that money was totally worth it, since I discovered there's this thing Ben does with his...

More later!

Love, Aislin

A BRIEF PEEK AT THE NEXT BOOK OF THE SERIES

BOOK 2, MOTHER LOVE

Irish girl Grainne Larkin wants three things for her thirtieth birthday: her mother's love, a baby, and dashing Irish-American Rafe Byrne—not necessarily in that order. When she encounters her longtime crush Rafe, sparks fly! But Grainne may discover that opening her heart—to Rafe, to the prospect of motherhood, and to her mother—is the biggest risk of all...

Prologue: Mother Love

The Gallagher Post: Gai Lannigan's Girl Talk

Baby Hunger

Lust for a guy is one thing. But lust for babies is a whole different story. And a lot harder to satisfy. The old cliché about biological clocks is just a polite way to describe waking up one morning, realizing you've wasted your youth, and now you can practically feel your eggs shriveling.

The viable ones, that is. The duds are probably sashaying merrily round your ovaries, snickering at their rapidly dissolving sisters.

If you've baby hunger but no daddy material on the horizon, you're probably thinking, how can I joke about this? I see your point. Your average baby fanatic is actually a bit of an addict, with a terrible craving for her fix. The trouble is, like other common addictions—say, drink, drugs and gambling—the temptations of babies are everywhere. (Which only increases the baby longing.)

Another painful truth is that baby-cravers often gravitate toward careers that provide maximum contact with babies, like pediatricians, or playschool teachers. Unfortunately, jobs like that give baby-lusters minimum contact with what they can't do without: unattached sperm-providers.

You might be one of the lucky ones, though, with several paternal prospects to choose from. But what if you're keener on having a baby than having a man? If word gets out, people will think you're quite heartless, if not altogether mad. Which bothers true baby-lusters not a whit.

Your road to motherhood couldn't be simpler: You pick a fellow you know will drop his drawers for you, no questions asked. Unfortunately, any guy who'll sleep with you at the snap of your fingers is a guy who's had it off with every available female who's crossed his path—not the sort you'd want condom-less.

You could always bide your time and wait for the perfect, baby-making love machine. But who knows how long that could take? So my advice is to go for a nice guy with a presentable gene pool, who won't make a scene when you cool the relationship. After the deed is done, that is. Trouble is, nice men want to do the decent thing...

MOTHER LOVE

CHAPTER ONE

"*Y*ou don't think Gai *really* wants a baby, do you?" Justine Egan tapped the screen of her mobile, then drained her pint.

"Don't tell me you're reading that blog again." Crunching a shortbread finger in a dim corner of O'Fagan's, I stared enviously at Justine's glass. A pity I'd no head for drink. Today of all days, I'd have liked something to take the edge off. "Aren't you meant to be checking recipes for birthday cake?"

"Not now." Justine thrust her phone across the scratched wood table. "Check out today's *Girl Talk*."

"I came to the pub to relax," I said as she went to the bar for a refill, "not read about angsty girls with too much time on their hands." But to please Justine, my flatmate and best friend, I scanned her favorite blog, helping myself to a third biscuit. As if a self-induced sugar coma might help me forget why I was mainlining the stuff in the first place.

You know how it is—the day your ex-boyfriend gets married, it's like a huge insect squished on the windscreen of your life. It's not like you *care* or anything, it's just that the oul' bugger is blocking your vision.

O'Fagan's wasn't the best place to clear your head either, with strings of Guinness flags hanging listlessly from the ceiling and ancient, smoke-stained paneled walls. And today, the place felt more claustrophobic than usual—a far cry from the flower-bedecked, sun-drenched nuptials I could see in my mind's eye half a world away.

Not that I wanted to be shackled to some guy for life or anything. But there's something about people you know tying the knot that gets you pondering your own future. Even if it's a wedding you'd no interest in attending, if they prostrated themselves at your feet and begged you—

"Is that *Girl Talk* you're reading?" Eamonn winked at us from behind the taps. "What's she on about today?"

"Getting pregnant," Justine told him. "With the right guy."

"And before your ovaries wither like raisins," I put in.

"Aw, Grainne." Eamonn shuddered. "Who wants to hear that female stuff?" In a former life, he'd attended seminary, even if he hadn't lasted long.

"Well, you asked." I took another bite of shortbread. "Although," I added under my breath, "there's something to be said for ignorance is bliss."

"Amen to that," said Eamonn. Really, the man had ears like underwater sonar. He resumed his glass polishing and pint-pulling and whatever else a barman does at Dublin's least trendy and most morgue-like pub, on a late spring afternoon. "Sure, I can't see why *The Gallagher Post* publishes such rubbish, though."

"Because it's trendy," Justine retorted. "And every girl I know reads it." She returned to the table with her second pint, and plucked her mobile from my hands. "So, what do you think of the post? The baby bit is rather strange, but when she mentioned the perfect man—"

"No such thing," I said. "That's why most girls end up settling for good enough…"

. . .

MOTHER LOVE IS available for **free** in ebook format at your local library—all you have to do is put in a request, or use your library's request app...And of course, you can find *Mother Love* at your favorite online retailer, in ebook or print!

ACKNOWLEDGMENTS

I dedicate this book to my daughters, Carrie and Meghann—and I am eternally grateful to them for their endless encouragement and belief in me. Thank you to Carrie Grant, for her generous reading of many versions of the manuscript, her title suggestions, and for my treasured *Roget's Thesaurus* that she gave me as a gift when she was twelve years old.

And to Meghann Gibson, who gifted me with loads of Irish knick-knacks and keepsakes, especially the miniature pair of step-dancing shoes featured in this story.

I've been blessed to have so much additional help in bringing this book to publication. Thanks to Courtney Lopes, who created a book cover that *exactly* matched what I imagined!

My family has been a tremendous source of support; I thank Patricia Davis, crackerjack copy editor and beloved sister. I also share big appreciation and hugs to my niece, Rachael Davis, for letting me talk her into posing for the original book cover.

Thank you to my Irish grandmothers, Hazel and Alice, Anne and Susan, and those whose names I do not know. Although these women are long gone from this world, I think their voices live on, traveling from the past onto the pages of this book.

And my deepest gratitude to John Browne, for his artistic talents, wise counsel, and inspiration.

One fun detail in *It Only Takes Once*: The fortunes in Chapter Seven, "The Step Dance," and Chapter Ten, "The Fortune Cookie," are all real—fortunes I personally received in the cookies I ate at Chinese restaurants. I have to wonder, though—did I choose these cookies, or did they choose me?

ABOUT THE AUTHOR

Susan Colleen Browne weaves her love of Ireland and her passion for country living into her Village of Ballydara series, novels and stories of love, friendship and family set in the Irish countryside. Her latest Irish novels are *The Little Irish Gift Shop, Becoming Emma,* and *The Fairy Cottage of Ballydara*!

Susan is also the author of an award-winning memoir, *Little Farm in the Foothills,* the first book of the Little Farm in the Foothills series, the sequel, *Little Farm Homegrown,* and a gardening guide, *Little Farm in the Garden.*

A community college instructor, Susan runs a little homestead with her husband John in the Pacific Northwest, USA.

When she's not tending vegetable beds or wrangling chickens, she's working on her next Irish story!

For more about the village of Ballydara and other fun Irish stuff, visit www.susancolleenbrowne.com.

You'll also find recipes, book excerpts and tales from Susan's "little farm" at www.littlefarminthefoothills.blogspot.com and www.susancolleenbrowne.substack.com !

BOOKS BY SUSAN COLLEEN BROWNE

The Village of Ballydara Series

It Only Takes Once, Book 1 (print and ebook)

Mother Love, Book 2 (print and ebook)

The Hopeful Romantic, Book 3 (print and ebook)

The Galway Girls, Book 4 (print and ebook)

The Secret Well, novelette ebook

A Christmas Visitor, novelette ebook and the sequel to *The Secret Well*

The Little Irish Gift Shop, Book 5

Becoming Emma, Book 6

Becoming Emma, Special Edition

The Fairy Cottage of Ballydara, Book 7

Little Farm in the Foothills Series

Little Farm in the Foothills: A Boomer Couple's Search for the Slow Life, Book 1 (print and ebook)

Little Farm Homegrown: A Memoir of Food-Growing, Midlife, and Self-Reliance on a Small Homestead, Book 2 (print and ebook)

Little Farm in the Garden: A Practical Mini-Guide to Raising Selected Fruits and Vegetables Homestead-Style, Book 3 (print and ebook)

The Morgan Carey Series for Tweens, set in the Pacific Northwest

Morgan Carey and The Curse of the Corpse Bride, Book 1, a lighthearted Halloween story (print and ebook)

Morgan Carey and The Mystery of the Christmas Fairies, Book 2, a gentle fantasy (print and ebook), set in the Foothills!

The Secret Astoria Scavenger Hunt, Book 3, a haunted house adventure

(print and ebook)

Susan's books are available for **free** in ebook format at your local library—all you have to do is put in a request, or use your library's request app!

The Little Farm books are available in print format at your local library too. You can also order them from your neighborhood bookstore or find them at your favorite online retailer!